Charles Leeson Prince

Observations Upon the Climate of Uckfield, Sussex

and its neighborhood from 1843 to 1870

Charles Leeson Prince

Observations Upon the Climate of Uckfield, Sussex
and its neighborhood from 1843 to 1870

ISBN/EAN: 9783337363581

Printed in Europe, USA, Canada, Australia, Japan

Cover: Foto ©Andreas Hilbeck / pixelio.de

More available books at **www.hansebooks.com**

OBSERVATIONS

UPON

THE CLIMATE OF UCKFIELD,

SUSSEX,

AND ITS NEIGHBOURHOOD,

FROM 1843 TO 1870.

SECOND EDITION.

WITH SOME ADDITIONAL OBSERVATIONS

AND

STATISTICS OF RAINFALL

TO THE END OF THE YEAR

1885.

BY

C. LEESON PRINCE,

MEMBER OF THE ROYAL COLLEGE OF SURGEONS, FELLOW OF THE ROYAL
ASTRONOMICAL AND METEOROLOGICAL SOCIETIES, MEMBER OF THE
SCOTTISH METEOROLOGICAL SOCIETY, &c.

—nisi persuadere nobis volunt, sanis quidem considerandum esse, quod cœlum,
quod tempus anni sit ; ægris verò non esse.

Lewes : H. WOLFF, 64, High Street.

1886.

PREFACE.

THE first edition of this work being now out of print, I am requested to issue a second, in which I have inserted a continuation of the monthly notices of the weather to the end of the year 1885.

My meteorological instruments having been removed to Crowborough in the spring of 1872, I have not added any tabular matter in respect of temperature since the date of publication of the former edition.

By the assistance of Miss Laura Day, since the year 1877, I am enabled to give a continuous register, in a series of tables, of the yearly, monthly, and seasonal rainfall at Uckfield for a long period; the results of which may be considered a very reliable record of the rainfall there, as well as, relatively, to its immediate neighbourhood. Chapters II. and III. have been revised, and for the most part re-written, in accordance with the continuation of the general observations for the district.

Chapters V. and VI. of the first edition have been omitted. As to the former, I contemplate its forming the basis of a separate work, and with respect to the latter I consider it has already answered the purpose for which it was written.

C. L. P.

THE OBSERVATORY, CROWBOROUGH,
    Nov., 1886.

INTRODUCTORY REMARKS.

THE interesting phenomena connected with the science of Meteorology have been found, from very early ages, to excite a lively interest in the human mind. This will occasion no surprise, when we consider how man is placed by nature in a state of dependence upon the various conditions of the atmosphere. To watch their vicissitudes therefore, and speculate upon their consequences, becomes almost a daily necessity. The beautiful scenery produced by the ever varying clouds, consequent upon their state of almost incessant change, contributes very largely to render the science increasingly attractive.

Meteorology, considered merely as a source of amusement and recreation, offers many pleasures to those who delight in observing everything which may be passing around them. In every part of the world atmospheric phenomena, with their respective causes and effects, are studied with great interest, whether we consider the electric storm near the equator, or the splendid scenery among the snow and ice of the polar sea.

We find that the ancient shepherds of eastern countries, people who were often, if not constantly, abroad both day and night, observed, and some few recorded with a certain amount of accuracy, various atmospheric phenomena. It would appear that to Aristotle should be given the credit of first observing and arranging systematically many natural objects, especially the changes of the weather. He described with accuracy the rainbow, solar halo, and various appearances of the clouds, rain, snow, &c. Shortly after him Theophrastus, the disciple both of Plato and Aristotle, collected and arranged many prognostics of the weather. Most of these prognostics Aratus, the Greek philosopher, introduced into his Diosemeia, while among both Greek and Roman historians are to be found many interesting allusions to the study of Meteorology.

The Romans who wrote principally upon this subject were

Pliny, Virgil, Lucretius, and Seneca. Pliny, however, was very apt to indulge in fabulous and often absurd notions; Virgil appears to have followed in the steps and to imitate Aratus; Lucretius labored very much to explain the causes of some atmospheric changes; and Seneca, in his natural questions, endeavoured to give some explanations, which are too lengthy and indefinite to be really interesting. It is remarkable that for many centuries the science should have remained in comparative neglect, when we consider that almost all the operations necessary for the support of human life depend upon various states of that medium in which we live and move and have our being. Little, if anything, was attempted in the way of investigating the great laws of atmospheric changes till the seventeenth century, when certain philosophical instruments were invented, which supplied important desiderata for observing and recording variations. About the middle of the last century, then, the science seemed to revive, and Saussure, Bertholin, Fahrenheit and others stirred up a few scientific men to an attentive study of meteorology. During the present century, and more especially during the last twenty years, the science has made steady and successful progress. The number of careful observers has wonderfully increased, and they are yearly contributing much useful information upon this important subject. In meteorology we should ever bear in mind that it is by recording as much as possible of the past that we are enabled, in a slight degree, to judge of the future; and let me advise those who possess an aptitude for the study of meteorology to cultivate it, not only for their own individual gratification, but for public usefulness. I need scarcely refer to its importance in relation to medicine, for the fact has been fully established that at all times and in all places, the common sense of mankind has ascribed to atmospheric changes the good or bad state of health of the whole human race.

The atmosphere and its changes which immediately surround us, and influence to a great extent our daily pursuits and avocations, are really less understood than many other subjects of far less interest and importance. The amount of evaporation from the skin and lungs is entirely regulated by the temperature and humidity of the atmosphere. Both the circulation of the blood and the absorption of food into the body, are accelerated by an increased amount of moisture, which fully establish the medical importance of meteorological enquiries. As another instance of the influence which the amount of evaporation from the body must exert upon the general health, I would state the following from Matteuci's observations, viz.—" That the generality of cutaneous exhalations from the body is sometimes ten times greater in dry than in moist air, and this is doubled in passing from 32° to 64° Fahrenheit."

Hippocrates says, in the opening paragraph of his treatise concerning earth, air, and waters, " Whoever desires properly to investigate the art of medicine must do this—first take into consideration the seasons of the year, and how each is capable of operating (on the system), for they not only do not resemble each other, but differ widely the one from the other in the changes (they bring about)," and in aph. i. he remarks " that the changes of the seasons are especially concerned in the production of diseases, and that great alternations from heat to cold and so forth, have also their due effect." Celsus also says near the commencement of his second book, " Sed antequam dico, quibus præcedentibus morborum timor subsit, non alienum videtur exponere, quæ tempora anni quæ tempestatum genera, quæ partes ætatis, qualia corpora maximè tuta, vel periculis opportuna sint, quod genus adversæ valetudinis in quoque timeri maximè possit. Non quòd non omni tempore, in omni tempestatum genere, omnis ætatis, omnis habitûs homines, per omnia genera morborum et ægrotent et moriantur; sed quòd frequentius tamen quædam eveniant; ideòque utile sit scire unumquemque, quid et quando maximè caveat."

At the present day so great an importance is attached, and interest taken, in the science of meteorology, that competent men are engaged in almost every civilized portion of the globe in observing, recording, and investigating the more common atmospheric phenomena. The results of such enquiries cannot be too highly appreciated. During the late war with Russia how many hundreds of valuable lives might have been saved had the climate of the Crimea been more thoroughly understood.

I consider that by climate is meant the temperature of the air near the surface of the earth, which, if not entirely influenced by the heat of the sun, is at least greatly dependent upon it. Temperature is found to be very unequally distributed over the globe on account of the various conditions which regulate the distribution of solar heat. 1st. From day to day and from season to season, by the earth's rotation. 2nd. By the degree of latitude of any given place. 3rd. By the distribution of land and water, places on the sea coast being less liable to sudden and great fluctuations of temperature than those situated more inland. 4th. By the character of the soil and colour of its component parts. This is a most important condition, and one too frequently overlooked; for certain soils have a marvellous power of absorbing and radiating the heat of the sun's rays. 5th. By the elevation of the land above the level of the sea. All these conditions are incessantly influencing the climate of every portion of the earth's surface, and have a tendency so to dissipate and counteract the solar heat, that they can only affect the earth's surface, not its mass, while at the same time they regulate the amount, character, and distribution of animal and vegetable life.

Some years ago, Sir John Leslie ascertained, by carefully conducted experiments, that the difference of temperature of the earth during summer and winter at the depth of one foot, amounted to three degrees, while at eight feet it was only half a degree; at one foot from the surface January was the coldest month and July the hottest; but at the depth of four feet March was the coldest and September the warmest. The heat of the sun, therefore, affects the soil to a very limited depth. Further experiments upon the same subject, made at the Paris Observatory, fully established the above facts, and it was also ascertained that there is a point at which the temperature remains constantly the same, and uninfluenced, therefore, by external causes.

It has become a well ascertained fact that the climate of places situated not far distant the one from the other varies considerably. The works of Howard and the system of observation so long taken at the Royal Observatory at Greenwich, give a very complete account of the climate of London and its vicinity, and it is at the request of scientific friends, impressed with the desirability of placing all meteorological facts on permanent record, that I have been induced to tabulate and arrange, on the following pages, the results of my observations upon the climate of Uckfield during the last twenty-eight years, a space of time sufficiently long to establish its prominent peculiarities, and the knowledge of which may prove important to both present and future residents. I trust it may be considered that the value of these observations are enhanced by the fact of the series having been conducted with scarcely any interruption, and that the whole have been recorded by myself, with the exception of some portions in the years 1843 and 1844, which, however, I consider to be quite trustworthy, and they have been incorporated with the series. Thus I hope to add a link to the chain of meteorological information respecting our ever-changing climate. The parish of Uckfield lies upon an undulating tract of country, situated about midway between the South Downs, and the highest point of Ashdown Forest. The surrounding neighbourhood is well wooded, and intersected here and there by a few small rivulets, while the scenery from several elevated spots is both interesting and picturesque. The principal part of the town stands upon a gentle slope in a direction from N.E. to S.W. The upper portion is 200 feet, and the lower, at the railway station, 66 feet above the level of the sea. With respect to its geological position, I shall merely observe that with the exception of some patches of clay on the southern side of the stream, the greater portion of the parish lies upon the stratum known as the Horsted beds of the Hastings sand, which begins at the foot of the hill on the south side of Horsted Church, and extends to the borders of the contiguous counties of Kent and Surrey.

The floor of the observatory is 144 feet above the level of the sea, in latitude 50° 58′ 25″ north, and in longitude 24 seconds east of Greenwich. A description of the building, by F. Brodie, Esq., may be seen in the sixteenth volume of the Monthly Notices of the Royal Astronomical Society. The maximum and minimum self-registering thermometers have been placed on a stand in perfect shade, a few inches distant from the northern side of the observatory. The stand is very similar to that known as Pastorelli's, but having a shelf at the bottom to prevent the possibility of the instruments becoming affected by any terrestrial radiation. This stand is affixed to a post, the lower end of which is sunk two feet in the ground, and surrounded by sand in order to prevent any vibrations being communicated to the thermometers from the rotation of the equatorial dome. The bulbs were situated at a mean distance of 4½ feet from the ground. The rain guage, as may be seen in the following engraving, was situated on the western side of the observatory, and about 20 feet from it.

SOUTH SIDE OF UCKFIELD OBSERVATORY.

The instruments were read every morning about nine o'clock, the maximum temperature reading was recorded for the previous day, and the minimum reading for the current day. It occasionally happened, however, that this minimum would have given an unfair reading for the succeeding day whenever a great rise of temperature had occurred during the current day. In such a case the instrument was adjusted again after sunset, when it very generally gave a correct reading for the next morning. The radiation thermometers were also read about nine o'clock, and the terrestrial radiator was subject to the same re-adjustment in extreme cases as that in the shade. The cistern of the standard barometer is suspended 146 feet above the level of the sea, and its readings recorded once a day. All necessary corrections have been applied to the readings of the several instruments.

Rainfall was measured at nine o'clock, and the amount set down to the previous day, except in a few instances, where I have been quite certain that the fall had occurred after the midnight at the close of any month, when it was recorded for the first day of the new month. The funnel of the rain gauge has a diameter of 12 inches, and is elevated six feet above the surface of the ground. This height above the ground has been maintained during the whole of the observations, without any appreciable difference in the amount collected in it, and from one of Glaisher's rain gauges, the funnel of which was only four inches above the ground.

CHAPTER I.

THE barometer is an instrument constructed for the purpose of ascertaining the weight or pressure of the atmosphere, by which means we are enabled to ascertain variations in the state of the weather, foretell, to a certain extent, its changes, as well as to measure the heights of mountains and the depths of mines. About the middle of the seventeenth century it was the common opinion among philosophers, that the ascent of water in pumps was owing to what they considered nature's abhorrence of a vacuum, and that fluids might be raised by suction to any height whatever. It was accidentally discovered, however, that water could not be raised in a pump unless the sucker reached to within thirty-three feet of the water in the well, and Galileo thought there might be some other cause for this ascent of water. Being unable to satisfy himself on this point, he referred the matter to his pupil, Torricelli, who entertained the idea that the *pressure of the atmosphere* was the real cause of the ascent of water in pumps, and that a column of water thirty-three feet in height was in exact balance with a column of air of the same base. His suspicions were fully confirmed by subsequent experiments, and it also occurred to him that as mercury was fourteen times heavier than water, a column of mercury thirty inches in height would be an actual balance to the much longer column of water. Subsequent experiments of filling a glass tube with mercury, and inverting it into a cistern containing the same metal, fully established the truthfulness of the idea, for the mercury descended to thirty inches.

Shortly after this discovery, Descartes, Pascal, and others, hinted. that if the mercury be sustained in the tube by the pressure of the atmosphere, it ought to descend lower in the tube if it were carried to a greater elevation above the sea, having a less column of atmosphere to sustain it. Pascal undertook to make the experiment by observing the height of the mercury in the tube first at the bottom of a mountain in Auvergne, and afterwards at different altitudes, by which it was found that the mercury fell lower and lower as the ascent increased, thus confirming the theory relating to the universal pressure of the atmosphere, and the consequent suspension of the mercurial column.

The circumstance of the column of mercury in the tube being narrower than the surface of the mercury in the cistern, makes no difference in the experiment, because the pressure of elastic fluids is as their density, not as their width of volume. The same result would occur if the surface of the mercury, presented to the atmospheric pressure in the cistern, were only equal to the width of the upright tube.

After the conclusion of these experiments, some time elapsed before it became known that the pressure of the air was different at different times in the same place. Further observation, however, soon discovered that with variations in its altitude there are also certain changes in the general character of the weather, and that the barometer informs us of what is taking place in the *upper* regions of the atmosphere, and seldom, at first, in that stratum which is nearest the earth.

At or near the level of the sea, atmospheric pressure is about fifteen pounds to the square inch, and as fluids press equally in all directions, upwards, downwards, and laterally, this pressure is equally intense over every shape and surface. The human subject bears this pressure over the body in an equal ratio, and estimating its surface at about fourteen and a half square feet, the pressure would vary to the amount of a ton weight, according as the barometer stood at its maximum or minimum. This great difference greatly affects us in respect to the natural functions of the body, and consequently our health, more especially when the change has been sudden ; and the fact that certain maladies are seriously increased by unusual depressions of the barometer, admits of no doubt. The barometer is one of the most useful of philosophical instruments to the gentleman, the farmer, and the mariner. It should always be borne in mind that its indications of atmospheric changes are frequently premonitory, not immediate, and therefore we must not find fault with the instrument because it does not inform us of the actual state of the weather at the time and place of observation. Barometric fluctuations indicate, and are often the result of, atmospheric changes extending over a very large area. A storm raging either in Spain, France, Belgium, Scotland, or Ireland, would seriously affect the barometer in the south of England without any atmospheric disturbance being apparent at the latter place. It thus becomes extremely difficult for an observer in any particular locality either to understand or predict what may be the result of such variations. Certain changes of the weather may undoubtedly be predicted by combined and careful observations of the barometer and the clouds; but these principles are comparatively few, and should be received as of general, but by no means universal application; moreover, great allowance should be made for local influences. The weather in the South of England is immensely influenced by the strong currents of wind so frequently coming up the Channel, and again by N.E. currents being deflected from continental shores, and rushing over the eastern and south-eastern counties.

Humbolt has said that "important changes of the weather do not actually arise from local causes situated at the place of observation itself; their origin is to be looked for in a disturbance of the equilibrium of the currents of the atmosphere, which has begun afar off, and generally not near the surface of the earth."

The ebb and flow of the atmospheric tide form not the least interesting portion in a series of meteorological inquiries, and carefully conducted observations furnish proof of the accuracy of other parts of the series. As localities vary in their relative conditions, so the indications of the barometer vary with geographical position. One set of observations will not, therefore, give the atmospheric pressure for all, as the range of the barometer varies with latitude, being least at the equator and greater in proportion to the distance from it. The permanency of pressure upon the surface of the globe must be dependant upon the equal balance of atmospheric currents, while its fluctuations must be traced to the destruction of this equipoise, either by local expansion of heat, by the increase and decrease of aqueous vapor, or by the natural progression of temperature, exerting its influence upon diversities of aerial currents.

There are three kinds of barometer in general use in this country.

1st. The upright standard barometer.

2nd. The wheel (or Dr. Hook's) barometer.

3rd. The aneroid barometer.

The first instrument is generally found in observatories and in the houses of scientific men, who can appreciate its valuable indications. It is always available, subject to certain known corrections, for comparison with similar instruments in any part of the world.

The wheel barometer is in use where accurate observations are not necessary, but its indications are sufficient for the agriculturist.

The aneroid barometer is a third form of the instrument, and, when occasionally corrected by a standard, is especially useful, on account of its great portability, for ascertaining the height of any place above the level of the sea.

Although I commenced barometric observations in 1842, yet it was not until January 1st, 1854, that I obtained a standard instrument. I have therefore rejected all readings previous to this latter date as not sufficiently trustworthy to be placed on record, and moreover, perfectly useless for comparison with standard instruments. In the following table I have given the results of observations made daily at 9 a.m., one reading daily being as much as my leisure would allow me to record with regularity. All the readings have been subjected to the usual corrections, viz., for index error, capillarity, reduction to the temperature of 32°, and to sea level :—

TABLE I.

MEAN MONTHLY READING OF BAROMETER AT 9 A.M.

	January.	February.	March.	April.	May.	June.	July.	August.	Sept.	Oct.	Nov.	Dec.	Mean.
1854	29.852	30.226	30.347	30.089	29.761	29.811	29.889	29.968	30.193	29.928	29.888	29.997	29.995
1855	30.199	29.781	29.747	30.141	29.871	30.055	29.946	30.067	30.170	29.715	30.012	29.954	29.971
1856	29.591	30.111	30.182	29.803	29.844	30.088	30.010	29.922	29.851	30.164	30.101	29.903	29.964
1857	29.826	30.205	29.939	29.812	29.968	30.048	30.047	30.022	29.979	29.890	30.124	30.368	30.019
1858	30.377	30.023	29.966	29.966	29.971	30.100	29.960	30.027	30.066	30.033	29.926	29.973	30.042
1859	30.268	30.045	30.026	29.820	29.958	29.970	30.140	30.019	29.909	29.737	30.021	29.820	29.977
1860	29.727	30.052	29.889	29.970	29.953	29.781	30.036	29.768	29.924	30.064	29.877	29.674	29.892
1861	30.203	29.896	29.841	30.182	30.116	29.965	29.814	30.079	29.939	30.040	29.776	30.174	30.002
1862	29.915	30.094	29.988	30.052	29.922	29.927	29.968	29.981	30.077	29.936	29.963	30.072	29.991
1863	29.813	30.347	29.926	30.007	30.043	29.930	30.156	29.953	29.904	29.838	30.078	30.157	30.012
1864	30.235	29.923	29.700	30.105	30.002	29.975	30.046	30.108	29.989	29.869	29.829	30.056	29.903
1865	29.616	29.915	29.927	30.154	29.968	30.220	29.993	29.918	30.262	29.613	29.888	30.269	30.025
1866	29.822	29.744	29.722	29.909	29.993	29.967	29.961	29.836	29.803	30.114	29.971	30.013	29.924
1867	29.728	30.118	29.808	29.862	29.914	30.124	29.922	30.024	30.108	29.768	30.310	30.055	29.979
1868	29.962	30.196	30.035	29.988	30.042	30.170	30.071	29.934	29.878	29.963	30.027	29.617	29.990
1869	30.076	30.031	29.811	30.027	29.829	30.106	30.124	30.159	29.860	30.063	29.976	29.757	29.985
1870	30.018	29.888	30.043	30.192	30.101	30.143	30.039	29.984	30.096	30.098	29.832	29.931	30.030
Mean .	29.954	30.035	29.935	30.004	29.955	30.022	30.007	29.986	30.000	29.931	29.976	29.928	29.982

From this table it will be seen that the annual mean height of the barometer during these seventeen years was 29.982, not much under 30.000 inches, and also that it was highest in the year 1858, and lowest in 1860, the former a dry, the latter a wet season. It is usually high as the season is calm, dry, and free from violent tempests during the spring and autumn months. The barometer stands very high in February. It is lowest in October and December, the former being by far the wettest month in the year in this county.

When it is desired to reduce the daily readings of the barometer to a monthly mean, the following method, described in Example 2, will be found a ready way of accomplishing it. We will suppose that you wish to find the mean daily reading of the following nine days, and the usual plan is given in Example 1:—

EXAMPLE 1.

Thus: October 1 . 30·215 inches.
    „ 2 . 30·105 „
    „ 3 . 29·764 „
    „ 4 . 29·210 „
    „ 5 . 28·810 „
    „ 6 . 29·200 „
    „ 7 . 29·411 „
    „ 8 . 30·102 „
    „ 9 . 29·900 „

9 ⌋ 266·717

Mean of the 9 days   29·635

EXAMPLE 2.

October 1 . 30·215 inches.
    „ 2 . 30·105 „
    „ 3 . 29·764 „
    „ 4 . 29·210 „
    „ 5 . 28·810 „
    „ 6 . 29·200 „
    „ 7 . 29·411 „
    „ 8 . 30·102 „
    „ 9 . 29·900 „

          3·717

For 3 observations   +   3·
above 30 inches

          6·717

For 1 observation   −   1·
below 29 inches

9 ⌋ 5·717

Mean of the 9 days   29·635

Example 2 is a method I discovered some years since, and which, for its brevity, I strongly recommend. The mean is obtained by adding up the decimal figures *only*. One whole number must then be added for every reading above 30 inches, and one subtracted for every reading below 29 inches. When the number of readings above 30 inches is sufficient to give a whole number in the quotient, the subsequent decimals must be added to 30 inches, and when not sufficient, to 29 inches. The mean monthly reading is never below 29 inches.

I have often been surprised to find an idea prevalent, that the pressure of the atmosphere is greater in wet weather, when the barometer is low, and least in fine weather, when the barometer is high. This notion must have arisen from a misconception of the construction of the instrument. The pressure of air cannot be exerted upon the top of the mercurial column, because the tube is there hermetically sealed. The pressure, therefore, must take place upon the mercury in the cistern, and in proportion as this pressure is there, greater or less, so does the mercury rise or fall in the upright tube. In fine weather, therefore, when the air is heaviest, the mercury will ascend; while in wet weather, when the air is lighter and less buoyant, the mercury will rise in the cistern and fall in the tube. In severe storms the atmosphere becomes lighter as the storm increases. The highest readings of the barometer are usually observed when the direction of the wind is from a point between N. and E., and lowest when from a point between S. and W.

The following table gives a few instances of unusually high and low readings of the barometer during the last seventeen years :—

TABLE II.

DATE.		ELEVATION.	DATE.		DEPRESSION.
1854	March 5...	30.579	1855	March 22...	28.902
1856	January 13...	30.721	1856	September 28...	28.788
1857	November 12...	30.770	1859	December 26...	28.610
„	December 12...	30.745	1860	January 24...	28.733
1858	January 17...	30.726	1864	November 15...	28.863
1859	January 10...	30.824	1865	January 14...	28.714
„	February 23...	30.733	1866	January 11...	28.769
„	March 11...	30.741	1867	January 8...	28.735
„	December 10...	30.818	1868	December 24...	28.863
1863	February 13...	30.725	1870	October 24...	28.973
1865	December 16...	30.725			
1867	March 2...	30.757			

The aneroid barometer is a most useful instrument for ascertaining the height of a position above the level of the sea. As we ascend a hill the height of the atmosphere above us is diminished, and consequently a lower reading occurs, and this in such regular gradation that by the aid of certain tables, calculated for the purpose, we are enabled to determine, with great exactness, comparative elevation. Although for strictly scientific purposes the standard barometer is to be preferred before any other, yet for ordinary occasions, and more especially for heights less than 1,000 feet, the aneroid will give a very close approximation to the truth. Its great portability renders it an agreeable and useful companion to the tourist, and a good instrument will show the difference of a few feet. No correction is necessary for any inconsiderable range of temperature. I would, however, caution those who are in the habit of using the instrument, frequently, not to omit comparing its readings occasionally with a standard. A sudden jar or too frequent "tapping" will derange the spring.

The following simple rules for ascertaining the relative height of any two places may perhaps be useful :—

Rule 1—Divide the difference between the readings of the upper and lower station by ·0011, and the quotient will give the height in feet.

Rule 2—Persons who take no delight in a multitude of scientific corrections, will be very well pleased with the simplicity of Mr. Strachan's method. It is as follows :— Read the aneroid to the nearest hundreth of an inch, subtract the reading at the upper station from that at the lower; multiply this difference by 9; the product is the elevation in feet.

EXAMPLE.

Lower Station	...	30.25 inches.
Upper „	...	29.02 „
		123
		9
Elevation	...	1107 feet.

Rule 3 is Mr. Symon's :—

TABLE III.

Rule 3.—Take from the table the value corresponding to the approximate mean of the upper and lower barometers, and to the mean temperature (which may be guessed at), divide the difference of the barometers by it; the quotient will be the height in feet.

EXAMPLE.

Base of Ben Lomond 29.890 ... Mean temperature 50°
Summit of   ,,   26.656 ... Mean barometer   28.27

    Difference   3.234

.00104) 3.234 (3110
   312

  .114   The true height being 3116 feet.
  .104   The rule gives   ... 3110 ,,

  .100   Error 6
  .104

Rule 4 is by Mr. J. M. Heath, who has given the following table or companion to the aneroid barometer :—

Bar.	Vert. Alt.	Bar.	Vert. Alt.	Bar.	Vert. Alt.
	90		96		102
30.9	4824	28.9	2955	27.3	1363
	91		97		103
30.5	4460	28.7	2761	27.0	1054
	92		98		104
30.2	4184	28.4	2467	26.7	742
	93		99		105
29.9	3905	28.1	2170	26.5	532
	94		100		106
29.6	3623	27.8	1870	26.2	214
	95		101		107
29.2	3243	27.5	1567	26.0	0.

This table is computed for temperature 62°, and therefore will need no correction in 9 cases out of 10. When the temperature is much above or below 62° the alteration of the readings of the barometer, at the rate of 1 inch for 15°, or ·2 for 3°, is very simple and easy. Three corrections only are required—(1), correcting bar, readings for temperature of air; (2), interpolation between the terms in the table; (3), subtraction.

Mr. Heath works out the height of Ben Lomond as an example :—

Reading	29.890	26.656
$62° - 50° = 12°$	+.800	+.800
Corrected reading	30.690	27.456
Tabular numbers	4633	1522
	1522	
Difference	3111 height in feet.	

A variety of other formulæ may be found in meteorological works, but either of the above rules will suffice for ordinary occasions. I will, however, add the following table, showing the geometrical progression of the volume and elasticity of the air for heights taken in arithmetical progression :—

Height in Miles.	Volume.	Height of Barometer.
0.000	1	30.000
2.705	2	15.000
5.410	4	7.500
8.115	8	3.750
10.820	16	1.875

As the force of gravity is exerted in a perpendicular direction, any increase or decrease in the two forces must at once pervade the whole of the vertical column in which it takes place, so that under every circumstance of disturbance the geometrical progression of the density will be maintained.

In the Ordnance Survey of 1861, one principal line of levelling passed through Uckfield, and I am, therefore, enabled to give the elevation above the sea of several points in this parish and neighbourhood. The levels established, on these lines, and marked by the surveyors upon permanent objects, furnish definite points all over the kingdom, from which the lines of levels for the contours and the detail plans of every part of the kingdom are carried, and thus all the levels of the Ordnance plans refer to one common datum level, which is the level of the sea at Liverpool. The difference between this level and that of the mean tide at Shoreham, in this county, is less than six inches (.461 foot).

These bench marks are found to be extremely useful, also, as starting points for barometric measurements, and estimating, so far as elevation is concerned, the probable climate of any particular locality. Of the numerous bench marks which have been made in the parishes of Maresfield, Uckfield, Isfield, Horsted, and Lewes, I have selected the following, in order that a general idea may be formed of their respective heights above the level of the sea :—

BENCH MARK.	WHERE SITUATED.	HEIGHT ABOVE THE GROUND.		HEIGHT ABOVE SEA LEVEL.	
No. 180	On front of Duddleswell Gate House	0.77	feet	615	feet
Maresfield 184	On the north gable of the Fox Inn .	3.83	„	418	„
„ 188	On east face of large stone pier near entrance to Lambpool . .	1.44	„	243	„
„ 192	On north corner of Maresfield Parish Church tower	4.76	„	182	„
„ 194	On north gable of Maresfield National School	1.69	„	151	„
„ 195	On north side of wall at Gateway, near Maresfield Mill . . .	2.32	„	106	„
„ 198	On north corner of Fillness' Cottage, Birdletts	0.86	„	110	„
Uckfield 201	On front of stone cottage, near Brown's Lane	2.63	„	199	„
„ 202	On S.W. face of wall, in front of Rock Hall Cottage	3.43	„	180	„
„ 203	On wall at junction of roads, near Rock Hall	2.52	„	151	„
„	Floor of Observatory at Uckfield .			144	„
„ 204	On wall at junction of fences opposite King's Head Inn . . .	2.70	„	117	„
	On North gable of Uckfield Church	2.97	„	138	„
„ 206	On north face of south pier of Uckfield Bridge	1.53	„	61	„
„ 207	On north side of cottage at the corner of Framfield Road . . .	2.49	„	94	„
„ 208	On front of Fir Cottage . . .	0.65	„	156	„
Horsted 215	On top of small stone pier at entrance to Horsted Place . . .	1.85	„	133	„
„ 216	On north face of Little Horsted Parish Church tower	3.88	„	149	„
Isfield	On south corner of Isfield Parish Church tower	2.16	„	36	„
„ 227	On front of Clay Hill House . .	1.52	„	85	„
Lewes 242	On north face of large pier of Lewes Bridge	2.21	„	19	„
„ 246	On south corner of St. Michael's Church	2.36	„	105	,
„ 248	Bolt in east face of St. Ann's Parish Church tower	2.92	„	158	„
Rotherfield	Floor of Observatory at Crowborough Beacon			825	„

CHAPTER II.

On the Meteorological Character of the Several Months of the Year, together with various Remarks in Reference thereto.

JANUARY.

"When all this uniform, uncoloured scene
  Shall be dismantled of its fleecy load,
  And flush into variety again.
  From dearth to plenty, and from death to life,
  Is Nature's progress, when she lectures man
  In heavenly truth; evincing, as she makes
  The grand transition, that there lives and works
  A soul in all things, and that soul is GOD.
  He sets the bright procession on its way,
  And marshals all the order of the year;
  He makes the bounds which winter may not pass,
  And blunts his pointed fury; in its case,
  Russet and rude, folds up the tender germ,
  Uninjured, with inimitable art;
  And, ere one flowery season fades and dies,
  Designs the blooming wonders of the next."   Cowper.

Previous observations stamp this month as the coldest period of the year, and in severe winters, when there has been little or no frost in the previous December, the cold usually commences during the first or second week, accompanied by a keen N.E. wind. Should a change not occur in the course of two or three days, we are nearly certain of having a fall of snow and a continuance of the frost. The mean temperature is about 38°. In continued frosty weather the temperature falls to 15°, and even lower on a clear night, after a fall of snow. It occasionally happens that these frosts are of short continuance, and are quickly succeeded by a sudden thaw; but such thaws frequently prove but temporary, and the wind soon changes by S.E. to E., and N.E., with a return of frost for perhaps a week or ten days longer. On these occasions the trees are beautifully decked with rime, and present a splendid appearance when dazzling in the solar rays of the early morning. In our very uncertain climate we occasionally find that great mildness prevails during the month, when the fall of rain is, almost invariably, above the average. This was especially the case in the years 1846, 1851, 1853, 1866, and 1877. In 1846 and 1866 the weather was often too warm to bear fires with comfort. Very strong S.W. winds are frequent in such a season, which increase to a hurricane if long continued, and occasion great depression of the barometer.

On the other hand, we had very cold weather in the years 1850, 1861, 1867, 1871, and 1881. The heaviest snow which we have had for many years occurred in 1881, which is still fresh in our memory. For many years past the fall of snow in this county has been trifling as compared with the Midland counties. On the high ground of Crowborough the snow lies sometimes for many days, in consequence of the dryness of the air. In very severe weather snow crystals fall in abundance, which are well worthy of attentive examination under a magnifying-glass. These crystals are wholly different from ordinary snow, and although they all, without exception, assume the hexagon form, yet their internal structure presents some wonderful varieties of crystallization.

FEBRUARY.

"From sunward rocks the icicle's faint drop
　By lonely river side is heard at times
　To break the silence deep, for now the stream
　Is mute, or faintly gurgles far below
　Its frozen ceiling. Silent stands the mill,
　The wheel immovable and shod with ice.
　The babbling rivulet at each little slope
　Flows scantily beneath a lucid veil,
　And seems a pearly current liquefied ;
　While at the shelvy side in thousand shapes
　Fantastical the frostwork domes uprear

Their tiny fabrics, gorgeously superb
With ornaments beyond the reach of art.
Here vestibules of state and colonnades,
There gothic castles, grottoes, heather fanes,
Rise in review and quickly disappear;
Or through some fairy palace fancy roves,
And studs with ruby lamps the fretted roof,
Or paints with every colour of the bow
Spotless parterres, all freaked with snow-white flowers —
Flowers that no archetype in nature own;
Or spreads the spiky crystals into fields
Of bearded grain, rustling in autumn breeze."   GRAHAME.

This is the last month of winter, and extremely variable in its character. There is an old proverb—

"February fill dyke, be it black or be it white,
But if it be white it's the better to like,"

but more recent observations tend to set aside the old proverb, as February, next to March, is the driest month of the year in Sussex. In severe winters, the frosts of the two previous months continue, or return, with great intensity; while on several occasions the greatest cold of the year has occurred in this month. It was a very cold month in the years 1845, 1847, 1855, and 1860. Very intense frosts occur occasionally; thus, at Uckfield, on February 12, 1845, the temperature fell to 3°, and on February 12, 1847, to 1°! as shown by thermometers protected from radiation. Snow falls occasionally, with strong N.E. winds, while at other times rain falls upon the frozen ground, so that walking or driving becomes almost an impossibility for a few hours. A very remarkable instance of this frozen rain occurred in February, 1855, particulars of which I have mentioned on page 128. The latter part of the month is often *very* dry, and Kirwan has said that he never knew a long drought but when it manifested itself at the end of this month and continued through the first part of March.

It was a very mild month in the years 1849, 1856, 1867, 1869, 1883, and 1884.

The sun now acquires considerable influence upon vegetation, and in mild weather some of our spring flowers come into bloom towards the end of the month.

MARCH.

> " While yet the spring is young, while earth unbinds
> Her frozen bosom to the western winds ;
> While mountain snows dissolve against the sun,
> And streams, yet new, from precipices run ;
> Ev'n in this early dawning of the year,
> Produce the plough, and yoke the sturdy steer,
> And goad him till he groans beneath his toil,
> Till the bright share is buried in the soil.
> That crop rewards the greedy peasant's pains
> Which twice the sun and twice the cold sustains
> And bursts the crowded barn with more than promised gains.
> But ere we stir the yet unbroken ground,
> The various course of Seasons must be found ;
> The weather, and the setting of the winds,
> The culture suited to the several kinds
> Of seeds and plants, and what will thrive and rise,
> And what the genius of the soil denies.
> This ground with Bacchus, that with Ceres suits,
> The other loads the trees with happy fruits."　　Georgic i., 43.

A marked meteorological feature of this month is the prevalence of boisterous weather and gales during the second or third week, just antecedent to the vernal equinox. Although these gales usually approach from the S.W., yet we sometimes have a strong current from the N.E., which, when it lasts many days, induces a rapid evaporation from the soil.

> " March dust is worth a King's ransom.
> A dry and cold March never begs its bread.
> March flowers never made summer bowers."

Should the N.E. winds not set in till April, March is often a somewhat wet month, with the wind veering frequently between N.W. and S.W.

March, however, is sometimes a cold month, and the driest of the year. It was particularly cold in the years 1845, 1855,

1865, and 1883. The first mentioned instance was the coldest on record, and its mean temperature was several degrees lower than the average for January. Snowstorms occur occasionally, which give a very wintry appearance to the landscape, but the sun begins at this time to acquire such power that the snow seldom remains long on the ground.

> " When Februeer is come and gone
> The snow lays on a hot stone."

It was a mild month in the years 1848, 1854, 1859, 1871, 1882, and 1884. Hence, it is more frequently mild than otherwise. In some years the latter part of the month is characterized by great warmth, and the temperature in the shade will rise to 70° and upwards. Upon the whole, however, vegetation makes but little progress, as any premature warmth is quickly followed by cold nights and chilling winds, to the great injury of any advancing foliage.

APRIL.

> " Whanne that Apryll with his shoures sote
> The drought of Marche had perced the rote
> And bathed every bayne in suche lycoure
> Of whiche bertue engendred is the floure
> Whan Zephicus eke with his sote breth
> Inspired hath every holte and heth
> The tendre croppes, and the yonge sonne
> Hath in the Ram halfe his course yronne
> And smale foules maken melodye
> That slepen of nyght with open eye
> So prycketh hem nature in her courage
> Than longen folke to go on pylgrymage
> And palmers to seken straunge strondes
> To serbe halowes conthe in sondry londes
> And specyally fro every shyres ende
> Of Englonde to Caunterbury they wende
> The holy blysful martyr for to seke
> That hem hath holpen whan they were seke."   CHAUCER.

Perhaps there is no other month in the year wherein we are exposed to such great and sudden changes of temperature as in

April. The increasing power of the sun's rays and easterly winds cause excessive evaporation. Some days may be warm and genial, while on the other hand days of wintry rigour are experienced with heavy showers of hail or snow. In April, 1849, a heavy fall of snow was followed by such a severe frost as to destroy all the garden fruits.

It was a very cold month in the years 1847, 1849, 1860, 1879, and 1881, and it was very mild in the years 1844, 1854, 1865, 1874, and 1882. In April, 1865, the sudden warmth, after the cold of the previous month, was very remarkable. Very wet weather seldom occurs, but the quantity of rain was above the average in the years 1848, 1856, 1871, and 1882. Towards the close of the month, whatever may have been the general character of the weather, a large number of our spring flowers come into bloom. During the third week it is usual for the wryneck, cuckoo, nightingale, swallow, redstart, willow wren, and other migratory birds to appear—the marten and swift come later. The earlier kinds of butterfly also appear, in addition to the sulphur species, which generally appear in March and occasionally in February. During warm evenings the common bat may be seen flitting round the house. Their appearance is always welcome, and usually indicates fine weather for two or three days.

The atmosphere is occasionally very clear during showery weather, and objects, twenty or thirty miles distant, can be seen very distinctly with a telescope of moderate power.

In this month we often see large masses of the Cumulo-stratus cloud, in various directions, which can scarcely fail to attract attention.

MAY.

" By zephyrs led comes genial May,
    With brighter green she decks the cheerful mead ;
    Breathes either bland to wake the genial seed,
    Bids the swoll'n buds their crimson folds disclose,
    And with her own warm blushes tints the rose ;

> Now the plumed tenants of the copse and grove
> Disport on circling wing, and chaunt of love,
> Swelling the melody of waking birds !
> The woodman's song, and low of distant herds !
> Where silv'ry riv'lets play through flow'ry meads
> And woodbines give their sweets, and limes their shades.
> Bathed in soft dew and fanned by western winds
> Each field its bosom to the gale unbinds ?
> The blade dares boldly rise, new suns beneath,
> The tender vine puts forth her flexile wreath,
> And freed from chilling blasts and northern shower
> Spreads without fear, each shoot, and leaf, and flower."

This month usually is characterized by a great increase of warmth and sunshine, while the still increasing power of the sun's rays manifests itself by the rapid advance of vegetation. The leafing season is now general, and is completed, for the most part, by the close of the month with the exception of the mulberry, whose foliage is seldom much advanced before the first week in June. The beauty of natural scenery becomes most attractive, and is much enhanced by the splendid varieties of cloud which adorn the sky.

As in April, so in this month, our climate is subject to great vicissitudes of temperature. It was a cold month in the years 1845, 1855, 1877, and 1879. In the latter instance vegetation was very generally injured, more especially the fruit, cereal, and hop crops.

It was a warm month in the years 1847, 1857, 1862, 1868, 1878, and 1882. On May 28th, 1847, the temperature in the shade rose to 87°, and on the 31st to 85°. It was a wet month in the years 1843, 1856, 1860, and 1878. The most prevalent winds are the N.E. and S.W. When easterly winds are prevalent they seriously affect the young and tender foliage, which suffers also from the accompanying dewless nights. This month alternates very frequently with September. Being the last month of the spring season, the weather is, for the most part, fine and pleasant for out-door exercise and amusements. Our migratory birds have very generally arrived, and most of them may be heard in full song.

Some butterflies are seen on the wing, after remaining long in the chrysalis state during an inclement season; also the field cricket, the chafer or maybug, the forest fly, and the large female wasp, &c. Bees, too, are very active, and have thrown forth their early swarms.

JUNE.

> " A thousand beauties lost to vulgar eyes
>   Now to the scrutinising search are spread;
>   The grasses elegant, though not proud robed!
>   The mallow purpling o'er the pleasant sides
>   Of pathways green, mixed with the helpless vetch
>   Each dry, entangled copse, enpurpled glows
>   That climbs for aid. Deceitful nightshade dressed
>   In hues inviting. Every splashy vale,
>   With orchis blooms; while in the moistened plain
>   The meadow sweet its luscious fragrance yields.
>   And then what odours from the hedgerow breathe
>   When the soft shower calls forth the hidden sweets!
>   The clover richly feeds the stealthful gale;
>   The strawberry, blushing, hides its modest face
>   Beneath the mantling leaves."   BIDLAKE.

The first of our three summer months is usually characterized from its commencement by a considerable increase of temperature. In rare instances only do we find summer attained before this date. The N.E. wind of the spring months now retires before that from the westward. Vegetation proceeds most rapidly towards perfection, and, by many, the general appearance of the landscape is considered to be the most beautiful of any period of the year. The dews are frequently very heavy, and compensate for the extra evaporation from the soil.

It was a rather cold month in the years 1852, 1855, 1860, 1869, 1871, and 1882. The temperature was very high in the years 1846, 1857, 1858, 1866, and 1877. A marked feature in the temperature is that in a series of years it departs very little from the average.

The month was very wet in the years 1852, 1860, 1871,

1872, and 1879; and very dry in the years 1844, 1858, 1870, and 1877. In 1844 the severe drought which commenced in April and May continued, with the exception of a few trifling showers, throughout the month of June. Accounts from all parts of the country represented the pasturage as being very seriously affected, and presenting a most sterile appearance. The wheat crop, as in almost every instance of drought in the spring months, alone maintained a healthy condition. The old proverb which says that "Drought never bred dearth in England" is generally correct. The driest June on record was that in the year 1858, but the drought was confined to that particular month. In June, 1852, after a considerable drought in the spring, rain fell more or less or 23 days, and the total amount was upwards of seven inches, while in the neighbourhood of Lewes it was nearly eight inches. This was the largest rain-fall which had occurred in June during the present century. It has been observed that from Midsummer day, to the end of the first week in July, we have rather showery weather, with occasional thunderstorms; facts which should be taken into consideration by the farmer.

Few birds continue their song after the end of this month. The yellow hammer, goldfinch, and golden-crested wren may chirp sometimes. The cuckoo's note also ceases. Innumerable insects are called into life by the heat of this month, and afford an endless amusement to the admirer of Nature's works.

JULY

"Calls forth the labouring hinds; in standing rows,
   With slow approaching step and levelled stroke,
   The early mower bending o'er his scythe,
   Lays low the slender grass; emblem of man,
   Falling beneath the ruthless hand of Time.
   Then follows blithe, equipped with fork and rake,
   In light array the train of nymphs and swains;
   Wide o'er the field, their labour seeming sport,
   They toss the withering herbage. Light it flies;
   The grateful sweetness of the new mown hay,

> Breathing refreshment, fans the toiling swain,
> And soon the jocund dale and echoing hill
> Resound with merriment. The simple jest,
> The village tale of scandal, and the taunts
> Of rude, unpolished wit, raise sudden bursts
> Of laughter from beneath the spreading oak,
> Where, thrown at ease, and sheltered from the sun,
> The plain repast and wholesome beverage cheer
> Their spirits."   OLD POEM.

July is the warmest month of the year. The winds are generally from the westward, but in very hot seasons an easterly current will sometimes prevail for a few days, which opposes the upper current of air from the westward, and eventually causes severe thunderstorms. Should the storm be violent, and extend over a large area, the weather becomes cooler for a fortnight or more; and when it happens towards the end of July, so great a change occurs that we have no return of really hot weather. Some of the most beautiful forms of cloud may be seen during this month, especially the cirrus, cirro-cumulus, and cumulo-stratus, which reminds us of the following lines by Bloomfield:—

> " To view the white-robed clouds in clusters driven,
> And all the glorious pageantry of Heaven,
> Low on the utmost bound'ry of the sight,
> The rising vapors catch the silver light :
> Thence Fancy measures, as they parting fly,
> Which first will throw its shadows on the eye,
> Passing the source of light, and *thence* away,
> Succeeded quick by brighter still than they :
> For yet above these wafted clouds are seen
> (In a remoter sky, still more serene)
> Others detached in ranges through the air,
> Spotless as snow, and countless as they're fair;
> Scattered immensely wide from east to west,
> The beauteous semblance of 'a Flock at rest.
> These, to the raptured mind, aloud proclaim
> Their mighty Shepherd's everlasting Name."

The excessive evaporation from the soil causes enormous masses of condensed vapour to be formed at no great distance from the earth. These constitute the cumulo-stratus cloud, which

is always present during heavy showers, and, when congregated,
generally discharge themselves in actual thunder-storms.

It was a very hot month in the years 1847, 1852, 1859,
1870, 1876, 1878, and 1881. In the last instance the temperature was supposed to have been higher than was ever recorded
in England. Such, however, was not the case, as the temperature was *higher* over the South of England in July, 1847,
when for three consecutive days the temperature was considerably above 90°—viz., 13th 95°, 14th 98°, and 15th 93°!

The month was gloomy and cold in the years 1845, 1860,
1862, 1867, 1875, 1879, and 1882. An excessive rainfall
occurred in 1865, 1875, 1879, and 1882 to the great injury of
the cereal crops. On the other hand the month was remarkably dry in the years 1847, 1852, 1863, 1864, 1869, and 1876.
In 1869 the drought was very unusual, and only two slight
showers fell during the entire month.

In early seasons the harvest has commenced about the 15th,
but it commences more usually about the end of this month or
in the first week in August. The weather is often showery during
the first ten days, and therefore unfavourable for the completion
of hay harvests in those seasons when much rain has fallen just
after Midsummer day. Should a storm be unusually severe, and
the clouds at a considerable elevation, large hail, or flattened
pieces of ice, will fall and commit great havoc among the
crops of corn, hops, hot-houses, &c. This precipitation differs
materially from that which occurs in the ordinary cold showers
of March and April.*

Notwithstanding this is the warmest month of the year,
most of the feathered tribe have nearly discontinued their notes.
Fresh flowers, in their natural order of succession, come into
bloom as the season advances ; while those which adorned the
fields in May and June hasten to ripen their seed.

The common snake may frequently be seen crossing the
dusty road in sultry weather. This reptile, having no fang, is

perfectly harmless ; nevertheless, every opportunity is generally taken of killing it. It feeds on insects, field mice, harvest mice, and many pests of the field, and should, therefore, be considered rather as a friend than a foe. The common bat is now very busy in warm weather, and destroys an enormous number of annoying insects, many tribes of which are now in full vigour.

AUGUST.

> " Here once a year, distinction lowers her crest ;
>   The master, servant, and the merry guest,
>   Are equal all ; and round the happy ring
>   The reaper's eyes exulting glances fling,
>   And warmed with gratitude he quits his place,
>   With sunburnt hands and ale enlivened face,
>   Refills the jug, his honoured host to tend,
>   To serve at once the master and the friend ;
>   Proud thus to meet his smiles, to share his tale,
>   His nuts, his conversation, and his ale."   BLOOMFIELD.

In this, the last month of summer, we find its mean temperature, upon the average, to be less than that of July, yet in some years the greatest heat is not attained till this month. The high temperature *at.night* constitutes a peculiar feature of this period. By the middle of the month the soil becomes so much heated by the continuance of summer heat that after a fall of rain a rapid evaporation occurs from the surface, and the atmosphere, thus loaded with moisture, becomes exceedingly oppressive. The maximum temperature in the shade is generally very uniform, and differs but slightly from that of the previous month. Westerly winds are the most prevalent, with but little variation. With respect to thunderstorms, the action of the wind is much the same as last month, and severe storms occasionally occur in different parts of the country. The beautiful scenery displayed among the ever-changing clouds is equal to that of the other summer months, and enhances the prospect in the now matured landscape. It was a very hot month in the years 1842, 1846, 1856, 1857, 1871, 1880, and 1884. In 1842 the heat was excessive, and on several days the temperature in the shade was 90° and upwards. There had not been any rain in July, and the surface of the ground had become so hard and dry, that reflected solar heat influenced that in the shade. During the first four days of August, 1856, the daily highest temperature ranged from 90° to 92° in the shade. This month was also very hot in the year 1857, and was supposed to have been the hottest August (1842 excepted) since the year 1780.

It was a cool month in the years 1845, 1848, 1860, and 1864. On the 10th in 1848 a frost occurred, after some showers of rain and snow had fallen during the day, and early on the following morning I saw some sheaves of corn so frozen together that they could not be readily separated, which I imagine to have been an unprecedented recorded occurrence in the South of England. The rainfall, upon the average, exceeds that for July, which is partly to be attributed to the large quantity which falls in thunder showers. It was, however, a particularly wet month in the years 1852, 1860, 1878, 1879, 1881 ; and very dry in the years 1849, 1855, and 1880. Harvest now becomes general, and in forward seasons hop-picking commences during the last week.

About the middle of the month the swift takes its departure to more southerly regions. Various birds, as the finches, linnets, lapwings, &c., congregate, and the note of the redbreast is heard again.

SEPTEMBER.

" When is the aspect which Nature wears
    - The loveliest and dearest ?   Say, is it in Spring ?
    When its blossoms the apple tree beauteously bears,
        And birds on each spray are beginning to sing ?
    Or is it in Summer's fervid pride ?
    When the foliage is leafy on every side,
    And tempts us at noon in the green-wood to bide,
        And list to the wild bird's warbling?

" Lovely is Nature in seasons like these :
        But lovelier when *Autumn's* tints are spread
    On the landscape round ; and the wind-swept trees
        Their shady honours reluctantly shed ;

> When the bright sun sheds a watery beam
> On the changing leaves and the glistening stream ;
> Like smiles on a sorrowing cheek, that gleam
> When its woes and cares for a moment are fled."   B. BARTON.

September, the first of the autumnal months, is very variable in its character.   In some years it has been like one of the spring months, while in some few instances it has proved the hottest month of the year, with brilliant skies and great drought. The mean temperature is materially affected by the reduction in the length of day; nevertheless, in warm autumns, after a rather cool season, its general character is that of true summer.   When the month is fine there is not a more delightful period of the year on account of that peculiar softness and serenity of atmosphere which is seldom experienced in any other month.   In such seasons the equinoctial gales * are usually deferred till October. It was a very warm month in the years 1843, 1846, 1857, 1858, 1865, 1875, 1880, and 1884.   September, 1843, was an extraordinary instance of late summer-like heat.   On the first day the temperature rose to 90° in thé shade; on the 2nd, 87°; and on ten other days the highest daily temperature ranged from 80° to 85·5°.   I believe there is no other instance on record of such continued heat at this period of the year.   The heat of September, 1846, was a continuance of the great heat of the two previous months, and it was not till the morning of the 29th that there was any warning of autumn's approach.   The daily temperature during the first three weeks ranged from 70° to 82·5°, and at night it very rarely fell below 50° till the 29th.   No rain fell during the first three weeks.

Another remarkable instance of splendid weather in September occurred in the year 1865.   With the exception of a very slight shower on the 21st no rain fell during the month, while on fifteen days the sky was absolutely cloudless.   It was a somewhat cold month in the years 1845, 1847, 1860, 1863, and 1877 ; hence it is oftener warm than otherwise.   A crisis generally occurs about

* See subsequent remarks on page   .

the time of the equinox, and wherever the wind happens to be at that time, from it we may frequently determine what will be its prevalent direction during the ensuing quarter. Westerly winds are by far the most frequent, but they occasionally yield to those from the N.E. In the course of a long series of years the rainfall is found to be heavier during the autumn than at any other season of the year, but September is the driest of the three months.

The phenomena attendant upon sunrise and sunset at this season of the year are well worthy our attention, for it is certain that we nowhere meet with a more pleasing show of Nature than at this time. The richest decoration that human fancy can imagine must sink into insignificance when compared with a spectacle in which radiance and beauty are so pre-eminent.

OCTOBER.

" And when the fields with scatter'd grain supply
  No more the restless tenants of the sty,
  From oak to oak they run with eager haste,
  And, wrangling, share the first delicious taste
  Of fallen acorns; yet but thinly found
  Till the strong gale has shook them to the ground.
  It comes, and roaring woods obedient wave.
  Their home, well pleased, the joint adventurers leave;
  The trudging sow leads forth her numerous young,
  Playful, and white and clean, the briars among,
  Till briars and thorns increasing, fence them round,
  Where last year's mould'ring leaves bestrew the ground,
  And o'er their heads, loud lashed by furious squalls,
  Bright from their cups the rattling treasure falls;
  Hot, thirsty food, whence doubly sweet and cool,
  The welcome margin of some rush-grown pool." BLOOMFIELD.

October is frequently stormy and wet. The decrease of temperature is considerable, being more than six degrees less than September; nevertheless, the month is often warm, considering the shortness of the days, thus compensating for the cold of the longer days in April and May. After heavy rains the sky is particularly blue, and in warm seasons is dotted with the beautiful cirro-cumulus cloud. The gossamer web decks the hedges and stubble of the cornfields, indicating thereby a further continuation of fine weather. On some of the finest evenings we still have some beautiful sunsets, and a deep rosy tint extends far along the horizon. The first frosty mornings now occur, which are often the precursors of rain. Thunderstorms rarely happen, unless the first half of the month has been warmer than usual.

During the latter half of the month gales of wind are frequent from S.W., which cause considerable depressions of the barometer, and a low mean daily reading. The cause of this depression is supposed to originate from the great change of temperature which usually takes place towards the end of the month. Hence there is a loss of balance in the amount of vapour contained in the equatorial and polar currents. When the latter gains any amount of vapour, which the former loses, the exchange will perhaps account for the great rainfalls and the frequent gales of wind with which we are visited at this season of the year. Instances of unusual warmth occurred in the years 1847, 1851, 1856, 1857, 1861, 1874, 1876, and 1878. On October 12th, 1847, the highest temperature in the shade was as much as 71°. This month continued very warm throughout, with a great prevalence of westerly wind, and a moderate rainfall. October, 1856, was a warm and pleasant month, when the average highest daily temperature was upwards of 62°, and it frequently ranged between 65° and 68° during the second and third weeks. In October, 1857, the heat was unusually great, and on three days the maximum temperature in the shade ranged between 70° and 74°, while it was 72° so late as the 16th. The warmest October, however, was that in the year 1861, when the mean temperature was 4·5° above the average. On four days the temperature in the shade was 70° and upwards. N.E. winds were prevalent, and the rainfall was below the average. Cold weather prevailed in the years 1844, 1850, 1867, and 1881. The mean temperature of October, 1844, was more than four degrees below the average. October, 1850, was also very cold, and the mean temperature was nearly six degrees below the average. October, 1867, was almost as cold as the previous instance, and unusually severe frosts were recorded during the first fortnight. On the morning of the sixth the temperature of radiation was fifteen degrees below the freezing point.

NOVEMBER.

" Look Nature through, 'tis revolution all;
   All change ; no death. Day follows night, and night
   The dying day ; stars rise, and set, and rise ;
   Earth takes th' example. See, the summer gay,
   With her green chaplet and ambrosial flowers,
   Droops into pallid autumn ; winter gray,
   Horrid with frost, and turbulent with storm,
   Blows autumn and his golden fruits away :
   Then melts into the spring ; soft spring, with breath
   Favonian, from warm chambers of the south,
   Recalls the first. All to re-flourish, fades ;
   As in a wheel, all sink to re-ascend ;
   Emblems of man, who passes, not expires."   YOUNG.

November is generally a very dreary month, and, with a few exceptions, the atmosphere is for the most part unsettled, gloomy, and damp. The S.W. wind is prevalent, and most of the heaviest gales of wind on record have occurred in this month. A sudden decrease of temperature may at any time be expected, with sharp frosts and slight falls of snow ; but very severe frosts seldom commence till the last week, and are not usually of long continuance. Although the month is characterized by a general cloudiness of sky, and a considerable number of wet days, yet great variation is observed in the actual amount of rainfall. In a series of years the mean quantity exceeds that for September, but is less than that for October. Instances of unusual warmth in November occurred in the years 1846, 1847, 1852, 1857, and 1881. During the first week in November, 1846, the temperature was at or above 60° on three days, and up to summer heat in the full rays of the sun. In November,

1847, the temperature of the two first days was remarkably high —higher, indeed, both in the shade and in the sun than on several days in the months of May and June. This high temperature, accompanied by genial winds, continued both day and night to the 17th, when the first sensible diminution of warmth was observed in consequence of the wind blowing suddenly, and with some violence, from the northward. November, 1852, was remarkable for high temperature, slight thunder storms, gales of wind, heavy rain and floods. November, 1857, was also very warm. The mean temperature was nearly three and a half degrees above the average.

Very cold weather seldom prevails in the southern counties during November, but a remarkable instance occurred in the year 1851, when the cold was greater than had been experienced in this month since the year 1786. It was also a cold month in the years 1861, 1867, 1871, and 1879. Our forest trees generally lose their leaves by the first week, and should a sudden frost occur, after a wet day, the foliage falls to the ground very suddenly; nevertheless the woodlands, here and there, exhibit a beautiful variety of rich mingling hues.

Nearly all our summer and autumnal flowers are gone save a very few in some sheltered spots, but in their absence the bright green of the ivy, holly, and mosses stand forth in all the vividness and freshness of a new vegetation.

The various kinds of fungi are now very abundant, and there is much to admire in their elegance of form and varying tints.

Great quantities of winter birds now hasten to our comparatively warmer region. The woodpigeon, the latest of the winter birds, arrives. The various tribes of insects seek their winter quarters. The more tender burrow in the earth, beneath the reach of frost, and as the cold increases, their animal functions appear to cease, so that they require neither food nor air. It is very pleasing to consider with what extraordinary instinct all these insects are provided for the purpose of their self-preservation during an inclement season, so that when plants cease to grow, and flowers to blossom, they require neither the protection of the one nor the juices of the other.

DECEMBER.

" Where waves the leaf,
Or rings with harmony the merry vale?
Day's harbinger no song performs, no song
Or solo anthem deigns sweet Philomel.
The golden woodpecker laughs loud no more.
The pye no longer prates, no longer scolds
The saucy jay.   Who sees the goldfinch now
The feathered groundsel pluck, or hears him sing
In bower of apple blossoms perched?   Who sees
The chimney-haunting swallow skim the pool,
And quaintly dip, or hear his early song
Twittered to dawning day?   All, all are hushed.
The very bee her merry toil foregoes,
Nor seeks her nectar to be sought in vain.
Only the solitary robin sings,
And, perched aloft, with melancholy note,
Chaunts out the dirge of autumn.   Cheerless bird,
That loves the brown and desolated scene,
And scanty fare of Winter."   OLD POEM.

When we examine the tables of temperature a considerable variation is found in that for this month; thus in 1879 it was 32°, and in the next year 41·7°, and upon the average of the last eleven years it has equalled that for January. Generally, this month may be said to be mild and rather stormy, for the real severity of winter seldom commences before the last week, while the month and year expire either in gloomy, damp weather, or in a state of frost and snow, according to the prevailing character of the season during the few previous weeks.   If the month should prove mild a considerable quantity of rain frequently falls, but if cold it is almost invariably dry.

The direction of the wind varies as much or more than in any other month.   Should the S.W. prevail the atmosphere is very much disturbed by severe storms of wind, heavy rain, and even lightning and thunder; but if north, settled frost accompanied by heavy snow may occur, even at the beginning of the month. The gales from the westward are now and then very heavy, accompanied by a great depression of the barometer. It was a very mild month in the years 1843, 1852, 1857, 1868, and 1876.

On the morning of Christmas Day, 1868, the thrush and lark were singing as in early spring, and swarms of gnats were observed in sheltered situations.

On the other hand December was a very cold month in the years 1844, 1846, 1855, 1878 and 1879.

In 1844 the cold was more severe than had been known in December since the year 1788, when the mean was eight degrees below the average.

As a rule the month of December is very dreary and unpleasant; " but every medal has its reverse," and winter has its charms and usefulness; in fact, the reduction of temperature and its accompaniments are absolutely necessary for our English constitutions. Let the consideration, then, of the unspeakable advantages which we enjoy in our island home not only banish every repining thought that we are not placed in still milder regions and serener skies, but teach us to regard the Divine Being with ever increasing love and unceasing adoration.

> " NATURE never did betray
> The heart that loved her; 'tis her privilege
> Through all the years of this our life, to lead
> From joy to joy; for she can so inform
> The mind that is within us, so impress
> With quietness and beauty, and so feed
> With lofty thoughts, that neither evil tongues,
> Rash judgments, nor the sneers of selfish men,
> Nor greetings where no kindness is, nor all
> The dreary intercourse of daily life,
> Shall e'er prevail against us, or disturb
> Our cheerful faith, that all which we behold
> Is full of blessings."   WORDSWORTH.

TABLE IV.

SHOWING THE MEAN TEMPERATURE OF EACH MONTH AND YEAR.

	January.	February.	March.	April.	May.	June.	July.	August.	Sept.	Oct.	Nov.	Dec.	Mean Annual.
	°	°	°	°	°	°	°	°	°	°	°	°	°
1843	39.56	35.98	43.20	47.51	52.12	57.43	62.64	63.32	62.53	49.09	44.00	43.29	50.05
1844	37.67	35.55	41.80	51.21	51.40	59.21	61.50	58.56	57.58	47.64	42.53	31.45	48.00
1845	36.30	31.19	34.70	46.83	48.82	60.66	60.06	57.14	54.11	48.27	42.91	38.50	46.62
1846	41.72	41.96	42.88	47.48	54.82	65.50	64.06	64.43	62.11	52.64	46.25	32.79	51.38
1847	36.43	34.92	42.37	46.41	56.96	58.81	66.87	63.59	54.21	53.51	46.60	41.29	50.16
1848	34.12	42.51	43.90	48.75	58.24	59.08	61.59	58.09	57.08	51.29	41.23	42.14	49.83
1849	39.33	42.62	42.50	45.50	55.61	60.46	61.90	63.24	58.85	51.90	43.38	36.82	50.17
1850	33.04	42.14	39.04	49.66	52.88	60.73	62.64	60.80	56.58	45.59	44.95	38.48	48.87
1851	42.01	40.30	43.20	46.98	53.29	60.35	62.98	63.62	57.76	53.26	37.78	40.12	50.13
1852	41.51	40.84	42.17	47.53	53.25	57.10	70.32	62.67	58.61	48.20	49.86	46.86	51.57
1853	42.10	34.18	38.93	47.33	53.70	60.51	61.28	61.40	56.54	52.30	42.80	34.20	48.77
1854	39.47	40.55	44.16	50.50	51.69	57.84	62.86	62.31	59.98	50.78	40.66	41.19	50.16
1855	36.34	30.87	38.83	46.76	49.54	56.61	62.91	62.10	57.70	51.96	42.19	36.22	47.66
1856	40.04	42.82	41.23	48.44	50.78	57.90	62.53	64.72	55.93	54.28	41.21	39.61	49.95
1857	36.94	39.96	42.75	47.23	55.75	63.21	64.03	66.68	60.56	55.33	46.11	44.61	51.93
1858	37.33	36.92	42.15	48.77	51.62	63.84	60.70	62.15	60.43	52.82	40.30	40.77	49.81
1859	39.64	42.05	45.92	47.44	54.87	62.99	68.18	63.16	57.51	52.25	42.54	36.56	51.09
1860	40.34	35.51	41.30	43.81	53.00	56.12	59.08	58.91	53.64	50.61	40.44	36.04	47.40
1861	33.51	41.48	43.74	45.84	52.77	60.94	60.84	61.76	56.12	55.81	39.52	40.47	49.40
1862	37.60	41.00	44.45	49.01	56.48	57.10	59.37	59.63	55.64	52.36	40.71	42.24	49.63
1863	41.52	40.93	43.28	49.18	52.52	59.15	60.55	62.20	53.09	52.58	45.64	40.89	50.12
1864	36.71	36.33	42.80	48.92	55.23	58.37	62.16	59.25	56.52	50.62	41.37	37.65	48.82
1865	36.16	37.06	36.72	50.25	55.25	61.08	63.39	60.37	63.48	52.79	44.26	42.10	50.29
1866	42.44	41.33	41.57	49.63	51.48	62.93	62.59	60.64	57.16	51.83	43.37	42.15	50.59
1867	33.29	44.32	38.24	49.20	52.57	57.40	58.35	60.60	56.55	46.86	39.94	35.96	47.77
1868	35.00	41.01	42.41	46.54	56.13	59.50	64.77	61.82	58.21	47.24	41.39	46.23	50.02
1869	40.88	44.80	38.44	50.95	51.98	55.57	64.16	60.16	58.62	48.84	43.11	37.15	49.55
1870	38.48	35.53	40.00	48.01	52.52	60.95	65.57	60.63	55.70	50.44	41.03	33.18	48.50

The result of table 4 informs us that the following are the mean temperatures of the several months :—

January, 38.19° February, 39.09° March, 41.52° April, 48.06° May, 53.40°
June, 59.69° July, 62.78° August, 61.57° September, 57.60° October, 51.11 °
November, 42.71° December, 39.24°—and the mean annual temperature 49.58°

The following are the values of the extreme mean temperature in each month :—

In January,	1850	the mean temperature was	33.04	and in January,	1866	42.44	Diff.	9.40
In February,	1855	,,	30.87	and in February,	1869	44.80	,,	13.93
In March,	1845	,,	34.70	and in March,	1862	44.45	,,	9.75
In April,	1860	,,	43.81	and in April,	1844	51.21	,,	7.40
In May,	1845	,,	48.82	and in May,	1848	58.24	,,	9.42
In June,	1869	,,	55.57	and in June,	1846	65.50	,,	9.93
In July,	1867	,,	58.35	and in July,	1852	70.32	,,	11.97
In August	1845	,,	57.14	and in August,	1857	66.68	,,	9.54
In September,	1863	,,	53.09	and in September,	1865	63.48	,,	10.39
In October,	1850	,,	45.59	and in October,	1861	55.81	,,	10.22
In November,	1851	,,	37.78	and in November,	1852	49.86	,,	12.08
In December,	1844	,,	31.45	and in December,	1852	46.86	,,	15.41

The coldest month was February, 1855, and the hottest, July, 1852.

The greatest variation occurred in December, and the least in April.

The mean annual temperature varies 5.3°, viz., from 51.93° in 1857, to 46.62° in 1845 ; and although at first sight this difference may not appear considerable, yet it is sufficient to exert an enormous influence upon the general character of the seasons, the produce of the soil, and the health of the population. The Registrar General's interesting returns have fully established the important fact that there is a very intimate connection between temperature and mortality. Whenever the mean temperature falls to 45°, or thereabouts, the number of deaths from diseases of the respiratory organs increases, and should it fall below 40° the death rate from such diseases is still higher. When a period of intense cold prevails, so that the temperature scarcely rises above the freezing point for two or three weeks, the number of deaths will be found to exceed what takes place during an epidemic of cholera or scarlet fever. But when the mean temperature rises to 55° there will be an increase in the number of deaths from diseases of the abdominal viscera, and this number will fluctuate as the temperature fluctuates between 55° and 65°. Hence we are informed that the mortality from all causes is least when the temperature is about 50°, which is very little above our mean annual temperature.

TABLE V.

A TABLE shewing the Highest and Lowest mean Monthly Temperature in each Year, together with the amount of Difference of Temperature.

Year.	Highest mean Temperature.		Lowest mean Temperature.		Difference.
		°		°	°
1843	August ...	63.32	February ...	35.98	27.34
1844	July ...	61.50	December ...	31.45	30.05
1845	June ...	60.66	February ...	31.19	29.47
1846	June ...	65.50	December ...	32.79	32.71
1847	July ...	66.87	February ...	34.92	31.95
1848	July ...	61.59	January ...	34.12	27.47
1849	August ...	63.24	December ...	36.82	26.42
1850	July ...	62.64	January ...	33.04	29.60
1851	August ...	63.62	November ...	37.78	25.84
1852	July ...	70.32	February ...	40.84	29.48
1853	August ...	61.40	February ...	34.18	27.22
1854	July ...	62.86	January ...	39.47	23.39
1855	July ...	62.91	February ...	30.87	32.04
1856	August ...	64.72	December ...	39.61	25.11
1857	August ...	66.68	January ...	36.94	29.74
1858	June ...	63.84	February ...	36.92	26.92
1859	July ...	68.18	December ...	36.56	31.62
1860	July ...	59.08	February ...	35.51	23.57
1861	August ...	61.76	January ...	33.51	28.25
1862	August ...	59.63	January ...	37.60	22.03
1863	August ...	62.20	December ...	40.89	21.31
1864	July ...	62.16	February ...	36.33	25.83
1865	September ...	63.48	January ...	36.16	27.32
1866	June ...	62.93	February ...	41.33	21.60
1867	August ...	60.60	January ...	33.29	27.31
1868	July ...	64.77	January ...	35.00	29.77
1869	July ...	64.16	December ...	37.15	27.01
1870	July ...	65.57	December ...	33.18	32.39

The above table represents in a tabular form the extremes of mean monthly temperature in each year; but in subsequent pages I have given descriptions of various current phenomena, not only in cases of extreme temperature, but also the more prominent phenomena, *in every month*, throughout the series.

TABLE VI.

THE FOLLOWING TABLE SHEWS THE MEAN TEMPERATURE OF THE
SEASONS.

YEAR.	WINTER.	SPRING.	SUMMER.	AUTUMN.
Commencing previous December.	December. January. February.	March. April. May.	June. July. August	September. October. November.
1843	39.56	47.61	61.13	51.87
1844	38.83	48.13	59.75	49.25
1845	32.98	43.45	59.28	48.23
1846	40.72	48.39	64.66	53.66
1847	34.71	48.58	63.09	51.44
1848	39.30	50.29	59.58	49.86
1849	41.36	47.87	61.86	51.37
1850	37.33	47.19	61.39	49.04
1851	40.26	47.82	62.31	49.60
1852	40.82	47.65	63.36	52.22
1853	41.05	46.65	61.06	50.25
1854	38.07	48.78	61.00	50.34
1855	36.13	45.04	60.54	50.62
1856	39.69	46.82	61.72	50.47
1857	38.83	48.58	64.64	54.00
1858	39.62	47.51	62.23	51.18
1859	40.82	49.41	64.77	50.76
1860	37.47	46.03	58.03	48.23
1861	37.01	47.45	61.18	50.48
1862	39.69	49.98	58.70	49.57
1863	41.56	48.32	60.63	50.43
1864	37.97	48.98	59.92	49.50
1865	36.95	47.40	61.61	53.51
1866	41.95	47.56	62.05	50.78
1867	39.92	46.67	58.78	47.78
1868	37.32	48.36	62.03	48.95
1869	43.97	47.12	59.96	50.19
1870	37.05	46.84	62.38	49.05

The mean difference of temperature between winter and summer is . . . . 22.38°

The mean difference of temperature between spring and autumn is . . . . 2.79°

The mean temperature of winter from all observations is . . . . 38.96°

The mean temperature of spring from all observations is . . . . 47.66°

The mean temperature of summer from all observations is . . . . 61.34°

The mean temperature of autumn from all observations is . . . . 50°.45

The five coldest winters were those of 1845, 1847, 1855, 1861, and 1865, and the mean of their temperatures was 35°.5. ·

The five warmest winters were those of 1849, 1853, 1863, 1866, and 1869; the mean of their temperatures was 41°.97.

The five coldest springs were those of 1845, 1853, 1855, 1860, 1867, and the mean of their temperatures was 45°.56.

The five warmest springs were those of 1848, 1854, 1859, 1862, and 1864; the mean of their temperatures was 49°.48.

The five coldest summers were those of 1845, 1848, 1860, 1862, and 1867; the mean of their temperature was 58°.87.

The five warmest summers were those of 1846, 1847, 1852, 1857, 1859; the mean of their temperatures was 64°.10.

The five coldest autumns were those of 1844, 1845, 1850, 1860, and 1867; the mean of their temperatures was 48°.50.

The five warmest autumns were those of 1843, 1846, 1852, 1857, and 1865; the mean of their temperatures was 53°.05.

The coldest winter was that of 1845; the warmest that of 1869.

The coldest spring was that of 1845; the warmest that of 1848.

The coldest summer was that of 1860; the warmest that of 1859.

The coldest autumn was that of 1867; the warmest that of 1857.

The difference between the coldest and warmest winter was 10°.99.

The difference between the coldest and warmest spring was 6°.84.

The difference between the coldest and warmest summer was 6°.74.

The difference between the coldest and warmest autumn was 6°.22.

The greatest variation in temperature occurs in winter, and the least in autumn, and this variation closely coincides with the results of the long series of observations conducted at the apartments of the Royal Society, together with those at the Royal Observatory at Greenwich, as deduced by Mr. Glaisher.

The hottest month in the year occurred four times in June, thirteen times in July, ten times in August, and once in September. The coldest month in the year occurred nine times in January, ten times in February, eight times in December, and once in November.　　　　　　　　　　E

TABLE VII.

SHOWING THE HIGHEST AND LOWEST TEMPERATURE OF THE AIR IN THE SHADE, AND OF SOLAR AND TERRESTRIAL RADIATION IN EACH YEAR.

Year.	Temperature of the Air in Shade.					Temperature of Radiation.				
	Date.		Highest.	Date.		Lowest.	Date.		Highest in the Sun.	Date.		Lowest on the Grass.
1843	September	1	90°.0	February	13	19°.2	...	...	...	...	...	...
1844	July	25	86.0	January	3	11.0	...	...	...	...	...	...
1845	June	17	85.0	February	12	3.0	...	...	...	...	...	...
1846	June	20	92.5	December	14	13.0	June	20	113°	December	14	12°
1847	July	14	98.0	February	12	1.0	July	14	113	February	12	—4*
1848	July	6	83.0	January	28	11.0	September	16	98	January	28	10
1849	June	5	84.0	December	29	14.0	June	24	100	December	29	8
1850	July	17	89.0	January	8	18.0	June	26	100	January	8	13
1851	June	27	90.0	November	19	19.0	August	8	105	November	19	13
1852	July	6	93.0	February	21	17.0	July	14	112	February	21	15
1853	July	8	85.0	December	26	14.0	July	8	98	December	26	9
1854	July	24	92.0	January	3	16.0	July	24	102	January	3	13
1855	May	26	82.0	February	11	9.0	June	29	99	February	11	2
1856	August	2	92.0	December	2	17.0	August	2	107	December	2	13
1857	June	28	92.0	January	30	16.0	August	23	101	January	30	14
1858	June	15	90.0	January	24	20.0	June	15	106	January	24	17
1859	July	12	90.0	December	17	16.4	July	12	107	December	17	14
1860	July	11	77.2	December	29	6.6	July	11	102	December	29	3
1861	June	19	83.6	January	11	14.2	June	19	114	January	9	6
1862	May	6	80.2	March	5	18.6	August	3	129	March	4	14
1863	August	13	83.2	February	18	22.0	July	9	121	February	18	15
1864	July	19	83.4	January	7	14.6	April	21	113	December	18	L3
1865	June	21	88.0	January	29	11.2	August	19	115	January	29	6
1866	July	12	86.4	January	12	22.4	July	11	108	January	12	15
1867	August	14	83.4	January	4	4.0	August	23	110	January	4	—2*
1868	July	22	91.6	January	1	17.0	July	21	113	January	1	6
1869	July	17	88.6	December	29	13.0	July	16	106	December	29	7
1870	June	22	88.6	March	14	13.0	June	21	112	December	30	6

* The only instances of the temperature of radiation falling below Zero ; the one being 36° and the other 34° below the freezing point of water.

TABLE VIII.

SHOWING THE MONTHLY AND YEARLY MEAN MAXIMUM TEMPERATURE IN THE SHADE.

	January.	February.	March.	April.	May.	June.	July.	August.	Sept.	October.	Nov.	Dec.	Annual.
1843	45.3	41.6	53.1	59.5	61.8	66.8	72.2	74.9	74.6	58.3	50.5	47.6	58.8
1844	43.3	42.3	49.7	63.7	63.9	71.8	74.1	69.1	68.6	57.2	48.1	35.4	57.2
1845	41.5	37.4	42.1	56.1	59.3	72.7	69.6	67.4	63.3	56.4	49.1	44.9	54.9
1846	45.7	47.3	50.9	55.3	66.0	78.8	74.7	74.1	72.5	58.2	50.3	38.0	59.3
1847	40.6	41.5	51.8	57.9	69.3	70.3	80.6	75.8	66.0	61.9	52.6	45.6	59.4
1848	37.5	47.9	51.4	57.9	72.5	68.0	71.5	66.5	67.1	58.0	47.1	46.4	57.6
1849	43.5	50.3	50.1	53.9	65.2	72.8	73.6	74.6	68.2	59.2	49.2	41.2	58.5
1850	37.0	48.3	48.3	58.1	63.3	74.0	73.7	71.1	67.4	54.4	51.3	43.0	57.5
1851	47.4	46.7	49.7	56.7	65.0	72.9	74.5	74.6	69.0	60.5	45.4	44.8	58.9
1852	47.9	47.7	53.0	57.9	63.8	66.7	82.8	74.2	69.5	57.3	54.9	51.8	60.6
1853	47.7	40.2	48.1	55.8	66.0	71.4	70.6	72.4	66.6	60.9	50.1	39.1	57.4
1854	44.8	47.7	55.0	64.1	63.1	67.8	75.5	75.1	72.3	60.4	47.4	46.7	59.9
1855	40.9	36.9	46.5	57.5	59.2	68.3	73.4	73.5	68.2	58.8	46.1	40.8	55.8
1856	44.4	48.2	48.7	57.6	59.8	67.8	74.0	75.5	67.0	62.5	48.5	45.1	58.2
1857	42.2	48.5	51.3	56.9	68.6	76.4	75.3	77.8	70.8	63.4	53.3	49.7	61.1
1858	44.0	44.1	51.9	58.0	61.0	75.3	70.5	72.7	68.7	61.0	45.7	44.8	58.1
1859	44.4	48.5	52.9	56.3	64.4	74.6	81.1	74.3	66.1	59.4	49.0	41.9	59.4
1860	45.4	41.4	47.9	52.7	61.9	63.6	68.9	66.5	62.0	57.7	45.5	40.6	54.5
1861	37.9	46.4	51.2	56.0	63.9	70.9	69.6	71.7	65.8	62.7	46.5	45.1	57.3
1862	42.6	45.6	50.4	57.1	65.1	66.3	69.1	69.8	63.1	59.1	46.0	46.9	56.7
1863	45.8	48.4	52.5	59.5	62.5	68.9	73.8	72.0	62.8	58.7	51.6	48.0	58.7
1864	41.6	41.9	50.8	59.3	66.7	69.3	74.6	71.3	65.9	57.8	48.9	42.4	57.5
1865	41.7	42.0	44.0	64.9	66.5	74.6	74.8	70.6	75.3	60.3	51.4	47.0	59.4
1866	48.0	46.3	49.2	58.7	63.3	74.4	73.7	71.4	64.8	59.3	51.6	49.0	59.1
1867	39.3	50.0	44.1	57.5	63.2	69.5	69.8	71.6	66.5	56.0	47.5	41.9	56.4
1868	41.2	48.8	51.3	57.6	69.2	74.6	78.8	72.8	69.5	56.3	46.7	50.8	59.8
1869	46.0	50.2	44.5	60.0	60.5	66.7	76.3	71.5	66.7	56.7	49.7	42.4	57.6
1870	42.9	40.2	46.2	60.8	65.2	73.9	77.1	70.5	65.6	58.2	47.7	37.7	57.2

TABLE IX.

SHOWING THE MONTHLY AND YEARLY MEAN MINIMUM TEMPERATURE AT NIGHT.

	January.	February.	March.	April.	May.	June.	July.	August.	Sept.	Oct.	Nov.	Dec.	Annual.
	°	°	°	°	°	°	°	°	°	°	°	°	°
1843	33.7	30.3	33.2	35.4	42.4	48.0	53.0	51.6	50.4	39.8	37.5	38.9	41.1
1844	31.9	28.7	33.8	38.7	38.8	46.5	48.8	47.9	46.5	38.0	36.9	27.4	38.6
1845	31.0	24.8	27.2	37.4	40.3	48.5	50.4	46.8	44.8	40.0	36.6	32.0	38.3
1846	37.6	36.6	34.8	39.6	43.5	52.1	53.3	54.6	51.6	47.0	42.1	27.5	43.3
1847	32.1	28.2	32.9	34.9	44.5	47.3	53.0	51.3	42.4	45.0	40.5	36.9	40.7
1848	30.7	37.0	36.3	39.5	43.9	50.1	51.6	49.6	47.0	44.5	35.3	37.8	41.9
1849	35.1	34.9	34.8	37.0	45.9	48.0	50.1	51.8	49.5	44.5	37.5	32.3	41.8
1850	29.0	35.9	29.7	41.2	42.4	47.4	51.5	50.4	45.7	36.7	38.5	33.9	40.2
1851	36.5	33.8	36.6	37.2	41.5	47.7	51.4	52.6	46.4	45.9	30.1	35.3	41.3
1852	35.0	33.9	31.3	37.1	42.7	47.4	57.7	51.1	47.6	39.0	44.8	41.8	42.4
1853	36.5	28.1	29.7	38.8	41.3	49.6	51.9	50.3	46.4	43.6	35.5	29.2	40.0
1854	34.1	33.3	33.3	37.1	40.1	47.8	50.2	49.5	47.3	41.1	33.9	35.6	40.2
1855	31.7	24.7	31.1	36.0	39.8	44.8	52.4	50.6	47.2	45.0	38:2	31.6	39.4
1856	35.6	37.4	33.7	39.2	41.7	48.0	51.0	53.9	44.8	46.0	33.8	34.0	41.6
1857	31.6	31.3	34.1	37.5	42.8	49.9	52.7	55.5	50.3	47.1	38.9	39.4	42.6
1858	30.5	29.7	32.3	39.5	42.2	52.3	50.9	51.6	52.1	44.5	33.7	36.6	41.3
1859	34.8	35.6	38.8	38.5	45.3	51.3	55.2	51.9	48.8	45.0	36.0	31.2	42.7
1860	35.2	29.6	34.6	34.8	44.0	48.6	49.2	51.3	45.2	43.4	35.3	31.4	40.2
1861	29.1	36.5	36.2	35.6	41.6	50.9	52.0	51.7	46.4	48.9	32.5	35.8	41.4
1862	32.5	36.3	38.4	40.9	47.8	47.8	49.5	49.4	48.1	45.5	35.3	37.5	42.4
1863	37.2	33.4	34.0	38.8	42.4	49.3	47.2	52.3	43.3	46.4	39.6	33.7	41.5
1864	31.7	30.7	34.8	38.5	43.6	47.3	49.7	47.1	47.1	43.3	33.8	32.9	40.0
1865	30.6	32.0	29.4	35.5	43.9	47.5	53.1	50.0	51.6	45.2	37.0	37.1	41.1
1866	36.8	36.2	33.9	40.4	39.6	51.4	51.4	49.8	49.4	44.2	35.0	35.2	41.9
1867	27.2	38.5	32.3	40.8	41.9	45.3	46.8	49.6	46.5	37.6	32.3	29.9	39.1
1868	28.7	33.1	33.4	35.4	43.0	44.3	50.7	50.8	46.8	38.1	36.0	41.6	40.2
1869	35.7	39.3	32.3	41.8	43.4	44.3	51.9	48.7	50.4	40.9	36.4	31.9	41.4
1870	33.9	30.7	33.7	35.2	39.8	47.9	53.9	50.7	45.7	42.6	34.2	28.5	39.7

TABLE X.

SHOWING THE MEAN DAILY RANGE OF TEMPERATURE IN EACH MONTH IN THE SHADE.

	January.	February.	March.	April.	May.	June.	July.	August.	Sept.	October.	Nov.	Dec.	Annual.
	°	°	°	°	°	°	°	°	°	°	°	°	°
1843	11.6	11.3	19.9	24.1	19.4	18.8	19.2	23.3	24.2	18.5	13.0	8.7	17.7
1844	11.4	13.6	15.9	25.0	25.1	25.3	25.3	21.2	22.1	19.2	11.2	8.0	18.6
1845	10.5	12.6	14.9	18.7	19.0	24.2	19.2	20.6	18.5	16.4	12.5	12.9	16.6
1846	8.1	10.7	16.1	15.7	22.5	26.7	21.4	19.5	20.9	11.2	8.2	10.8	16.0
1847	8.5	13.3	18.9	23.0	24.8	23.0	27.6	24.5	23.6	16.9	12.1	8.7	18.7
1848	6.8	10.9	15.1	18.4	28.6	17.9	19.9	16.9	20.1	13.5	11.8	8.6	15.7
1849	8.4	15.4	15.3	16.9	19.3	24.8	23.5	22.8	18.7	14.7	11.7	8.9	16.7
1850	8.0	12.4	18.6	16.9	20.9	26.6	22.2	20.7	21.7	17.7	12.8	9.1	17.3
1851	10.9	12.9	13.1	19.5	23.5	25.2	23.1	22.0	22.6	14.6	15.3	9.5	17.6
1852	12.9	13.8	21.7	20.8	21.1	19.3	25.1	23.1	21.9	18.3	10.1	10.0	18.2
1853	11.2	12.1	18.4	17.0	24.7	21.8	18.7	22.1	20.2	17.3	14.6	9.9	17.3
1854	10.7	14.4	21.7	27.0	23.0	20.0	25.3	25.6	25.0	19.3	13.5	11.1	19.7
1855	9.2	12.2	15.4	21.5	19.4	23.5	21.0	22.9	21.0	13.8	7.9	9.2	16.4
1856	8.8	10.8	15.0	18.4	18.1	19.8	23.0	21.6	22.2	16.5	14.7	11.1	16.6
1857	10.6	17.2	17.2	19.4	25.8	26.5	22.6	22.3	20.5	16.3	14.4	10.3	18.5
1858	13.5	14.4	19.6	18.5	18.8	23.0	19.6	21.1	16.6	16.5	12.0	8.2	16.8
1859	9.6	12.9	14.1	17.8	19.1	23.3	25.9	22.4	17.3	14.4	13.0	10.7	16.7
1860	10.2	11.8	13.3	17.9	17.9	15.0	19.7	15.2	16.8	14.3	10.2	9.2	14.3
1861	8.8	9.9	15.0	20.4	22.3	20.0	17.6	20.0	19.4	13.8	14.0	9.3	15.9
1862	10.1	9.3	12.0	16.2	17.3	18.5	19.6	20.4	15.0	13.6	10.7	9.4	14.3
1863	8.6	15.0	18.5	20.7	20.1	19.6	26.6	19.7	19.5	12.3	12.0	14.3	17.2
1864	9.9	11.2	16.0	20.8	23.1	22.0	24.9	24.2	18.8	14.5	15.1	9.5	17.5
1865	11.1	10.0	14.6	29.4	22.6	27.1	21.7	20.6	23.7	15.1	14.4	9.9	18.3
1866	11.2	10.1	15.3	18.3	23.7	23.0	22.3	21.6	15.4	15.1	16.6	13.8	17.2
1867	12.1	11.5	11.8	16.7	21.3	24.2	23.0	22.0	20.0	18.4	15.2	12.0	17.3
1868	12.4	15.6	17.9	22.1	26.2	30.3	28.0	21.9	22.7	18.2	10.6	9.2	19.6
1869	10.2	10.8	12.2	18.1	17.1	22.4	24.4	22.8	16.2	15.7	13.3	10.5	16.1
1870	8.9	9.5	12.4	25.6	25.4	25.9	23.2	19.8	19.9	15.6	13.4	9.2	17.4

TABLE XI.

SHOWING THE MONTHLY MEAN HIGHEST TEMPERATURE IN THE SUN AT FOUR FEET ABOVE THE SURFACE OF SHORT GRASS.

	January.	February.	March.	April.	May.	June.	July.	August.	Sept.	Oct.	Nov.	Dec.	Annual.
1846	48.6	53.5	58.1	63.0	75.4	93.6	85.1	80.2	85.0	70.6	58.2	46.3	68.1
1847	46.2	48.5	58.1	65.4	75.8	78.8	91.2	84.6	76.5	70.0	59.4	50.6	67.1
1848	44.0	53.6	58.0	64.1	81.9	71.5	78.1	74.4	76.9	68.9	55.2	52.3	64.9
1849	48.3	57.8	54.1	59.7	70.4	82.0	80.5	80.4	75.5	66.0	58.0	46.2	64.9
1850	40.8	54.5	57.2	65.0	70.7	83.1	84.0	80.3	78.8	63.2	58.4	49.9	65.5
1851	54.5	55.9	55.6	66.2	73.7	88.0	84.9	85.5	83.8	67.9	55.5	49.2	68.4
1852	54.5	53.7	63.5	66.9	70.2	72.7	96.5	86.2	77.7	63.3	57.4	54.7	68.1
1853	50.9	44.7	54.2	61.0	74.1	76.3	76.1	79.2	74.1	65.9	55.4	41.5	62.8
1854	47.7	52.7	61.8	72.0	70.2	73.7	83.6	81.5	80.6	66.0	50.4	49.2	65.8
1855	43.4	43.2	54.9	70.9	69.9	78.7	85.7	84.3	81.0	67.9	51.8	46.7	64.8
1856	48.7	52.8	57.6	68.5	68.3	80.5	81.3	85.2	76.8	71.4	53.1	48.2	66.0
1857	46.4	56.3	58.1	65.1	78.8	87.0	85.3	88.3	81.2	71.9	58.1	52.7	69.1
1858	47.9	52.8	61.1	70.5	72.5	91.1	80.1	86.5	81.4	70.6	55.3	48.3	68.2
1859	47.7	53.7	58.6	65.9	74.3	88.2	97.7	89.7	82.6	70.6	60.2	49.0	69.8
1860	51.1	. 50.4	57.4	64.8	79.0	76.8	87.0	82.6	78.4	69.9	56.7	47.7	66.8

TABLE XII.

SHOWING THE MONTHLY MEAN HIGHEST TEMPERATURE IN THE SUN AT FOUR INCHES ABOVE THE
SURFACE OF SHORT GRASS.

	January.	February.	March.	April.	May.	June.	July.	August.	Sept.	Oct.	Nov.	Dec.	Annual.
	°	°	°	°	°	°	°	°	°	°	°	°	°
1861	47.7	57.8	66.2	78.4	88.7	93.1	86.2	89.8	84.2	82.6	58.8	57.4	74.2
1862	56.7	60.2	69.0	75.3	88.8	95.7	100.9	101.0	93.0	71.7	53.1	51.0	76.3
1863	53.6	69.6	76.0	86.4	91.1	94.1	105.7	94.8	86.7	73.1	63.3	56.2	79.2
1864	55.3	58.9	76.9	91.0	90.7	86.6	93.0	85.2	81.6	69.3	59.1	49.9	74.8
1865	49.9	49.4	59.0	80.0	82.0	93.5	94.5	98.9	94.9	73.0	60.4	51.4	73.9
1866	53.8	55.5	62.9	74.0	79.9	90.4	93.3	87.0	84.1	77.5	59.4	53.4	72.6
1867	45.9	56.9	55.1	73.4	79.0	86.0	87.3	91.7	84.1	69.2	58.4	50.7	69.8
1868	46.1	59.5	66.6	74.1	85.5	92.4	97.2	88.2	86.6	69.0	53.5	56.0	72.9
1869	53.6	60.8	58.7	76.7	75.1	82.9	92.4	89.8	81.9	70.0	60.2	49.8	71.0
1870	50.5	49.3	60.2	80.0	85.4	96.8	97.2	92.6	87.6	77.4	61.2	47.0	73.8

TABLE XIII.

SHOWING THE MONTHLY AND ANNUAL MEAN LOWEST TEMPERATURE *UPON* THE SURFACE OF SHORT GRASS.

	January.	February.	March.	April.	May.	June.	July.	August.	Sept.	Oct.	Nov.	Dec.	Annual.
	°	°	°	°	°	°	°	°	°	°	°	°	°
1846	36.3	34.1	29.5	33.8	38.2	47.7	50.0	50.4	44.4	41.3	38.6	25.0	39.1
1847	30.4	26.2	28.9	31.8	40.2	42.0	48.9	46.1	38.5	41.4	37.1	34.4	37.2
1848	28.8	34.5	34.6	36.9	42.5	46.9	48.6	45.9	42.3	40.8	30.9	33.6	38.8
1849	32.1	32.7	31.8	33.3	43.1	44.0	46.7	48.3	45.1	41.6	33.9	30.2	38.6
1850	26.3	34.1	26.6	38.3	39.6	44.6	48.9	47.6	43.3	33.8	35.7	31.5	37.5
1851	34.3	30.2	33.4	35.0	35.1	45.8	49.4	48.1	43.0	43.0	26.7	32.5	38.0
1852	31.6	31.2	28.3	31.3	39.3	45.1	52.7	47.8	44.1	37.5	42.4	39.2	39.2
1853	33.9	25.1	26.7	36.1	38.6	47.0	49.3	47.4	44.1	41.1	33.3	26.1	37.4
1854	31.2	30.0	29.9	34.2	36.7	44.2	46.6	45.5	42.7	38.9	30.1	31.7	36.8
1855	28.2	20.8	27.9	31.7	36.0	42.6	48.2	46.2	43.0	41.6	33.0	27.7	35.6
1856	32.8	34.8	30.2	35.6	38.9	44.5	47.4	48.2	40.7	40.0	29.8	31.4	37.8
1857	29.4	27.8	31.4	35.1	39.0	46.3	48.6	51.8	46.1	43.3	37.6	35.8	39.3
1858	27.0	26.1	27.7	35.7	38.4	48.5	43.3	47.4	48.3	40.8	30.8	34.7	37.4
1859	32.1	33.2	35.8	38.7	41.8	47.7	51.8	47.1	43.3	41.0	30.9	27.8	39.2
1860	33.7	27.3	32.7	31.8	40.6	46.0	45.5	47.4	40.5	37.0	30.1	25.4	36.5
1861	24.5	32.4	30.1	30.5	35.4	46.2	48.9	48.5	43.0	44.6	29.9	31.7	37.1
1862	29.2	33.7	37.2	37.1	45.0	44.6	45.5	45.1	45.2	40.3	30.8	33.3	38.9
1863	33.2	28.3	27.7	33.8	36.0	44.1	40.5	46.9	39.3	41.5	35.8	32.1	36.6
1864	28.7	28.7	31.2	34.8	40.0	43.6	45.2	42.4	43.6	37.8	29.2	29.7	36.2
1865	26.7	29.3	24.9	34.0	39.0	41.2	47.7	44.4	44.1	38.9	31.3	33.2	36.2
1866	33.4	29.6	28.9	35.2	33.8	45.8	45.8	44.8	44.0	38.3	28.9	30.4	36.3
1867	22.7	34.6	28.7	36.2	38.3	41.0	42.4	45.7	41.8	31.7	26.0	24.8	34.5
1868	25.2	27.8	29.3	31.8	38.8	40.5	47.0	46.6	42.8	35.2	33.7	39.0	36.5
1869	33.0	36.2	29.1	38.5	41.8	43.3	50.0	45.6	47.1	36.6	31.6	26.1	38.2
1870	28.4	26.8	28.6	28.4	33.3	42.1	49.4	46.2	40.6	37.0	28.8	23.5	34.3

TABLE XIV.

SHOWING THE EXTREME MEAN RANGE OF TEMPERATURE, OR THE DIFFERENCE BETWEEN THE MONTHLY MEAN HIGHEST TEMPERATURE IN THE SUN AT FOUR FEET *ABOVE*, AND THAT *UPON* THE SURFACE OF SHORT GRASS.

	January.	February.	March.	April.	May.	June.	July.	August.	Sept.	Oct.	Nov.	Dec.	Annual Mean.
1846	12.3	19.4	28.6	29.2	37.2	45.9	35.1	29.8	40.6	29.3	19.6	21.3	29.0
1847	15.8	22.3	29.2	33.6	35.6	36.8	42.3	38.5	38.0	28.6	22.3	16.2	29.9
1848	15.2	19.1	23.4	27.2	39.4	24.6	29.5	28.5	33.6	28.1	24.3	18.7	26.0
1849	16.2	25.1	22.3	26.4	27.3	38.0	33.8	32.1	30.4	24.4	24.1	16.0	26.3
1850	14.5	20.4	30.6	26.7	31.1	38.5	35.1	32.7	35.5	29.4	22.7	18.4	27.9
1851	20.2	25.7	22.2	31.2	38.6	42.2	35.5	37.4	40.8	24.9	28.8	16.7	30.3
1852	22.9	22.5	35.2	35.6	30.9	27.6	43.8	38.4	33.6	25.8	15.0	15.5	28.9
1853	17.0	19.6	27.5	24.9	35.5	29.3	26.8	31.8	30.0	24.8	22.1	15.4	25.4
1854	16.5	22.7	31.9	37.8	33.5	29.5	37.0	36.0	37.9	27.1	20.3	17.5	28.9
1855	15.2	22.4	27.0	39.2	33.9	36.1	37.5	38.1	38.0	26.3	18.8	19.0	29.2
1856	15.9	18.0	27.4	32.9	29.4	36.0	33.9	37.0	36.1	31.4	23.3	16.8	28.1
1857	17.0	28.5	26.7	30.0	39.8	40.7	36.7	36.5	35.1	28.6	20.5	16.9	29.7
1858	20.9	26.7	33.4	34.8	34.1	42.6	36.8	39.1	33.1	29.8	24.5	13.6	30.7
1859	15.6	20.5	22.8	27.2	32.5	40.5	47.9	42.6	39.3	29.6	29.3	21.2	30.5
1860	17.4	23.1	24.7	33.0	38.4	30.8	41.5	35.2	37.9	32.9	26.6	22.3	30.2

F

TABLE XV.

SHOWING THE EXTREME MEAN RANGE OF TEMPERATURE, OR THE DIFFERENCE BETWEEN THE MONTHLY MEAN HIGHEST TEMPERATURE IN THE SUN AT FOUR INCHES *ABOVE*, AND THAT *UPON* THE SURFACE OF SHORT GRASS.

	January.	February.	March.	April.	May.	June.	July.	August.	Sept.	Oct.	Nov.	Dec.	Annual Mean.
	°	°	°	°	°	°	°	°	°	°	°	°	°
1861	23.2	25.4	36.1	47.9	53.3	46.9	37.3	41.3	41.2	38.0	28.9	25.7	37.1
1862	27.5	26.5	31.8	38.2	43.8	51.1	55.4	55.9	47.8	31.4	22.3	17.7	37.4
1863	20.4	41.3	48.3	52.6	55.1	50.0	65.2	47.9	47.4	31.6	27.5	24.1	42.6
1864	26.6	30.2	45.7	56.2	50.7	43.0	47.8	42.8	38.0	31.5	29.9	20.2	38.5
1865	23.2	20.1	34.1	46.0	43.0	52.3	46.8	54.5	50.8	34.1	29.1	18.2	37.6
1866	20.4	25.9	34.0	38.8	46.1	44.6	47.5	42.2	40.1	39.2	30.5	23.0	36.2
1867	23.2	22.3	26.4	37.2	40.7	45.0	44.9	46.0	42.3	37.5	32.4	25.9	35.3
1868	20.9	31.7	37.3	42.3	46.7	51.9	50.2	41.6	43.8	33.8	19.8	17.0	36.4
1869	20.6	24.6	29.6	38.2	33.3	39.6	42.4	44.2	34.8	33.4	28.6	23.7	32.8
1870	22.1	22.5	31.6	51.6	52.1	54.7	47.8	46.4	47.0	40.4	32.4	23.5	39.5

TABLE XVI.

OF THE SIX PRECEDING TABLES THE FOLLOWING IS A SUMMARY :—

	A	B	C	D	E	F	G	H
January ...	43.2	33.0	10.2	48.0	51.3	30.1	16.8	22.8
February ...	45.2	32.8	12.4	52.3	57.7	30.2	22.4	27.0
March ...	49.5	33.4	16.1	57.9	65.0	30.0	27.5	35.4
April ...	58.1	37.9	20.2	65.9	78.9	34.3	31.3	44.9
May ...	64.3	42.5	21.8	73.6	84.6	38.7	34.4	46.4
June ...	71.0	48.2	22.8	81.4	91.1	44.6	35.9	47.9
July ...	74.0	51.4	22.6	85.2	94.7	47.5	36.8	48.5
August ...	72.2	50.4	21.8	83.2	91.9	46.8	35.5	46.2
September ...	67.6	47.4	20.2	79.2	86.4	43.2	35.9	43.3
October ...	58.9	43.1	15.8	68.2	73.2	39.4	28.0	34.9
November ...	48.9	36.3	12.6	56.2	58.7	32.2	22.8	28.1
December ...	44.2	34.1	10.1	48.8	52.2	30.8	17.7	21.9
Annual Mean ...	58.1	40.9	17.2	66.6	73.8	37.3	28.7	37.3

Column A shows the monthly and yearly mean maximum temperature in shade during 28 years.

  ,, B   ,,   ,,   ,, minimum   ,,   ,,

  ,, C   ,,   ,,   ,, mean daily range of   ,,

  ,, D   ,,   ,,   ,, mean maximum temperature in the sun at four *feet* above the surface of short grass, from fifteen years' observations.

  ,, E shows the monthly and yearly maximum temperature in the sun at four *inches* above the surface of short grass, from ten years' observations.

  ,, F shows the mean monthly and yearly temperature of radiation from the surface of short grass from twenty-five years' observations.

  ,, G shows the difference of temperature between the mean monthly and yearly temperature of solar radiation at four feet *above* the surface of short grass, and that of terrestrial radiation *upon* the surface of short grass, from fifteen years' observations.

  ,, H shows the difference of temperature between the mean monthly and yearly temperature of solar radiation at four *inches above* the surface of short grass, and that of terrestrial radiation *upon* the surface of short grass, from ten years' observations.

Upon examination of column A in preceding table, it will be seen that the day temperature is highest in July and lowest in January; that the least increase of temperature from month to month occurs from January to February, and the greatest from March to April, while the least decrease occurs from July to August, and the greatest from October to November. In column B it will be seen that the night temperature is lowest in February, but that there is not much difference between the night temperatures of January, February, and March. The warmest night temperature occurs in July. The night temperature of August is sometimes very oppressive, but upon the average is 1° less than that of July. Night temperature is nearly six degrees higher during the last, than during the first, six months of the year. In column C is recorded the mean daily range of temperature in the shade, which is equalled by very few localities in England. This large amount of daily range of temperature constitutes an important feature in the climate of Uckfield. It is probably owing to the geological position of the parish and its neighbourhood, upon either the Hastings or Ashdown Sand. I could enumerate many instances wherein the range of shade temperature has amounted to 35° and upwards, between the hours of sunrise and noon. Again, the temperature often declines very suddenly, and to a great extent, immediately after sunset, or as soon as terrestrial radiation commences. There is a very considerable difference in the daily average during the corresponding month of different years. Thus in June, 1860, the mean daily range amounted to 15° only, but in June, 1865, to 27.1°! Again, in July, 1861, it was only 17.6°, but in July, 1847, 27.6°. The greatest annual variation is 5.4°, which was the difference between that in the year 1860 or 1862, and 1854. In column D the mean results are given of the first series of observations of solar radiation, which extend over a period of fifteen years. The instrument employed for these observations was an ordinary blackened bulb thermometer, made by Negretti and Co., which has the bulb quite uncovered, and fully exposed to every viscissitude of temperature, sunshine, and wind. I consider that the colour of the bulb, with its power of absorbing *a certain amount* of heat, sufficiently compensates for any loss of heat by reflection. I prefer this kind of thermometer for the purpose of ascertaining the *natural* intensity of the sun's rays to another kind, which has the blackened bulb enclosed in a glass sphere or jacket. I am unable to comprehend what practical usefulness can result from observations taken with this latter instrument. Its readings indicate a temperature far too great for the latitude of London and its vicinity, but they cannot indicate the amount of accumulated solar heat which *may* be obtained in England by other contrivances. I have occasionally seen readings from such an instrument given at 160° and upwards, which is about the temperature of the engine room of a steamer off the coast of Aden. Can it be fair to quote any such reading as the true indication of solar heat in this country? It very rarely happens that bodies exposed to the direct rays of the sun attain, in this latitude, a higher temperature than 120°; but De Saussure, by means of a little box constructed of wood, and lined with charred cork, obtained a temperature of 221°, the temperature of the external air not being higher than 75°. Professor Robinson, of Edinburgh, by means of a somewhat similar contrivance, frequently obtained an indication of 230°, and once, under favourable circumstances, 237°! The sun's rays, therefore, not concentrated in any way, but merely accumulated, *can be made* to indicate a temperature above that of boiling water. In a course of experiments made some years ago by Colonel Sabine the remarkable fact was elicited that the intensity of the sun's rays (the excess of temperature above that in the shade) is least at the equator, and increases with the distance from it. In July, 1822, the maximum effect of a nearly vertical sun was 57°. On Melville island in March, a thermometer placed in the sun, at a distance from the ship's side, and the weather calm and clear, indicated an effect of 55°. At the time this experiment was made the temperature in the shade was 25°, and in the sun, + 30°. The greatest effect in the vicinity of London in the same month upon a thermometer covered with black wool was only 49°. In Captain Scoresby's account of the Arctic regions are several remarks upon the intensity of the sun's rays. He says, " The force of the sun's rays is sometimes remarkable where they fall upon the snow-clad surface of the ice or land, for they are, in a great measure, reflected without producing any material elevation of temperature; but when they impinge on the black exterior of a ship; the pitch on one side occasionally becomes fluid, while ice is rapidly generated at the other; or, while a thermometer placed against the black paint work on which the sun shines indicates a temperature of 80° or 90°, or even more, on the opposite side of the ship a cold of 20° is sometimes found to prevail." In his last voyage to Greenland the radiating power of the sun was found to be nearly 80° in the month of April.

Humbolt often endeavoured to measure the power of the sun between the tropics by two mercurial thermometers, one of which remained exposed to the sun, while the other was placed in the shade. The difference of their readings never exceeded 6.6°, while sometimes it was not more than one or two degrees. But to return to table 16. In column E are given the mean results of the second series of observations upon solar radiation, which extends over a period of ten years. The removal of the thermometer from four *feet* to four *inches* above the surface of grass caused a very large increase in the readings in column E over those in column D. It varied from rather more than 3° in January to 13° in April, 11° in May, and nearly 10° in June and July; the greatest variation occurred in April. In column F are given the results of twenty-five years' observations upon the mean monthly temperature of radiation upon the surface of short grass. In columns G and H are given the differences of temperature respectively between columns F D and F E. The latter shows the enormous range of temperature to which vegetation is exposed in this locality, which will be still more apparent by consulting table 15, where may be seen the extraordinary ranges of temperature which occurred in several months. Among the numerous meteorological registers which have been kept in this country during the last twenty years we rarely find that regular observations have been made of solar and terrestrial radiation. So great is its value in the general economy of nature, that without a certain proportion of its genial influence the fruits of the earth do not come to perfection. Moreover, the public health is affected to a greater or less extent by a peculiar type of disease which may be referable to a deficiency of intensity in the solar rays, the full influence of which is an advantage, for which no elevation of temperature, under a cloudy sky, can compensate. But if the power of solar radiation, when tested by the work it does, is inconceivably enormous, its exact adjustment to the measure of that work is no less wonderful. There is just enough of radiant force poured down upon the earth to keep its intricate machinery in proper motion—no less, no more. The latent and specific heat of water, with all its other properties, are each exactly fitted to the amount of heat received.

THE OLD BRIDGE AT UCKFIELD.   TAKEN DOWN, FEBRUARY, 1859.

CHAPTER III.

THE RAINFALL AT UCKFIELD.

THE fall of rain in any district constitutes a very important feature in the history of its climate, as it exercises a considerable influence upon the public health, the fertility of the soil, and the purity of the atmosphere.

The position of Uckfield is somewhat peculiar with respect to rainfall, as the amount is probably much influenced by the heavier falls which occur on the Forest Ridge to the north, and on the Downs to the south.

Subsequent tables will show details of this rainfall, and how great has been the variation in the several months, seasons, and years. These tables exhibit the results of observations at my Uckfield observatory from 1843 to 1877, both inclusive; while from the year 1877 to the end of the year 1885 the register was continued by Miss Laura Day, of Uckfield House. In consequence of the alteration in the position of the gauge during the latter period, amounting to an increase in the elevation above sea level of fifty feet, it must be taken into consideration, by the scientific observer, that this increase of elevation would give, theoretically, an increase of 1·7 inch per cent. upon the rainfall as compared with the first period.

This correction has not been applied, and the tables show the amount actually registered by Miss Day. Throughout the entire series October maintains its character of being, upon the average, the wettest month, while March is the driest, although the difference between it and the amount for April is very trifling.

If we consider the four decades of years the gradual increase of rainfall becomes apparent; thus from 1843 to 1852 the yearly average was 28·99 inches; from 1853 to 1862, 29·76 inches; from 1863 to 1872, 30·08 inches; and from 1873 to 1882, 32·16 inches. Whether this steady increase will be maintained during the current decade is very doubtful; at all events since the year 1882, *i.e.*, for the years 1883-84-85, there has been an accumulating deficiency of 7·65 inches, or a yearly average of 2·55 inches. Three consecutive dry years have not been recorded since the years 1869-70-71, when the accumulated deficiency was 10·98 inches, or a yearly average of 3·66 inches, but this decrease was in a great measure compensated for by an excess of 8·58 inches in the year 1872.

Upon examination we find a remarkable difference in the annual quantity of rain; thus in the wettest year, 1852, 50·55 inches fell at Uckfield, but in 1847 only 17·58 inches, showing an extreme difference in the yearly amount of nearly 33 inches!

The average annual rainfall at Uckfield during the last forty-three years has been 30·05 inches. The average for Winter has been 7·46 inches; Spring, 5·65 inches; Summer, 6·91 inches; and Autumn, exactly 10 inches.

Mr. Glaisher, in his remarks upon the rainfall at Greenwich, has stated that, generally speaking, the times of heaviest rainfall are —

In Winter, during the morning and afternoon hours.

In Spring, during the afternoon and early morning hours.

In Summer, during the afternoon hours till after midnight.

In Autumn, during the afternoon and early morning hours.

And he further states that rain falls most *frequently* —

In Winter, during the six hours preceding and following noon.

In Spring, during the three hours following noon.

In Summer, during the three hours following six p.m.

In Autumn, during the six hours following noon, which are the *most frequent* of any in the year.

It falls least frequently —

In Winter, during the three hours preceding midnight.

In Spring, during the three hours from 6 to 9 p.m.

In Summer, in the six hours before noon, which are the *least frequent* of any in the year.

In Autumn, during the three hours preceding noon and from 6 to 9 p.m.

With respect to the average frequency of rain at the different hours throughout the year, it is found that rainfall is most frequent between the hours of 2 and 3 p.m., and least frequent between the hours of 10 and 11 a.m. Also that rainfall is heavier by day than by night in spring, autumn, and winter; but in summer it is heavier by night than by day. Table (20) gives the instances of very heavy rains during each year—*i.e.*, when the amount of rainfall during any twenty-four hours ending 9 a.m. has nearly amounted to, or exceeded, one inch and a quarter.

Previous to the removal of the old bridge at Uckfield, in the year 1859, these heavy rains would generally produce a flood over the brook land between it and Buxted. Upon reference to the engraving, it will be seen how much the two heavy piers must have obstructed the current. Our heaviest rains occur in Autumn, which are very prejudicial to the ripening of fruit buds, the preparation of the soil for grain crops, and the crop of hops for the ensuing year. The effect of saturated soil upon the roots of hops is very injurious; and I have never known a heavy crop to be obtained, when, during the previous autumn, the rainfall has much exceeded the average. The next point of interest to the amount of rainfall is the number of wet days in the course of the year.

Table (19) gives the monthly and annual number, and shows how slight a variation occurs, during a series of years, in the number of wet days for the several months. The least number will be found in June, and the greatest in October.

The greatest monthly number of wet days occurred in Oct.,

1885, and Nov., 1872. The greater or lesser number of wet days is no criterion of the *amount* of rainfall.

With reference to the amount of moisture in the atmosphere, we find that if a mass of air be gradually cooled, it will descend to a degree of temperature at which it will be saturated by the quantity of vapour contained in it. This temperature is called the "Dew Point." Dew is the visible form of aqueous vapour, which it assumes under circumstances favourable to its production. This occurs when the sun is absent, the sky clear, and when the atmosphere, replete with moisture, is chilled by contact with any surface colder than itself. The interposition of clouds almost invariably prevents the continued formation of dew. For a long time it was supposed that dew dropped "like gentle rain from heaven," and it was not until a comparatively recent period that any other theory was believed. The dew drop is familiar to everyone. Resting in luminous beads upon the surface of leaves, or pendant from the finest blades of grass, or threaded upon the floating lines of the gossamer, it varies in size from the diameter of a small pea to a very minute atom. Each of these, like the rain-drop, have the properties both of refracting and reflecting light; and hence, as from so many prisms, the unfolded rays of the sun are sent up to the eye in brilliant colours similar to those of the rainbow. When the sunbeams traverse horizontally a very thickly bedewed grass plot, these colours are so arranged as to form an iris or dewbow; and if we select any one particular drop for observation, and steadily regard it while we change our position, we shall find the prismatic colours follow each other in their regular order. The deposition of dew was first satisfactorily explained by Dr. Wells. "When the sun is below the horizon, or for a short period before sunset, bodies upon the surface of the earth, exposed to the aspect of a clear sky, cool by the radiation of the particles of heat absorbed, and at a more rapid rate than the atmosphere. The air in immediate contact with these bodies, replete with humidity in the form of transparent aqueous vapour, is chilled by their cold embraces ; and, owing to the increase of its density, it becomes incapable of holding in suspension the moisture with which it is charged in the same quantity as before. The surplus is, therefore, disengaged, and appears upon the surface of the refrigerating object in globules of dew. It is essential to this process that the night should not be a cloudy one; because when the sky is overcast, the radiant heat proceeding from the surface of the earth, and which would otherwise go off into free space, is interrupted by the clouds, and returned by them in sufficient quantity to prevent the decrease of temperature necessary to compel the atmosphere to surrender a portion of its hoard of aqueous particles. On nights which are perfectly cloudless, therefore, the deposition of dew is greater than when the sky is partially overcast; on those which are both cloudy and windy there is none whatever formed ; but a gentle motion in the air on a clear night is favourable to its production in the greatest quantity, by bringing fresh portions of the atmosphere, laden with moisture, into contact with the colder bodies at the surface. In opposition to the moisture of dew, that of mists is deposited upon all substances exposed to it alike ; while another distinction is, that the moisture of mists exists previous to any deposition, in a visible state, and is produced quite independent of the bodies which receive it."

With the object of ascertaining the amount of moisture existing in the atmosphere, I made some very careful observations at Uckfield during eight consecutive years, ending with 1857, with the following results, viz. :—The average mean temperature of the Dew Point for January was $34°·9$; Feb., $32°·9$; March, $34°·0$; April, $40°·6$; May, $45°·4$; June, $53°·1$: July, $57°·1$; August, $56°·9$; Sept., $52°·1$; Oct., $47°·2$: Nov., $38°·2$; Dec., $35°·6$; and the annual mean was $44°·0$; which was $5°·8$ below that of the air.

TABLE XVII.

THE MONTHLY AND YEARLY RAINFALL AT UCKFIELD, SUSSEX. (IN INCHES.)

Year.	Jan.	Feb.	March.	April.	May.	June.	July.	Aug.	Sept:	Oct.	Nov.	Dec.	Total.
1843 .	2·35	2·50	0·62	2·21	5·69	1·71	3·11	3·84	0·28	4·75	2·71	0·32	30·09
1844 .	3·03	3·84	2·32	0·37	0·18	0·79	1·47	2·23	0·60	5·11	2·99	0·44	23·37
1845 .	2·97	1·25	0·57	1·53	2·65	1·08	1·43	2·95	3·12	1·89	2·99	0·60	23·03
1846 .	3·25	1·37	1·90	1·62	1·43	0·92	2·23	2·30	1·50	5·53	1·69	1·37	25·11
1847 .	1·81	1·73	0·67	0·69	1·63	1·77	0·22	1·08	1·80	1·57	2·12	2·49	17·58
1848 .	1·49	3·00	2·56	3·11	0·79	3·91	3·01	6·05	2·63	6·03	2·27	3·18	38·03
1849 .	2·21	2·51	0·64	3·82	2·67	0·85	1·69	0·76	3·37	5·08	1·92	3·81	29·33
1850 .	1·47	2·47	0·18	3·27	2·78	2·03	2·44	2·37	2·62	1·96	4·39	2·64	28·62
1851 .	4·25	1·11	4·01	2·23	0·35	1·62	3·50	1·56	0·21	4·11	0·81	0·50	24·26
1852 .	5·56	1·42	0·47	0·48	2·59	7·04	0·50	6·01	6·54	8·70	6·52	4·70	50·55
1853 .	4·34	0·84	1·70	2·80	1·56	1·61	3·97	3·17	2·88	7·25	0·99	0·59	31·70
1854 .	2·21	0·51	0·11	0·25	3·87	2·22	2·19	1·43	1·45	4·28	2·29	2·34	23·15
1855 .	0·23	0·97	3·19	0·51	2·29	1·77	3·44	0·67	0·88	6·05	1·76	2·04	23·80
1856 .	2·67	1·62	1·62	4·54	4·77	1·72	2·67	1·97	6·06	1·63	1·03	3·29	33·59
1857 .	3·65	0·38	2·23	2·21	1·45	3·45	2·08	3·24	4·67	4·61	2·84	0·93	31·74
1858 .	1·16	0·71	1·21	2·05	2·03	0·16	3·26	1·85	1·14	1·83	1·37	2·59	19·36
1859 .	2·57	2·16	1·79	2·28	1·02	1·48	1·67	1·59	3·82	4·33	5·67	5·10	33·48
1860 .	4·75	1·50	3·00	2·53	4·20	4·80	3·00	5·84	3·75	2·97	2·95	3·17	42·46
1861 .	0·23	1·78	2·51	0·69	1·56	2·88	2·85	1·16	3·70	1·85	7·50	1·64	28·35
1862 .	2·27	0·80	4·05	1·63	2·61	2·03	1·43	1·90	2·31	7·00	0·94	3·04	30·01
1863 .	3·67	0·88	0·91	0·46	1·96	3·81	0·79	2·18	3·44	3·23	1·68	2·73	25·74

Year.	Jan.	Feb.	March.	April.	May.	June.	July.	Aug.	Sept.	Oct.	Nov.	Dec.	Total.
1864 .	0·94	1·03	3·64	1·04	1·94	1·01	0·46	1·73	3·06	2·09	5·56	0·98	23·48
1865 .	5·26	1·63	1·82	0·33	3·37	1·38	4·86	3·76	0·02	11·23	3·06	2·28	38·97
1866 .	6·22	4·35	1·95	1·25	0·70	2·77	2·83	2·07	6·12	1·61	1·89	2·03	33·79
1867 .	3·15	1·70	3·02	2·24	2·07	1·87	5·25	1·96	2·33	3·41	1·41	2·07	30·48
1868 .	4·35	1·03	1·52	2·30	1·03	0·59	2·96	3·18	3·01	2·64	1·37	6·51	30·51
1869 .	3·00	2·53	2·28	1·52	3·98	0·96	0·08	1·30	4·33	1·86	2·65	4·08	28·57
1870 .	1·83	1·56	1·73	0·31	1·05	0·34	2·12	2·14	2·29	5·50	2·24	3·88	24·99
1871 .	2·61	1·64	1·19	3·90	0·62	3·87	2·68	1·34	3·07	2·50	0·70	1·52	25·64
1872 .	5·36	1·80	1·94	0·61	3·16	2·72	1·59	1·80	1·83	5·05	6·92	5·88	38·64
1873 .	3·60	2·02	2·18	0·64	1·02	2·79	2·35	3·62	3·07	4·67	3·16	0·94	30·06
1874 .	2·22	1·90	0·69	2·29	0·59	2·10	0·58	1·97	3·15	4·18	2·66	2·32	24·65
1875 .	3·88	1·15	0·71	0·87	1·28	3·74	3·40	1·45	1·80	4·74	4·82	1·18	29·02
1876 .	0·96	3·05	3·07	2·63	0·91	1·88	0·45	3·92	4·23	1·09	3·23	7·95	33·37
1877 .	7·07	2·25	2·49	2·51	2·15	1·02	3·49	3·34	1·28	3·79	7·68	2·51	39·58
1878 .	1·60	2·05	1·65	3·12	3·86	1·55	1·03	4·13	1·78	4·37	4·03	2·08	31·25
1879 .	3·32	4·13	0·95	3·52	3·11	3·29	3·53	4·80	3·28	0·77	1·27	1·03	33·00
1880 .	0·49	3·05	0·88	1·81	0·20	2·02	3·50	1·08	4·16	6·72	4·26	3·62	31·79
1881 .	1·40	4·43	2·71	0·80	1·22	2·19	1·46	5·18	3·24	2·54	4·36	3·52	33·05
1882 .	1·51	1·80	1·43	3·10	1·06	2·11	4·57	2·14	3·27	7·78	3·82	3·26	35·85
1883 .	2·73	4·27	1·24	1·38	2·62	2·32	2·31	0·63	3·13	2·88	4·59	1·39	29·49
1884 .	2·85	1·69	2·03	1·31	0·23	2·28	1·62	1·22	3·64·	1·08	1·07	4·14	23·16
1885 .	2·81	4·20	2·46	1·37	2·91	0·82	0·67	0·68	4·57	4·22	3·88	1·29	29·88
Mean of 42 years.	2·867	2·014	1·810	1·817	2·027	2·121	2·297	2·502	2·870	4·057	3·071	2·604	30·05

TABLE XVIII.

THE RAINFALL DURING THE SEVERAL SEASONS OF THE YEAR
AT UCKFIELD, IN INCHES.

Year.	Winter.	Spring.	Summer.	Autumn.
Commencing previous December.	December. January. February.	March. April. May.	June. July. August.	September. October. November.
1843 .	6·14	8·52	8·66	7·74
1844 .	7·19	2·87	4·49	8·70
1845 .	4·66	4·75	5·46	8·00
1846 .	5·22	4·95	5·45	8·72
1847 .	4·91	2·99	3·07	5·49
1848 .	6·98	6·46	12·97	10·93
1849 .	7·90	7·13	3·30	10·37
1850 .	7·75	6·23	6·84	8·97
1851 .	8·00	6·59	6·68	5·13
1852 .	7·48	3·54	13·55	21·76
1853 .	9·88	6·06	8·75	11·12
1854 .	3·31	4·23	5·84	8·02
1855 .	3·54	5·99	5·88	8·69
1856 .	6·33	10·93	6·16	8·72
1857 .	7·32	5·89	8·77	12·12
1858 .	2·80	5·29	5·27	4·34
1859 .	7·32	5·09	4·74	13·82
1860 .	11·35	9·73	13·64	9·67
1861 .	5·18	4·76	6·89	13·05
1862 .	4·71	8·29	5·36	10·25
1863 .	7·59	3·33	6·78	8·35
1864 .	4·70	6·62	3·20	10·71
1865 .	7·87	5·52	9·97	14·31
1866 .	12·85	3·90	7·67	9·62
1867 .	6·88	7·33	9·08	7·15
1868 .	7·45	4·85	6·75	7·02
1869 .	12·04	7·78	2·34	8·84
1870 .	7·47	3·09	4·60	10·03
1871 .	8·13	5·71	7·89	6·27

Year.	Winter.	Spring.	Summer.	Autumn.
Commencing previous December.	December. January. February.	March. April. May.	June. July. August.	September. October. November.
1872 .	8·68	5·71	6·11	13·78
1873 .	11·50	3·84	8·76	10·90
1874 .	5·06	3·57	4·65	9·99
1875 .	7·35	2·86	8·59	11·36
1876 .	5·19	6·61	6·25	8·55
1877 .	17·27	7·15	7·85	12·75
1878 .	6·16	8·63	6·71	10·18
1879 .	9·53	7·58	11·62	5·32
1880 .	4·57	2·89	6·60	15·14
1881 .	8·45	4·75	8·83	10·14
1882 .	6·83	5·59	8·82	14·92
1883 .	10·26	5·24	5·26	10·60
1884 .	5·93	3·57	5·12	5·79
1885 .	11·15	6·74	2·17	12·67
Mean of 43 years.	7·46	5·65	6·91	10·00

TABLE XIX.

THE MONTHLY AND ANNUAL NUMBER OF WET DAYS,

i.e., wherein the Fall of Rain and Melted Snow amounted to One Hundredth of an Inch and upwards during the 24 hours ending at 9 a.m.

Year.	Jan.	Feb.	March.	April.	May.	June.	July.	Aug.	Sept.	Oct.	Nov.	Dec.	Total.
1843 .	17	18	7	18	23	13	15	12	4	16	25	10	178
1844 .	15	18	17	4	5	8	10	14	9	21	15	4	140
1845 .	16	11	11	13	25	11	18	17	14	11	18	19	188
1846 .	16	11	16	15	7	5	12	11	8	21	9	6	137
1847 .	10	10	7	8	12	11	4	10	11	13	13	13	122
1848 .	10	18	20	17	6	18	13	23	9	23	15	16	188
1849 .	19	10	10	21	11	6	11	8	12	19	10	14	151
1850 .	9	11	6	14	14	10	12	15	8	11	15	13	138
1851 .	20	7	16	13	5	6	14	5	6	13	7	8	120
1852 .	17	12	2	3	11	23	4	19	15	16	23	23	168
1853 .	17	7	5	10	9	11	14	7	10	20	8	3	121
1854 .	16	6	4	5	16	9	8	9	5	11	13	15	117
1855 .	3	5	14	7	12	10	15	10	6	23	11	10	126
1856 .	19	10	3	14	21	7	10	13	17	12	9	12	147
1857 .	16	7	13	14	7	9	11	11	18	16	13	8	143
1858 .	6	7	6	11	17	4	15	8	12	11	6	14	117
1859 .	10	13	10	12	9	11	8	8	17	15	14	14	141
1860 .	18	10	19	11	15	18	12	23	17	13	10	13	179
1861 .	2	15	17	4	7	13	20	8	15	10	18	11	140
1862 .	17	5	20	10	14	14	13	10	12	20	11	16	162
1863 .	19	9	8	9	8	13	2	15	12	17	10	11	133

TABLE XIX—Continued.

Year.	Jan.	Feb.	March.	April.	May.	June.	July.	Aug.	Sept.	Oct.	Nov.	Dec.	Total.
1864 .	18	11	13	6	7	8	4	6	13	7	14	6	113
1865 .	15	12	11	3	9	5	11	14	1	16	13	10	120
1866 .	15	15	12	10	8	10	8	14	20	9	12	16	149
1867 .	17	12	15	13	13	5	15	11	9	15	5	10	140
1868 .	13	7	18	11	5	4	6	11	10	12	7	23	127
1869 .	17	16	14	10	16	5	2	7	12	7	9	16	131
1870 .	16	9	7	4	6	4	8	11	7	17	11	13	113
1871 .	15	14	10	17	3	12	16	6	8	12	7	11	131
1872 .	21	17	13	7	15	13	11	13	8	20	26	19	183
1873 .	18	7	13	13	11	10	9	16	9	19	13	7	145
1874 .	10	18	10	10	5	9	5	13	12	17	10	11	120
1875 .	20	10	5	5	8	10	13	5	10	17	18	12	133
1876 .	10	15	21	15	7	11	6	12	16	8	15	24	160
1877 .	25	18	18	16	14	7	17	16	12	15	24	16	198
1878 .	16	13	10	18	22	14	10	24	10	15	20	15	187
1879 .	12	23	12	21	23	23	23	19	11	12	11	13	203
1880 .	7	21	5	17	4	18	24	8	15	19	17	21	176
1881 .	12	18	13	15	11	11	12	24	19	21	24	22	202
1882 .	9	13	17	16	11	19	21	18	19	23	22	23	211
1883 .	23	17	17	8	12	14	18	13	20	15	22	17	196
1884 .	16	18	11	14	7	10	15	7	14	14	6	21	153
1885 .	16	23	12	14	18	10	8	12	25	26	15	13	192
Mean of 43 years.	14·7	12·7	11·8	11·5	11·4	10·7	11·7	12·4	12·0	15·5	13·8	13·8	152

TABLE XX.

THE FOLLOWING ARE INSTANCES OF HEAVY RAINFALL,
TOGETHER WITH THEIR DATE AND THE AMOUNT. (IN INCHES.)

Year.	Month.	Rainfall.	Year.	Month.	Rainfall.
1843	Aug. 23	1·47	1871	June 14	1·41
1849	April 19	1·40	1872	Jan. 23	1·02
,,	Oct. 4	1·69	,,	May 17	1·11
1850	Nov. 14	1·47	1873	Jan. 18	1·05
1851	Aug. 28	1·30	,,	July 13	1·33
1852	Oct. 4	2·12	1874	Feb. 26	1·04
,,	,, 25	1·77	,,	Oct. 6	1·17
1853	July 14	1·79	1875	June 30	1·23
,,	Aug. 23	1·29	,,	July 14	1·20
,,	Sept. 21	1·27	,,	Nov. 7	1·04
1854	Oct. 7	1·42	1877	Jan. 2	1·06
1856	Sept. 27	2·38	,,	Oct. 24	1·30
1857	June 11	1·41	,,	Nov. 24	1·05
1861	Nov. 5	1·27	1878	Oct. 25	1·32
,,	,, 13	1·52	1879	Jan. 1	1·29
1862	Oct. 20	1·53	,,	May 28	1·34
1864	Nov. 15	1·30	,,	Aug. 19	1·17
,,	,, 23	1·40	1880	Sept. 14	1·25
1865	July 23	1·30	,,	Oct. 9	1·72
,,	Oct. 18	2·40	,,	,, 26	1·12
,,	,, 26	1·41	1881	Feb. 19	1·95
,,	,, 30	1·22	,,	June 5	1·06
1866	Jan. 11	1·89	,,	Oct. 22	1·10
1867	June 2	1·47	,,	Nov. 26	1·30
,,	July 25	1·33	1882	Sept. 19	1·05
1868	,, 11	2·10	,,	Oct. 21	1·50
,,	Aug. 17	1·18	1884	,, 3	1·84
1869	Dec. 16	1·16	1885	Sept. 15	1·14
1870	Oct. 22	1·26			

CHAPTER IV.

MONTHLY REMARKS RESPECTING ATMOSPHERIC PHENOMENA FROM THE YEAR 1843 TO 1870, BOTH INCLUSIVE.

THE following remarks upon the prevalent weather during the several months will, I trust, be interesting to those who may have kept similar journals in other parts of the country, as well as to those who will consider them worthy of record, if for reference only. They were written, for the most part, at the close of each month respectively.

A slight difference may occasionally be observed between the averages of temperature, rain, &c., now given, and those which I have previously published in my annual meteorological reports, but this difference has arisen from the fact of my having obtained, from a longer series of observations, more correct results.

1843.

JANUARY.

The first few days of the month were fine and frosty; nevertheless, *thunderstorms* visited several parts of the country. On the 7th a very remarkable depression of the barometer commenced, which continued, more or less, for ten days. On the 11th we had a heavy snowstorm for three hours. On the 13th the wind suddenly shifted from N.W. to S.W., and blew a tremendous hurricane all day. The barometer fell in some places on the south coast to nearly 28 inches. At Holyhead it was reported to have fallen below 28 inches. Upon the whole the month was stormy and mild. The mean temperature was more than one degree above the average, and the wind was westerly on 22 days.

FEBRUARY.

The month began mild and stormy, the barometer constantly fluctuating. On the 3rd there were some heavy showers of rain and hail with thunder, at 4 p.m. From the 4th to the 19th the weather was much colder, but the frost was not severe. The 15th was the coldest day, when the temperature remained below the freezing point. From the 24th to the end of the month the weather was damp and unpleasant. There was a considerable depression of the barometer on the 27th. The mean temperature of the month was nearly three degrees below the average. Easterly winds were prevalent on twenty days.

MARCH.

The first eleven days of the month were very fine and dry, but the frosts at night were rather severe for the season. With the exception of some trifling showers, on 13th and 15th, there was no rain till 21st, and the total rainfall for the month did not much exceed half an inch. From 16th to 24th the weather was very warm for the season. The maximum temperature in the shade on 18th was 66°! Southerly winds were the most prevalent. It was a very fine seed-time for the farmers in this neighbourhood.

APRIL.

The first week was mild and wet, the rain coming in heavy showers. In consequence of the warmth of the previous month vegetation had considerably advanced. During the evening of the 8th the wind veered suddenly to the north, from which date to the 13th, inclusive, we had very cold weather with snow, hail, and severe frosts at night. On the morning of the 14th there was a sudden rise of temperature, and the remainder of the month was, upon the whole, mild. On the 20th the temperature reached 74° in the shade with some thunder at noon. The mean daily range of temperature for the month was very great.

MAY.

This month was, for the most part, cold and wet. The first four days were fine and mild, but on the 5th a wet season commenced, which continued for nearly five weeks. On the 17th, heavy thunderstorm with much rain. Thunderstorms occurred also on 24th, 28th, and 29th. It was the wettest May of which I have any record. The wind was extremely variable throughout the month.

JUNE.

The mean temperature of this month was more than two degrees below the average. The weather during the first nine days was showery, with considerable fluctuation of the barometer; but the remainder was fine, dry, and for the most part rather warm. A sudden rise of temperature occurred on 14th, and we had a slight thunderstorm on 18th. In consequence of the heavy rains in May and at the beginning of this month, there was an immense crop of hay, which was secured in good condition. The last three days of the month were cool. The winds were extremely variable, and the rainfall was below the average.

JULY.

The month began with warm, sultry weather. The 4th and 6th were very hot days, followed by slight thunderstorms and some rain. The second and third weeks were fine and warm, but there was no unusual heat. On the 23rd there was a great increase of atmospheric pressure during the night, which was followed by a rise of temperature on the following day, notwithstanding the wind was northerly. On the 31st a remarkably heavy but extremely local shower passed over this parish about mid-day; nearly three quarters of an inch of rain fell in less than an hour. There was scarcely any rain in the parishes either north or south of Uckfield. The mean temperature was about equal to the average, and the rain rather in excess.

AUGUST.

The first three days of the month were cool and showery. On the 4th two severe thunderstorms with torrents of rain.

From this time to the 19th the weather was very hot and sultry. On the 23rd a very heavy rain came up from the S.W., which continued from 1 p.m. till midnight, with high wind. The depth of rain was nearly one and a half inches, but in some parts of the country it was upwards of two inches. This occurred about the middle of corn harvest, and the rain was very injurious to wheat in the sheaves, a great part of which was just ready to be carried. On 30th and 31st there was a great rise of both pressure and temperature, indicative of approaching fine weather. There were some fearful thunderstorms in various parts of England during this month, with loss of life both to man and cattle.

SEPTEMBER.

The mean temperature of this month was nearly five degrees above the average. Great heat, drought, and clear skies continued to the 24th day. The heat was excessive on the 1st day, having been 90° in the shade! On eleven other days the highest temperature in the shade was at or above 80°!! The barometer fluctuated but little till the last week, when the weather became suddenly cold with a northerly wind. The fall of temperature on the morning of 28th was very remarkable—viz., to 30°—there was a sharp hoar frost, and ice was formed on the surface of small pools as thick as a penny piece. The winds were chiefly northerly and easterly. The depth of rain scarcely exceeded a quarter of an inch. The mean daily range of temperature was very great.

OCTOBER.

The first week was fine, and even hot for the season. During the second week the weather was stormy and wet, with great fluctuations of the barometer. On the morning of 17th we were visited by a severe thunderstorm, accompanied by a hurricane of wind, torrents of rain and hail. A severe frost on the morning of the 20th quite stripped the trees of their foliage. The 23rd was a remarkably fine warm day; highest temperature in shade 63°! On 31st continued heavy rain. The mean temperature was more than two degrees below, and the fall of rain a quarter of an inch above, the average.

NOVEMBER.

This was a very damp and gloomy month. Although rain fell more or less on 25 days, yet the total amount did not equal the average. Very stormy weather prevailed on 7th, and from 20th to 23rd, both inclusive. Heavy rain fell on 23rd, when the low grounds were flooded. The mean temperature was above the average.

DECEMBER.

This month was remarkable for drought, mildness, and great atmospheric pressure. The temperature was very equable, and on some days varied only one degree in the course of the twenty-four hours, and twice only throughout the month did it fall below the freezing point. The winds were westerly. The weather was so mild on Christmas day that the birds sang as in early spring. The mean temperature was four degrees above the average.

1844.

JANUARY.

The first three days of the month were extremely cold, with some snow. A remarkable rise of temperature occurred on the 4th, amounting to as much as forty degrees in the course of thirty hours. Mild weather continued throughout the greater part of the month; nevertheless, the mean temperature was rather below the average. A thunderstorm passed to the westward on the 29th. On 30th and 31st there were showers of snow, rain, and hail.

FEBRUARY.

This was a cold month, and the mean temperature was more than three degrees below the average. There were frosts more or less severe on twenty-four nights. The lowest temperature was recorded on the morning of the 6th. There was a heavy fall of snow on the 2nd to the depth of nearly seven inches. During the last ten days of the month the weather was stormy and wet, with great depression of the barometer. On the 23rd a heavy gale and rain from S.W. The fall of rain was more than double the average.

MARCH.

March came in "like a lion," the weather being very stormy and wet to the 5th day. During the evening of the 4th there was a very high flood over the brooks, and the old bridge was only passable by horse and cart. From the 8th to the 13th the weather was again very stormy with dashing showers of rain and hail; wind W. and N.W. During the remainder of the month the weather was extremely variable. The last three days were very warm, notwithstanding easterly winds. The fall of rain was nearly half an inch above the average.

APRIL.

This month was remarkable for heat, drought, great atmospheric pressure, and splendid skies. The mean temperature was more than three degrees above the average, while the fall of rain was less than half an inch. The highest temperature in the shade on 26th was 80°! and on several other days the temperature was at or above 70°. The winds were variable. There were fewer frosty mornings than usual at this season.

MAY.

To the 9th day the weather was fine and hot. A severe drought continued throughout this month, and there was an extraordinary prevalence of N.E. wind. The temperature fluctuated considerably. On the 14th the highest temperature in the shade was 75°, while on the 18th it fell to 27°, or five degrees below the freezing point. The amount of evaporation from the soil was immense.

JUNE.

The month commenced with rather cold weather, and continuance of the drought which had prevailed during the two previous months. From the 8th to the 18th the weather was mild and dry; but in Suffolk great heat prevailed on the 11th, 12th, and 13th. Some showers fell on the 18th, but we had no very hot weather till the 23rd and 24th, when the temperature, in the shade, ranged from 82° to 85°. There was a great decrease of temperature on the 25th with some heavy showers. The amount of rain at Thwaite, in Suffolk, on this day was 1·72 inches; at London, 1·23 inches; while here it was only 0·23! Thunderstorms occurred in some districts on 27th. The month ended with fine, hot weather, and excessive drought; for the trifling showers which fell occasionally were scarcely sufficient to revive the drooping vegetation. The winds were chiefly westerly and the mean temperature about equal to the average. Grass and clover were very short this season.

JULY.

The temperature of this month was variable, and the mean one degree below the average. The fall of rain was also below the average. All grass land was much burnt up by the drought, which had been prevalent for the most part since the end of March. Accounts from all parts of the country conveyed universal complaints of its daily increasing injurious effects upon the crops. The wheat crop alone maintained its healthy condition. The heat was very great from 22nd to 25th, both inclusive. Thunderstorms prevailed occasionally.

AUGUST.

The first half of this month was cool and showery. There were thunderstorms on the 5th and 6th. During the storm on the 5th the lightning set fire to a barn at Nutley, which was burnt to the ground. Another thunderstorm occurred on the 8th, and the weather was very showery till the 15th. The latter half of the month was fine and dry, with no unusual heat for the season. The highest temperature in the shade was observed on the last day. The mornings of 28th and 29th were cool, and on low grounds there was hoar frost.

SEPTEMBER.

This month was fine, warm, and dry. The total amount of rainfall was little more than half an inch, which is two inches less than the average. There was a considerable reduction of temperature on the 9th, after the severe thunderstorm of the previous evening. From 12th to 17th it was again very warm, particularly on the latter day. From 18th to 25th it was colder in consequence of a continued prevalence of N.E. wind. The 27th and 28th were rather warmer days, and the temperature in the shade was upwards of 70°! The mean temperature of the month was about equal to the average.

OCTOBER.

After a very long drought we had from the 11th to the close of this month very heavy rains, which thoroughly soaked the ground, and prepared it for wheat sowing. Although westerly winds prevailed during the greater part of the month, yet the temperature fluctuated very considerably. The mean, however, was about equal to the average. A sudden frost on the morning of the 8th stripped the more tender trees of their foliage. On the following morning the temperature was 18° higher. On 13th, 14th, and 15th we had heavy rains, amounting in the whole to near two and a half inches. On the morning of the 19th there was another severe frost, and also on 23rd and 24th. That the summer and early part of autumn had been unusually dry, may be inferred from a letter dated Chichester, Oct. 10th :—" The weather still continues dry in this neighbourhood. The bed of the Lavant is as dry as the high road, which is a very unusual circumstance at this season of the year. To a stranger Charles Crocker's lines—

> " ' I've seen thy waters with a torrent's force,
> Resistless and with loud and rushing sound,
> Dash forward in their wild, impetuous course,
> As if they scorned thy channel's narrow bound.'

would very probably appear a poetical fiction, although the inhabitants of this neighbourhood well know their truth."

NOVEMBER.

The first half of this month, like that of August, was stormy and wet—and this was the general character of the weather over the whole of England. On the 1st we had a gale and unusually heavy rain from the eastward. With the exception of the 4th, rain fell more or less every day to the 15th. On the 13th, the whole of the brook land, between Uckfield and Buxted bridges, presented one sheet of water. The latter half of the month was fine and dry, with great prevalence of easterly winds. Severe frosts occurred on the mornings of 26th, 27th, and 28th.

DECEMBER.

This was the coldest December since the year 1799. In both instances there was an extraordinary prevalence of easterly winds. On the present occasion southerly winds were recorded for 36 hours only during the entire month. The mean temperature was nearly eight degrees below the average. From the 5th to the 15th the frost continued without intermission both day and night. No rain fell till the 28th and 29th! the whole of which, together with a small quantity of melted snow, did not amount to half an inch. This severe weather was very general throughout Europe. The day before Christmas day, 120 vessels, outward bound, were detained in various parts of the Thames. At Venice the lagoons were frozen, and all communication by water was stopped. In the South of France a greater quantity of snow had fallen than was remembered by anyone living; while the cold was so intense that wolves were forced from their lurking places and approached, much nearer than usual, human habitations.

1845.

The year 1845 was remarkable for its low temperature and generally overcast state of the sky. The mean temperature of every month, with the exception of June and November, was considerably below the average. The annual mean temperature, too, was as much as three degrees below the average, and is the lowest annual mean which I have recorded. The fruit and grain crops never attained perfection, and the year will be especially remembered as that in which the potatoe disease first appeared in this county. The following are a few remarks upon the several months :—

JANUARY.

This month was not remarkable for any extreme temperature, and although the depth of rain on some days was considerable, yet the total amount very slightly exceeded the average. More than half the nights were frosty, but the temperature was never below 22°. The mean temperature was nearly two degrees below the average, notwithstanding a great prevalence of southerly wind in the second and third weeks. The barometer fluctuated considerably. Very cold weather commenced on the 29th, and continued with great severity for eight weeks.

FEBRUARY.

With the exception of the last three days, the weather throughout the whole of this month was intensely cold. The mean temperature was below the freezing point, and nearly eight degrees below the average. It was probably the coldest February since the year 1785. There was frost more or less every night from the 1st to 25th, both inclusive. The following were the lowest temperatures :—1st, 19°; 9th, 19°; 12th, 3°! 13th, 14°; 20th, 17°. The winds were variable. The weather became milder during the last three days. On the 26th the temperature rose to 50° in the shade—a genial warmth after the previous cold. Most of the tender and half hardly plants were destroyed, but the common laurel did not suffer so much as it did in the great frost of January, 1838.

MARCH.

The cold weather returned on the 4th, and continued with great severity till the morning of the 21st. The mean temperature was seven degrees below the average, and, altogether, it was the coldest March since the year 1789. The average daily temperature of the first three weeks was two degrees below the

freezing point. The greatest cold was registered on the morn-
ning of the 14th, viz., 12°! At Thwaite, in Suffolk, the lowest
was 5°! The cold on many days was felt very keenly in consequence of bitterly cold winds from north and east. The lats
ten days of the month were mild and warm. The temperature
rose to 60° on the last day.

APRIL.

The first week was remarkably fine, dry, and mild—a delightful change after the great severity of the two previous months.
From 8th to 15th the weather was unsettled and showery. On
the 9th and 10th the barometer was low, and the temperature
fluctuating; although the highest temperature, on the 8th, was
55°, yet on the 9th it was not higher than 37°! A thunderstorm
occurred on 14th, during which a barn at Hailsham was struck
by the lightning, and burnt to the ground. From 17th to 23rd
the weather was very fine, with brilliant sunshine; but the winds
were easterly, and the mornings cold. The latter part of the
month was overcast and showery. The mean temperature of
this month was more than one degree below the average.

MAY.

This month was gloomy, cold, and wet throughout; although
rain fell on 25 days, yet the total rainfall for the month did not
much exceed the average. In consequence of the continued
overcast sky, the evaporation of moisture was much less than
usual, and caused a very unhealthy condition of atmosphere.
The mean temperature was nearly five degrees below the
average.

JUNE.

This month proved to be the warmest and most genial of the
year. The mean temperature was above the average, and some refreshing showers fell during the first and fourth weeks. The
winds were, for the most part, westerly. From 12th to 17th, both
inclusive, the heat was very great, and proved to be the only hot
weather during the year. The remainder of the month was, for
the most part, fine, but there were occasional showers, which
were of great service to the growing crops.

JULY.

There were a few fine days in the first week, but, upon the whole, the month was gloomy, cold, and showery. The crop of grass was most abundant, but very little of it was harvested and carried in good condition. Haymaking, generally, was not finished till the 28th. The only good hay made this summer was that which was harvested during the few hot days just before midsummer. Throughout England there was a remarkable absence of sunshine, which produced disastrous effects upon the grain and other crops. The potatoe disease made its first appearance in this parish during the fourth week. I first observed it on the 28th, and within ten days of this time it was generally observed throughout the county. In the North of England it was not apparent till quite the beginning of September. The mean temperature of the month was nearly two degrees and a half below the average. The amount of rainfall was deficient nearly one inch.

AUGUST.

During the first fortnight the weather was very wet, and rain fell more or less every day but one. There was much electrical excitement on the 6th and 7th, with but very little rain in this locality. Some large hail stones fell during a shower on the 7th. The mean temperature of the month was low for the season, and as much as four and a half degrees below the average. The rainfall slightly exceeded the average. There was a general absence of sunshine throughout the month.

SEPTEMBER.

The weather was fine, dry, and warm during the first fortnight, but during the remainder of the month it was overcast, cool, and very showery. There was a severe gale on the 18th, with some heavy showers. On the 21st, another severe gale and a very heavy rain, which seriously injured the hops; very few at this time having been picked in consequence of the unusual lateness of the season. By the end of this month the greater part of the potatoe crop had become completely diseased, and unfit for food. The mean temperature was three degrees and a half below, and the rainfall a little in excess of, the average. Winds extremely variable, but they were for the most part easterly at the beginning, and westerly at the end of the month.

OCTOBER.

Throughout this month the weather was cold and dry for the season. The mean temperature was three degrees, and the fall of rain nearly two inches and a half below the average. The winds were chiefly westerly. There was a great prevalence of cirro-stratus cloud, and on several days there were some beautiful solar halos, particularly on the 6th, when the prismatic colours were very distinct. Very little rain fell after the 10th, and the latter part of the month was very favourable for all agricultural operations.

NOVEMBER.

The mean temperature of this month was slightly above the average; although rain fell more or less on eighteen days, yet the total amount very little exceeded the average. The winds were variable, but chiefly westerly. A splendid double lunar halo was visible during the evening of the 11th, with prismatic colours very distinct. A thick fog and frost on 14th, and severe hoar frosts occurred on the mornings of 23rd, 24th, and 25th.

DECEMBER.

The mean temperature was nearly one degree below, and the rainfall half an inch above the average. Rain fell more or less on nineteen days. The mornings were very frequently frosty, but the cold was not severe at any time during the month. The barometer was low on 20th and 23rd—weather stormy and unsettled. Rather severe gales occurred on 26th, 27th, and 28th. During the last night of the year, the wind at intervals blew quite a hurricane, with heavy showers of rain.

1846.

JANUARY.

This month was remarkably mild. The mean temperature was three degrees and a half above the average. During the last fortnight heavy rains were frequent, and caused some high floods in various parts of the country. The winds were chiefly westerly, and there were only five frosty mornings. On the 27th the birds were singing as in early spring, and I observed the crocus, snow-drop, violet, primrose, and polyanthus in full bloom. The barometer was high on the 9th and low on the 19th.

FEBRUARY.

The mild weather which prevailed throughout the previous month continued throughout this month also, and the mean temperature was three degrees above the average. Rain was registered on eleven days, but the total amount was not quite equal to the average. On many days the mildness of the weather was such that fires were not only unnecessary but uncomfortable, and a walk round the garden was preferable to the fireside. Notwithstanding the general mildness of the season northerly winds were very prevalent. On the last day of the month the highest temperature in the shade was as much as $61°$, and wide beds of the cirro-cumulus cloud adorned the sky. A large female wasp appeared, and sulphur butterflies were basking in the sunshine. The common ant was abroad and very busy. Hops had sprouted five or six inches, the gooseberry tree was in leaf, and vegetation generally was advancing most rapidly. Many persons regarded this state of the vegetable world with great anxiety, and prognosticated that this sudden advance of life would be checked, and perhaps destroyed before May-day. If, however, we look into former records of unusually mild seasons, we may discover some grounds for more cheerful expectations. It will at least appear that there is no necessary connection between a very early spring and a failure in the autumnal produce.

Newhaven Bridge in the Year 1786.

C.L.P.

MARCH.

The mean temperature of this month was also considerably above, and the fall of rain about equal to, the average. Upon the whole this month was less pleasant than the last, in consequence of the frequent showers and the fall of snow on the 19th and 20th. On the latter day there was much lightning and thunder during the evening. Again, on the 26th, a thunder storm passed to the eastward of this place, and was very severe at Chiddingly, where a house was struck, and a man and child very much injured. The only severe gale occurred on 16th. The winds were chiefly from the westward, and the barometric variations were trifling. The highest temperature recorded for this month was one degree less than that for February !

APRIL.

Although the mean temperature for this month was slightly below the average, yet it must be considered to have been mild for the season. There were fewer frosty mornings than usual, and the rainfall was very nearly equal to the mean amount. The greater part of it came during the first week. On the 3rd there was much thunder, heavy· rain and hail to the south of this place. Much electrical disturbance again on the 12th. Westerly winds were the most prevalent.

MAY.

The mean temperature of this month was rather above, and the rainfall nearly one inch below, the average. The winds were variable. In consequence of the high temperature of the previous months, the foliage became fully developed quite early in the month, and presented a strong contrast to the corresponding week in the preceding year. On the 22nd there was a somewhat sudden increase both of temperature and pressure, which proved to be the introduction to a long and splendid summer. During the last week the weather was very brilliant and dry, but with great honey dews on a variety of plants. Fruit trees suffered dreadfully from this blight, particularly the plum, cherry, and peach. As for the rose trees, they were so covered with aphides that they could scarcely come out into leaf. The fly infested the hop bines, and fears were entertained of a complete blight in this plant. Grass was very abundant, and some persons began to cut it at the close of the month.

JUNE.

From the 1st to the 22nd of this month, both inclusive, the weather was uninterruptedly fine, dry, and excessively hot. On several days a parching easterly wind prevailed, and vegetation drooped from the intense heat of the solar rays. During these three weeks the highest temperature was at or above 80° on ten days, and at or above 90° on four days. The heat in the sun's rays was very great on the 18th, when a thermometer placed on a slate indicated a temperature of 143°! although in the shade it was only 83°. The 20th was the hottest day, viz., 92°.5! in the shade. Again on the 22nd it was 91° in the shade, and at 6 p.m. 84°! Distant lightning and thunder during the evening and night. A dense blue haze was very perceptible over the landscape during this great heat, which is often an indication of a further continuance of hot weather. The hay harvest was nearly completed by the 15th, and a large crop was secured in very good condition. The mean temperature of the month was as much as five degrees and a half above the average, while the total rainfall was less than an inch. Thunder storms occurred in various parts of the county on the 20th and 22nd, particularly at Horsham, Lewes, and Newhaven.

JULY.

Although the mean temperature of this month was one degree and a half above the average, yet it was equal to that of the previous month. There were fewer days of intense heat, but the nights were warmer. The hottest day was the 5th, when the temperature in the shade was 87°.5. On the last four days of the month the temperature ranged from 83°.5 to 85° in the shade, and from 92° to 105° in the sun. The winds were westerly. On the 18th gale and rain, with great depression of temperature on this and succeeding day. From 28th to 31st the heat was most oppressive both day and night. The fall of rain was a little below the average.

AUGUST.

The warm weather at the close of last month continued during the first week. On the first day the temperature reached 91° in the shade, which was the greatest heat since June 22nd. Fearful thunderstorms occurred in various parts of the kingdom, especially in London* and the eastern counties. Several persons were struck dead by lightning, and much damage done by hailstones of large size. During the night of the 4th, and nearly all day of the 5th a severe storm visited this county. There was much electrical disturbance again on the 5th, and the atmosphere was most oppressive. The remainder of the month was, upon the whole, warm and seasonable; heavy showers on the 18th and 20th, and again during a slight thunderstorm on 29th. The winds were westerly till the last week. The mean temperature was nearly three degrees above the average.

SEPTEMBER.

During the first three weeks we had a continuance of fine, warm weather, the temperature in the shade ranging from 61° to 82°.5, and in the sun from 78° to 104°. No rain fell till the 21st, but from this time to the end of the month the weather was cool and showery. The change came precisely at the equinox, after nearly five months of magnificent weather. The mean temperature was nearly five degrees above, and the fall of raiu little more than half the average. The winds were extremely variable. In some parts of the country there was very heavy rain during the night of the 23rd, but scarcely half an inch fell at Uckfield. Notwithstanding the splendid weather which had prevailed throughout the summer, our autumnal fruits were sadly deficient, more especially apples, which either rotted on the trees or were devoured by myriads of wasps, which had previously destroyed much of the wall fruit. It is also worthy of record that there were very few swallows this season, but a greater number of swifts than usual.

OCTOBER.

After such fine weather as we had in September, a consider-

* See "Illustrated London News," of August 8th.

able amount of rain was to be expected this month, independently of the fact that October is the wettest month in the year. Rain fell more or less on twenty-two days, and the total amount exceeded the average by a fifth. The mean temperature was more than one degree above the average. With the exception of the last week the winds were westerly. The barometer fluctuated very frequently, and the lowest reading was on the 15th. Heavy gales from S.W. occurred on the 5th, 6th, 7th, 10th, 15th, 21st.

NOVEMBER.

During the first sixteen days of this month the weather was remarkably fine and dry for the season, and the wind kept constantly between east and south. There was not a trace of frost, while in many days the highest temperature in the shade exceeded 60°, and that in the sun 70°! The roads were dusty once more, and the weather calm and pleasant. On the 18th the wind shifted to S.W., and brought on a heavy sea fog, and subsequently some slight showers of rain. The next ten days were showery and cool. On the 28th cold weather set in, followed by sharp frost at night. 29th and 30th, fine, clear, frosty weather. In the northern and eastern counties snow fell to a considerable depth. The mean temperature was nearly three degrees and a half above the average, and there was not the usual quantity of rain by one inch. There was a great prevalence of easterly wind.

DECEMBER.

The cold weather which commenced just at the close of November continued with but little intermission to the close of this month. There was a great prevalence of northerly and easterly winds. The mean temperature was as much as six degrees and a half below the average, although not so low as it was in December, 1844. The following are the lowest temperatures which I recorded, viz., 14th, 13°; 15th, 15°; 16th, 18°; 31st, 19°. Snow showers fell occasionally during the month, but the amount was very trifling. In some parts of the country there were heavy falls of snow on 12th, 13th, and 17th. On the 21st there was a heavy gale and rain from S.W., with great depression of the barometer. The last few days were brilliantly clear, for the most part, with sharp frosts at night. The fall of rain would have been much below the average had not so much fallen during the gale on the 21st. There was a brilliant lunar halo at midnight of 31st.

1847.

JANUARY.

The year commenced with hard frost till the afternoon of the third, when sleet, snow, and rain fell, intermingled. A thaw commenced during the night, and the temperature attained its maximum for the 24 hours at midnight. On the 4th a rapid thaw, and very damp, unpleasant weather continued till the evening of the 10th, when the frost returned. To the 16th, inclusive, very clear skies, with slight frosts at night. 17th and 18th were very gloomy with a cold N.E. wind. 19th, a very cold day and the atmosphere loaded with moisture. 21st, the wind shifted to S.E., with a little rain. 22nd and 23rd, gloomy and damp. 24th, very stormy with heavy rain from the S.E. 27th, showery. 28th, very stormy, with heavy hail showers. 30th, hard frost in the morning, but the temperature rose to 46° during the day. 31st, fine, and milder.

As an illustration of the variable nature of our climate in its seasons, I may observe, that in the third week of Jan., 1846, the snowdrop, crocus, primrose, anemone, polyanthus, and wall-flowers were in bloom, while during January, 1847, even the snowdrop scarcely ventured to lift its head above ground.

FEBRUARY.

The month began clear and frosty, a little snow fell on the evening of the first, and showers of sleet and snow were frequent on the 2nd and 3rd, and accompanied by a cold N.E. wind. A sudden rise of temperature on 6th, the maximum being as high as 51°, whilst the previous day it was only 39°. On the 7th an equally sudden fall of temperature, the wind having veered to the eastward, and snow fell during the greater part of the day, a clear frosty night followed, and on the morning of the 8th the thermometer had fallen to 14° which (with the exception of Dec. 14th, 1846), was hitherto the most severe frost during the present winter. At mid-day a little granular snow commenced falling, the flakes increasing in size till near sun set, when a severe snow storm came on from S.S.W., but subsequently from N.E., and continued with great violence till past 10 p.m. During these few hours the snow attained a depth of eleven inches, making an average depth of fourteen inches, since the morning of the 7th. This was the heaviest fall of snow which has occurred in Sussex since the memorable storm on the night of Dec. 25th, 1836. Severe weather continued until early in the morning of the 14th, when a very sudden thaw, with heavy rain, took place, causing considerable floods over the low grounds in this neighbourhood. On the morning of Friday, the 12th, the frost was intense, and my self-registering thermometer fell to 1° at 7½ a.m. Such intense frost has not been experienced in this county since Jan., 1838, when the temperature was 4° lower than on the 12th. 18th stormy, with misty rain. 20th a fine day. During the last week the weather was very cold.

MARCH.

The cold and dry weather which set in on February 23rd continued till March 13th, the wind blowing from N.N.E. and E. for nearly three weeks. The amount of rain during this period was very trifling, and scarcely exceeded a quarter of an inch. On the 9th a little snow fell, followed by a sharp frost at night and some more snow. Heavy snow was also very prevalent in the afternoon; the evening was clear and frosty; the temperatature fell to 20° during the night. Snow showers were frequent on the 12th and 13th, and there were sharp frosts every morning to the 15th inclusive. On the 16th a rise of temperature occurred during the day, the maximum being 56°, and on the 17th, 60°. Owing to clear skies, as well as the increasing power of the sun's rays, the daily maximum of temperature during the remainder of the month was about the average; but the mornings and evenings were very cold throughout, with some severe frosts on several mornings particularly on the 31st, the minimum being as low as 26°.

The wind was very variable after the 13th, and the equinox passed by without its accustomed gales. Upon the whole it has been a fine and dry month, and an excellent seed-time.

Vegetation, generally, was at least five weeks later than in the corresponding period of 1846.

APRIL.

The month began with a cool westerly wind, and sharp, frosty mornings; sleet and snow showers were frequent during the first three days. From the 5th to the 12th inclusive, the atmosphere was a little warmer. 13th, much colder, the wind having veered to the eastward, and the maximum temperature was 16° lower than on the previous day. 17th, the minimum temperature this morning was as low as 23°, which was an unusually severe frost for the month of April. 18th, another severe frost; and sharp frosts occurred also on the mornings of 19th, 20th, and 21st. These frosty mornings, followed by an almost cloudless sky during the day, necessarily exposed vegetation to so great a range of temperature that it scarcely advanced throughout the month. Easterly wind prevailed till the morning of the 24th, when it once more veered to the westward. 25th, a slight frost again, followed by a fine, clear day. 30th, very fine morning, but the wind veered to the N.W. during the afternoon, when it became rather colder again. The nightingale was first heard in this parish on the 21st, and the cuckoo on the 22nd. Which was one week later than usual.

MAY.

The weather was very showery to the 3rd, and on this day some heavy showers of hail, with thunder, occurred during the afternoon and evening. From the 4th to the 8th, inclusive, the weather was rather stormy and unsettled, with frequent showers. On the 9th, there was a very decided rise of temperature. From the 10th to the 19th, in consequence of the genial change, vegetation,which had been so long retarded by the continued low temperature at night, seemed at length to advance with unusual rapidity and vigour, so that the whole face of the country presented quite a different appearance during these few days. 21st, a very fine day, the maximum temperature rose to 72°, and in the sun to 80°. The barometer had also risen very considerably, and this occurring simultaneously with a fall of the dew-point, was a sure indication of approaching fine weather. The 24th was much cooler, and a slight shower of rain fell in the evening. The last seven days were unusually hot for the month of May, and the temperature was equal to the hot weather of July. On the 28th the heat was intense, the maximum in the shade being as high as 87°, and in the sun 98°; while a thermometer on a south wall stood at 110° for two hours. 31st, another extremely hot day, and the barometer very high: such continued heat has not occurred in May since the year 1833.

JUNE.

The weather, during the first five days of the month, was very fine and seasonable. On the morning of the 7th there was a slight frost and small crystals of ice were found at the edge of some water in a metallic basin. 8th, a cloudy morning, and the day proved showery, thunder being heard at intervals; a little before 5 p.m. the wind shifted suddenly from W. to N.W., and brought up a severe, but short, thunder storm with heavy rain and hail—the stones varying in size between a large pea and bean, doing very serious injury to the young foliage, as well as to the hop bines. 9th, clear and very cold morning, and a few flakes of snow fell from a passing nimbus at 6 a.m. 11th and 12th fine days, but the morning very cold for the season. From 13th to 25th inclusive, very cool showery weather prevailed. The remainder of the month was very warm and dry.

JULY.

The temperature of the first three days of the month was very near the average of the season. On the 4th, the wind veered to the S.E. accompanied by a considerable rise of temperature, and large beds of the cirro-cumulus cloud. On the night of the 6th there was much lightning with thunder in this locality. From this date to the 24th the weather was extremely hot, while from

11th to 16th inclusive, the heat was more continued and intense than has been experienced in the south of England since the year 1808, and it is somewhat singular, that in both instances, the highest temperature should occur on the same days of the month, viz., July 13th and 14th. The daily highest temperature in the shade from 12th to 16th, both inclusive, was as follows: 12th, 89°; 13th, 95°; 14th, 98°!!; 15th, 93°; 16th, 88°. Mean for week ending 16th, 73°.2! From the night of the 16th to evening of the 17th, there was much electrical display. On the 24th a brilliant solar halo was visible from 1 to 3 p.m. The 25th was much cooler, the maximum for the day was not higher than 69°, a slight shower fell at noon. From the 26th to the close of the month, the weather was again very hot and dry, the temperature varying between 76° and 87° in the shade, and from 86° to 106° in the sun. It has been the driest month since May, 1844, and hitherto less rain has fallen than in any summer season since the year 1835, when there was scarcely a shower during the months of July and August.

AUGUST.

The intense heat which prevailed during the last week in July continued till the 2nd of this month. On the morning of the 4th the minimum was down to 39°, which is an unusual degree of cold so early in the month, for the night temperature is generally higher now than during any month in the year. Much heavy rain fell during the night of the 5th. The weather was cool and pleasant to the morning of the 10th. The 11th, 12th, and 13th were extremely hot, sultry days. On the 12th, large swarms of Myrmica Rubra and Formica Rubra were extremely troublesome. The air for several miles being apparently quite filled with them. 14th to 16th very fine and dry. From the 17th to 21st it was again very hot and sultry, and the maximum temperature for the month occurred on the 18th, being half a degree higher than on the 2nd. It was suddenly cool, damp, and showery from the 22nd to the 24th inclusive. Throughout the month the weather was most favourable for the harvest, and it is many years probably since the corn has been so fine, and secured in such excellent order.

SEPTEMBER.

The morning of the 1st was cold for the season, but as the power of the sun's rays was still considerable, the maximum temperature rose to 71° in the shade. 4th to 7th very fine weather. Early on the 6th the temperature fell to 31°, and on the grass to 26°. Such a sudden and severe frost so early in September, is a most unusual occurrence in Sussex. In many places the French beans, out-door cucumbers, vegetable marrow, &c., were quite destroyed, and ice was observed a tenth of an inch in thickness. On the evening of the 7th the wind veered suddenly from N.W. to S.W., rain began to fall about 7 p.m., and continued uninterruptedly for 12 hours, to the depth of nearly nine-tenths of an inch. This was a truly acceptable visitation, after the long drought, for the pasture lands were become quite bare, and in some districts of the county the supply of water, for general purposes, was very deficient.

The 8th was an oppressively sultry day, till the evening, when the wind veered to the northward, and the air became drier and cool. 19th, fine, a gale from S.W. with heavy rain came on during the night. The remainder of the month was, upon the whole, fine and seasonable, the nights, however, were cold, and on the morning of the 27th the temperature fell to the freezing point. The month has been remarkable for frequent and sudden variations in the temperature at night.

OCTOBER.

The drought, which has been very remarkable throughout the present year, may still be said to continue, for the comparatively small quantity of rain which fell during the past month served merely to refresh vegetation, without being sufficient to replenish our ponds and springs. The first four days of the month were gloomy. 9th, densely overcast all the morning, and the sun being hid by a double tier of cloud, nothing could be seen of the great solar eclipse. On the 12th the temperature rose to 71° in the shade, and 86° in the sun, being very unusual warmth for the second week of October—during this day there was a very beautiful display of the cirro-cumulus cloud, reminding us of hot summer weather. 17th, very fine—much lightning at night. 18th showery—frequent lightning during the evening. 23rd, stormy, with heavy showers and a gale from S.W. 24th, showers of rain and hail—during the evening and night a very beautiful Aurora Borealis was visible, having a fan-shaped appearance, and exhibiting, at intervals, various shades of colour from deep crimson to bright orange. Such a brilliant display of this phenomenon has not been seen in the South of England since that on the night of February 18th, 1837.

NOVEMBER.

The temperature of the two first days of the month was remarkably high—higher indeed both in the shade and in the sun than on several days in May and June ; the temperature continued high both night and day till the morning of the 17th. A very keen wind continued all day on the 18th. A beautiful double halo surrounded the moon in the evening. Several pairs of wild ducks were seen in the neighbourhood. 19th, hard frost. On the 20th a sharp frost before sunrise. 24th, a slight frost, and a considerable rise of the barometer occurred, which had previously been gradually falling since the morning of the 19th. From 23rd to 28th more rain fell than in any week for twelve months past.

DECEMBER.

1st, very clear sky with a cold breeze from north. 5th, fine, and the wind blowing strongly from the westward. 6th, a slight frost early in the morning, but at 4 a.m. the sky became suddenly overcast, and a very severe gale came on from the S.W., which had been preceded by a rapid fall of the barometer during the previous forty-eight hours ; the wind at intervals blew a complete hurricane ; this gale continued throughout the day and night, accompanied by frequent lightning and thunder ; large masses of electric clouds frequently collected, and after precipitating copious showers, again dispersed ; at 9 p.m. the barometer had fallen to 28.63 inches, but it was even lower than this during the night. The morning of the 9th was very stormy, with some heavy rain. 10th and 11th overcast and damp. From 12th to 15th inclusive the weather was remarkably fine and pleasant, and the temperature much above the average for the season. 18th, a very dark wet day throughout; some of the low grounds were flooded during the night. On the 21st a very sensible decrease of temperature had occurred, the maximum being only 34°. From this time to the end of the month the weather was very gloomy and monotonous. During the last week, the anemone, auricula, violet, primrose, &c., were in bloom in many gardens in this neighbourhood.

1848.

JANUARY.

1st, very fine day, followed by rain at night. 4th, very fine, and several of the spring flowers in bloom, including the polyanthus, violet, anemone, auricula, wall-flower, stock, &c. 7th, sharp frost, much rain at noon, a splendid rainbow visible at four p.m. 8th to 12th, very cold. 12th to 17th, milder. On the 16th a sudden change took place at midnight, and the 17th was a very wet day, followed by a heavy gale from S.W. at night. 20th to 23rd, very cold, cloudy weather. On the 22nd a damp misty rain fell at intervals, so that everything was cased with ice, and travelling rendered very dangerous. From 25th to 29th inclusive the weather was very severe, accompanied by cutting N.E. and E. winds. During the afternoon of the 27th several very brilliant meteors were observed in this neighbourhood; at night the frost was very severe, and on the morning of the 28th the temperature had fallen to 11°, being the most severe frost during the present winter.

FEBRUARY.

The first three days of the month were very fine and pleasant, but the mornings were frosty, particularly on the 7th, when the temperature fell 24°. To the 7th very damp and unpleasant weather, with much rain on the 5th. 10th, very heavy rain during the evening. 11th, a very high flood over the low grounds in this neighbourhood, nearly an inch of rain having fallen in twelve hours. 12th, a very warm, spring-like day. 13th, very damp and unpleasant weather. 18th, very fine, and the atmosphere remarkably clear, distant objects seen very distinctly. From the night of the 21st to the end of the month the atmosphere was unusually stormy and unsettled, and the gales were very severe during the nights of the 24th and 25th. The gale on the 27th was the most severe, however, and much rain fell during the morning. The month was very mild, but wet, rain having fallen more or less on 17 days. The mean temperature was high.

MARCH.

The month commenced with very wet, stormy weather, and a low atmospheric pressure. 10th, very stormy, with heavy showers of rain, hail, and snow. 18th, a severe gale, with showers of rain and hail, accompanied by a very low state of the barometer. 16th and 17th, almost continual rain. 18th, finer, with large masses of the cumulo-stratus cloud, presenting a very beautiful appearance in their various changes of nimbification. 19th, fine morning, but rain fell in the afternoon, and a heavy squall with rain and hail came on about ten p.m. 21st, overcast morning, with some severe snow storms from the westward, accompanied by the lowest state of the barometer during the month. The last three days of the month were fine, with a considerable rise of temperature.

APRIL.

The first five days of April were remarkably fine and hot for the season, and the heat was more sensibly felt in consequence of the previous long-continued wet and gloomy weather. On the 6th the wind veered to the north, causing a rapid and sudden diminution of temperature, there being a decrease of 20° in the maximum as compared with the previous day. From the 6th to the 28th the weather was very overcast, gloomy, and wet, there being scarcely any sunshine, while the quantity of rain was so much above the average that the soil in many districts was quite saturated, and agricultural operations much suspended. On the 29th the wind veered to the northward, the atmosphere became much drier, and the dew point fell from 42.6 to 38.9. The cuckoo and nightingale were heard in this parish on the 17th.

MAY.

After three wet months, very hot and dry weather set in on April 29th, and continued almost uninterruptedly until May 30th. During the first sixteen days of the month the sun was never obscured by a cloud, so that this cloudless state of sky, being for the most part accompanied by a parching easterly wind, caused the daily amount of evaporation from the almost saturated soil to be very considerable, and in consequence the surface soil soon became very dry and hard for agricultural labour. On the 17th and 18th, some slight showers of rain fell, and on the latter day a rather severe hail storm passed over during the afternoon. From this time to the 30th the weather was again very fine and warm for the season. On the 31st the barometer fell considerably, which was followed by some heavy showers during the afternoon, which proved extremely beneficial to vegetation, which, on some soils, was beginning to suffer from the sudden drought.

JUNE.

.The mean temperature of June was below the average. To the 8th, fair, but the nights were very cold for the season. 12th, a severe thunder storm during the afternoon, and much heavy rain. The lightning struck two large oak trees near Fletching. 21st and 22nd, warmer, and the sky very electric. 23rd, sultry, and heavy rain fell during the afternoon, while distant thunder was heard at intervals. The storm appeared to be much more severe to the eastward. From this time to the close of the month the weather was very showery, and unfavourable for the hay harvest, a considerable quantity having been stacked in very bad condition.

JULY.

July has been very remarkable for deficiency of sunshine and frequent gales of wind, accompanied at intervals by very heavy rains, which have materially tended to delay both the hay and corn harvests—of the former very little was secured in good condition after the 18th. On the morning of the 1st the temperature at this place fell to 40°, and on the low grounds there was a frost upon the grass. On the 4th, cirro-cumuli clouds were very numerous, indicating an early rise of temperature. The maximum on the 5th was 73°, and on the 6th, 83°. 7th, very sultry, with thunder storms passing to the eastward and westward. On the evening of the 14th frequent thunder and lightning in N.W., which continued almost incessantly till 2 a.m. of the 15th, when a severe thunder storm approached from S.W., opposed by a strong current from N.E., which rendered the lightning very forked and dangerous. The rain here was very trifling, but a few miles to the east, south, and west, it fell in torrents, with much hail. This storm did considerable damage in this and the adjoining counties. To the 19th, fine dry weather. 20th, stormy, with rain. 23rd, showery, and much rain at night. 25th and 26th, very wet days. To the 29th fine. 30th, wet night. 31st, fine, rain at night.

AUGUST.

The mean temperature of August was below the average, and the weather extremely wet and cold to the 30th day, when the wind shifted suddenly to the N.W., and the atmosphere at once became drier and more pleasant. It presented a striking contrast to the corresponding month in last year, which may be seen by reference to the monthly summary. On three days only was the maximum temperature in the shade above 70°. The morning of the 10th was very cold for the season, and there was a white frost over the brooks and low grounds in this locality; in some counties, particularly the eastern, the rain was not so continuous and heavy, and the greater part of the corn was secured in tolerable condition. It now appears probable that the potatoe disease has been caused entirely by atmospheric influence, viz., the presence of a superabundance of moisture around and in the roots and foliage of the plant, while a comparatively small amount has been exhaled by the stomata. It is the natural property of a plant to absorb a certain portion of carbonic acid from the atmosphere during the day time, which is then decomposed under the stimulus of light; the carbon is fixed, and the oxygen is given out; but if a plant which has been kept for some time in the dark is suddenly exposed to a strong light, it becomes choked with carbon and dies. The same process appears to take place with regard to the potatoe disease; for if, after a long continuance of wet and cloudy weather, the plant is subject to hot sunshine for a day or two, the sap becomes too much inspissated, exhalation from the stomata becomes impeded, and the foliage of the plant soon perishes.

SEPTEMBER.

The month of September was, upon the whole, very fine to the 23rd, and proved a most agreeable change after the heavy and continued rains which fell in August. There were slight frosts over the brooks every morning from 12th to 19th; but subsequently, and even to the end of the month, the nights were unusually warm for the season. The 16th was a remarkable day, inasmuch as the barometer attained its maximum, and the extreme range of temperature occurred during the 24 hours; early in the morning the temperature on the grass had fallen 31°, and by two p.m. the maximum in the sun in the same situation was 98°, thus proving that in a few hours vegetation was exposed to a range of 67°! The 22nd was a fine day, but exhibited a great variety of cloud, particularly the cirro-cumulus. On the S.W. horizon lightning was very frequently observed during the night, the upper current from S.W. being opposed by a lower one from the eastward. On the 23rd heavy showers fell during the day.

OCTOBER.

The first three days of October were very showery. The 6th and 7th were very fine and hot days for the season, the maximum being as high as 71° and 74° respectively, and during these two days there were some beautiful specimens of the cirro-cumulus cloud, reminding us of hot summer weather. 9th, a strong gale from S.W., with incessant rain during the afternoon. 10th to 12th, very fine, with a cool wind from N.E. 13th, very heavy rain from N.E., and there was rain every day, more or less (26th excepted) from this time to the end of the month. On the 18th there were some heavy snow showers during the morning, and a large flight of wild ducks were seen wending their course towards the N. W., which many persons would consider to be a prognostic of an early and severe winter. · October has been a very wet month nearly throughout, the depth of rain having been almost equal to the enormous quantity which fell in August.

NOVEMBER.

November was, upon the whole, a fine month, and a good seed time from the 6th to the 16th inclusive. The depth of rain was below the average, and the quantity less than in any month since May. There were some sharp frosts on several mornings, more particularly on the 5th, 8th, 9th, 15th, 16th, 20th, and 25th. On the 5th the thermometer fell to 24°, a temperature which proved quite sufficient to strip the more tender trees of their foliage. From 6th to 16th very fine, with drying winds on many days. 17th, damp overcast day. There was a brilliant display of the Aurora Borealis during the evening. It was seen, however, to much greater advantage between 2 and 3 a.m. of the 18th, the atmosphere being then much clearer, the auroral arch was well defined with eight beautiful columns of light, ascending nearly to the zenith. 26th, an unusually severe hoar frost, with much rime on all radiating surfaces : fine day and cold, but followed by a great rise of temperature at night, with rain and wind. 27th, very heavy rain till 8 a.m., and low grounds, consequently, much flooded.

DECEMBER.

December was, upon the whole, a mild month, with rather more than the average quantity of rain, and scarcely any appearance of winter until the 21st. The first week was very stormy, with some heavy gales and rain from the S.W. On the 5th and 6th very heavy showers of rain and hail, accompanied by much lightning and an occasional peal of thunder. A brilliant lunar halo appeared at 9 p.m 10th to 13th, very fine and mild, the temperature on each day being above the average for the season. 21st, a brilliant morning, severe frost, and a very keen wind from the eastward : the temperature not rising higher than 30° during the day; to 24th hard frost. On the 25th, a change early in the morning with some heavy rain, the wind having veered suddenly from S.E. to S.W. A brilliant solar halo appeared during the afternoon of the 27th, followed by some heavy rain at night. 31st, dark overcast day. The weather was so unusually mild during the second week, that primroses might be seen in full bloom in warm and sheltered situations.

1849.

JANUARY.

The month began with hard frost during the first week; but during the remainder of the month, the weather was unseasonably mild, gloomy, and wet—rain fell more or less on 16 days, between 8th and 31st. 1st, densely overcast—a cold freezing wind blowing from N.E. 2nd, very hard frost, fine day, lunar halo at night. 3rd, hard frost. 4th, cold and damp. 5th, overcast. 6th, overcast; a large solar halo appeared at 1 p.m., and a lunar halo at 8 p.m., through a cirro-stratus cloud. 11th, densely overcast, and a very cold gale, blowing quite a hurricane at intervals from N.W. 14th, stormy morning, showers of rain and hail p.m.; the Aurora Borealis was very splendid at 11 p.m. 15th, dull day, clear evening; Aurora Borealis again visible in N.N.W. at 11 p.m. 16th, overcast, with rain at intervals. 28th, heavy rain during the night, and the low grounds much flooded. During the second week, in consequence of the great mildness of the season, the primrose, polyanthus, violet, snowdrop, crocus, mezereon, &c., were in full bloom.

FEBRUARY.

The mean temperature of February was much above the average. During the first eight days of the month, the sky was uniformly overcast, and the atmosphere, for the most part, very calm. To the 19th, very fine clear weather, and a considerable daily amount of evaporation; up to this day, the barometer had been very high, and Mr. Thompson, of Chiswick, states that on the 11th, it stood higher than at any time since Feb. 7th, 1798. A very heavy rain fell on the morning of the 25th, causing a considerable flood over the brooks. 28th, densely overcast, with a severe gale and driving rain from S.W.; from 6 to 7 p.m. the wind blew a hurricane, with torrents of rain, when veering from S.W. by W. to N.W. In consequence of this hasty rain, there was a very high flood over the brooks soon after midnight. It is remarkable that, with the exception of four days, the wind has blown constantly from the western points of the compass, from Jan. 9th to Feb. 28th. As a further proof of the great mildness of the season, I may remark that some large toads were observed hopping about on the evening of the 6th, as if it were summer —their earliest appearance, noticed by White in his History of Selbourne, was on the 28th. On the 13th, two brimstone butterflies *(Gonepteryx Rhamni)*, and a cabbage butterfly *(Pontia brassicæ)*, the earliest appearance of the latter noticed by White was on April 28th; on the same day, a robin's nest was found nearly built. On the 23rd, a considerable quantity of frog spawn was seen; and on the 27th, a large female wasp in full vigour. The wallflower and polyanthus have been in bloom throughout the winter.

MARCH.

The month of March, to the 21st day, was very dry and mild, with a high state of the barometer. It was a very good seed time, and on light soils the ground worked well, notwithstanding its saturated state and the absence of any severe frost. 24th, very cold, and some heavy showers of snow and sleet fell during the afternoon. 25th, a gale from the N.E., and snow fell between 8 and 10 a.m. to the depth of one inch, the temperature of the atmosphere being below the freezing point. This was more snow than had fallen at any time throughout the last winter. The maximum temperature in the shade on this day was not higher than 38 degs., but on the 17th, it was 61 degs.—so changeable is our climate! 28th, heavy showers of hail, rain, and sleet. 30th, a bright solar halo at 5 p.m., and a large lunar halo at 9 p.m. 31st, a very fine morning, and the atmosphere much warmer. Many electric groups of cloud were visible throughout the day, which ended in a short but severe thunder storm between 7 and 8 p.m., with some heavy showers of rain and hail. From the 12th to the 18th, the weather was very fine and mild, and the common bat *(Vespertilio)* might be seen flying about as in the summer evenings.

APRIL.

The month of April was very wet and showery to the 29th day, until which time, the 21st and 22nd, were the only two consecutive days without rain or snow. 17th, snow showers in the morning, and some heavy snow also fell in the afternoon. 18th, very severe frost, and the ground covered with snow—fine day; heavy snow and rain fell again at night. 19th, very heavy rain fell early in the morning—fine till about 3 p.m., when the wind veered suddenly to the N.E., and a gale came on with very heavy snow, rain, and sleet, which continued for eight hours; most of the snow melted as it fell, and laid only upon radiating surfaces, but upon more exposed situations it accumulated to the depth of several inches, and drifted under hedge-rows, to the depth of nearly two feet. So much snow at this season of the year is unusual, but not unprecedented. 28th, fine morning—frequent thunder storms in the neighbourhood, with heavy showers of rain and hail; in some places the hail stones were as large as a man's thumb! The severe frosts on the mornings of the 6th, 12th, 14th, 18th, and 21st, almost totally destroyed the blossom of the wall fruit trees in this locality, and even in sheltered situations it has been very much injured. The cuckoo was first heard in this parish on the 20th, and the nightingale on the 23rd.

MAY.

The first few days of May were very warm, with dry parching winds. The 3rd and 4th were unusually hot for the season, and the atmosphere highly charged with electricity. On the 6th, the air became suddenly much cooler, and so continued till the 13th. 15th to 18th, very showery, and the wind boisterous at times. 20th, very heavy rain all day—the quantity fallen being upwards of one inch, during the twenty-four hours. 21st, very showery. This heavy and almost continued rain caused a considerable flood over the brooks in this locality, which much injured the grass, and many acres were, in consequence, scarcely worth mowing. 22nd and 23rd, very showery. 24th to 31st, very warm growing weather, with heavy showers on the mornings of the 28th and 29th.

JUNE.

The month of June commenced very seasonably, and the temperature was many degrees above the average. On the morning of the 4th, from 5 a.m. to 7 a.m, continued thunder was heard in the south-west, when the storm appeared to pass off in a north-westerly direction. A shower of rain fell here at 9 a.m., and another about noon. This storm visited Brighton with great severity, the hail-stones being unusually large, and breaking many thousands of panes of glass in the green-houses, &c. 5th, very hot and sultry, the temperature rising to 84° in the shade. 8th, distant thunder was heard occasionally. The mornings of the 10th, 11th, 12th, and 14th, were most unusually cold for the season, the temperature falling to 39°, 37°, 35°, and 36°, on each morning, respectively. On the 12th, the frost was sufficiently severe to form ice on the low grounds. From 18th to 28th, the weather was uniformly fine and dry, during which time the greater part of the hay crop was secured in excellent condition. The fall of rain was not half the average for June.

JULY.

A remarkably low temperature occurred on the morning of the 1st, the minimum being down to 38°; there was a slight frost over the brooks, and even upon higher situations the ferns were much injured. The hot and dry weather which commenced on June 8th, continued with but little interruption until July 17th, when the wind veered to the southward, and some rain fell during the evening. 19th, frequent showers of rain and hail, with occasional peals of thunder. 20th, frequent but slight thunder storms occurred during the day. 27th, fine morning and very sultry; a very heavy shower of rain fell soon after 1 p.m., but was much heavier at Maresfield and Buxted Park; at the latter place, upwards of half an inch of rain fell in a short time, while the depth at Uckfield was not more than ·34 inch. This heavy shower was very partial, for scarcely a drop of rain fell either at Horsted or in the northern portion of Maresfield and Buxted parishes. The late rains were of very material benefit to the turnips and oats, and were not sufficiently heavy to injure or lay the wheat, the crop of which was both abundant and of good quality, the ears being very fine and well filled.

AUGUST.

The fall of rain during the three summer months was a little more than fell in the dry summer of 1847. Although the heat was not excessive during any part of the month, yet the atmosphere was very warm and dry, consequently the harvest was secured in excellent condition throughout the southern and midland counties. This month, too, presents a remarkable contrast to August, 1848, when a much greater quantity of rain fell in three weeks than the total quantity registered for the three summer months of 1849. 7th, very sultry, and the sky obscured by large electric masses of cloud; much lightning was visible during the evening over the downs. 8th, a severe thunder storm from 1 to 3 a.m.; the lightning was very vivid, and almost incessant, but the fall of rain was comparatively trifling in this locality. 11th, very fine, with much lightning and distant thunder in the south-west, at 9 p.m. From the 20th to the end of the month, the weather was very fine, dry, and hot, the maximum temperature ranging from 71° to 81°, and the minimum from 50° to 60°.

SEPTEMBER.

September was a very fine month, and although heavy rain fell at intervals, yet it was not so continuous as materially to impede the completion of harvest. A severe thunder storm occurred on the morning of the 1st, with heavy rain; a second storm passed over at 9 p.m., with some heavy showers. 2nd, fine day; much lightning and distant thunder in S.W. during the afternoon and evening. 3rd, very sultry day, with occasional lightning and thunder, particularly during the evening and at night. 4th, heavy showers and much lightning early in the morning—fine day—a severe storm raging to the northward of this place during the afternoon. 17th to 20th, very fine, with cool breezes from the northward. On the morning of the 19th, the temperature fell to 36°, and there was a white frost over the brooks.

OCTOBER.

The weather during the month of October was changeable. Much heavy rain fell during the first week, otherwise the month would have been drier than usual. Both the barometer and thermometer have fluctuated considerably, and consequently much sickness prevailed. 4th, very heavy rain from 1 to 8 a.m., when more rain fell than has been registered for one day during the last seven years. There was a high flood over the brooks and low grounds. 5th, a slight frost early in the morning— fine day. 18th and 19th, very fine weather, with a great many meteors visible at night. During these last three days the foliage changed colour and fell rapidly.

NOVEMBER.

This was very fine autumnal month, and the weather unusually mild and dry, consequently very favourable for all agricultural operations. 10th, unusually fine and mild for the season. 12th, a dense fog all day. 18th, frosty morning. 19th to 23rd, gloomy and damp. 24th, fine. 25th, very fine—frosty at night. 26th, a cold day, and a little granular snow fell during the night. 27th, hard frost. 28th, hard frost, and a thick rime upon the trees ; a very clear cold day and evening, but the temperature rose during the night. 29th, a brilliant lunar halo at 9 p.m. 30th, continual rain throughout the day.

DECEMBER.

The month was seasonable, and, upon the whole, mild to the 20th, when the winter commenced with some severity, and the cold continued to the close of the month. 11th to 16th, very changeable weather, and for the most part the sky was densely overcast throughout. 17th, heavy rain and gale early— fine day. 18th, very stormy, with heavy rain at intervals. 20th, a clear and cold day, the temperature not being higher than 39°, and winter commenced. 21st, a dull day, with snow and showers at intervals. 22nd, much snow. 28th a heavy gale and snow from 6 to 8 a.m.; a very cold freezing wind continued all day, and the max. temperature was not higher than 27°; this is an unusually low maximum temperature, and is generally the commencement of much continued cold weather. 29th, very severe frost, the temperature fell to 14° and on the grass to 8°. 31st, hard frost, and the atmosphere very hazy and dark.

1850.

JANUARY.

The frost which commenced on December 20th, 1849, continued with scarcely any intermission to the morning of January 25th, when the atmosphere became milder and foggy—the wind veered to the westward, and much rain fell during the night. Although the frost continued so long, yet the cold was not so intense as is frequently observed during a severe winter in the south of England, for the temperature (with the exception of the 8th day) was never more than 9° below freezing point. In consequence of the continued frost some rare winter birds were shot in this county, including several specimens of the Bohemian Waxwing *(Ampelis Garrulus)*, also a larger number of wild geese (probably *Auser Palustris)* were seen in this immediate locality than had been observed for many years previously. On the 14th and 15th a piercingly cold gale continued to blow from the eastward. 31st, densely overcast, with misty rain during the afternoon, much rain at night, and the temperature rose considerably.

FEBRUARY.

February was a very mild month—but its mean temperature was not quite so high as the corresponding month in 1848 and 1849. It was remarkable that there were only three frosty nights throughout the month. The weather during the first week was very stormy, with much rain at intervals. A severe gale came on during the evening of the 5th, and continued with great violence for twenty-four hours. 11th, a very splendid meteor was visible throughout the southern and midland Counties, at about a quarter to 11 p.m. 11th, Frost during the morning, which was followed with much rain during the day. 22nd, a very fine, mild day, and the temperature rose to 56° in the shade.

MARCH.

The mean temperature of March was 3° below that of February. It was an unusually dry month, and therefore extremely favourable for all agricultural operations. During the fourth week, the frosts for several nights were very severe, but as the weather had been both cold and dry since February 20th, the blossoms of the fruit trees were not sufficiently forward to receive any serious injury. Upon the whole, it has been the most seasonable March for some years, and by far the coldest since 1845. 26th, a very severe frost occurred early in the morning, when the temperature fell to 14° below the freezing point of water; the atmosphere throughout the day was remarkably diaphanous, and distant objects were seen very distinctly.

APRIL.

During the first three weeks the weather was for the most part stormy, with a considerable fall of rain, and the temperature was more equable than is usual at this season of the year, there being a total absence of frost during the above period. March having been dry and favourable for agricultural labour, the heavy rains of April were beneficial to the grain and other crops. From 26th to 30th, the temperature was much lower, a cold easterly wind prevailing. The nightingale was first heard in this parish on the 7th, and the cuckoo on the 11th. There were some slight frosts on several mornings during the last week, but not severe enough to injure the progress of vegetation.

MAY.

After the first week it was a very seasonable month; the warm growing showers, which fell at intervals, hastened vegetation considerably, and also proved very beneficial to all crops situated upon the dry soils in this neighbourhood.

JUNE.

The temperature of this month during the first three weeks was variable, the thermometer in the shade having varied from 32° to 84°. The extreme range for the month, however, was 70, viz: 30° in the morning of the 16th, and 100° in the sun on the 26th; the low temperature just noticed is very unusual at this season of the year, and would have injured the fruit to a great extent had it not been protected by the foliage. The temperature was highest on 26th, and the atmosphere highly charged with electricity. A thunder storm passed over about 6 p.m., and in its course the lightning struck a tree at Isfield, under which some labouring men had, a short time previously, been sitting. A much more severe storm visited this place soon after midnight, when the lightning was extremely vivid and forked, and the thunder unusually loud. A house at the lower part of the town was struck by the electric fluid, which much injured the roof, and removed a considerable quantity of Horsham stone roof, besides splitting some large rafters; descending to the ground floor it burnt some children's clothes, &c.—although thirty persons were under the roof at the time, fortunately no one was injured.

JULY.

During the month of July the weather was variable, with frequent and sudden fluctuations of temperature, while the hasty showers which fell at intervals knocked down the wheat to a considerable extent. During the first three days the weather was cold and gloomy. 6th, a brilliant solar halo appeared during the afternoon. 8th, fine, much lightning to the east at night. 9th, overcast day, and thunder was heard occasionally. From 15th to 18th, both inclusive, the weather was excessively hot and sultry. The storm which visited Brighton with such severity commenced about 1 p.m., to the south of East Grinstead; taking a S.E. direction, it reached Hailsham about 3 p.m.; it then passed on slowly towards the sea, and reached Brighton soon after 6 p.m., having described in its course rather more than a semicircle; on reaching Brighton it was met by a large mass of cumulo stratus cloud, which for some hours previously had been apparently stationed in the north-west. It was probably the junction with this cloud which caused the immense fall of rain at Brighton. Although the storm lasted scarcely an hour, yet the depth of rain was 1.81 inch.

AUGUST.

August was a very showery month throughout, and consequently very unfavourable for the completion of harvest. The variations of the barometer were inconsiderable, while the fluctuations of temperature were both sudden and frequent. The first four days were very sultry, with occasional showers. 5th, very hot, and the atmosphere highly chárged with electricity. 12th, showery, and thunder was heard at a distance. 13th, thunder storms. 21st, continual rain all day, and a very cold air at night. 22nd, a slight frost early in the morning, wheat sheaves were frozen together, and even ice was observed in some situations, a circumstance which has not occurred in August for many years.

SEPTEMBER.

During the first three weeks the weather was very fine and dry, with a high barometer and an easterly wind. The earth was drier and the evaporation greater at this period than at any time during the summer, while the temperature on many days was much above the average for the season, particularly at night. This beautiful weather was most acceptable for the completion of harvest after the very showery month of August. On the nights of the 10th, 11th, and 12th, small meteors were numerous.

OCTOBER.

This was a very seasonable month in the South of England. The quantity of rain two inches less than the average. The mean temperature, in consequence of the number of frosty nights and the great absence of sunshine during 17 days of the month, was low.   From the 8th to 22nd, the weather was very dry and favourable for all agricultural operations.   1st, overcast, and thunder shower in the afternoon.   23rd, continual rain all day, with a heavy gale and rain from S.W.

NOVEMBER.

During the first fortnight of November the weather was, for the most part, very fine, with the wind almost constantly from the westward.   The temperature was higher and more equable than is usual at this season.   A few small meteors might be seen during the evening of the 11th, but the state of the atmosphere was not favourable for observation.   A severe hoar frost occurred on the morning of the 15th, when the temperature of radiation was 14° below the freezing point.   From 19th to 26th inclusive the weather was extremely stormy, with a fall of three inches and a half of rain during the week.   The 24th was probably the most boisterous and stormy day which has been experienced in this county for some years, and the depth of rain was nearly an inch and a half in little more than twelve hours.

DECEMBER.

The mean temperature of December was about the average of the last nine years, with a great prevalence of westerly winds and a very damp, foggy atmosphere. During the first fortnight the weather was very gloomy, with fog more or less every day. From the 14th to the 18th inclusive there was more electrical disturbance in the atmosphere than is usual at this season of the year, and showers of rain and hail were very frequent. From 18th to 25th the temperature was below the average, and hoar frosts were observed every morning.   The 25th was a particularly clear and mild day, and to the end of the month the temperature continued much above the average for the winter months.   During the last week the primrose, violet, polyanthus, and snowdrop were in bloom in sheltered situations. The common bat *(vespertilio)* might be seen every afternoon, and an adder *(aspera vulgaris)* was killed at Maresfield on the 28th, moving slowly across a path in a semi-torpid state.

1851.

JANUARY.

The first four days of the month were gloomy with showers. 5th, a fine day—there were some showers in the evening, from large masses of cumulo-strati clouds. 16th, fine early—a gale and heavy showers in the evening and night. 17th, stormy. 20th, very heavy rain, and gale in the evening. 21st, fine—heavy showers of rain and hail at night. 23rd, hoar frost—fine day—showers to the North in the afternoon, and a very large rainbow. 24th, hoar frost, and frequent hail-showers during the afternoon. 27th, very fine—a splendid orange-coloured meteor visible at 10 p.m. 30th, hail showers—very heavy rain and gale in the evening and at night. With the exception of 1834, the temperature of January had not been so high since the year 1796.

FEBRUARY.

The weather has been unusually fine and dry throughout the month, while the slight frosts which occurred on twelve nights were of essential service in checking the too rapid progress of vegetation.

MARCH.

During the first week the weather was dry and cold, with slight frosts at night, but the remainder of the month was remarkable for very severe gales of wind, heavy falls of rain, and a stormy, unsettled atmosphere. In the South of England it was probably the wettest March since the year 1821. The fall of rain on Saturday, the 15th, throughout the southern counties was very remarkable; at Southampton the depth was 1.06 inch; at Uckfield, 1.20; at Greenwich, 1.45; at Lewisham, 1.72; at London, 1.04. It was also singular that this unusually large fall of rain was confined to places situated south of latitude 52°; North of this parallel the weather was generally fine.

APRIL.

The month of April was cold and showery, while both the mean temperature and the fall of rain were below the average.

On several nights both at the beginning and end of the month the temperature fell below the freezing point, which very much retarded the progress of vegetation. Although the winter had been so mild and damp, yet the spring was decidedly later than usual. 27th, showers of snow and rain in the afternoon, and much lightning visible on south horizon during the evening. 30th, frequent thunder showers during the day, cool evening and night. A farm house was struck by lightning at Heathfield this day. The cuckoo was heard at Isfield on the 16th, and the nightingale on the 17th. Some glow-worms were seen during the night of the 20th, which is much earlier than usual.

MAY.

The mean temperature of May was about the average of the last eight years, and a very small quantity of rain fell. The barometer during the last three weeks was high, whilst the very dry state of the atmosphere caused a considerable amount of evaporation from the soil. An occasional frosty morning during the first week still kept vegetation backward; some of the fruit blossoms were much injured, particularly in damp and cold situations. Ice was observed a considerable thickness on the mornings of the 1st, 4th, 5th, 7th, 15th, and 16th. 26th to the 31st, for the most part fine. At the close of the month rain was much wanted for the grass and other crops.

JUNE.

The mean temperature was above, and the fall of rain below the average; the former, however, would have been much higher had it not been for general coolness of the nights. The heat was very great during the last week : the daily maximum temperature ranging from 80° to 90° in the shade, and from 90° to 102° in the sun. Notwithstanding this great heat, there was a remarkable absence of thunder storm or any electrical display. Westerly winds prevailed throughout the month, and at intervals the weather was more stormy than usual at this season, particularly on the 9th, 12th, 15th, and 16th. There was no rain after the 15th. From the 23rd to the end of the month the weather was very hot, with an almost cloudless sky.

JULY.

With the exception of a thunder shower on the 1st, the dry weather which commenced on June 16th continued to July 8th, during which period the greater part of the hay crop was secured in excellent condition. From the 8th to the close of the month the weather was for the most part showery, and the daily temperature scarcely equal to the average. After the 5th, westerly winds prevailed throughout the month with an overcast sky and great humidity of the atmosphere.

AUGUST.

This was a remarkably fine month throughout. The mean temperature was above the average, and the fall of rain only 1.56 inch, 1.30 inch of which fell early in the morning of the 28th. In consequence of this almost uninterrupted succession of fine weather, the corn crops were secured in excellent condition throughout the southern counties. From 15th to 26th the weather was very fine and dry. 28th, very heavy rain came on early in the morning, and in *five* hours 1.30 inch fell. 29th, thunder storm with rain and hail. The barometer was high throughout the month.

SEPTEMBER.

With the exception of March, 1850, this was the driest month since May, 1844. Notwithstanding the very fine weather which continued to the close of the month, and the high daily maximum temperature both in the shade and in the sun, its mean temperature scarcely exceeded the average. This was occasioned by the comparative coldness of the nights, and the constant prevalence of N. and N.E. winds for nearly three weeks. The barometer, which had been high throughout the summer, began to fall immediately after the equinox, and although the weather continued fine in the southern counties, yet a fearful gale visited the eastern coast, from Essex northwards.

OCTOBER.

Since the autumn of 1842, October has been by far the wettest month in the year. In the present instance, upwards of four inches of rain fell. The temperature was very equable for the season. The night temperature was remarkably high; while the almost entire absence of frost allowed the trees to retain their foliage but little changed; many of our summer flowers continued in bloom throughout the month. The last ten days proved an excellent seed time, in consequence of the mildness of the season, and the land having been much benefited by the heavy rains which fell during the last three weeks. Notwithstanding, however, this large amount of rain, a great scarcity of water prevailed throughout this district, and many water mills were unable to continue their work for several weeks past.

NOVEMBER.

Instead of the damp and stormy weather which usually characterises November in the south of England, the month was remarkable for its low temperature, comparatively clear skies and drought. The mean temperature was *five* degrees below the average, and upon reference to the valuable tables compiled by James Glaisher, Esq., of the Royal Observatory, Greenwich, and published in the Philosophical Transactions, part 2nd, 1850, it appears that so low a temperature has not been observed in November since the year 1786. During the present century the following are the only instances of continued frost at this period, which I here insert, together with their respective mean temperature—

Year				Mean Temperature of November.
1807 ...	...	...	...	... 38·7 degs.
1809 ...	...	...	...	... 39·5
1815 ...	...	...	...	... 38·9
1826 ...	...	...	...	... 39·9
1829 ...	...	...	...	... 39·3

It is worthy of remark that much severe weather prevailed during the subsequent winter months in every instance. A general idea is prevalent in this neighbourhood that it is many years since there was such continued drought and scarcity of water during the autumnal months. I therefore state the fall of rain during the past five months, ending Nov. 30th, together with the quantity which fell in the corresponding months in 1847, and the average for the same period during the last eight years—

FALL OF RAIN IN INCHES.

	1851		1847		Average of 8 years.
July	3·50	......	0·22	......	1·95
August	1·56	......	1·08	......	2·69
Sept.	0·21	......	1·80	......	1·99
Oct.	4·11	......	1·57	......	3·99
Nov.	0·81	......	2·12	......	2·63
	10·19		6·79		13·25

From this table it is manifest that although the fall of rain in the present instance is rather more than three inches below the average, yet it is nearly three and a half inches more than fell in 1847, proving that it is not safe to trust to the " memory of man" in these matters.

DECEMBER.

The mean temperature of December was above the average, but the most remarkable features of the month were the continued drought and the absence of any gales of wind from the westward, which usually occur when the temperature exceeds the average of the season. Upon reference to the records which I possess of the monthly fall of rain since the year 1727, I find it has frequently occurred that when November has been very dry, December has been wet, and *vice versa;* but the following are the only instances of continued drought during the consecutive months of November and December throughout this long period.

FALL OF RAIN IN INCHES.

	1756	1762	1767	1788	1812	1822	1851
Nov	·97	·92	·92	·45	·18	·63	·81
Dec	·94	·23	·40	·89	·76	·67	·50
Total,	1·91	1·15	1·32	1·34	·95	1·29	1·31

The scarcity of water throughout this neighbourhood became a most serious inconvenience, not only to the farmers and millers, but the supply for domestic purposes was very scanty, while in some villages it could only be purchased by the pailful.

1852.

JANUARY.

The winter of 1851-52 was remarkably mild, and its mean temperature nearly two degrees above the average. The drought which had continued throughout the months of November and December, 1851, came to a close during the first week, and before the end of January upwards of five inches and a half of rain had fallen. The weather continued mild, stormy, and unsettled throughout the month. The mean temperature was upwards of three degrees above the average. Lunar halos were frequent, and during the evening of the 5th a splendid meteor was seen near the zenith. The 16th was a remarkably fine day, and I saw a sulphur butterfly on the wing. The winds were westerly.

FEBRUARY.

This month began with a spring-like temperature; highest on the 1st, 57°! which was only once exceeded, viz., 58° on 17th. From this date to the end of the month the weather became much colder, with N. and E. winds. The mean temperature was nearly two degrees above the average. Both solar and lunar halos were frequent during the first fortnight. Westerly winds were the most prevalent. On the 19th, about half-past ten, I observed a beautiful display of the aurora borealis. Three rose-coloured columns extended from N.E. horizon to nearly the zenith. At 11 p.m. a well defined arch extended from Aldebaron to Corona Borealis, the convexity of which almost reached Polaris. Beneath was a fainter arch. From the superior arch innumerable evanescent columns were apparent, emitting at intervals clouds of electric light. I counted thirty of these columns at 11.14 p.m. At 11.30 p.m. the whole of the northern portion of the sky, as far as the tail of Ursa Major, was of a splendid rose or pink colour. Clouds soon came over, but there was still a very strong light to the northward. After midnight the aurora was again very magnificent.

MARCH.

Although the mean temperature of this month was slightly

above the average, yet it was cold in its general character, with a great prevalence of E. winds, frosty nights, and continued drought, till the evening of the 29th. 21° was the lowest temperature. A sudden interval of summer-like weather occurred from 21st to 24th, both inclusive. On the latter day the highest temperature in the shade was 72°, and that in the sun 86°. It was quickly succeeded by a return of N.E. wind and frosty nights. The barometer continued very high till the last week.

APRIL.

The drought continued till the 28th, when a little rain fell, and also on the two succeeding days. The barometer was very high, and the winds easterly every day till the 28th. There were frequent frosts at night, but the mean temperature was very little below the average. The rainfall was less than half an inch.

MAY.

The mean temperature of this month was about equal to the average. The drought of the previous months may be said to have continued till the 9th. The pressure then began sensibly to diminish, and was followed by some refreshing rains, of which the parched ground stood much in need. Thunder storms occurred on the 14th, 16th, and 17th. The winds were variable, but N.E. during the first and last weeks. The weather was for the most part very gloomy and cold during the day, from continued absence of sunshine. The rainfall slightly exceeded the average.

JUNE.

Throughout this month the barometer continued very low, and the rains were heavy and almost incessant. The total rainfall exceeded seven inches, which is an unprecedented amount for June in the south of England. In consequence of the previous fine, dry weather, the grain crops did not suffer quite so much as might have been expected, but many thousand acres of grass land were so repeatedly flooded as to render the crop of hay from thence almost valueless. The peas were also much injured by the excessive moisture, and many acres of beans were thrown into the farmyard for manure. Thunder storms occurred on 14th, 19th, and 24th. On the latter day it was very severe to the northward of Uckfield. As usual in wet periods, solar and lunar halos were frequent.

JULY.

After the heavy rains and low temperature of June, a very sudden change to drought, bright skies, and a rapid increase of temperature, occurred on July 3rd. The remainder of the month was excessively hot, and its mean temperature ¡the highest I have ever registered for any month. On six days the temperature was at or above 90° in the shade, and on 16 days it was at or above 80°. As might be expected, the actual mean temperature was nearly eight degrees above the average, while the rain did not exceed half an inch. The barometer continued high, with very little fluctuation. The winds were variable.

AUGUST.

On the 3rd of this month a rainy period commenced, and continued with but little intermission during the remainder of the year. From 3rd to 17th the rains were heavy and almost incessant. The total rainfall for the month was more than double, and the mean temperature one degree above the average. The winds were westerly. There was much electrical disturbance on many days. On the 11th we had a violent gale from S.W. for some hours, which very much shattered the corn and fruit; many trees were blown down in this neighbourhood. By the 18th the grain crop had become so saturated with moisture, that the corn began to grow as it stood in the sheaves. The weather, during the remainder of the month, was rather finer, with occasional showers only, till the storm on the last day.

SEPTEMBER.

The mean temperature of this month was one degree above the average, and the rainfall larger than I have ever registered for September. Although rain fell on fifteen days only, yet the total quantity was rather more than six inches and a half. On some days we had summerlike weather, more particularly during the first and fourth weeks. On the 2nd the highest temperature in the shade reached 81°·5, and on the 24th, 74°. The winds were westerly, and the sky much covered by cloud. There was much electrical disturbance. During the storm of 7th a boy was killed by lightning near Ashcombe.

OCTOBER.

The month commenced stormy, with very heavy rains on 1st and 4th. On the latter day 2·12 inches of rain fell in the course of 24 hours, and from the previously saturated state of the ground, caused an immense flood all over the brook lands between Buxted and Lewes. During the second and third weeks the rains abated, and the weather became tolerably fine and warm for the season. On the 22nd, however, the atmosphere was again loaded with moisture, and rain fell heavily during the remainder of the month. The water rose on the north side of Lewes bridge to 13 feet 6 inches above low water mark, which was higher than it had been for 55 years. The height of the spring tides is rarely more than ten feet. At Uckfield bridge the water was highest during the evening of 26th, when the flood very nearly reached the front of the "Bell Inn."

NOVEMBER.

The general character of the three previous months was maintained throughout the whole of November. Rain fell on 23 days, to the amount of 6.52 inches. The mean temperature of the month was extraordinarily high, having been as much as seven degrees above the average. On the 5th the temperature was 64°, and on several other days it was at or about 60°. The winds were westerly. A strong gale from S.W. on 7th. The brook lands were frequently flooded.

DECEMBER.

A very high temperature continued throughout this month, and the S.W. wind blew constantly, with frequent heavy rains and gales. On the 17th we had a very severe thunder storm, with heavy rain and hail at intervals, for upwards of thirty hours, after which the brook lands were much flooded again. Solar and lunar halos were frequent. On the 27th a severe gale came on from S.W., which was felt throughout the kingdom, causing much damage to property both on land and sea.

———

During the last five months of this year the immense fall of rain was equally great and injurious both throughout this country and Ireland, while the continued and serious floods had been unprecedented in the present century. Sudden thaws, after heavy snows have occasionally been the cause of disastrous inundations in some parts of the kingdom, but which have been generally more dependent upon sudden changes of temperature than any extraordinary falls of rain. In the present season, however, the great floods have been entirely due to the *actual quantity of rain which has fallen;* indeed, the ground for many weeks before the close of the year became completely saturated, and refused to imbibe any more moisture. The rain, therefore, ran off the ground into the natural channels, which were already swollen by the unusual rise of springs throughout the country, rendering the bye roads and lanes in many instances quite impassable, and the arable land unfit for sowing wheat; therefore, at the close of the year a comparatively small breadth had been sown in the neighbourhood. In some few instances, where the grain was sown during a few fine days in the middle of October, it came up much better than might have been anticipated.

During the past century the following are instances of heavy rains in six consecutive months contrasted with the present season :—

	Inches.
1774—April to September both inclusive.........	22.28
1775—July to December inclusive..................	22.65
1782—April 12th to October 11th inclusive......	24.30
1792—April to September inclusive	20.25
1848—July to December inclusive..................	23.17
1852—August to December (five months only)	32.47 !

No further proof is required to show that the present wet season far exceeds any instance on record.

The year ended with remarkably mild weather, and without a trace of winter, many of our spring flowers being in bloom during the last week.

.

1853.

With the exception of the months of January, June, and October, the mean temperature of every month throughout the year was below the average. During the preceding ten years the mean annual temperature of Uckfield was $49°.67$—the lowest temperature during the above period having been $46°.62$ in 1845, and the highest $51°.57$ in 1852. Although this variation is scarcely $5°$, yet the range of these few degrees of temperature has a very marked influence upon vegetation. Should the mean prove to be below the average value, and especially when continued month after month, very serious effects are produced upon vegetation generally, for the earth, partaking of the low temperature of the air, chills the roots of all cereal plants, and either perishes a large portion of the seed or retards its growth to such an extent as to produce a thin and impoverished crop. For the above reasons cold seasons usually precede periods of scarcity. It appears that the mean temperature of 1853 was nearly $1°$ below the average, the lowest since 1845, and that to the end of May it corresponded to the worst of seasons, viz., 1816; but the weather so far improved in the months of June, July, and August, as to prevent the serious consequences which would otherwise have ensued.

The heavy rains of 1852, and January, 1853, saturated the earth with moisture, and as the temperature of December, 1852, and January, 1853, was unusually high, vegetation during these two winter months was kept in a very warm and moist condition, which rendered it the less able to withstand the cold weather which prevailed in February, March, and April the temperature of even the latter month scarcely exceeded that of the previous December.

Frost occurred in every month except June, July, and August. The following are a few particulars of each month :—

JANUARY.

Was very mild and wet; the temperature was 4°, and the depth of rain 1.51 inches above the average. Three-fourths of the sky were overcast, and the wind was chiefly from west and south-west. It was the warmest January since 1834.

FEBRUARY.

Colder weather set in early this month. On the morning of the 1st there were 8° of frost, with a cold north wind. There were severe frosts on the mornings of the 15th, 19th, and 22nd, when the temperature fell to 17°, 18°, and 19° respectively. Solar and lunar haloes were frequent. The depth of snow was very trifling, although the wind was generally from N., N.E., and E., and the sky was more than three-fourths covered by cloud.

MARCH.

This was a cold month. Frost occurred on twenty nights, and so late as the 19th and 27th the temperature fell to 20° and 19° respectively; the mean temperature was more than 2° below the average. North and N.E. winds continued during the greater part of the month, with occasional showers of snow.

APRIL.

The temperature of this month was also below the average, the rain nearly one inch in excess, and of the whole amount more than two inches fell in the fourth week. S. and S.W. winds were the most prevalent, but at intervals the atmosphere was dry and seasonable, particularly from 6th to 19th, inclusive. Solar and lunar haloes were frequent, as the sky was much covered by cloud. During the afternoon of the 20th a severe thunder storm passed over, with a heavy shower of rain and hail. On the 25th the brooks were much flooded. The cuckoo was first heard on the 19th, and the nightingale on the 20th.

MAY.

The greater part of this month was cold and dry, with a great prevalence of N. and N.E. winds. The mean temperature, however, was not much below the average. A frost occurred on the morning of the 9th, which severely injured the blossoms of the wall fruits, and the more so on account of the showers of rain and hail which fell on the previous day. Thunder storms passed over on the 16th, 27th, and 30th. The depth of rain was half an inch below the average.

JUNE.

This was a warm and seasonable month, the temperature being above and the fall of rain below the average. The showers were distributed at such intervals as materially to improve the grass crops, which subsequently proved abundant. A severe thunder storm passed over Lewes on the 26th, where a house was struck and much injured by lightning. Heavy rain fell on the 26th. The wind was chiefly from S. and S.W., and the sky was more overcast during the day than at night.

JULY.

The mean temperature of July was more than 2° below, and the depth of rain more than two inches above, the average ; the wind was almost entirely from S.W. and W. A thunder storm passed over on the 1st, with some heavy rain. On the evening of the 7th a most severe thunder storm passed over a portion of the county west of Brighton, in a line from Worthing to Henfield and Eastgrinstead. Many houses were struck, and serious accidents occurred throughout the course of the storm. Hail stones fell upwards of five inches in circumference. The *ascertained* loss by the tenant farmers was £8,577 ; and by market gardeners, £521 12s. 8d. Rabbits, hares, ducks, and various birds were killed in the fields. Nearly the whole of the fruit was destroyed, the apples and pears being cut in halves upon the trees. On the 14th there was a very heavy fall of rain to the depth of 1.79 inches. At Thwaite, in Suffolk, it was 2.20 inches, and at the Royal Observatory, Greenwich, 2.80 inches ! From this time to the end of the month the sky was generally overcast, and crops suffered much from continued absence of sun.

AUGUST.

During the first fortnight the weather was very fine, warm, and dry, while the sun shone more constantly than at any time of the year. The winds were more equally distributed than usual. The mean temperature of the month was, however, below the average, and the depth of rain a little in excess. Very heavy rain fell on the night of the 22nd, accompanied by frequent lightning and thunder.

SEPTEMBER.

Upon the whole this was a fine month for harvest, especially in the north; the mean temperature was below the average, and the depth of rain about half an inch in excess. There was a slight frost on the morning of the 27th, otherwise the temperature at night was higher than usual at this period of the year. The sky was about half covered by cloud.

OCTOBER.

This month was remarkable for continued and very heavy rains throughout. Three times during the month the fall of rain exceeded an inch in the course of 24 hours. The atmosphere and the earth were nearly saturated with moisture, which together with the almost entire absence of the sun told most injuriously upon vegetation; a severe thunder storm, accompanied by heavy rain and hail, occurred on the 27th. Meteors were very abundant during the evening of the 30th, and there was a brilliant display of the Aurora Borealis on 31st; the temperature was above the average, and only twice during the month did it fall below freezing point. The depth of rain was nearly three inches above the average, which for this month is nearly $4\frac{1}{2}$ inches. October during the last ten years having been by far the wettest month in the year.

NOVEMBER.

This month was mild and foggy—its mean temperature was a little below the average, and the total depth of rain was less than an inch, the usual quantity being nearly three inches. Solar and lunar haloes were frequent. The sky was rather more than half covered by clouds. The barometer was high during the month; there was very little rain to the 25th. The wind was generally from N. and N.E.

DECEMBER

Was very cold, dry, and frosty—its mean temperature was 5° below the average, and lower than any December since 1846, severe weather set in on Dec. 15th, and continued to the close of the month. The temperature fell below 20° on 17th, 26th, 29th, 30th, and 31st. The wind was chiefly from N. and N.E. No rain fell between 7th and 30th, but snow showers were frequent during the fourth week. The barometer was very low considering the coldness of the weather and the prevalence of N.E. and E. winds.

1854.

The mean temperature of the year 1854 exceeded the average by little more than half a degree, and in its general character was exceedingly favourable to the products of the soil. The fall of rain was more than six inches below the average. The winds from the S.W. and W. have been by far the most prevalent.

The following are a few particulars of each month.

JANUARY.

The cold weather which commenced on Dec. 15th, 1853, continued to the 5th of this month. On the 3rd the temperature fell to 16°, which was the minimum for the year. In the northern and midland counties the cold was much more severe, and at many places the temperature fell several degrees below Zero. Less snow fell in Sussex during this winter than in any other county. Upon the whole this month was mild and damp, its mean temperature was 1° above, and the fall of rain half an inch below the average.

FEBRUARY.

During this month the barometer was high, with but little

fluctuation. The mean temperature was 2° above the average, and the fall of rain only one-third the usual quantity. The wind was generally from the North and West; although there were frosts on several mornings, the only severe one was on the 14th, when the temperature fell to 19°.

MARCH

Was another fine and dry month, the barometer was uniformly high, notwithstanding the prevalence of westerly winds. The dew point was low. The mean temperature was 3° above the average, and the fall of rain scarcely exceeded the tenth of an inch. It was by far the driest March during the last twelve years; a severe frost occurred on the morning of the 6th, when the temperature fell to 19°. A comet appeared near the western horizon on the evening of the 29th.

APRIL.

The drought which commenced at the end of January continued to the 28th of this month. The mean temperature was nearly three degrees above the average, and the fall of rain was only a quarter of an inch. The winds were generally from the eastward. The amount of ozone was considerable. The weather was very fine, warm, and dry, particularly during the first fortnight, and in some places the scarcity of water was severely felt. Swallows appeared in this locality on the 10th, the nightingale on the 14th, and the cuckoo on the 18th. The lilac was in full bloom so early as the 17th.

MAY.

This month was gloomy, cold, and wet. The temperature was more than two degrees below, and the fall of rain above the average. The winds were generally from the S.W. and W., and the barometer unusually low for this season of the year. The Aurora Borealis was visible during the evenings of the 16th and 25th. There was a slight frost so late as the 20th, which materially injured the more forward vegetables in many situations. Thunder showers with hail were frequent on the 8th and 9th. It was the coldest May since 1845.

JUNE

Was a very gloomy, cold month, although there was not much rain till the last week. The sky was three-fourths covered by cloud, and the amount of ozone considerable, but not more than was registered in April. The mean temperature was $2°$ below, and the fall of rain very nearly the average. The wind was generally from the westward. During the second week the atmosphere was full of aphides, which nearly destroyed the hop plants in some districts. There was a thunder storm to the N.W. on the 30th, and two bullocks were struck dead by lightning at Isfield Place.

JULY.

After the first twelve days this month was very fine, warm, and dry, and most of the hay in this neighbourhood was harvested without a shower. The mean temperature was a little below the average, but the heat was excessive from 20th to 25th, both inclusive. During these six days the daily maximum temperature in the shade ranged from $83°$ to $92°$. The 24th was the hottest day. The fall of rain was little more than the average. The greater part fell on the 1st, 9th, 11th, and 26th. The barometer was rather low, and the winds generally from the westward.

AUGUST.

Although the mean temperature was not quite $1°$ above the average, yet it was remarkably fine summer weather throughout the month, and extremely favourable for the corn harvest. The fall of rain was only the average. The wind was generally from the westward, and very calm. The amount of ozone was small, and the sky was rather more than half covered by clouds. Thunder storms occurred on the 3rd and 16th, and the atmosphere was very hot and oppressive during the last five days, particularly on the 27th.

SEPTEMBER.

This was another remarkably fine, warm, and dry month. The mean temperature was more than two degrees above the average, and the highest since 1846. The barometer was uniformly high. The wind variable. The amount of ozone and cloud small. The fall of rain was only 1.45 inches, the whole of which fell between the 13th and 17th. The temperature at night was unusually high, and more resembling July than September. The corn harvest was completed before the close of the month, and the grain crops, both in quantity and quality, were very superior.

OCTOBER.

The mean temperature of this month was a little below the average. The barometer fluctuated considerably, and the winds were variable. The fall of rain was about equal to the mean for October, which has been the wettest month in this locality for several years past. The temperature, both at the beginning and end of the month, was much above its average value, and there were very few frosts at night. The amount of ozone was small, but rather more than in the three previous months. There was a very great fall of rain on the 6th to the depth of nearly two inches. Heavy rain fell on 17th, 19th, and 25th.

NOVEMBER

Was very foggy, cold, and damp; its mean temperature was nearly three degrees below the average. The fluctuations of the barometer were remarkable and frequent, particularly on the 16th, 22nd, and 29th. The wind was variable, and so much ozone had not been observed since June. The fall of rain was rather less than the average. During the fourth week there were some sharp frosts at night.

DECEMBER

Was very mild, gloomy, and damp. On several days the atmosphere was almost saturated with moisture. The mean temperature was 41°.19, the average being 39°.24; the wind was variable, and the sky overcast. Very little ozone was observed, and the fall of rain slightly exceeded the average. Meteors were very abundant on several nights. Solar and lunar haloes were observed during the month. The barometer was very low again on the 18th.

1855.

The mean temperature of the year 1855 was 47°.66, and it was the coldest year (1845 excepted) since 1816.

This low temperature must not be ascribed to the severe frost in January and February, inasmuch as every month was below its average value, with the exception of August and October. The fall of rain was considerably below the average, and had it not been for the heavy rain which came in October, it would have been one of the driest years on record.

The following are a few particulars of each month respectively :—

JANUARY.

During the first fortnight of this month the barometer was high, and the weather unusually mild and dry, but the sky was generally overcast both day and night. A few primroses might be seen in bloom on warm banks, and on the 10th bees and gnats were flying about as if it were autumn instead of mid-winter. The long and severe frost of this year commenced on the 15th, the temperature falling to 26 deg., although the sky was overcast. Snow fell in small quantities on several days. The 31st was an exceedingly cold day, with a gale and drifting snow from the N.E. In consequence of the high temperature which prevailed during the first fortnight, the mean was 36°.34. The depth of rain and melted snow did not amount to a quarter of an inch; the average being upwards of two and a half inches. The sky was, for the most part, densely overcast.

FEBRUARY.

The severe frost which commenced on January 15th continued with but little intermission to the 24th of this month, when the wind veered to the S.W.—some rain fell, and a general thaw commenced. Snow showers were frequent on several days, but the depth was never more than about five inches on a level. Snow crystals fell occasionally, but in great abundance on the 17th. These crystals differ very materially from ordinary snow; a very interesting account of them by James Glaisher, Esq., of the Royal Observatory, Greenwich, will be found in the *Illustrated London News* of February 24th.

On the morning of Saturday, 3rd, such a remarkable frost occurred as few persons probably ever remember to have seen. A piercingly cold wind prevailed on Friday morning from E.N.E., which at noon veered to east, and in the evening to E.S.E. The maximum temperature for the day had not been higher than $27°$, and the minimum $21°$.

The barometer, which at 9 a.m. stood at 29.875 inches, had fallen to 29.650 at midnight. At 1 a.m. on Saturday the wind increased almost to a hurricane, and the atmosphere indicated a heavy fall of snow. At 2 a.m., however, a little sleet commenced falling, and at 3 a.m. a very heavy rain, which continued for upwards of two hours; while the temperature of the air for several feet above the earth remained below the freezing point.

By day light, the pavements, roads, as well as every tree and shrub, were completely enveloped with a coating of ice one-sixth of an inch in thickness. All houses on their S.E. aspect were entirely covered in the same way. The effect was very extraordinary on the leaves of evergreens; and at 10 a.m., just as a thaw was commencing, an entire ice-leaf might, with care, be removed from their upper surface with all the veins and form of the true leaf delineated thereon with the accuracy of a photograph. The branches of many of the smaller shrubs were broken by the weight of the ice. At mid-day most of the trees had lost their transparent covering, when it was interesting to pick up the various forms of ice-branches which had fallen from the trees and hedges. This frozen rain stopped the hands of the church clock. It is recorded that a somewhat similar phenomenon happened in the day time in the month of January, 1771, and again in 1807; on the latter occasion rooks, when attempting to fly from the trees, fell to the ground with their wings completely frozen: and for the same reason larks, plovers, and other birds were caught in the fields.

The frost was most severe on the morning of the 11th, when the lowest reading of my thermometer was $9°$, and the radiating instrument $2°$. On nine days during the month the minimum thermometer readings were less than $20°$.

It was the coldest February on record, the mean temperature not being higher than 30° 87. The depth of rain was considerably below the average, but the amount of ozone was greater than for any other month throughout the year.

The phenomenon of the frozen rain, just described, reminds me so much of Phillips' poetical description of this occurrence, which frequently happens in northern climates, that I have quoted the following lines from his " Letters from Copenhagen."

> " Ere yet the clouds let fall the treasured snow,
>   Or winds begun through hazy skies to blow,
>   At evening a keen eastern wind arose,
>   And the descending rain unsullied froze.
>   Soon as the silent shades of night withdrew,
>   The ruddy morn disclosed at once to view
>   The face of Nature in a rich disguise,
>   And heightened every object to my eyes.
>   For every shrub, and every blade of grass,
>   And every painted thorn, seemed wrought in glass ;
>   In pearls and rubies rich the hawthorns show,
>   While through the ice the crimson berries glow.
>   The thick sprung reeds the watery marshes yield
>   Seem polished lances in a hostile field ;
>   The stag in limpid currents, with surprise,
>   Sees crystal branches on his forehead rise.
>   The spreading oak, the beech, and tow'ring pine,
>   Glaz'd over, in the freezing ether shine ;
>   The frighted birds the rattling branches shun,
>   That wave and glitter in the distant sun.
>   When, if a sudden gust of wind arise,
>   The brittle forest into atoms flies ;
>   The crackling wood beneath the tempest bends,
>   And in a spangled shower the prospect ends."

MARCH.

This month was cold and wet; both temperature and pressure were below the average and the depth of rain in excess. The wind was extremely variable; frosts occurred more or less on twenty nights, so that the mean readings of the minimum thermometer were below the freezing point. The barometer was unusually low on the 3rd, 12th, 22nd, and 23rd. The sky was much covered by cloud, and the amount of ozone considerable.

On account of the lateness of the season, the following notes may, perhaps, prove interesting:—Frogs spawned about 14th, bees appeared on 19th, the sulphur butterfly (Gonepteryx Rhamni) on 20th, gnats were playing about under a south hedge on 26th.

APRIL.

Upon the whole this was a fine and dry month, but the mean temperature was below the average, and there were some frosty mornings both in the first and last weeks. With the exception of the second week the barometer was high, and the wind frequently from the eastward; the depth of rain was rather more than half an inch, the average being nearly two inches.

MAY.

With the exception of the fourth week, this month was gloomy and cold—the mean temperature having been as much as four degrees below the average. There were sharp frosts on the mornings of the 5th, 6th, 9th, and 13th. On the morning of the 9th the reading of the minimum thermometer was 27°, and the radiating thermometer 22°. Fortunately vegetation was very backward, or it must have been injured; very few fruit trees were in bloom at this time. The barometer was rather low, and the wind blew generally from the eastward; the depth of rain slightly exceeded the average.

JUNE.

During this month also, the mean temperature was considerably below the average, and upon the whole it was the coldest June for many years. The mornings of the 18th, 20th, and 21st were unusually cold for the season; the readings of the minimum thermometer being only 4° above the freezing point; indeed, slight frosts did occur on these mornings upon the low grounds in this locality. The only really warm days were 6th, 26th, 27th, 28th, and 29th. The mean temperature of January 2nd was warmer than June 1st. Very little ozone was observed, and the sky was much covered by cloud. The wind blew generally from the S.W. and W. The depth of rain was below the average.

JULY.

The weather during this month was showery and unsettled. The hay crop was deficient and not well harvested. The mean temperature was below the average, and the temperature frequently very low for the season. The wind blew generally from the westward, and the sky was very much covered by cloud; scarcely any ozone was observed. Heavy rains fell on the 11th, 12th, and 13th, and the total depth for the month was considerably above the average. Slight thunderstorms occurred on the 9th, 14th, and 23r .

AUGUST.

This was a very fine, warm, dry month, and very favourable for the corn harvest. The mean temperature exceeded the average of eleven years, and with the exception of the 20th, the daily highest temperature in the shade was above 70°, while in the sun it was frequently above 90°. Slight thunderstorms occurred on 7th and 8th, but a very severe one visited this neighbourhood on 23rd. The morning was overcast, and the day sultry; distant thunder was heard in S.W. at 4 p.m., and at 9 p.m. very vivid lightning was visible along the whole horizon from S.W. to S.E.; at 10·30 a storm came up against the lower current from the eastward; and at 10·45 a short shower of rain fell, and very large hail. The hail stones were ordinarily the size of pullets' eggs, and some much larger; several measured from three to six inches in circumference. Many thousand panes of glass were broken in this neighbourhood, but I think the greenhouses at Buxted Park received the greatest injury. Birds were killed, fruit knocked off the trees, and the hop-bines much injured.

The storm appeared to be still more severe both to the eastward and westward of this place, but I think the hail storm was very local.

The depth of rain was not equal to a fourth part of the average. Westerly winds were by far the most prevalent. The amount of ozone was very trifling.

SEPTEMBER.

Was a remarkably fine, dry, and pleasant month, and although there was a considerable prevalence of N.E. and E. winds, yet the mean temperature was nearly equal to the average. The barometer was high, and the amount of rain only 0·88 of an inch, 0·54 of which fell on the last two days. The morning of the 9th was cold for the season, and the temperature of radiation fell two degrees below the freezing point. This is unusually cold for September. The amount of cloud and ozone was small. Thunder storms passed over on the 29th.

OCTOBER.

During this month, and particularly during the last week, th barometer was very low and fluctuating. The weather was very stormy on the 4th, 5th, 6th, and 26th. The depth of rain was considerably above the average, although October is the wettest month in the year in the South of England. There was a remarkable absence of frost, and the mean temperature exceeded the average by nearly two degrees. Westerly winds were by far the most prevalent, and the amount of ozone trifling. A beautiful solar halo was visible during the afternoon of the 27th.

NOVEMBER.

The great prevalence of N.E. and E. winds, and the low temperature of the dew point were the most remarkable features in this month. Both the mean temperature and the depth of rain were also below the average, notwithstanding which there were few frosts at night. The sky was for the most part overcast, and the amount of ozone equal to the average.

The foliage remained on the trees later than usual, as it was not until the 15th that it began to fall. On 30th at 7 p.m. a brilliant meteor about 15 minutes in diameter appeared close to the star B. Aurigœ, and moved somewhat slowly and horizontally to the star A. Draconis in about ten seconds. It was of a globular form, and the light which it emitted was so intense that the smallest print might have been read with facility. As it disappeared it left a beautiful train of blue light along its path. This was by far the most splendid meteor which I had ever seen.

DECEMBER.

The temperature of this month was extremely variable, and the mean value more that three degrees below the average. During the first fortnight there was an unusual prevalence of N. and N.W. wind, and the atmosphere for the most part gloomy and cold. On the evening of the 18th a short but severe frost commenced, and the temperature continued below the freezing point till the morning of the 23rd, when a sudden and very extraordinary rise of temperature occurred.

At 10 p.m. on 22nd my self-registering thermometer stood at 19° *below* the freezing point, and at 9 a.m. of 23rd it had risen to 13° *above*, thus indicating a rise of 32° in less than twelve hours.

So sudden a change has not been observed since January, 1843. During the last week the weather was unusually mild and damp. On the 24th a sulphur butterfly (Gonepteryx Rhamni) was observed, enticed out probably by the great rise of temperature.

The depth of rain was a little below the average. The amount of ozone, which had been very trifling at the beginning of the month, was considerable during the last fortnight. A thunder storm with heavy showers of rain and hail passed over on 24th.

It is worthy of record that several swallows were seen in this locality towards the end of November, and during the first week of this month. I have ascertained also that they were seen in other counties at the end of November; it must not be considered, therefore, as a merely local or solitary instance of the late appearance of these birds.

1856.

The mean temperature of the year 1856 was a little above the average. The weather throughout was not remarkable for any particular excess, either of heat or cold. The fall of rain was rather more than four inches above the mean annual amount in this neighbourhood.

The following are a few particulars of each month respectively :—

JANUARY.

During this month, the weather was for the most part overcast, mild, and damp—rain having fallen, more or less, on 19 days; the total amount, however, did not equal the average quantity for the month. The mean height of the barometer was very low on the 7th, 8th, 21st, and 24th. The mean temperature was above the average. There were only eight frosty mornings, while on many days the temperature was at or above 50° in the shade. The wind was very variable, and the sky generally overcast. A specimen of gonepteryx rhamni appeared on the 3rd; the aconite was in flower on the 17th, and the hazel on the 19th.

FEBRUARY.

The mean temperature of this month was unusually high, and the maxima especially so on the 9th, 26th, and 27th. It was the mildest February during the last fourteen years. Although the degree of humidity was high throughout the month, yet the fall of rain was considerably below the average. As a proof of the great mildness of the season, I may remark that the birch tree was in flower on 5th, snowdrop on 6th, mezereon on 8th, red hepatica on 10th, primrose on 16th, crocus and polyanthus on 22nd, and the willow on 28th. I noticed some lambs in an adjoining parish on the 1st; the missel thrush sang, and bees appeared in considerable numbers on the 10th; the lark sang on 11th; frogs spawned about 17th; and the bat (Vespertilio) appeared on 24th.

MARCH.

Both the mean temperature and the fall of rain were about the average value for the month; the latter would have been very deficient but for the very heavy rains which fell during the night of the 16th, when upwards of an inch fell in a few hours. Upon the whole it must be considered to have been a dry month, and extremely favourable for all agricultural operations. East and north-east winds were very prevalent, both during the first fortnight and the last week. The amount of ozone was considerable. The zodiacal light, which is occasionally seen at this period of the year was very conspicuous during the evening of the 7th. The daisy flowered on the 12th, and the mercurialis perennis on the 15th.

APRIL.

This month was for the most part overcast, mild, and wet. The mean temperature was a little above, and the fall of rain more than double the average. It was the wettest April during the last fifteen years. East and north-east winds were very prevalent, and there were some frosty mornings between the 16th and 23rd. On the morning of the 29th also the temperature fell to 29°, which somewhat injured the young foliage, which was coming out very fast. Vanessa Urticœ appeared on the 1st; nightingale and swallow on the 12th; the cuckoo on the 18th.

MAY.

This month had not been so gloomy, cold, and wet since May, 1843. Its mean temperature was 3° below the average, and the fall of rain more than double the usual quantity. East and north-east winds were again very prevalent, with an overcast sky during the first fortnight. Ozone was abundant on several days, but the mean amount did not equal that of January and March. A severe gale of wind blew from S.W. on 18th with occasional showers of rain, snow, and hail. On the 29th a severe thunder storm passed over this locality; the lightning struck an elm tree in a brook to the south of the town, stripping off a considerable portion of the bark, as well as splitting a portion of the hard wood. The rain and hail on this occasion was not of long continuance, but nearly half an inch of rain fell in about ten minutes. Vegetation advanced very slowly throughout the month.

JUNE.

Although the mean temperature of this month was more than two degrees below its mean value, yet the weather upon the whole was fine and pleasant. Rain fell on seven days only, and the total amount was below the average. The winds were chiefly from the westward, and the amount of ozone was very trifling.

JULY.

The mean temperature of this month was about its average value, but (with the exception of 23rd) there was no really hot summer weather till the last few days. On the 30th and 31st the maximum temperature in the shade was 86° and 87° respectively, and on the latter day 104° in the sun. The amount of ozone was very trifling, and the depth of rain about one third more than the average. During the evening of the 15th a very severe thunder storm passed over this place, with very heavy rain and large hail. I have been credibly informed that some of the hail stones measured seven inches in circumference. A large quantity of glass was broken in the various greenhouses of this and the adjoining parishes. A slight thunder storm also occurred on the evening of the 23rd.

AUGUST.

The great heat which commenced at the close of July continued during the first week of this month. The maximum temperature in the shade on 1st, 2nd, 3rd, and 4th, was 90°, 92°, 90°, 90° respectively, and the temperature at night never fell below 61°. During these four days the temperature in the sun ranged from 103° to 107°; the bulb of this thermometer is suspended in the air, and not influenced by the reflection of heat from any wall or building. The mean temperature of this month was more than 3° above its average value, and the fall of rain one-third less than usual. Slight thunder storms occurred on the 11th, 14th, 16th, and 22nd. Scarcely any ozone was observed, and during the last fortnight the sky was much covered by clouds.

SEPTEMBER.

Throughout the first three weeks of this month the weather was tolerably fine and dry, with a good proportion of sunshine; but during the last week the weather became so suddenly stormy, cold, and wet, that the mean temperature was nearly two degrees below the average. Upwards of six inches of rain fell, 2.38 inches of which fell during the day and night of the 27th. This heavy rain was accompanied by a great depression of the barometer, the reduced reading of which, at 9 a.m. of 28th, was 28.625 inches. It had not been so low since February, 1848.

OCTOBER.

This was the driest month of October which has been observed in the South of England for some years past. The readings both of the barometer and thermometer were considerably above their average value. The fall of rain was very little more than a third of the usual quantity. During the last fortnight scarcely any rain fell, and the sky on several nights was extremely clear and favourable for astronomical observations. Very little frost was observed, which is an unusual circumstance at this period of the year.

NOVEMBER.

In consequence of the frequent frosts and low temperature at night, the mean temperature was considerably below the average. The weather, however, was very dry, with an unusual prevalence of N.W. winds. The depth of rain scarcely exceeded one inch. A great many meteors were observed during the evening and night of the 24th, none during the second week.

Sharp frost commenced on the morning of the 29th, and the temperature fell to 19° at 9 a.m. of 30th. The amount of ozone was more than had been observed for several months. The foliage fell very gradually during the second and third weeks.

DECEMBER.

This month was remarkable for the very frequent and sudden fluctuations of the barometer. The temperature also varied considerably. The severe frost which commenced at the close of November continued to the 4th of this month. The weather then became suddenly very mild and wet. The amount of ozone was rather more than last month, and the sky was much covered by cloud.

The night of the 24th was remarkably clear, and favourable for astronomical observations, although the barometer was low and the temperature below the freezing point. Upon turning the telescope to Saturn the planet was observed in great perfection when near the meridian.

On the 25th very heavy masses of cumulo-strati, cirro-strati, and nimbi clouds were observed towards the S.E., at noon, and distant thunder heard. During the afternoon and night, I understand there was a considerable fall of snow along the coast, east of Brighton.

––––––

1857.

The year 1857 was remarkable for a very high temperature, it having been, upon the whole, the warmest year of which we have any authentic record.

The valuable tables upon temperature, published by James Glaisher, Esq., F.R.S., of the Royal Observatory, Greenwich, which extend over a period of seventy-nine years, do not confirm the generally received idea that a hot summer is either preceded or followed by a cold winter, or *vice versa:* on the contrary, it would appear that any hot or cold period has been generally accompanied by weather of the same character. The hot year of 1779 was preceded by one warm year and followed by two others. The warm year of 1806 was preceded by a warm winter. The hot year of 1818 was preceded by a moderate winter, and was followed by a warm one. The year 1822 was preceded by a warm winter, and was followed by a moderately cold one. The year 1834 followed a very mild winter, and was followed by another. The year 1846 was preceded by a warm winter, and was followed by a moderately cold one.

The mean temperatures of the warm years 1779, 1806, 1818, 1822, 1834, 1846, 1852, and 1857, were as follows, the year of the highest temperature being 1857 :—

	Mean Temp.			Mean Temp.
1779	51·2	1834		51·0
1806	50·5	1846		51·3
1818	50·8	1852		51·5
1822	51·0	1857		51·9

The years which were distinguished by unusually hot summers were 1778, 1779, 1780, 1781, 1818, 1826, 1831, 1834, 1835, 1842, 1846, and their average mean temperature was 63.2.

With the exception of the months of January and April, the temperature of every month exceeded the average, and this excess was particularly to be observed during the months of June, August, September, October, November, and December. During the summer months the rains were not frequent, but considerable in amount, and fell at such intervals as to be of the greatest possible benefit to the growing crops. It was an early harvest, and the grain crops were abundant, of good quality, and well secured.

Fruit was more abundant, and of better flavour, than for some years past, but when gathered it did not keep well.

During the last few weeks of the year a very maligant form of scarlet fever (diptheria) prevailed in this neighbourhood, of a very infectious character. It proved rapidly fatal to a large number of persons under twenty years of age. Instead of running the ordinary course of scarlet fever, the eruption, in the majority of cases, was suppressed, and a deposit of lymph was formed upon the tonsils, uvula, and pharynx; the inflammation, in some cases, extending to the trachea, and producing a species of croup. Unless the early symptoms could be detected and arrested, such immediate prostration of the system was induced that the disease frequently proved fatal in less than a week, and occasionally so early as the fourth day.

The following are a few particulars of each month respectively :—

JANUARY.

The mean temperature of this month was below, and the fall of rain considerably above, the average. The fluctuations of the barometer were frequent. The low grounds were flooded on the morning of the 10th, after the heavy rains during the previous night. The frost was severe on the morning of the 15th, and from that date to the close of the month the temperature fell below the freezing point on almost every night. The most severe frost happened on the morning of the 30th, when the temperature fell to 16°. The sky was much covered by clouds, and the amount of ozone considerable. I observed some primroses in bloom on 12th, the hellebore on the 26th, and snowdrop on 29th.

FEBRUARY.

This was a remarkably fine and dry month, and set aside the old proverb, "February fill dike—be it black or be it white." The mean temperature was considerably above the average, and the fall of rain very trifling. There was a great deficiency of ozone, although the wind was variable. With the exception of sharp frosts during the nights of the 2nd and 4th, the night temperature was much higher than usual at this season of the year. During the first fortnight, although the weather was so mild, yet scarcely any rain fell, and the wind remained perfectly calm.

MARCH.

During the first week the weather was very fine and dry, with a high barometer, but subsequently the weather became showery, with frequent slight frosts at night, frequent fluctuations of the barometer, and variable winds. The sky was much covered by cloud, the amount of ozone was considerable, and the fall of rain nearly an inch above the average. On the evening of the 7th I noticed a very brilliant lunar halo, which was followed on the 8th by showers of rain, hail, sleet, and snow. A very heavy hailstorm passed over at mid-day of the 15th, followed by sharp frost at night. On the morning of 22nd the temperature fell to 25°, and there were some heavy snow showers during the day.

The two known periodic comets of D'Arrest and Brorsen appeared this month. I saw the former for the first time on the evening of the 22nd, and the latter on the 26th.

APRIL.

This month was, upon the whole, rather cold and showery. The mean temperature was below, and the fall of rain above the average. The sky was much covered by cloud, but a larger amount of ozone was present in the atmosphere than during any month of the year. The barometer was low and the wind variable. After the first week, the temperature at night was very low, with frequent frosts at night. So late as the 30th the temperature fell to 25°. The nightingale was first heard on the 10th, and the cuckoo on the 11th. Swallows appeared on the 19th.

MAY.

This was a very fine and dry month for all the grain crops. During the first eight days the weather was rather cold, with a great prevalence of N.E. wind, but subsequently, the day and night temperature being considerably above the average, vegetation advanced rapidly and was not retarded by late frosts, which for several years past have so much injured the young foliage at its first appearance. The winds were variable, and the amount of ozone considerable. The fall of rain was more than half an inch below the average, the only wet day being the 22nd, when nearly an inch of rain fell during the 24 hours. Brilliant solar haloes were observed both on the 26th and 27th.

JUNE.

The mean temperature of June was more than 3° above the average, and the mean highest temperature in the shade exceeded 76°. The hottest day was the 28th, when the maximum temperature rose to 92° in the shade. On the 25th it was at 90°, and on the 26th 91°. It was the warmest June since that in the year 1846. The amount of rain was considerably above the average, but the greater portion of it fell during the 9th, 10th, and 19th, in very heavy thunder showers. The amount of ozone on several days was considerable, and the wind very variable. The latter part of the month was particularly favourable for securing the hay crop, the sky being almost cloudless from 23rd to 27th, both inclusive, and the air extremely hot and dry. Brilliant solar haloes were visible on the 2nd and 6th. Thunder storms occurred on the 10th, and at midnight of the 19th.

JULY.

This was another fine summer month, with the continuance of a high daily temperature, both in the shade and in the sun, although not quite so high as in the preceding month. The fall of rain was a little above the average, in consequence of the heavy thunderstorm on the 1st, otherwise it would have been an unusually dry period. Westerly winds were prevalent, with a deficiency of ozone.

AUGUST.

This was a month of real summer weather, both the day and night temperature having been exceedingly high. It was the hottest month during the summer, and with the single exception of August, 1842, it was the warmest August since that in the year 1780. On thirteen days the temperature was at or above 81° in the shade, while on several nights the temperature did not fall below 61°. Although the night of the 23rd was cloudless, and radiation, therefore, going on freely, yet the temperature was never lower than 66°.5, which is the highest night temperature which I have ever recorded. The amount of rain was above the average, the greatest portion falling in heavy showers. From the 17th to the 31st scarcely a drop of rain fell, and the weather was most favourable for the harvest, the greater portion of which must have been secured in excellent condition throughout the southern counties. Thunder storms occurred on the 6th, 9th, 13th, and 16th.

SEPTEMBER.

Although the fall of rain was more than double the average amount, yet there were some intervals of very fine weather, particularly during the last fortnight. The mean temperature was nearly 3° in excess, and the temperature at night was unusually high for the season. It was the mildest September since that in the year 1846; and the equinox passed over without the accustomed gales. An immense number of wasps appeared this autumn, and the fruit was much injured by them.

OCTOBER.

The mean temperature of this month exceeded the average by 5°, and was the warmest October since that in the year 1831. The maximum temperature on the 1st was 74°, and so late as the 16th it was 72°. The temperature at night was extremely high, and not a trace of frost was visible till the morning of the 31st, when the temperature fell to 30°. The fall of rain slightly exceeded the average, and was particularly heavy on the 6th, 7th, 8th, and 21st. On the 29th a thunder storm passed over towards the N.W. about 1 p.m. A splendid lunar halo was visible during the evening.

NOVEMBER.

There was an unusual prevalence of N.E., E., and S.E. winds this month; and had it not been for the heavy rains which fell during the day and night of the 23rd the amount for the month would have been very much below the average. The mean temperature was more than 2° above the average, while on six days the temperature was at or above 60°, and only on the mornings of the 13th and 25th was there any appearance of frost. Many of the tender annuals and perennial flowers continued in bloom till the close of the month. The sky was much covered by cloud, and dense fogs were frequent, particularly on the 5th, 20th, and 21st.

DECEMBER.

The extraordinary mildness of this season continued to the close of this month, the mean temperature of which was nearly 6° above the average. The 20th and the 31st were the only frosty mornings. Throughout the month the barometer was remarkably high, and the fall of rain very trifling. If the month of December is mild it is generally *wet,* but it very seldom happens to be both mild and *dry.*

There was an entire absence of easterly winds. The sky was much covered by cloud, and there was a great deficiency of ozone.

As another proof of the great mildness of the season, I should mention that I saw the following flowers in bloom on Christmas-day :—Anemones, verbenas, violets, roses, helleborus niger, penstemon, scarlet geranium, fuschias, primroses, daisies, rhododendrons, and dandelions. The buds of the yellow jessamine and pyrus japonica were almost expanded, and even the leaves of the snowdrop and jonquil were appearing above ground. The haulm of some potatoes, which had been left in the ground, was from 6 to 8 inches high.

1858.

The temperature of the year 1858 was slightly above the average, but there was a great deficiency in the rainfall, which was very marked in the months of February and June. The year was not characterised by any particular excess or deficiency of temperature throughout the various months. June was the warmest and February the coldest. The following are a few particulars of each month respectively :—

JANUARY.

The mean temperature was below the average. Sharp frosts occurred on fifteen nights, but the temperature never fell below 21°. There was scarcely any rain or snow till the last two days, although the sky was very frequently densely overcast. The winds were westerly.

FEBRUARY.

This was the coldest month of the year, and the mean temperature was 2° below the average. There was a great prevalence of easterly winds, and on many days clear, bright weather. The lowest temperature was 21°·6 on the morning of 19th.

MARCH.

This was a dry month, and the mean temperature was slightly above the average. During the first fortnight there were frequent frosts at night, cold northerly winds by day, and very little sunshine. The temperature rose considerably in the second and third weeks, and on the 24th reached 71°·6 in the shade. The winds were variable. On 6th and 7th a rather severe gale from N.W. 10th, hard frost and some snow. 12th, hard frost. 15th, much overcast, and weather very unfavourable for observing the solar eclipse. The latter part of the month was warmer. The equinox passed by without any particular gale, in fact, the atmosphere was calm and almost free from cloud.

APRIL.

Throughout the whole of this month the temperature was variable. During the first fortnight the weather was, for the most part, overcast and showery, with thunder occasionally. There were few frosts at night, notwithstanding the great prevalence of easterly winds. The latter half of the month was much finer, with clear skies, and an absence of rain till the last two days. Both the rainfall and the mean temperature were above the average.

MAY.

This was a cold, showery month; the mean temperature was nearly 2° below, and the rainfall about equal to the average. Vegetation advanced very slowly. Westerly winds were the most prevalent. It was not till the last few days that we had really warm weather. On the 26th there was a sudden and great rise of the barometer, which was a precursor of the beautiful weather about to follow. On the 29th the highest temperature in the shade was 70°, and on the 31st 80°!

JUNE.

The mean temperature of this month was 63°·8, which is the highest mean temperature recorded for June (with the exception of that in the year 1846) during the last 86 years. The mean maximum reading of my thermometer in the shade was unusually high, while the reading of a thermometer, with blackened bulb, placed in the full rays of the sun, and not influenced by reflection from any wall or building, was as high as 91°.

The highest temperature in the shade was exactly 90° both on the 15th and 16th, and in the sun 106°.

During the last few years, however, as high, and even higher temperatures have been observed in the month of June. The following are the dates :—

		In the shade.				In the sun.
1846, June 19th	...	...	91.5	...	...	...	112
„ „ 20th	...	...	92.5	...	...	...	113
„ „ 22nd	...	...	91.0	...	...	...	110
1850, June 27th	...	...	90.0	...	...	...	102
1857, June 25th	...	...	91.0	...	...	...	100
„ „ 26th	...	...	90.0	...	...	...	101
„ „ 28th	...	...	92.0	...	...	...	101

The month of June was very hot in the years 1775, 1781, 1818, 1822, 1826, 1842, and 1846, and it is worthy of remark, that in every instance the hot weather continued during the subsequent months of July and August.

The most remarkable feature of the past month has been the almost entire absence of rain in this locality, although some heavy thunder showers have fallen along the eastern borders of the county, and in Kent.

June was also an exceedingly dry month in the years 1743, 1757, 1765, 1775, 1782, 1791, 1806, 1818, 1825, and 1827. The following table will show the amount and the deficiency of rain during the last seven months.

	Fall of rain at Uckfield in inches.	Average fall of rain at Uckfield during the last fifteen years.
1857, Dec.	0.93	2.08
1858, Jan.	1.16	2.76
,, Feb.	0.71	1.70
,, March	1.21	1.51
,, April	2.05	1.97
,, May	2.03	2.31
,, June	0.16	2.16
Total	8.25	14.49

The spring of 1844 was remarkably dry, and the total fall of rain during the months of April, May, and June, was only 1.34 inches, but in the previous three months 9.19 inches had fallen, making a total of 10.53 inches for the six months. The following list of dry seasons, which continued during the first six months of each year respectively, may perhaps be interesting :—

Number of inches of rain which fell during the first six months.

	Inches.		Inches.		Inches.
1741	4.32	1794	7.17	1822	5.89
1742	7.21	1798	7.25	1823	6.06
1760	7.10	1801	5.52	1825	5.35
1762	6.28	1802	6.06	1834	7.07
1771	6.41	1806	5.44	1840	6.12
1785	4.46	1814	7.06	1847	8.30
1788	7.27	1815	6.49	1858	7.30

JULY.

This month was much cooler than the last, with frequent showers and occasional heavy rains. It proved the wettest month of this dry year. Its mean temperature was 2° below the average, and therefore unfavourable for bringing the grain crops to maturity. Thunderstorms occurred in this county on 7th, 15th, 16th, and 18th. During the storm of the 16th, the vane on the church steeple was struck by lightning and slightly injured. On 25th a violent gale from S.W. did much injury to the hop gardens.

AUGUST.

Fine weather prevailed during the first three weeks, with very little rain. The winds were extremely variable,; the mean temperature was rather above, and the rainfall considerably below the average. Thunderstorm on 18th. The 21st was stormy and heavy rain. With the exception of 30th, the latter part of the month was fine and dry.

SEPTEMBER.

This was a fine and very pleasant month. The mean temperature was nearly $3°$ above the average. Although rain fell on twelve days, yet it was very trifling in amount. The winds were variable from points between east and west. From 12th to 17th, both inclusive, the weather was extremely warm for the season, and the daily temperature ranged between $72°$ and $79°$ in the shade, while in the sun it was nearly $100°$. This fine weather continued to the end of the month. The temperature at night was higher than that in the months of July and August. A strong southerly wind blew on the 23rd, otherwise the atmosphere was very calm about the time of the equinox.

OCTOBER.

Was another fine month. The mean temperature considerably above, and the fall of rain below the average. There were only two frosty mornings. Winds chiefly westerly, and the month passed away without any gales.

NOVEMBER.

On the 1st the wind veered to the eastward, and caused a very considerable diminution of temperature. Cold weather prevailed, for the most part, throughout the month, the mean temperature of which was more than $2°$ below the average. Winds were easterly, with great atmospheric pressure till the 24th. Hoar frosts were frequent at night. The rainfall was scarcely half the average for the month.

DECEMBER.

Upon the whole this was a mild month, with both the mean temperature and rainfall above the average. The sky was densely overcast and the winds westerly. There was scarcely any frost, and the mean daily range of temperature was very small.

At the end of November and beginning of December the drought, which had been a remarkable feature in the weather of this year, was found to be of serious inconvenience throughout the county. The springs, wells, ponds, and water courses were drying up. Many cottagers found difficulty in obtaining the necessary supply for domestic purposes, while farmers were obliged to send long distances to obtain a supply for their cattle. The great dryness of the soil interfered also with the wheat sowing in some districts. A long drought occasionally brings about a formidable train of evils, not the least of which is the probable prevalence of low fever and other diseases, which are referable to scarcity of water, and its consequent unfitness for drinking and culinary purposes.

1859.

JANUARY.

The mean temperature of this month was above, and the rainfall nearly equal to, the average. Frosty mornings were few and not severe. Winds were chiefly westerly, and at intervals almost amounting to a gale from S.W. The sky was much covered by cloud.

FEBRUARY.

This was also a mild month, with the mean temperature considerably above the average. There were a few slight frosts, but the winds were for the most part westerly, and the weather showery. The rainfall was a little above the average. The 21st was a very mild day, and two or three kinds of butterflies were on the wing. A beautiful display of the Aurora Borealis was visible during the evening of the 22nd.

MARCH.

This was a fine, mild month, and the temperature higher than for many years past. The weather was showery during the third week, but the equinox passed by without any particular gale. The only stormy period was during the second week. There was an entire absence of easterly wind throughout the month, which is remarkable at this season of the year. The common bat was flying about on the 3rd. Snakes appeared on the 4th, and the willow was in flower on the 5th. Some young thrushes were seen in the garden at Uckfield House on 24th.

APRIL.

The temperature of the month was rather below the average, and some heavy showers fell occasionally. A severe frost occurred on the 1st, when the temperature fell 10° below the freezing point. There were fewer frosts than are usual at this season. There was some electrical disturbance during the evenings of 7th, 10th, and 16th. Also a brilliant Aurora Borealis on 21st. The latter part of the month was cold, with more wind from eastward than during the two preceding months.

MAY.

This was a fine, dry month, and notwithstanding an extraordinary prevalence of N.E. and E. winds, the mean temperature was above the average. The rainfall scarcely exceeded an inch. Vegetation advanced but slowly, and it was near the end of the month before the oak trees had completed their foliage. Slight thunder storms occurred on 19th, 20th, 30th, and 31st. The weather became quite summer-like during the last week, and on several days the temperature was considerably above 70° in the shade.

JUNE.

This was a warm and dry month, but the heat was not intense. There was again a considerable prevalence of N.E. and

E. winds during the first fortnight. Slight thunder storms occurred on the 6th, 26th, and 27th; the mean temperature was nearly 3° above, and the fall of rain considerably below, the average. The night temperature was high, and the weather calm and favourable for the grain crops. At the close of this month there was a great scarcity of water in this locality, and many wells had been dry for some weeks. I believe this was to be attributed more to the deficiency of rainfall during the previous, than to the current year, inasmuch as the rainfall for the past six months has been nearly equal to the average.

JULY.

With the exception of that in the year 1852, this was the hottest July for many years past. From the 3rd to the 20th, both inclusive, the daily highest temperature in the shade ranged from 80° to 90°, and in the sun from 97° to 107°. With the exception of that which fell during thunder storms on 18th, 20th, and 21st, the amount of rainfall was very trifling, while vegetation generally became very parched and drooping, from the excessive heat of the sun. The mean temperature was as much as 5° and a half above the average. The barometer continued high, and the winds were, for the most part, westerly.

AUGUST.

This month was also warm and dry; the greatest heat was from 19th to 25th, both inclusive, but it was moderate compared to the excessive heat of the previous month. The rainfall was much below the average, and vegetation suffered so much from the continued drought, that many shrubs and small forest trees died. Very slight thunder storms occurred on the 14th, 25th, and 30th, but the accompanying rainfall was trifling, and scarcely sufficient, even temporarily, to refresh the exhausted foliage. Winds were westerly and calm.

SEPTEMBER.

The temperature of this month was about equal to the average. The first fortnight was fine, with occasional showers. A wet season commenced at the middle of the month, and continued with but little interruption to the close of the year. The 17th was rather a stormy day, otherwise the period of the equinox again passed by without any particular gale. The temperature at night was frequently very high, and more than equal to many of those in July. Winds still continued westerly, with but little variation.

OCTOBER.

The mean temperature of this month slightly exceeded the average, which was chiefly occasioned by the high night temperature which prevailed during the first three weeks. After this date the weather became colder, both day and night, with sharp frosts at intervals. The fall of rain, although it amounted to more than four inches, was scarcely equal to the average for this wet month. Winds were variable, with an unusual prevalence of S.E. A severe gale came on during the night of 25th and morning of 26th; the weather was also very stormy and unsettled on 28th and 31st. On the 12th, about 8 p.m., two patches of Aurora appeared to the westward; the upper one extended from A cygni to B Lyræ, and the second from A Herculis nearly to the horizon. The colour was rosy pink, and very conspicuous in the strong moonlight. It faded away in about half an hour. At 9 o'clock a beautiful lunar corona was visible, and at 9.30 another patch of Aurora became visible to the westward, between A Herculis and A Serpentis, and extended vertically about 15°.

NOVEMBER.

This was a mild and very wet month. The mean temperature was nearly equal to the average. Upwards of four inches of rain fell during the first week. The weather was very boisterous, with heavy rain, on 1st and 5th. On the 6th we had a severe thunderstorm for four hours, with torrents of rain; and the wind at intervals blew quite a hurricane. All the low grounds were much flooded on the 7th, and a portion of the railway was under water for some hours. Lunar halos were frequent. The barometer was very low on the 1st, and high on the 18th. Winds were variable.

DECEMBER.

The weather was very changeable. During the first ten days it was mild, with westerly winds—from 11th to 22nd very cold, with hard frosts—while during the last nine days it was again mild, with constant heavy rains. The mean temperature was below the average by nearly 3°; the barometer fluctuated considerably, and its reading was very low on 26th. The lowest temperature during the frost was 16°.4 on the morning of 17th. The year ended with gloomy, damp weather, and rain. Several of the gales and rain came from S.E., which is a very unusual circumstance in the South of England.

1860.

The mean temperature of the year 1860 was 47°.40, which is two degrees and a quarter below the average of the last eighteen years.

With the exception of January and October, the mean temperature of every month was below the average. It was a cold ungenial year throughout, and the wet period, which commenced in September, 1859, continued with but little interruption to December 9th, 1860.

The depth of rain for the year was considerable, and although the total amount is upwards of four inches more than fell in 1848, yet it is eight inches *less* than fell in the wet year 1852.

The rains in the latter year were frequently very heavy, but there were considerable intervals of fine weather (July in that year having been the hottest month on record), and, without reference to a meteorological journal, it might have been supposed that the wet days of 1860 would far exceed in number those of 1852.

The following table, however, will show both the fall of rain and number of wet days in each year respectively, from which it will at once be seen that the excess of wet days in 1860 was not so great as many persons have supposed :—

	No. of wet days.		Fall of rain in inches.	
	1852	1860	1852	1860
January ...	17 ...	18 ...	5.56 ...	4.75
February ...	12 ...	10 ...	1.42 ...	1.50
March ...	2 ...	19 ...	0.47 ...	3.00
April ...	3 ...	11 ...	0.48 ...	2.53
May ...	11 ...	15 ...	2.61 ...	4.20
June ...	23 ...	18 ...	7.04 ...,	4.80
July ...	4 ...	12 ...	0.50 ...	3.00
August ...	19 ...	23 ...	6.01 ...	5.84
September...	15 ...	17 ...	6.54 ...	3.75
October ...	16 ...	13 ...	8.70 ...	2.97
November...	23 ...	10 ...	6.52 ...	2.95
December ...	23 ...	13 ...	4.70· ...	3.17
Total ...	168	179	50.55	42.46

It is also worthy of remark that the mean maximum temperature in the sun has only been three degrees ; and the amount of cloud only a fraction less than the warm year of 1859.

JANUARY

Was a mild and wet month. The barometer was low, and S.W. winds were the most prevalent. The mean temperature was above the average. There were but few frosty mornings, and the temperature never fell so low as seven degrees below the freezing point. A large lunar halo was visible during the evening of the 5th. 23rd—severe gale from S.W., with frequent lightning and heavy rain. 24th—stormy; frequent lightning at night. With the exception of 25th there was rain every day from 19th to 31st.

FEBRUARY.

This was the coldest month throughout the year. The temperature was three degrees below the average, and on several nights the frost was very severe. On the morning of the 11th the temperature was nearly 14 degrees below the freezing point. The winds were variable, and the sky was much covered by cloud. During the night of the 5th, a thunderstorm passed over, with a heavy shower of rain and hail. From 11th to 15th frequent snow storms, and the drifts of snow were greater than had been observed in this neighbourhood since February, 1847. 28th—strong gale from S.W., and many trees blown down.

T

MARCH.

The mean temperature was a little below, and the fall of rain nearly double the average for this month. The sky was much covered by cloud, and the winds blew generally from the westward. Hoar frost occurred on several mornings, particularly on 1st, 3rd, 9th, and 10th. 21st—severe gale again from S.W. 23rd—stormy, and the barometer low. On 31st another severe gale at night, and by 11 p.m. the barometer had fallen to 28.661.

APRIL.

This was the coldest April for many years, the mean temperature was nearly four degrees below the average. N.E. wind was very prevalent, and the sky much covered by cloud. Sharp frosts occurred on the mornings of 21st, 22nd, and 23rd, that on 22nd being more severe than any frost we had in January. A thunder storm, with some heavy rain, passed over during the night of 24th.

MAY.

A considerable quantity of rain fell during this month, and the temperature was below the average. The wind blew generally from the S.W., and the atmosphere was frequently almost saturated with moisture. 26th—a thunderstorm during the afternoon. 28th—stormy; notwithstanding the heavy fall of rain, the sky was less covered by cloud than during any month in the year.

JUNE.

This was probably the coldest June during the last forty years. The mean temperature was nearly four degrees below the average, and rain fell more or less on 18 days—it fell heavily on the 3rd, 9th, 12th, and 25th, and the total amount was more than double the average. The wind blew on 24 days from the S.W., and the atmosphere was unusually damp and gloomy for the season. On the 2nd there was the most severe gale which had occurred in June since the second of that month in the year 1809. Many trees were blown down in this neighbourhood, and much injury done to the standing crops.   29th, frequent thunderstorms, with showers of rain and hail.

JULY.

The mean temperature of this month was also several degrees below the average. The wind was variable, and the sky was much covered by cloud. The driest period of the year was during the first fortnight of this month, and some persons were able to secure the hay in excellent condition. From 15th to 24th rain fell every day, and it was very heavy on 21st and 23rd. Thunderstorms occurred on 28th and 29th.

AUGUST.

The temperature had not been so low in August since 1848. The sky was almost always covered by cloud, and rain fell on 23 days. It was the wettest month during the year, and scarcely any progress could be made with the harvest. There was a slight thunderstorm on 24th, followed by a gale from S.W., with incessant rain for many hours.

SEPTEMBER.

This was probably the coldest September since the year 1803. The land, having become saturated and chilled by the heavy rains and gloomy weather of the preceding month, remained in a very sad state, and it was with difficulty that the corn could be secured in even a tolerably dry condition. The winds were variable and the sky much covered by cloud. A severe gale from S.W. came on during the night of the 24th, with very heavy rain, causing a high flood over the brooks.

OCTOBER.

The temperature of this month a little exceeded the average, and during the first ten days the weather was fine and dry, but subsequently rain again commenced, and continued nearly every day till the 26th. The total fall of rain for the month, however, was below the average—this being usually the wettest month in the year. The last few days were fine and dry.

NOVEMBER.

After the first few days the weather was for the most part overcast and cold—the mean temperature was below the average, and the fall of rain a little in excess. Rain fell on ten days only during the month. The wind blew generally from the N.E., yet there were but few frosts at night. The sky was much overcast, and the month ended with gloomy, cold weather.

DECEMBER.

In consequence of the severe weather during the fourth week of this month, the mean temperature was more than two degrees below the average. The first few days were mild and wet, and the barometer was very low on the 8th and 9th. On the 15th a dense fog. On the morning of the 18th the frost commenced, and continued till the night of the 29th, when a severe gale came on from S.E., with torrents of rain and sleet, which continued till the afternoon of 30th, when a rapid thaw commenced, which caused, during the evening, the highest flood over the low grounds in this neighbourhood since October, 1852. The month ended with mild and damp weather.

The frost on Christmas day was very severe in many parts of England; and in some of the Midland and Northern counties the temperature fell several degrees below zero.

In Sussex, however, the lowest temperature did not occur on Christmas day, but on the morning of the 29th, when my thermometer indicated nearly 26° of frost.

1861.

The mean temperature of the year 1861 was only a quarter of a degree less than the average. The only meteorological features worthy of remark are, the great cold and drought in January, the frequent storms of wind and rain in March, and the low temperature, heavy rains, and floods in Nov. The spring, upon the whole, was cold and dry, and had it not been for the showery and somewhat cold weather in July, the harvest would have been early and of good quality. The crop of hops was almost an entire failure in this district, and but few gardens would pay for the picking.

JANUARY.

The severe frost which commenced on Dec. 18th, 1860, continued to the 17th of this month. The mean temperature was 5° below the average—and had not been so low since January, 1850. The second week was the coldest period. During the last fortnight the weather was much milder, accompanied by a generally overcast sky and very dense fogs. Very little rain or snow fell throughout the month. The wind blew frequently from the eastward, and the average height of the barometer was upwards of thirty inches. On the 29th some larks were singing very gaily, and a few primroses were seen in full bloom on warm banks.

FEBRUARY.

This was a mild month, with but little variation in temperature. The only severe frost was on the morning of the 12th, and was followed by rain at night. Lunar haloes were very frequent during the third week, in consequence of the humid state of the atmosphere. The 21st was a very stormy day, with a severe gale at night from the S.W. Throughout the month the sky was generally overcast, with a great prevalence of S.W. wind. The mean height of the barometer was below the average. Thrushes began to sing on the 5th, blackbirds on the 11th. Snowdrops came into bloom on the 8th, daisies on the 13th, crocuses on the 16th.

MARCH.

The atmosphere was remarkably stormy at various times during this month, particularly on the 1st, 2nd, 17th, 20th, and 21st. The fall of rain was more than the average, and the winds were chiefly from the westward. The sky was less covered by cloud than during the previous months. The mean height of the barometer was considerably below the average, and on the night of the 18th the reading was 28.882 inches. The mean temperature was 2° above the average, and there were but a few slight frosts at night. On the morning of the 2nd there was a very splendid solar halo in the S.E., with the prismatic colours very distinct; during the evening of the 9th there was a beautiful display of the Aurora Borealis.

APRIL.

The weather throughout this month was unseasonably cold and dry, with an almost constant prevalence of N.E. winds. There were some sharp frosts at night, particularly on the 4th, 10th, 21st, and 29th, and had not the atmosphere been dry, vegetation would have suffered severely. The mean temperature was nearly two degrees below the average. The barometer was very high throughout the month, particularly during the second week. The cuckoo was first heard on the 17th, and the nightingale on the 18th.

MAY.

During this month there was again a prevalence of northerly and easterly winds, which, together with hot sunshine on many days, caused excessive evaporation from the earth, which soon became very parched. The tender foliage suffered much from want of moisture, and many of the young shoots perished. The mean temperature in the shade was a little below the average, but in the sun it was nearly $90°$, which is very unusual at this season of the year. The fall of rain was below the average, and *none* fell from the 12th to the 27th. A slight thunderstorm occurred on the 11th, with heavy rain. Martens did not appear till the 3rd of this month.

JUNE.

This was a very warm and pleasant month, the 14th, 15th, 18th, and 19th having been the warmest days in the year; on the latter day the maximum temperature in the sun was $114°$. The mean temperature was considerably above the average, and the nights were warmer than usual. The sky was much covered by cloud, and the winds were very variable. Thunder showers occurred on 2nd, 3rd, 4th, 18th, 21st, 27th, and 29th. On the 18th the air was full of insects of various kinds, and the wall fruit trees were dreadfully infested with their respective kinds of aphis, which threatened seriously to injure the crops. I first observed the magnificent comet of this year during the evening of the 30th.

JULY.

This month was cool and showery. The mean temperature was nearly two and a half degrees below the average. The wind blew almost constantly from the S.W., and the sky was much covered by cloud. The barometer was very low, and with the exception of the first day it never attained the height of 30 inches. Slight thunder storms occurred on the 7th, 8th, and 27th.

AUGUST.

The mean temperature was very nearly equal to the average of the last eighteen years, and it was the finest and warmest month during the year. The barometer was considerably above the average. Although the winds blew almost constantly from the westward, yet the fall of rain was very trifling. Slight thunder storms occured on the 2nd, 7th, 16th, and 20th. On the evening of the 31st, I observed a great number of small meteors.

SEPTEMBER.

This month was cool and showery. The rains were very heavy on the 22nd, 24th, and 25th, and the total amount for the month considerably exceeded the average. The wind blew generally from the westward, and the sky was not much covered by cloud. A severe thunder storm passed over during the night of the 24th, and lunar haloes were frequent on the 19th and 20th. The mean temperature was nearly two degrees below the average, and there was no frost at night.

OCTOBER.

This was the warmest October for many years past. The high temperature at night was very remarkable, and the month passed away without the slightest frost, notwithstanding the wind blew very frequently from the eastward. The fall of rain was very much below the average, and the sky not much covered by cloud. The mean temperature in the shade was upwards of 55° (or four and half degrees above the average), and that in the sun upwards of 82°. Slight thunder storms occurred either here or in the neighbourhood on the 1st, 8th, and 10th, but the only heavy rains were on the 11th and 22nd. The leaf did not fall during the month, and the oaks remained as green on the 31st as they were in September.

NOVEMBER.

With the exception of that in the year 1851, it has been the coldest November for many years. The mean temperature was nearly four degrees below the average of the last eighteen years. Frost occurred more or less on fifteen nights, and was severe from the 16th to the 19th, both inclusive. On the morning of the latter day the temperature fell to 18°.2, and a radiating thermometer indicated a temperature three degrees lower. The fall of rain was greater than I had ever previously recorded in Nov., and amounted to more than three times the average. During the evening of the 1st lightning was frequently observed from large masses of cumulo-stratus cloud over the sea, and was followed on the morning of the 2nd by heavy snow for above an hour. Very heavy rain fell on the 5th and 6th, causing a high flood over the low grounds in this neighbourhood.

DECEMBER.

Although there was a great prevalence of easterly wind during this month, yet the mean temperature was nearly 2° above the average. The fall of rain was less than usual, and on many days the sky was clear and almost free from cloud, which is very unusual at this season of the year, except in periods of hard frost. There was no severe frost at night, and the weather could not be considered cold till the last four days of the month.

1862.

The mean temperature of the year 1862 has been almost identical with the average of the last twenty years. In consequence of the heavy rain in October, the amount of rain for the year was in excess. The winter of 1861-62 was very mild, and followed by a somewhat cold and cheerless spring and summer, if we except the month of May. With the exception of October, the autumn was, upon the whole, mild, fine and dry. The year closed with very mild, stormy and wet weather.

JANUARY.

During this month the weather was for the most part seasonable, without any extreme cold. Indeed, the only really cold period was from the 16th to 21st, both inclusive, when the temperature was scarcely ever above the freezing point. The mean temperature was rather below the average, and the winds variable. The sky generally overcast, and the fall of rain below the average, although rain fell more or less on seventeen days. None of our winter flowers were in bloom during the month.

FEBRUARY.

This was a mild month, with a temperature 2° above the average. The sky was much overcast, and the winds variable. The only severe frost was on the morning of the 9th. Rain fell on five days only, and the total amount was less than an inch. Snow fell in slight showers on 7th and 8th, but the ground was never covered by it. Primroses were in bloom on the 1st; snowdrops on 2nd; dandelion on 4th; hepatica on 8th; mezereon on 10th; winter stock 11th; anemone on 13th. Bats were flying about on 3rd; the lark sung on 5th; missel-thrush on 19th; and blackbird on 26th.

MARCH.

The weather was very cold during the first five days of the month, with occasional snow showers, and the most severe frost during the winter. The remainder of the month was unusually mild, stormy and wet. The fall of rain was more than double the average quantity. With the exception of that in the year 1859, it was the warmest March for more than twenty years. There was a short thunder storm during the evening of the 8th; a lunar corona on the 9th; lunar halo on 10th; and a thunder shower during the evening of the 16th; and from the 19th to the end of the month rain fell more or less every day. Polyanthus was in flower 3rd; dog's mercury on 5th; japonica on 6th; sterile strawberry on 7th; palma christi on 11th. Several large female wasps appeared on 16th.

APRIL.

This was also a mild month, with the temperature considerably above the average, and had it not been for the severe frosts during the nights of 12th, 13th, and 15th, the weather would have been most favourable for the fruit blossom; the winds were variable, the S.W. preponderating, and the sky was more free from clouds than during any month in the year. Rain fell more or less on ten days, but the total amount was below the average. The cuckoo appeared on 7th; swallow on 9th; the common sulphur butterfly and vanessa urticæ in great numbers on 17th; vanessa Io, or the peacock butterfly on 25th; glow worms on 18th. I did not hear the nightingale till 21st, which was rather later than usual; the corncrake was very noisy at night on and after the 28th.

MAY.

Although this month must be considered to have been showery, yet the mean temperature was upwards of 3° above the average; on the 1st we had two slight thunder storms, during which the lightning was unusually vivid, red, and diffused; the 6th was the *warmest day* of the year, and during the evening we had another thunder storm, with vivid forked lightning, and a few drops of rain, but the rain did not fall heavily till the next day; the winds blew generally from the westward, and the sky was much covered by cloud; the amount of rain for the month was a little below the average.

JUNE.

This was a cool, showery, and gloomy month for the season;

the mean temperature was much below the average, and very little above that of the preceding month. On three days only was the maximum temperature in the shade upwards of 70°, while on three nights the temperature fell below 40°. Although on the morning of the 10th the temperature of radiation was only 1° above the freezing point, yet a few hours afterwards it rose to 103° in the sun for a short time! The weather was unusually stormy on the 6th and 11th.

JULY.

The weather during this month was merely a continuance of the cold and very unseasonable temperature of June; the only fine weather happened during the last week, when the daily temperature in the shade was upwards of 70°, and that in the sun 100°; the winds were generally from the westward, and the sky much covered by cloud; the mean temperature was more than 3° below the average, and, with the exception of that in 1860, it was the coldest July during the last twenty years; the fall of rain was below the average.

AUGUST.

Very similar weather to that of June and July prevailed throughout this month, and the mean temperature was again below the average; the absence of sunshine was remarkable till a few days towards the end of the month; the fall of rain was below the average; the weather was unusually stormy on the 7th and 8th, with some heavy showers. Harvest progressed but slowly, and was *not finished* by the end of the month. It is worthy of remark that very few wasps appeared this autumn.

SEPTEMBER.

Very fine weather was prevalent during the greater part of this month, which was most acceptable for the completion of harvest and the occasion of hop-picking; the latter was scarcely inter-rupted by a shower, as the little rain fell generally at night; towards the end of the month the ground became dry, and the heavy rain which fell during the last three days proved most useful for the root crops; the mean temperature was, however, below the average, and there was a deficiency in the amount of rain. An immense number of acorns came to perfection this autumn, and four or five oak apples might be frequently found upon a leaf. A large party of swallows took their departure on the 11th, which is ten days or a fortnight earlier than usual; others left about the 29th, and a few young ones were seen in the subsequent months of October and November.

OCTOBER.

The mean temperature was a little above the average, and the weather was very fine during the first ten days, but subsequently heavy rains commenced and continued daily throughout the month; the night temperature was very warm for the time of year, and the only frost was on the morning of the 25th. Rain fell very heavily on the 18th and 19th, the amount being 1·24 inch and 1·53 inch respectively; the total quantity for the month exceeded the average by nearly 3 inches. After the fine and mild day of the 10th, a short thunderstorm passed over this place, and it appeared to be much more severe to the westward. At midnight of the 14th the temperature was 63°, which exceeded by several degrees that of any night in June, July, or August. On the evening of 21st glow-worms appeared in great numbers. On the 26th at 11 p.m., a brilliant meteor passed from Cassiopœia towards the planet Mars. The winds were very stormy during the latter half of the month, and generally from the westward.

NOVEMBER.

During this month the weather was variable, but upon the whole, fine and dry; the night temperature was rather low for the season, and frosts were frequent during the second and fourth weeks; the mean temperature was 2° below the average, and the sky was much covered by cloud. Fogs were frequent, and the winds changeable. A brilliant parhelion appeared soon after 9 a.m. of the 25th, which was visible for about half-an-hour. On the 2nd, 3rd, and 4th the foliage changed very suddenly, but did not fall for some time afterwards. Large flights of plovers were seen on the 5th, some woodcocks on 6th, and some wild ducks on 7th.

DECEMBER.

The chief character of this month was its unusual mildness and humidity; both the mean temperature and the fall of rain were above the average; although the sky was much overcast, yet there were a few bright days, particularly on the 8th, 12th, 14th, 25th, and 31st. On the evening of the 8th I observed a lunar burr, on the 11th a solar halo, and on the 14th, for some hours, a magnificent display of the Aurora Borealis, which appears to have been very generally seen in England. On the 20th some lightning and thunder at 3 a.m., which was followed by a very cold N.W. wind for upwards of 48 hours. The 25th was a remarkably fine and mild day; the temperature in the shade rose to 50°, and in the sun to nearly 70°! Some large flies were buzzing about in warm situations, and the bats were very busy among some gnats in the early part of the evening. A lunar corona and halo were visible during the evenings of 29th, 30th, and 31st, indicating a very humid state of the atmosphere, and the near approach of stormy, wet weather.

1863.

During the year 1863, the weather was, upon the whole, very favourable to the public health, in rural districts, and especially to the products of the soil. Very fine weather prevailed during both hay and corn harvest, and the crops were secured in excellent condition. The crop of fruit was also abundant, and of good quality.

The mean temperature of the year was half a degree above the average. The most remarkable features of the year were the unusual mildness of the winter of 1862-63; the very high atmospheric pressure throughout the month of February; the fine dry weather during the months of July and August; the unusual phenomenon of frost on the morning of July 19th; and the frequent very severe gales of wind during the autumnal months. The following remarks will point out the chief phenomena connected with the weather in each month.

JANUARY.

This month was remarkably mild, and the warmest since that in the year 1853; the mean temperature was upwards of three degrees above the average; it was, upon the whole, a wet month in this county; more rain having fallen in Sussex than in either of the adjoining counties; a severe gale occurred early on the morning of the 2nd; a lunar halo on the 3rd; a thunderstorm on the 4th; another gale on the 5th, with a great depression of the barometer; a severe gale also on the morning of the 20th, when slates, tiles, and lead were blown off from several houses in this parish; another lunar halo was visible on the 28th; the wind blew chiefly from the S.W., and the greater part of the rain fell during the first fortnight.

FEBRUARY.

This was a mild and dry month; the mean temperature was considerably above, and the fall of rain below, the average; the barometer was remarkably high, considering the great prevalence of westerly winds; there were frequent slight frosts at night, but the day temperature was high for the season, with much sunshine. Lunar haloes were visible on the 1st and 3rd; a sulphur butterfly made its appearance on the 28th; thrushes were frequently singing during both this and the preceding month.

MARCH.

Very seasonable weather prevailed throughout this month, the atmosphere being both mild, dry, and extremely favourable for agricultural operations. There were but few frosts at night, and vegetation, not being so forward as might have been expected, did not suffer therefrom; the usual easterly winds did not prevail, and at the equinox, especially, westerly winds were by far the most prevalent.

APRIL.

During this month the weather was again both mild and dry; the mean temperature was above, and the fall of rain much below, the average; rain fell on nine days only, and the total amount was less than half an inch. After the first week, vegetation advanced rapidly, and the fruit blossom was not injured by any late frosts. I saw the cuckoo on the 7th, swallow on the 12th, and the nightingale on 17th. The lilac was in bloom on the 20th, which is the earliest time I have ever observed it.

MAY.

From 1st to 27th the weather was cold and dry; both the temperature and the fall of rain were below the average; the sky was much covered by cloud, and the temperature of many days was more like March than May. N.E. winds were prevalent; the last three days were warmer, and the barometer higher than at any time during the month. The feathered tribe appeared to suffer much from the cold. I never heard them sing less, especially the nightingales, at this season of the year; the corn advanced but slowly, in consequence of the frequent low temperature at night.

JUNE.

Very ungenial weather prevailed, for the most part, throughout this month, after the 4th, with frequent heavy rain from 6th to 25th; the mean temperature was below, and the fall of rain considerably above, the average. High winds were frequent during the second week, with an overcast sky, and great depression of the barometer for this season of the year; thunderstorms, with heavy rains, occurred on 19th and 24th. The wheat was not in flower much before midsummer, which is a fortnight later than usual.

JULY.

This was a remarkably fine summer month, without any excessive heat; the weather was most favourable for the completion of hay and commencement of corn harvest. In consequence of the great radiation at night, causing a low night temperature, the mean temperature for the month was 2° below the average. On twenty-three nights the sky was cloudless. Rain fell on two days only, and the total amount was less than one inch. On the morning of the 19th there was a hoar frost, which injured some tender plants and vegetables in this neighbourhood; this unusual phenomenon at this season appears to have occurred very generally both in England, Scotland, and Ireland. An Aurora Borealis was visible in the evening.

AUGUST.

This was another very fine summer month, and scarcely any rain fell during the first fortnight, when the ground had become much parched in many situations; the mean temperature was a little above, and the fall of rain below the average; the night temperature was much higher than that in July; the winds were variable, the S.W. being the most prevalent. A beautiful display of meteors happened on the 10th, and following evening; on the 16th a very large one was visible in the N.W. at 9 p.m. Slight thunderstorms occurred on the 19th and 28th.

SEPTEMBER.

A colder state of the air commenced during the first week, and continued throughout the month; the mean temperature was as much as $4\frac{1}{2}°$ below the average. Heavy rains fell occasionally, particularly on the 6th, 20th, and 24th, and the total amount exceeded the average by nearly an inch; there was a remarkable absence of easterly wind, which is sometimes so prevalent either just before or after the equinox. The barometer fluctuated considerably, and was very low on the 22nd and 23rd. A large company of swallows congregated on the house tops both on the 18th and 26th, and probably took their departure on the 27th or 28th, as there were very few seen subsequently.

OCTOBER.

During this month the weather was, for the most part, overcast, mild, and damp; the mean temperature was above the average; the night temperature was very high for the season, being higher by several degrees than that in September, and not much under that of July. Although rain fell more or less on seventeen days, yet the total amount was considerably less than the average. Westerly winds were the most prevalent, and there was an entire absence of frost. A great many meteors were visible on the evening of the 10th; there were slight thunder-storms both on the 7th and 8th, with very heavy rain. A few swallows were seen on the 24th, and a few were seen flying about between the Church and The Rocks, on the 31st.

NOVEMBER.

This month must be considered to have been both mild and dry. S.W. winds were most prevalent. On the 2nd there was a very severe gale from S.W., with torrents of rain and great depression of the barometer; the mean temperature was nearly $3°$ above the average, and there were only five frosty mornings. Rain fell more or less on ten days, but the amount was consider-ably less than the average. The Aurora Borealis was visible during the evening of the 25th. This was a very wet month in the West of England, Scotland, and Ireland.

DECEMBER.

The mean temperature of this month was nearly $2°$ above the average, and there were but few frosts; the sky was much covered by cloud, but after the very severe gales on the 2nd and 3rd, the weather continued, for the most part, very dry till the 31st; the fall of rain was above the average, and the greater portion of it fell on the 1st, 2nd, and 3rd; on the latter day there was a high flood over the low grounds in this parish. Westerly winds were the most prevalent. On Christmas Day the primrose, polyanthus, wall-flower, violet, stock, and the yellow auricula were in bloom. On the 27th both a sparrow and a starling were seen feeding their young, the common bat was seen on several evenings during the month; and on the 30th swarms of gnats were enjoying themselves in the sunshine.

1864.

Notwithstanding the fine weather which prevailed, for the most part, during the year 1864, the mean temperature was nearly $1°$ below the average—the daily maximum having been much influenced by the very unusual prevalence of N.E. wind; the fall of rain was six inches below the average, and less than that in any year since 1858. November was the wettest month, and July the driest.

The summer was remarkable for the long drought, which may be said to have commenced about May 10th; the barometer continued, upon the whole, rather high throughout this period, with but little fluctuation; there was a remarkable absence of thunder storms in this locality, which may, perhaps, be attributed to the very dry state of the atmosphere, and the temperature not having been so high as usual. Another peculiar feature of this summer was the very low temperature which, at intervals, was observed at night. Upon nine nights in June, seven in July, and ten in August, the temperature of radiation was at, or very nearly down to, the freezing point; while on the morning of August 17th the minimum temperature was 31°.6.

The following list of unusually dry summers during the present century, together with the amount of rain, in inches, which has fallen during the summer months, in each instance, contrasted with that for 1864, may perhaps be interesting. Had the heavy rain which fell during the third week in August been delayed till after the close of that month, the summer of 1864 would have been the driest on record.

	June.	July.	August.	Total.
1800	0.99	0.00	1.46	2.47
1818	0.53	1.94	0.53	3.00
1825	0.69	0.05	1.25	1.99
1835	2.10	0.40	0.48	2.98
1840	0.83	1.22	0.94	2.99
1847	1.77	0.22	1.08	3.07
1849	0.85	1.69	0.76	3.30
1864	1.01	0.46	1.73	3.20

JANUARY.

The year commenced with a sudden but somewhat severe frost, to the 8th, inclusive. Ice upon the ponds attained an average thickness of from three and a half to four inches, and skating became very general on the 6th, 7th, and 8th. Although a thaw commenced on the 9th, yet the wind prevailed from the eastward till after the 18th, when it veered to the S.W., and a permanent thaw ensued; the weather continued very mild, for the most part, with occasional showers to the 30th, when the atmosphere became colder, with hoar frosts on the two last mornings of the month. Both the mean temperature and the fall of rain were below the average. On the 27th the season was so mild that the thrush and lark sang frequently, and several of the insect tribe appeared to be actively preparing for the spring. The Christmas rose was the only flower which I observed in bloom during the month.

FEBRUARY.

This was a cold month, without any excessive frost or heavy fall of snow; the N.E. wind was the most prevalent, and rendered the weather more sensibly cold to the feelings than the thermometer indicated; the mean temperature was 2°, and the fall of rain half an inch below the average. Much more snow fell in various parts of this county than in this immediate neighbourhood. The barometer fluctuated considerably. Notwithstanding the coldness of the season, the snowdrop was in bloom on the 2nd, crocus on the 6th, mezereon and blue and pink hepatica on 26th. Primroses were in bloom in warm situations, throughout the month.

MARCH.

This month was mild, stormy, and wet, with great depression of the barometer from 6th to 9th, both inclusive; the mean temperature was 1° above, and the fall of rain more than double the average; the N.E. wind was the most prevalent, particularly at the equinox. During the last week the weather was cold for the season, with frequent snow showers during the day and sharp frosts at night. The lark, blackbird, and thrush, were singing on the 2nd; the sulphur butterfly appeared on the 4th; the willow, alder, and hazel, were in bloom on the 19th.

APRIL.

Upon the whole this was a fine and dry month; the mean temperature was nearly one degree and a half above, and the fall of rain about half the average; the N.E. wind was again very prevalent, and the barometer high for the season; there were some brilliant days during the third week, when the temperature in the sun was higher than at any time during the summer. The cuckoo was heard on the 15th. I heard the nightingale, and observed some swallows flying about on the 16th; the large female wasp appeared in considerable numbers on 21st.

MAY.

This was another fine and dry month; the mean temperature was 2° above, and the fall of rain nearly half an inch less than the average. Rain fell on seven days only, and the greater part on the 7th, 8th, and 9th; the barometer fluctuated but little, and the mean was above the average. Easterly winds were by far the most prevalent, and on many days the sky was almost cloudless; the temperature in the sun, however, was not so high as that in April; there were slight frosts on the mornings of 25th, 30th, and 31st, which slightly injured the tender foliage.

JUNE.

The weather was again fine and dry throughout this month; the mean temperature, however, was rather below the average, and the fall of rain was not equal to half the usual amount. After the first four days the wind blew almost constantly from the westward; the barometer fluctuated but little, and its readings were about equal to the average; there was a slight thunder storm on 15th, accompanied by some heavy showers of rain and hail.

JULY.

This was a month of splendid summer weather, without any excessive heat, either in the shade or in the sun; the mean temperature was about equal to the average; the maximum temperature in the shade was very seldom so much as 80°. Rain fell on four days only, and the total amount was less than half an inch; the wind was very variable, the most frequent being the N.E.; the barometer remained nearly stationary throughout the month, and the reading was above the average.

AUGUST.

This was also a fair and dry month, but the temperature was

considerably below the average during the day as well as at night; the present instance was a remarkable exception to the warm nights which usually prevail at this season; the mean temperature was nearly 2°, and the fall of rain nearly one inch below the average. Had it not been for the heavy rain which fell on the 23rd, the month would have been a remarkably dry one. In this neighbourhood, and still more so in other parts of the country, water had become very scarce; the pastures were quite withered, and in some districts almost parched, on account of the great deficiency of rain since the month of March; the barometer remained high throughout the month, and the atmosphere was unusually dry; the amount of cloud was less than during any month of the year.

SEPTEMBER.

During the first three weeks of this month the weather was mild and showery, the wind blowing generally from the westward; the quantity of rain which fell during the three weeks was nearly equal to that of the previous three months; the equinox passed without any particular gales : the mean temperature was about 1° below the average, and the fall of rain nearly half an inch in excess. In consequence of the long drought the foliage of many trees, and especially the oaks, began to assume the autumnal tint after the heavy rains during the third week; the nights continued warm throughout the month, and the only indication of frost occurred on the morning of the 12th.

OCTOBER.

From Sept. 23rd to the 19th of this month, both inclusive, the weather was again remarkably fine and seasonable, without a shower of rain, while, during many days together the sky was cloudless. Easterly winds were again very prevalent; the mean temperature was a little below the average, and the fall of rain less than half the usual amount; the barometer was low both on the 19th and 23rd.

NOVEMBER.

From the 12th day to the end of this month the weather

was for the most part very stormy, with heavy rains; the total quantity which fell on the 15th and 23rd was nearly three inches; very heavy rain fell on the 17th; the mean temperaature was 1° below, and the fall of rain three inches above, the average; the barometer was very low on the 14th, 15th, and 26th, and with the exception of that in March, the mean reading was lower than during any month in the year; the wind was variable; the N.E. was the most prevalent during the first, and the S.W. during the latter part of the month.

DECEMBER.

The mean temperature of this month was nearly 2°, and fall of rain nearly one inch and a quarter below the average; the weather was rather severe from 15th to 19th, and again from 22nd to 27th. Upon the whole, however, it was a fine and seasonable month; there was a considerable fall of snow on the 18th, which was succeeded on the following day by showers of rain and hail; on 21st a dense fog during greater part of the day; from the 25th to the 31st the atmosphere was, for the most part, very gloomy and cold.

1865.

JANUARY.

This month was cold, stormy, and wet; the mean temperature was 2° below, and the fall of rain nearly double, the average; the barometer was very low from 12th to 17th both inclusive; and again during the heavy rain and snow on 26th and 27th. Much heavy rain fell during the evening and night of the 12th, which occasioned a high flood over the brooks on the following morning. On the 27th, after some heavy rain the previous day, we had a heavy snow storm for some hours, which soon reduced the temperature to the freezing point; more snow and rain fell again on the 30th; the winds were variable. Lowest temperature on the morning of 29th, 11°.2.

FEBRUARY.

The mean temperature was nearly 2° below the average, and the month was, for the most part, gloomy and cold, with a considerable prevalence of N.E. wind; the barometer was again very low during the first week, but subsequently it was rather high for the season; the frosts were rather severe from 11th to 15th both inclusive. On the 16th the weather became milder, and the remainder of the month was rather stormy and wet, with occasional frosts at night; the lowest temperature, 17°.2, occurred on the morning of 15th.

MARCH.

This was a very cold month throughout; the mean temperature was as much as 5° below the average; there were frosts more or less on 20 nights; the lowest temperature was 22°.2, on 21st. Easterly winds were by far the most prevalent; the equinox passed without any particular storm, and the atmosphere continued particularly dry and calm. Snow showers were very frequent, but slight.

APRIL.

A rather sudden change of temperature occurred on the first day, while from the 7th to the close of the month the weather continued remarkably fine and dry. Rain fell on three days only; the mean temperature was $2\frac{1}{4}°$ above the average. Easterly winds were very prevalent, notwithstanding which, the temperature on many days was upwards of 70° in the shade. The cuckoo and nightingale appeared on 8th. At the close of the month vegetation generally was making very rapid progress.

MAY.

The commencement of the month was fine, with a southerly wind; the mean temperature was 2° in excess. A considerable amount of rain fell on 7th, 10th, and 11th, and the total for the month was quite one-third above the average; the barometer fluctuated very frequently, and the winds were variable. A slight thunderstorm occurred on 22nd, after the great heat (81°.2 in the shade) of the previous day; there was also much electrical disturbance on 23rd. At the close of the month the season was far advanced, even the mulberry trees had acquired their foliage.

JUNE.

This was a very splendid summer month, and no rain fell between the 3rd and 28th; the sky was cloudless for several days and nights together. Notwithstanding this beautiful weather, the mean temperature was little more than 1° above the average. Winds were extremely variable. The 21st was the hottest day, viz., 88° in the shade, and 107 in the sun ; there was scarcely any electrical disturbance throughout the month. The crop of hay was secured in good condition.

JULY.

The mean temperature of this month was above the average, although there were very few days when the shade temperature exceeded 80°; the night temperature was high. There were some heavy thunderstorms on 6th, 16th, 23rd, and 25th, in consequence of which the rainfall was more than double the average. The 6th was the hottest day, when the temperature was 84°.4 in the shade, and 100° in the sun. On several days the atmosphere was most oppressive, without any great excess of temperature. Fruits of all kinds were very abundant, particularly pears, plums, cherries, and peaches. A few mulberries were ripe at the end of the month, which is quite a month earlier than usual.

AUGUST.

From the 1st to 23rd, the weather, for the most part, was cool and showery, but during the last week it became warmer, and the rain ceased ; the mean temperature was considerably below the average, and the rain upwards of an inch in excess ; the 27th was the hottest day. Winds were generally westerly, and the barometric readings very low for the season. A thunderstorm, of short duration, occurred during the evening of the 10th, otherwise the month was tolerably free from electrical disturbance. Harvest operations were frequently impeded by heavy rains, but the wheat crop was finally secured in good condition.

SEPTEMBER.

This was one of those delightfully fine months which seldom occur in our climate, and was probably the warmest and driest September of which we have any satisfactory record. On fifteen days the sky was cloudless! With the exception of a very slight shower on the morning of 21st, no rain fell during the month. The mean temperature was 5°.8 above the average, and this excess was observable both day and night; the highest temperature in the shade on 2nd was 81°.0; 7th, 82°.8; 8th, 81°.6; 15th, 80°; 16th, 83°.2, while on several other days it was upwards of 76°. There was a great prevalence of N.E. wind during the equinoctial period, which, however, passed off without any particular gale; this high temperature and brilliant skies appear to have been very general throughout Europe, especially at Paris, where the heat was described as having been excessive. The following is a list of warm Septembers since the year 1771, from which it will be seen that the present season exceeded all others :—

Years.					Mean Temperature.
1779	...	...	...	...	60.7
1795	...	...	...	...	60.8
1815	...	...	...	...	62.3
1818	...	...	...	...	60.7
1843	...	...	...	...	62.5
1846	...	...	...	...	62.1
1857	...	...	...	...	60.5
1858	...	...	...	...	60.5
1865	...	...	...	...	63.4!

OCTOBER.

The splendid weather which had prevailed throughout the previous month continued to the end of the first week. A severe thunder storm during the evening and night of the 8th completely changed the character of the weather from that of true summer to a period of drenching rains, low atmospheric pressure, and great electrical disturbance. Thunder storms occurred on 8th, 27th, and 30th; the mean temperature was nearly one degree and a quarter above the average; there was scarcely any frost at night, and the winds were extremely variable and stormy. During the day and night of the 18th no less than 2.40 inches of rain fell at my observatory, which was the greatest quantity I have ever registered during any twenty-four hours; the rainfall was again very large on 26th and 30th; there was a very high flood over the brooklands during the evening of 26th, when the water swept over the bridge, and advanced very nearly to "The Bell Inn." As I believe such heavy rains to be unprecedented in the South of England, I shall give a statement of daily amount—

October.		inch.
8th	...	0.65
9th	...	0.95
10th	...	0.80
11th	...	0.25
15th	...	0.10
17th	...	0.55
18th	...	2.40
19th	...	0.30
21st	...	0.34
22nd	...	0.86
24th	...	0.24
26th	...	1.41
27th	...	0.08
29th	...	0.68
30th	...	1.22
31st	...	0.40
Total	...	11.23

Previous instances of Heavy Rains in October, contrasted with the present season.

October.		inches.
1848	...	6.03
1852	...	8.70
1853	...	7.25
1855	...	6.05
1862	...	7.00
1865	...	11.23 !!

Aurora Borealis visible during the evenings of 19th, 20th, and 26th. The hop-picking was finished, fortunately, just before the break up of the fine weather; the crop was an exceedingly good one. The Jerusalem artichoke came into flower this autumn, which I have always considered to be a very faithful indication of the great warmth of the summer and autumnal seasons.

NOVEMBER.

The first half of this month was fine and dry, with much northerly wind, and a rather high atmospheric pressure; the mean temperature was considerably above the average, and there were but few frosts at night; the latter part of the month was very showery and stormy, with much electrical disturbance; the gale on 22nd was very severe, and the barometer fell to 29°.123 at 9. a.m. A slight aurora was visible on the 12th. The winds were variable.

DECEMBER.

The mean temperature was nearly 3° above the average; the winds were variable, and atmospheric pressure high, with the exception of a few days at the beginning and end of the month; the weather throughout was, for the most part, gloomy and dark, with occasional gales and rain; the rainfall was rather above the average, the greater part of which fell during the very violent gale on 31st. At Liverpool the force of the wind was 24 pounds on the square foot during this storm. Severe gales occurred also on the 29th and 30th.

1866.

JANUARY.

This month was very mild, stormy, and wet; the mean temperature was more than 4° above the average, and consequently the mildest January for many years past; the rainfall was more than double the average. Heavy gales of wind occurred on 2nd, 7th, 8th, 9th, 10th, and 11th; the fearful effects of the gale on the 11th will long be remembered. It was altogether a very remarkable day, the atmosphere was so dark and loaded with moisture, that gaslight was necessary till nearly noon. At 9 a.m. a severe thunderstorm commenced, which lasted about 50 minutes. The rain came down in torrents. At 11 a.m., the wind shifted suddenly to the northward, and a severe snow commenced, and continued till nearly dusk, when the rain and melted snow amounted to 1.59 inch, while the amount from 10 p.m. of the 10th, to 4 p.m. of the 11th, was not less than 2.75 inches! On the morning of the 12th we had more heavy rain and sleet, and subsequently a slight frost, so that the roads and pavements were coated with ice. On the 13th there was a gale from S.E., with heavy rain, and a great rise in temperature; the remainder of the month was mild and rainy, with great fluctuations of the barometer. Westerly winds were the most prevalent.

FEBRUARY.

This month was, for the most part, overcast, mild, and wet;

the mean temperature was nearly $2\frac{1}{2}°$ above the average, and the atmospheric pressure very low. Rain fell on 15 days, and the total amount was nearly three times the average. Very stormy weather prevailed during the first eleven days. A fine auroral arch was visible on the evening of the 7th. The gale on the 11th was the most severe, many trees were blown down, and slates, tiles, and lead were blown off several houses. The lowest reading of the barometer was 28.625. From 16th to 24th the weather was drier, with variable but calm winds. More rain fell on 26th and 27th, and the barometer was very low again on 28th.

MARCH.

This month was colder than January, and very little warmer than February. Its mean temperature was below, and the rainfall rather more than, the average. Winds were variable, but, for the most part, easterly. On the 7th, frequent snow showers and distant lightning. On the night of the 23rd a severe gale from S.W. Notwithstanding some rather sharp frosts at night, vegetation continued to advance satisfactorily. A northerly wind was prevalent at the equinox.

APRIL.

The mean temperature was considerably above the average; there was scarcely any frost registered during the month—in fact the average temperature of the night was high for the season—and vegetation continued to advance with great rapidity; the rainfall was half-an-inch below the average. Much distant lightning was observed on the 1st, 5th, and 6th. Winds were variable, but inclined to the eastward. On the 26th, 27th, and 28th, we had quite summer weather, and at night the nightingales were in full song. On the morning of 29th the wind veered suddenly to N.E., with cold rain; the highest temperature this day was only $47°$, while, on the previous day, it had been $72°.2$! a remarkable instance of variability of climate. Both the cuckoo and nightingale were first heard on the 14th.

MAY.

This month was cold and dry, and vegetation received a

decided check during the first fortnight; the mean temperature was nearly 2°, and the rainfall scarcely one-third the average. The winds were extremely variable, and the barometer fluctuated considerably; the temperature of radiation was frequently below the freezing point, but the only severe frost occurred on the morning of the 5th, when the temperature of the air fell to 28°, and that of radiation to 21°. Shallow pools were covered over by ice as thick as a penny piece. The tender foliage and fruit blossom was very much injured by this frost, the potato haulm was quite blackened, as well as the foliage of the hazel, ash, and oak.

JUNE.

The first few days of the month were fine and warm. Slight thunderstorms with heavy showers occurred during the nights of 3rd and 4th. The greater part of the month was fine, with the mean temperature nearly 3° above the average; the rainfall rather exceeded the average, but the greater part fell in heavy thunder showers; the winds were chiefly westerly. A thunderstorm occurred in this county on the 28th, which was very severe at Lewes, Brighton, and Eastbourne. In this immediate locality we had nothing of it, beyond a slight shower, and intensely vivid lightning from two large masses of cumulo-stratus cloud. Several casualties were reported—two barns and three stacks were burnt to the ground, a horse was killed at Shortbridge, and three men struck down, but not seriously injured. The barometer was not affected by this storm, which appeared to be very local.

JULY.

During the first eight days the weather was rather cool for the season, and nearly 2½ inches of rain fell, but subsequently we had fine, hot summer weather, and scarcely any more rain to the end of the month. From the 10th to 15th, both inclusive, the heat was intense, and ranging from 83°.6 to 86°.4 in the shade, and from 101° to 108° in the sun. The mean temperature, however, scarcely exceeded the average; the winds were variable, and the barometer rather low, both at the beginning and end of the month.

AUGUST.

Although this month was cool and showery, yet the total rain-fall was below the average; the mean temperature was deficient 1°. Winds were variable, and the barometer very low for the season. Solar and lunar haloes were frequent, in consequence of the great prevalence of cloud, particularly at mid-day.

SEPTEMBER.

This was a very overcast, wet, month; upwards of six inches of rain fell, and the mean temperature was below the average; the winds were generally easterly, and the barometer very low. On the morning of the 18th there was a slight hoar frost, and the temperature of radiation was 4° below the freezing point· During the last week the weather was comparatively finer, and warm for the season, particularly on 30th, when the highest temperature in the shade was 74°.6, and in the sun, 104°.

OCTOBER.

Upon the whole this was a fine autumnal month, with bright skies at intervals, and very little rain; the mean temperature was half a degree above the average. N.E. winds were very pre-valent. Atmospheric pressure showed little fluctuation; through-out the month there was a remarkable absence of S.W. gales, which are often so violent at this period. The night temperature was high.

NOVEMBER.

The mean temperature was above the average; the weather was extremely variable; the sky was much less overcast than is usual at this season, as several days were almost cloudless; the rainfall was below the average. Westerly winds were by far the most prevalent; on several occasions the barometric readings were low, without any apparent cause in this immediate locality.

DECEMBER.

This was a very mild month, with the mean temperature nearly 3° above the average. There was a great prevalence of westerly winds, and a stormy, unsettled state of the atmosphere, both at the beginning and end of the month. The frosts at night were few and slight; the lowest temperature (23°.2) occurred on the last morning. There was much electrical disturbance and vivid lightning on the 15th and 26th; the barometer fluctuated considerably, and its mean reading was below the average.

1867.

JANUARY.

The month commenced with a very severe frost, which continued till about noon of the 5th. The mean temperature of these five days was nearly 11° below the freezing point. From 6th to 9th, both inclusive, the weather was very mild, stormy, and wet, accompanied by great depression (28.728) of the barometer. Frost returned on the 11th, and continued, without intermission, to the evening of the 22nd, when rain commenced falling on the frozen ground, which for some hours rendered walking or driving extremely dangerous. At noon on the 18th, I observed, for the first and only time during the frost, a shower of snow crystals of various sizes and beautiful forms. Some of them were a quarter of an inch in diameter, and not accompanied by any snow flakes. The following are the lowest temperatures recorded by me :—Jan. 3rd, 7°.8; 4th, 4°.0; 5th, 9°.8; 14th, 7°.4; 15th, 9°.4; 19th, 10°. On the morning of the 4th, the temperature of radiation was 2°.6 below zero, and every tree and shrub splendidly decked with rime. In this immediate neighbourhood snow did not fall in such large quantities as was reported from various places in the south-eastern portion of the kingdom, and travelling was scarcely at all interrupted. The sudden change of temperature on the 22nd proved to be a complete break-up of the frost, and during the remainder of the month the weather was very mild, stormy, and wet. The mean temperature of the month was more than 5° below the average, and the lowest since January, 1850. The depth of rain and melted snow was above the average; the wind variable, and the sky much covered by clouds. The lauristinus, bay, furze, and several other shrubs were in most places killed to the ground; but their roots were preserved, for the most part, by a covering of snow.

FEBRUARY.

This month was unusually mild—in fact there is no record of such continued high temperature in February during the present century. February 1848-49-50 and 56 were all mild months; but the temperature was not equal to the present instance; the mean temperature was 44°.3, which is 6° above the average, and more than 2° higher than that for March; this high temperature was, for the most part, very constant, both day and night; there were slight frosts on two mornings only; the winds were chiefly westerly; the amount of rain was about equal to the average, and nearly all of it fell during the stormy weather which prevailed from the 4th to the 12th. The barometer was very low on the morning of the 6th, and high on the 21st.

MARCH.

This month was remarkable for its low temperature, frequent falls of snow, sleet, and great prevalence of N.E. winds, with occasional gales from the same quarter, so that many persons felt the cold more severely than during the intense frost of January. The mean temperature was more than 3° below the average, and there were frosts more or less severe on twenty nights; the barometer was very high during the first four days, but fell rapidly a few hours after the solar eclipse, and during the latter half of the month was very fluctuating. The sky was again much covered by cloud, and the fall of rain and melted snow nearly double the average.

Vegetation, which had shown a tendency to advance very rapidly in February, sustained a severe check by the severity of the cold, both day and night; and, considering the forward state of the fruit trees, it was very remarkable that the buds were not entirely destroyed. It was the coldest March since 1845.

APRIL.

During this month the weather was, for the most part, over-cast, mild, and showery, with occasional gales of wind from the westward. The mean temperature was nearly 2°, and the fall of rain about a quarter of an inch above the average. There were only two frosts throughout the month—namely, on the 1st and 12th, but they did not appear to injure either the fruit blossoms or vegetation generally. The barometer continued low after the first three days, and there was an unusual prevalence of westerly winds; the flowers, which were almost in bloom at the end of February, came into flower rapidly during the first week of this month. The wryneck appeared on the 6th, willow wren on the 12th, cuckoo on the 13th, swallow on the 14th, and the nightingale on the 15th.

MAY.

The extraordinary vicissitudes of the weather throughout this month arrested general attention in the South of England, accustomed as we are to very great variations of temperature during the spring months. Thus, after a cold January we had an extremely warm February; after a cold March a comparatively warm April, and then we had in May a repetition of the alternations of the four previous months. From the first to the tenth day summer weather was prevalent, the temperature in the shade on the 7th reached 82°, and in the sun just 100°. This fine weather was arrested on the evening of the 10th by a somewhat severe thunder storm, which, however, appeared much more violent to the westward. After the storm had passed over this parish a loud explosion was heard in the air, about five miles S.E. of us, which was not preceded or accompanied by a flash of lightning. From the 11th there was a sensible decrease of temperature, and a prevalence of cold N.E. wind; but there was no actual frost till the morning of the 17th, when the temperature outside my observatory fell to 32°, and on the grass to 28°. Subsequently very wintry weather prevailed to the 26th, as the following table and remarks will show :—

	Lowest temperature of the air.	Lowest temperature on grass.
17th	32.0	28.0
18th	29.4	26.0
22nd	32.0	27.6
23rd	29.2	26.0
24th	26.4	23.8
25th	32.4	28.4

On the 22nd and 23rd frequent snow storms occurred, accompanied by piercingly cold winds. I noticed some swallows so chilled by the cold that they could scarcely fly more than a yard from the ground, and then only under trees or sheltered banks. In this state many of them were knocked down and killed by boys. The nightingales were scarcely heard from the 12th to the 28th; this severe weather was felt very generally throughout England. In Yorkshire the wolds were white with snow, and the keen and boisterous north-east wind blew with the full rigour of winter. During the last six days the temperature was again warmer, so that the mean for the month was not more than $1°$ less than the average. The severe frost on the morning of the 24th killed the potato haulm nearly to the ground, and injured extensively the young shoots of the wisteria, walnut, chestnut, and even the hazel, while the first fronds of the common brake were almost destroyed. The fruit blossom was not so much injured as might have been expected. The ash tree came out into leaf very late this spring, and the oak rather sooner than usual.

JUNE.

Although the mean temperature of this month was rather more than $2°$ below the average, yet the month must be considered to have been fine, dry, and a very favourable time for the hay harvest; the coldness of the night temperature was, however, a very remarkable feature in the weather. On eleven nights there were slight frosts over the brooklands in this parish, while on the morning of the 29th the temperature of radiation fell to $27°$, or $5°$ below the freezing point. It was reported that ice as thick as a shilling was noticed on a pond near Cooksbridge. The growing shoots of the hop plant and the upper blade of the wheat stem were slightly injured, causing the latter to assume a rusty brown appearance in many situations. Notwithstanding the great fall of rain during the severe thunder storm on the 2nd, the total amount for the month was below the average. Scarcely any rain fell after the 6th; the winds were variable, N.E. was the most prevalent.

JULY.

With the exception of some thunder showers on the 1st and 3rd, the weather was very dry from June 6th to July 13th. After this date to the close of the month there were such frequent and heavy rains that the total quantity amounted to more than double the average. The month, upon the whole, was unseasonably cold, the mean temperature having been four and a half degrees below the average. Such low temperature had not been recorded for July since the year 1841. On several mornings—particularly on the 6th, 8th, 9th, 10th, and 29th—there were white frosts on the low grounds. The wind was chiefly westerly, and at intervals very stormy for the season. Slight thunder storms occurred on the 1st, 13th, 25th, and 28th. During the night of the 25th and morning of the 26th a very heavy rain commenced falling over Sussex, Surrey, and Kent, varying in amount from 1.25 inches at Chichester; 1.14 inches at Hastings; and 1.85 at Uckfield; to 5.04 inches at Sittingbourne, in Kent! This last return shows probably the heaviest fall of rain which has ever occurred in the southern part of England during the present century. A most interesting account of this rainfall will be found in "Symons' Meteorological Magazine" for August.

AUGUST.

Both the mean temperature and fall of rain were below the average. The temperature at night was unusually low for the month of August. On several occasions the low grounds were white with frost. The weather, however, for the most part, was favourable to harvest operations, and the greater portion of the grain was secured in excellent condition. The barometer remained tolerably high throughout, with but little variation. Westerly winds were the most prevalent. The 13th and 14th were the only very hot days, and the temperature in the shade on the latter day was the highest for the year. On the same day, at 10 p.m., a very brilliant lunar halo was visible.

SEPTEMBER.

This was a fine month, with a temperature somewhat lower than the average, but tolerably uniform till the last week, when the temperature at night fluctuated considerably. The fall of rain would have been much below the average had it not been for the heavy rain which fell during the thunder storm on the 9th. The most prevalent wind was the S.W. The equinox passed over without any particular storm; the S.W. wind was at that time prevalent.

OCTOBER.

This month was much colder than usual, the temperature not having been so low since 1850. During the first week there were severe frosts at night, and a prevalence of northerly wind. On the 6th much rain fell at night, and the weather continued very wet till the 18th; the total fall of rain was below the average; the barometer continued low throughout the month.

NOVEMBER.

Although the mean temperature was nearly 3° below the average, yet this month was unusually fine, dry, and favourable to agricultural operations. Rain fell on five days only, and the total amount was much less than usual; the barometer continued very high throughout, with but little fluctuation. Northerly winds were the most prevalent, and the sky frequently almost cloudless. Some swallows were observed flying about during the last week.

DECEMBER.

This was a cold but seasonable month; the mean temperature was 2° below the average; there were frosts, more or less severe, on twenty-one nights; consequently the average night temperature was rather more than 2° below the freezing point; the temperature of radiation, too, was unusually low. On the morning of the 9th it indicated 24° of frost, and on four other nights it ranged from 17° to 21°; there was an unusual prevalence of N. and N.W. wind; the fall of rain was rather less than the average; the month ended with hard frost, and the maximum temperature of the last day was 3° below the freezing point.

1868.

JANUARY.

The weather at the commencement of the month was very cold, and the mean temperature of the first eleven days was more than 4° below the freezing point. A gradual thaw commenced on the afternoon of the 11th, and the weather, with the exception of an occasional frosty night, was subsequently mild, very stormy, and wet. The mean temperature was 3° below, and the amount of rain considerably above, the average. The wind was variable, and the barometer very fluctuating between 16th and 24th. Early in the morning of the 1st a splendid meteor passed from E. to S.W., and a small white cloud was visible at the point of disappearance, which remained nearly stationary for five minutes. Snow crystals fell in considerable numbers on 1st and 4th.

FEBRUARY.

Although this month was not so warm as that of last year, yet the mean temperature was nearly 2° above the average; the fall of rain was trifling till the last day. The month was ushered in by a severe gale from S.W., which did not entirely subside till the evening of the 3rd. The barometer was not much affected by this storm. A rather rapid increase of pressure occurred on the 4th, and, with the exception of 19th, the readings of the instrument were high during the remainder of the month. The weather generally was considered to have been unusually pleasant for the season, and there was no interruption to outdoor occupations. Frosts occurred on several mornings, but were not so severe as usual. The winds were chiefly westerly. Primroses, hepaticas, violets, and other spring flowers were in bloom at the close of the month.

MARCH.

The mean temperature was nearly 1° above the average. Although the weather was somewhat cold and showery during the first half of the month, yet the total rainfall was below the average. Severe frosts occurred on several mornings, particularly on

25th and 31st. The wind was chiefly westerly. The barometer fluctuated less than usual, and the equinox passed by without any particular gale. Hail storms were frequent on 23rd, and there were some brilliant solar haloes on 24th and 25th.

APRIL.

During the first week the weather was, for the most part, warm and pleasant, but subsequently it became very cold, with the mean temperature much below the average. On several nights the frosts were very severe for the season, varying from 2° to 7° below the freezing point. The fall of rain was above the average, in consequence of the heavy rain on 19th.

MAY.

The mean temperature was more than 2° above the average, and so early as the first week vegetation had considerably advanced. During the third week the temperature was very high for the season, especially on 19th, when the temperature in the shade was 84°.2. A dry season commenced from the last week in April. Rain fell on five days only, and the total amount for the month was rather more than an inch, which is less than half the average amount. The night temperature was warm for the season; the only frost was on the morning of the 2nd. Several fine meteors were seen during the evening of the 18th. A severe thunder storm visited the western portion of this county on 29th.

JUNE.

This was a splendid summer month and very dry; but curiously enough, the mean temperature of this district was slightly below the average. Rain fell on five days, and only to a quarter of the average. The winds were, for the most part, westerly and calm; the sky was frequently cloudless for several consecutive days and nights. The hottest day was the 13th, the maximum temperature of which was 83°.6. There was very little electrical display. By the end of the month the drought occasioned the farmer considerable anxiety. The hay crop was light, but of good quality; the wheat was very forward, and looked remarkably well.

JULY.

This was a remarkably brilliant and hot month, although the heat was not so excessive in this neighbourhood as I have had to record in former years. The great prevalence of N.E. wind in this district materially lessened the heat from the sun's rays. In some parts of the country fabulous reports of the heat were circulated, but in the majority of these instances there must have been some defect, either in the instruments employed, or in the method of observing. The mean temperature of the month was 2°, and the fall of rain half an inch above the average; the latter is entirely due to the severe storm which visited this neighbourhood on the 11th. N.E. winds were the most prevalent. The temperature of solar radiation was not equal to that of July, 1862, and 1863.

AUGUST.

Both the mean temperature and fall of rain were above the average. The great heat of the previous month continued to the 10th, which was the hottest day. The temperature then suddenly declined. Rain fell frequently in heavy showers, and the 22nd was an unusually stormy, boisterous day for the season. The hops were much injured, and many blown down. On the 17th the fall of rain was very great, exceeding one inch in depth, but in some districts more than two inches fell. Winds were chiefly westerly, and the sky was much covered by cloud during the middle and latter part of the month.

SEPTEMBER.

This was a fine autumnal month; very hot weather prevailed during the first eight days, during which time the sun was never obscured by a cloud, and each bright day was followed by a bright moonlight night and very heavy dews, which refreshed vegetation after its exposure to the scorching rays of the sun. Both the mean temperature and fall of rain were above the average; the latter chiefly in consequence of the boisterous and wet weather which prevailed during the last week. With the exception of the 18th, scarcely any rain fell to the 25th.

OCTOBER.

Although the mean temperature was nearly 4° below the average, yet the weather was very fine for the season of the year. The fall of rain was much less than usual, but distributed throughout the month very equally. There were occasional, but not severe, frosts ; the night temperature fluctuated considerably, and varied as much as 17° on two consecutive nights. Winds were for the most part westerly.

NOVEMBER.

The mean temperature was below the average. During the second and third weeks the winds were generally from the northward, and this cold weather was very severely felt after the continued warmth of the summer months. Frosts at night were frequent, but not severe. The greatest cold occurred during the night of the 6th, 23°.4. Rain fell on seven days to the depth of 1.37 inch, which is very little more than half the average quantity. During the latter part of the month the sky was much covered by cloud. Gales of wind occurred on 3rd and 22nd.

DECEMBER.

The weather during this month was characterised by a succession of violent gales, and heavy continuous rains. Rain fell more or less on 23 days, to the depth of 6.5 inches, which was probably the largest amount recorded for December during the present century. The temperature was remarkably high, and as much as 7° above the average. The barometric readings were low, particularly on 24th and 27th. The winds were almost entirely westerly, and the sky overcast throughout. There was much electrical disturbance of the atmosphere on 13th, 24th, 27th, and 30th.

1869.

JANUARY.

This month was mild, and both the mean temperature and fall of rain were above the average. There were but few frosty nights, and the readings of the barometer were high. The winds fluctuated very much between S.E. and S.W. Gales occurred on the 3rd, 5th, and 31st. A thunder storm passed over on the 30th, with some heavy showers of rain and hail.

FEBRUARY

Was remarkably mild, with frequent but not heavy rains. The barometer fluctuated very little, and the S.W. winds were by far the most prevalent. The mean temperature was nearly 6° above the average.

MARCH.

This was a cold month, with rather more than the average quantity of rain. The mean temperature was upwards of 3° below, and the fall of rain rather in excess of, the average. N.E. winds were very prevalent, and the sky much covered by cloud. There was a fall of snow during the night of 13th, to the depth of about two inches. There were frequent, but not severe frosts, at night. The lowest temperature was 22°.4 on the morning of the 8th.

APRIL.

The mean temperature was considerably above the average. On many days bright sunshine and drying winds prevailed, so that vegetation advanced rapidly. Winds were chiefly westerly, and the fall of rain, distributed throughout the month in showers, was rather less than the average. The mean temperature of solar radiation was rather more than 76°.

MAY.

This month was cold and wet; indeed, there was scarcely a warm day throughout the month. Rain fell heavily in the first and last weeks, and the total amount was considerably above the average. It was the wettest May since 1860. The 28th was a particularly cold day, and the maximum temperature was not more than 47° in the shade and 51° in the sun.

JUNE.

This was a dry, but rather cold month, with a considerable prevalence of northerly winds during the latter half. The mean temperature was 4° below the average. The two warmest days were the 6th and 7th, when the temperature in the shade rose to 80° and 83°.4 respectively. The sky was much covered by cloud, but rain fell on five days only.

JULY

Was a fine, hot summer month, with a mean temperature of 64°.1, which is above the average. Rain fell on two days, but only to the amount of .08 inch. The barometer did not fluctuate much, and the winds were variable. The hottest day was 17th, when the temperature rose in the shade to 88°.6. The 12th, 16th, 18th, and 22nd were also excessively hot.

AUGUST.

After the first three days very little rain fell, and the month proved extremely favourable for all harvest operations. The heat was very great during the last week, when the temperature in the shade varied between 81° and 86°. There was a great prevalence of N.E. wind, and for many days together the sky was cloudless.

SEPTEMBER.

The mean temperature was 1° above the average, and some heavy rains fell during the second and third weeks. The readings of the barometer were low and very fluctuating. Westerly winds were prevalent, and the sky was much covered by cloud. A severe thunder storm passed over on the 10th, with torrents of rain for half an hour. Another thunderstorm on 29th.

OCTOBER.

This month was both cold and dry, the mean temperature and rainfall having been much below the average. During the first fortnight the night temperature was high for the season, but after the 17th the nights became suddenly cold, with frequent frosts. On the morning of the 28th the temperature fell to 25°, and terrestrial radiation to 18°! In the evening there was a strong Auroral light in the N.W. The winds were chiefly from the N.W., and on several days and nights the sky was cloudless.

NOVEMBER.

The mean temperature was a little above, and the rainfall about equal to, the average. It would have been a very dry month but for the heavy rains on the 22nd and 27th. The sky was less covered by cloud than usual; the nights were cold, with frequent frosts; the mean temperature on the surface of grass was below the freezing point. On the night of the 18th there was a brilliant lunar halo for several hours.

DECEMBER.

This month was cold, stormy, and wet, with a great prevalence of northerly wind, particularly during the first and fourth weeks. Severe gales occurred on 15th and 16th, with great depression of barometer on the latter day. The weather was very cold during the last week. The lowest temperature was 13° on the morning of the 29th.

1870.

JANUARY.

The mean temperature of this month was slightly above the average, but there was a deficiency of rainfall to the amount of nearly an inch. The weather was very stormy and unsettled on 6th, 7th, and 8th, the wind increasing to almost a hurricane for several hours on the latter day, with considerable depression of the barometer. On the morning of the 12th a slight thunder storm was observable to the southward; the latter half of the month was cold, with great prevalence of N.E. winds and high atmospheric pressure. The 20th and 21st were the coldest days, and the maximum temperature on each day was only 33°.

FEBRUARY.

The mean temperature was nearly three and a half degrees below the average. The weather was mild during the first week, but from the 9th to 26th, both inclusive, very cold and gloomy, with piercingly cold wind at intervals from N.E., especially from 9th to 13th. There were frequent snow showers, but the depth was not great. The fall of rain (and melted snow) was rather below the average. The N.E. wind was the most prevalent.

MARCH.

During this month both the mean temperature and rainfall were below the average. There were frequently severe frosts at night, particularly on 14th, when the temperature of the air fell 19° below the freezing point, and that of radiation 22°. The sky was much overcast. Rain fell on seven days only. On the morning of 13th occurred the heaviest snow during the winter —six inches on the level.

APRIL.

With the spring equinox commenced the long drought which continued during this and the two subsequent months. The mean temperature was equal to the average, but the nights were rather cold for the season, and severe frosts were recorded during the first fortnight. Rain fell to a trifling amount, on four days only. The weather was very fine, and although for many days together the sky was cloudless, yet the temperature in the shade was much influenced by the prevalence of either N. or E. winds. The dew point temperature was often many degrees below that of the air. Solar haloes were frequent.

MAY.

The mean temperature was nearly 1° below the average, and with the exception of some showers on 11th and 13th, the drought of the previous month continued. During the first week unusually severe frosts, for the season, occurred. On the morning of the 3rd the temperature in the shade fell rather more than 5° below freezing point, and that of radiation to 19°.8! On other nights some sharp frosts occurred, and so late as the 26th the temperature fell to 32°, and on grass to 27°! The sky was less covered by cloud than is usual at this season. The winds were variable, but the S.W. was the most prevalent.

JUNE.

The drought which had prevailed during the two previous months continued throughout this month also, for with the exception of some slight showers on the 1st, 16th, 22nd, and 24th, no rain fell. The mean maximum temperature in the shade was not quite 74°. The greatest heat was as follows:—16th, 87°; 21st, 84°.2; 22nd, 88°.6. The mean monthly temperature was rather more than 1° above the average, and the mean daily range 25°.9! The winds were, for the most part, westerly, and the sky not much covered by cloud. The readings of the barometer were high, with little fluctuation. A slight thunder storm occurred during the night of 16th.

JULY.

The mean temperature was nearly 3° above the average, and nearly the whole month was characterised by hot summer weather. The long drought which commenced towards the end of March may be said to have continued with little interruption to the 8th of this month. This was the most remarkable drought which had been experienced in the South of England since the year 1844. Such long droughts are rare during these months, as the following table, which gives all similar instances since the year 1740, testifies:—

	April.	May.	June.	Total.	
1741	0.27	0.44	1.36	2.07	inches of rain.
1762	0.59	0.73	0.76	2.08	„
1806	0.24	1.02	0.50	1.76	„
1844	0.37	0.18	0.79	1.34	„
1870	0.31	1.05	0.34	1.70	„

The heat was very great on the 8th, and from 19th to 26th, both inclusive, the 8th being the hottest day, when the temperature in the shade rose to 87°.2. After some showery weather from 8th to 11th, a quarter of an inch of rain fell on 15th, half an inch on 26th, and three-quarters of an inch on 31st. Slight thunder storms occurred on 16th and 26th. The wind was variable. It was remarkable that with such high temperature in the shade, the temperature in the sun was not so high as might have been expected, a much higher temperature having been recorded in previous years. The harvest was early, and all secured in excellent condition.

AUGUST.

After the thunder storm which occurred on the 26th of July, the great heat of the summer gradually declined, and throughout this month the temperature in the shade only once exceeded 76°. There was an unusual prevalence of N. and N.E. wind, which prevented excessive heat accumulating from solar radiation. The mean temperature and rainfall were somewhat below the average; the mean daily horizontal movement of the atmosphere was 233 miles. Slight thunder storms occurred on 8th, 9th, 18th, and 20th. During a hasty shower on the 9th, 0.33 of an inch of rain fell in six minutes, which was at the rate of 3.30 inches an hour! On the 20th two waterspouts were seen in the Channel.

SEPTEMBER.

Some heavy rains fell during the first eight days, but the remainder of the month was remarkably fine, dry, and seasonable; the last eleven days were almost cloudless, nevertheless the mean temperature was nearly 2° below the average, and the rainfall half an inch. The night temperature fluctuated in a remarkable manner. Thus, on the night of the 13th the lowest temperature of radiation was 51°, but on the subsequent night 29°, or three degrees below the freezing point. It was also below the freezing point on 16th and 25th; the 28th was the warmest day. During the storm of wind on the 9th, the mean hourly horizontal movement of the air was 26.3 miles. Westerly winds were prevalent during the first half, but easterly during the equinox, and to the end of the month. Aurora Borealis was visible on 24th and 25th.

OCTOBER.

The easterly winds which commenced on the 19th of the previous month, continued to the 6th. On the latter day a cold fog occurred, the wind shifted to the westward, and the weather, during the remainder of the month, was stormy, with heavy rains. The barometer was low on the 9th and 13th, while on the 24th, the reading was below 29 inches. During the evening of this day occurred a very brilliant display of the Aurora Borealis,* which was also visible, to a less extent, on the subsequent night. The mean temperature was below the average, although there were very few frosts at night. The depth of rain was considerably above the average, and fell more or less on 17 days. Westerly winds were by far the most frequent, and the mean daily horizontal of the air was 306 miles. The Aurora Borealis was visible also on the evening of the 14th.

NOVEMBER.

The mean temperature was below the average, with frequent sharp frosts at night. The mean night temperature of radiation was more than $3°$ below the freezing point. The weather, which was tolerably fine and dry during the first fortnight, was succeeded by a wet, stormy period, till the 26th, when the wind veered to the eastward, and the temperature rapidly decreased. The fall of rain was nearly half an inch less than the average. Easterly winds were the most prevalent. Lightning was visible during the evening of the 17th, and throughout the night of the 22nd, a continued storm of lightning, thunder, and wind prevailed over this county. Hartfield parish church was struck by lightning, which partially destroyed the spire and roof. Such a storm is of rare occurrence at this season of the year.

DECEMBER.

The weather during the greater part of this month was of a wintry character, and the temperature very much below the average. During the milder weather which prevailed from 11th to 20th much rain fell, and the barometer was low on the morning

* See " Astronomical Register" for February, 1871.

of the 14th. The fall of rain was considerably above the average; the severe Christmas frost commenced during the night of the 20th, and continued throughout the remainder of the month; the temperature remaining below freezing point both day and night, with the exception of two or three hours on the 26th. As it may be interesting to compare the daily temperature at this period with that of other places, I will append the following table :—

	IN SHADE.		
Dec.	Highest.	Lowest.	Radiation.
	°	°	°
21 ...	29.2 ...	29.0 ...	27.0
22 ...	26.0 ...	23.2 ...	18.0
23 ...	25.0 ...	18.0 ...	13.0
24 ...	31.6 ...	14.0 ...	8.6
25 ...	27.2 ...	15.6 ...	11.2
26 ...	33.2 ...	21.6 ...	12.6
27 ...	30.4 ...	19.6 ...	12.4
28 ...	32.0 ...	22.6 ...	20.0
29 ...	31.2 ...	25.6 ...	21.0
30 ...	30.0 ...	13.8 ...	6.2
31 ...	30.0 ...	15.2 ...	8.8

The mean temperature was nearly 6° below the average, while that of radiation fell to 23°.5. It was the coldest December since 1846, which had also been preceded by a hot summer. On the 27th snow crystals fell at intervals throughout the day; the heaviest snow occurred on the morning of the 28th, when it was between four and five inches thick on the level. This frost continued till the morning of January 5th, 1871, when the lowest temperature during the winter occurred. Aurora Borealis was visible on the evening of 17th.

THE OLD CHURCH AT UCKFIELD.

With the exception of the basement of the Tower and the Chancel Window, it was taken down in the year 1839, and the present edifice erected the following year.—C. L. P.

1871.

JANUARY.

The severe weather which commenced and continued throughout the previous month prevailed throughout this month also, and its mean temperature was as much as five degrees below the average of the last twenty-eight years; in fact, it was the coldest January during that period. On the morning of the fifth the temperature fell to 10°·4, and on the 14th to 14°·8. The highest temperature was 46°·4 on the 16th. Frost occurred on every night but five. The rainfall was slightly below the average. The winds were, for the most part, easterly. A beautiful double solar halo, with very distinct prismatic colours, was visible about one o'clock on the 10th. Snow fell more or less on the 9th, 11th, 24th, and 25th, but the amount was trifling.

FEBRUARY.

After the severe weather of the two preceding months, a period of warmer temperature set in, and continued, for the most part, throughout this month. The readings of the barometer were high, and the rainfall below the average of forty years. The wind was chiefly from the westward, with very little stormy weather. Some fine prismatic haloes were visible on the 2nd, 4th, and 11th. The 22nd was a remarkably fine day for the season, and the temperature in the sun's rays reached nearly 70°. A great variety of cloud was observable during the last week.

MARCH.

With the exception of an occasional frosty night, the weather was fine, dry, and mild for the season. The mean temperature was above the average by nearly three degrees, and the rainfall much less than usual. The weather during the last week was very trying for many invalids, as the temperature in the sun's rays was high, but very low in the shade in consequence of continuous cold easterly winds. Some rather heavy rain, accompanied by snow, fell on the 15th, followed by a slight frost at night. On nine days during the month the sky was cloudless and very dry. The barometer was somewhat higher than in February.

APRIL.

The mean temperature of this month was again above the average, and very dry; fine weather prevailed during the first ten days without any rain whatever, and the sky was frequently cloudless. Slight frosts were registered on two nights only, and then the amount was less than 1°. From the 10th a considerable amount of rain fell, and the total quantity for the month was rather more than two inches above the average. Upon the whole it was the wettest April since the year 1856. The wind was chiefly westerly. A solar halo was visible on the 14th, and a slight thunderstorm passed over on the 30th. The nightingale was first heard on the 10th, and the cuckoo on the following day.

MAY.

This was a very cold, dry, and unseasonable month, until the last week. Its mean temperature was four degrees below the average, so that it was the coldest May since 1845. North-easterly winds were very prevalent, with cloudless skies on many days, causing a very rapid evaporation from the soil, and low temperature at night, so that vegetation advanced slowly and imperfectly. Rain fell on three days only, and the total scarcely exceeded a fourth part of the usual quantity. The barometer fluctuated very slightly, and the mean readings were above the average. A thunderstorm occurred on the eighth with a slight shower. I particularly noticed that the holly trees were remarkably full of blossom—both the standard trees and those in hedge-rows.

JUNE.

The month came in with a very low temperature and a great prevalence of N.E. wind. Many persons had recourse to fires on the 2nd, 3rd, and 4th, the temperature having been very low both day and night, and the monthly mean three degrees below the average. The rainfall was nearly two inches above the average, but this excess was almost entirely due to the large amount which fell during a thunderstorm on the 14th. Thunderstorms occurred also in this district on the 20th and 21st, but on Midsummer-day the temperature was lower than it was on April 14th.

JULY

Was also a rather cool summer month, and the mean temperature was nearly one degree below the average. The only warm days were the 17th and 18th, when the highest temperature in the shade was 83°·6 and 80°·6 respectively. South-westerly wind was the most prevalent, and the rainfall slightly above the average. The sky was much overcast during the day, but frequently quite clear at night. The barometer was low throughout the month, and on two days only was the reduced reading above 30 inches. I observed a mock moon, which exhibited prismatic colours, during the evening of the 1st, and swarms of winged ants on the 7th.

AUGUST.

It must be recorded of this month that it was one of the finest, warmest, and most brilliant summer months of which we have any satisfactory record. The sky was absolutely cloudless on eighteen days and twenty-one nights. The mean temperature was about four degrees above the average. For eight consecutive days the maximum in the shade varied from 81°·8 to 89°·4. On the 12th a bright bulb thermometer, in the full rays of the sun, but suspended in free air, registered a temperature of 102°! The rainfall was about equal to half the average amount of 42 years, and the greater part fell during the night of the 17th. The wind was chiefly southerly and westerly. A bright parhelion was visible at 6 p.m. on the 22nd.

SEPTEMBER

Was, upon the whole, a fine month, although the rainfall slightly exceeded the average. The mean temperature was about equal to the average of thirty years. A marked feature was the great prevalence of N.E. wind, with scarcely any variation from the 10th to the 21st inclusive. The weather was very stormy on the 27th. Swallows commenced congregating on 22nd.

OCTOBER.

This was a somewhat dry month for the time of year, and rather cold. The mean temperature was 2° below the average, and frost occurred on one night only. The weather was very fine during the second week, with some warm breezes from the S.E. The wind was very fluctuating between S.E. and N.W. The rainfall was an inch and a half below the average. It should be recorded that on the morning of the 1st 0°·54 of an inch fell in about five minutes.

NOVEMBER.

This was a very cold month, with a great prevalence of N.E. wind. The temperature was more than five degrees below the average, and proved to be the coldest November for many years past; nevertheless, there were a few fine autumnal days, which are always appreciated at this season of the year. The readings of the barometer were very uniform. The rainfall was not equal to a fourth of the average amount. Brilliant Auroræ were visible on the 9th and 10th, and to a less extent on the 11th. From the 8th to the 16th Eucke's Comet was an interesting object on account of its peculiar fan-shaped appearance.

DECEMBER.

The weather during the first half of this month was extremely cold and dry, and the mean temperature was nearly three degrees below the average. The frost on several nights was severe, particularly on the 7th and 8th. The wind during this period was chiefly northerly and north-westerly, but during the latter part of the month westerly, with stormy weather on the 20th. The rainfall was much below the average, and the greater part fell during the third week. Jupiter's fourth satellite was quite dark during its transit on the night of the 30th.

1872.

JANUARY.

This was a very mild, stormy, wet month throughout, particularly on the 1st, 4th, 7th, 17th, 23rd, 24th, and 25th. Lightning and thunder occurred on the 6th and 23rd. The barometer fell to 28·765 inches (reduced) on the 24th. The mean temperature was more than two degrees, and the rainfall two and a half inches, above the average.

FEBRUARY

Was also a very mild month, but with less than the average quantity of rain, and passed away without any particular atmospheric disturbance; in fact it was quite a calm after the stormy weather of the previous month. The mean temperature was four degrees above the average, while many days were warm and pleasant for the season of the year. The wind was chiefly from southward, and the sky was much covered by cloud both by day and by night. During the evening of the 4th there was a remarkable display of the Aurora Borealis, which almost equalled the grand appearance of October, 1870. About midnight of the 6th there appeared a very strong auroral light over the whole of the northern horizon. Fine solar haloes were formed on the 9th and 19th, and lunar haloes on the 19th and 23rd. At the end of the month peach trees and the willow were in bloom, as well as many spring flowers. A credible neighbour informed me that he certainly heard the nightingale in January, and a person living in Barcombe parish asserts that he heard the bird at the latter part of this month. I believe these to be the only instances on record of the nightingale having been heard at this season of the year if we except the instance of Cowper when he says in his letter to Johnson: "You talk of primroses which you pulled on Christmas Day, but what think you of me who heard a nightingale on New Year's Day? Perhaps I am the only man in England who can boast of such good fortune."

MARCH

Must be considered to have been another mild month, the mean temperature having been nearly three degrees above the average; nevertheless, there were frequent slight frosts at night, which proved a salutary check to the prematurely advancing foliage. The rainfall was slightly in excess of the average. A small quantity of snow fell on the 21st, 22nd, and 23rd, but the total quantity for the three days was only ·12 of an inch. The wind was chiefly from the southward, and very stormy on the 27th and 28th, with some heavy rain. Many small meteors were seen during the evening and night of the 31st.

APRIL.

The mean temperature of this month was about equal to the average, and there were only two slight frosts at night. The wind was very equally distributed. From the 20th to 24th, both inclusive, was a somewhat stormy period, and thunder showers occurred on the 17th and 25th. On the latter day some remarkable masses of highly electric clouds appeared over the Channel during the evening. The rainfall was about a third of the average quantity, and was distributed over seven days. The cuckoo and nightingale were both heard on the 13th, and I saw a swallow on the 19th.

MAY.

This month was, upon the whole, somewhat cool and showery, with an excess of more than an inch in the amount of rainfall. This excess, however, was due to the heavy rain on the 17th. The mean temperature was nearly two degrees below the average. The wind was chiefly from the S.W., and at intervals boisterous, with heavy rain. Unusually severe frosts occurred during the nights of the 12th and 18th, which in many places were very injurious to the young foliage.

JUNE.

With the exception of three hot days about the middle of the month the weather was cool and showery. The mean temperature was two degrees below the average, but the rainfall was nearly two inches in excess, distributed over fifteen days. Very stormy weather prevailed from the 7th to 11th, both inclusive, with occasional showers of hail. A remarkable hailstorm passed over the Observatory about 6 p.m. on the 24th. The hailstones were of large size, and the circumference of most of them equalled that of a halfpenny. They were irregularly-pointed pieces of ice, having several nuclei. The ground was quite covered with them for some time after the passage of the storm. This storm was very much more severe at Heron's Ghyll, an estate situated about three miles to the south of the Observatory. It has been thus described by Coventry Patmore, Esq. :—The "hailstorm was quite unlike anything I have ever before or since seen or heard of. The afternoon was fine and quiet, when I saw a dense grey veil, apparently a furlong or so in breadth, approaching the house from the south. It was about a mile off when I first noticed it, as I knew by its obscuring in its course certain objects which lay at that distance. Sunshine was on either side of it. In a few minutes it reached the house. There was one clap of thunder, whether at the time of its arrival or a little while before I do not recollect. For somewhat less than two minutes the hail came down, with a sudden but not very violent blast of wind, in such quantities that nothing could be seen thirty yards from our windows. In those two minutes my rain-gauge measured nearly one inch and a quarter—that is to say, about as much as falls in an ordinary heavy downpour of twenty-four hours' duration. The forms of the hailstones and their way of falling were not less remarkable than their quantity. About half of them were ordinary hailstones as to spherical shape and construction, in concentric layers, only they were about the size of ordinary marbles. The other moiety were clear discs of ice of about the diameter of a penny piece and twice as thick, perfectly well formed, and in numberless cases having small projections on one or both sides, which made them look like the covers of small stewpans with their handles. Here and there was a mass of clear ice of a different form. The largest I picked up was about the size of a bantam's egg, hollow, and formed with spiral ridges. I did not weigh any of these hailstones, but a neighbour told me that he had picked up eight which weighed an average of two ounces each. I do not think that I saw any of more than half that weight. But what surprised me more than their size was their way of coming down. In my eagerness to examine the stones I hastened out of the window from which I was looking without my hat on. I felt the blows of the ice-balls almost as little as if they had been snowflakes. No glass was broken, no trees or shrubs injured; and a friend who was driving two high-spirited horses through the thickest of it told me that they took no notice of it whatever, though he should have been sorry to have been driving them through an ordinary hailstorm. The only way I can see of accounting for this extraordinary fact is the supposition that these masses of ice were formed and sustained in a funnel of wind, of which the extreme point or nose did not reach the earth, although it passed close above it; so that when the weight of the stones overcame the sustaining force of the hurri-

THE CHARLESES.

BEACHY HEAD. A.D. 1786.

cane they had only a hundred or two feet to fall through."
After the passage of this storm the temperature decreased considerably, as the highest temperature of the 25th was 13 degrees lower than that on the 24th. The month closed with fine, bright weather.

JULY.

This month was characterized by greater heat, both day and night, than had occurred in July since the year 1859. The mean temperature was nearly three degrees above the average. On twelve days the highest temperature in the shade ranged from 80° to 88°·2. The wind was extremely variable. The rainfall was below the average. On several days the atmosphere was highly charged with electricity, and thunderstorms occurred in this district on the 6th, 11th, 12th, 13th, 22nd, 23rd, 24th, 25th, 28th, and 30th. During the evening of the 11th two storms came off the sea, one of which passed from Cuckmere to the westward, and the other from Beachy Head to the eastward. On several days the atmosphere was very diaphanous for the time of year, and very distant objects were unusually distinct. A strong auroral light was visible in the N.W. at 10 p.m. on the 7th.

AUGUST.

The first part of this month was cool, with almost daily rain to the 11th, but the total amount for the month was considerably below the average. The mean temperature was low, and as much as 1°·5 below the average. The wind was variable. Thunderstorms occurred on the 7th and 8th, after which came a heavy gale from the S.E. The weather was very stormy and unsettled both on the 9th, 10th, and 11th. On 30th an Aurora was visible to the northward at 9 p.m.

SEPTEMBER.

This was a fine and agreeable month, although its mean temperature was more than a degree below the average. The rainfall was one inch below the average. The only heavy rain fell on the 23rd and 24th. The wind was chiefly westerly, and blew with the force of a hurricane on the 27th. The 28th was also a very stormy day. On the morning of the 23rd a frost occurred on the lower ground, which did much injury to dahlias and other tender plants.

OCTOBER.

This month was cold, stormy, and very wet. The mean temperature was more than 4° below the average, and the rainfall one inch in excess. Nearly three inches of rain fell during the last week. The wind was very frequently from the eastward. A strong gale prevailed from S.W. on the 29th and 30th, with heavy rain. Very vivid but distant lightning was visible on the 4th, 11th, and 26th.

NOVEMBER.

The mean temperature was slightly below the average, and the rainfall more than double the usual quantity. Throughout the month there were only four days free from rain. There was a strong gale from the south on the 1st, and from the S.W. on the 26th. The weather was also very stormy on the 6th, 10th, 15th, 24th, 25th, and 29th, with heavy rain. Thunderstorms occurred on the 2nd, 20th, and 30th, with hail showers. A bright Aurora was visible on the 12th, notwithstanding the moonlight.

DECEMBER.

This was a month of heavy rain also, and the total fall was three inches and a quarter above the average. In consequence of the great rains during the last three months the soil was completely saturated, which seriously delayed agricultural work. Heavy floods occurred in various parts of this county. A terrific gale burst over this district on the 8th. The weather was also very stormy on the 5th, 25th, and 31st. The mean temperature was above the average, and there were only three frosty nights throughout the month. Lightning was seen on the 9th. The barometer was very low on the 10th.

———

1873.

JANUARY.

The heavy rain, and stormy, unsettled weather, which commenced on October 15, 1872, continued, with but little interruption, to the 23rd of this month. The rainfall during this period, of rather more than three months, amounted to 22·78 inches. This was the heaviest rainfall which I have ever recorded in the like space of time, within the last thirty years, with the exception of that in the year 1852. The mean temperature was considerably above the average. The only frosty weather occurred during the last week, but the temperature was never lower than 25°·2. The barometer fluctuated considerably during the first three weeks in consequence of the frequent gales. On the 19th, at 11 p.m., the actual reading of my barometer was as low as 27·670 inches, which, corrected to sea level, was 28·541 inches. The depression was still greater during the night, accompanied by a great decrease of temperature. An Aurora was visible during the evening of the 7th. A thunderstorm passed over during the evening of the 20th. The last few days were cold and frosty.

FEBRUARY.

This month was very cold and frosty throughout, and the mean temperature was considerably below the average; while for several days together the mean daily temperature was below the freezing point, as shown by a thermometer protected from radiation. Snow fell to a considerable depth on 2nd, 9th, 22nd, 23rd, and 24th. The barometric readings were high, and on the morning of the 18th the mercury stood at 30·825 inches, which was the greatest pressure recorded for many years past. On the 2nd a peculiar frosty efflorescence on the windows rendered every object in the landscape of a beautiful violet colour. I am inclined to believe that this phenomenon was due to the prismatic effect of certain saline particles deposited during the gales of the preceding month. On the 3rd a few snow crystals fell occasionally. On 21st every tree and shrub was beautifully decked with rime. This phenomenon, which was confined almost exclusively to the neighbourhood of Crowborough Hill, continued throughout the day. The maximum temperature of the twenty-four hours was only 27°·8. The latter part of the month was somewhat milder, but frost occurred on several nights.

MARCH.

The mean temperature was considerably above the average, more particularly during the last ten days, notwithstanding the prevalence of easterly winds. The rainfall slightly exceeded the average of the last thirty years. During the first three weeks strong westerly winds prevailed at intervals, causing an occasional daily horizontal movement of the air to the extent of 400 miles and upwards. Showers of hail and snow were frequent, more particularly on the 10th and 11th. From 6 to 8 p.m. on 30th frequent thunder was heard to the westward of the Observatory, and vivid lightning was visible over the English Channel.

APRIL.

The mean temperature was rather below the average, for although the middle of the month was fine and warm for the season, yet very cold weather prevailed during the last week; while the frost on the night of the 25th was more severe than any which had occurred during the months of January and March. The rainfall was less than half the average, although it fell more or less on 13 days. The barometer fluctuated considerably, but without any extreme readings. At 6.45 a.m. on the 3rd a mock sun was visible on either side of the sun, which was surrounded by a halo of 35° in diameter. At 6.50 they disappeared, and almost immediately afterwards the entire halo became beautifully prismatic. The 6th was remarkable for much electrical disturbance, particularly during the afternoon. At 3.45 p.m. a shower of snowballs fell, each being equal in size to that of an ordinary marble. On 15th and 16th frequent lightning was visible ; also on the latter day a very violent squall of wind came on from E.N.E. about 10 a.m., and having continued for about ten minutes subsided as suddenly as it had commenced. At this time a thunderstorm was passing from S.E. to E. over the Channel. On 25th bright Aurora 7 p.m. 26th, severe frost for the season.

MAY.

The mean temperature was about two degrees below the average, but it was very equable throughout the month, with entire freedom from the frosts which occurred, on several nights, in localities situated 400 or 500 feet below the level of the Observatory. The rainfall was less than half the average, and the greater part of it fell during the first nine days. The barometer fluctuated considerably. On the morning of the 3rd a heavy hail-shower passed over. The morning of 26th was not favourable for observing the progress of the solar eclipse, which was visible by glimpses only. There were many irregularities observable upon the moon's limb, and, as usual, the moon's disc appeared much darker than the nuclei of the solar spots. On 27th violent thunder in S.W. during the forenoon.

JUNE.

The mean temperature was about the average of the last thirty years. The two warmest days were the 4th and 19th, when the maximum temperature in the shade was 76° and 79°·6 respectively. Although the rainfall considerably exceeded the average, yet the month could not be considered to have been of a wet character, because the excess of rain was due, chiefly, to the heavy rains on 4th, 12th, 17th, and 30th. The sky was more overcast than is usual at this season of the year, a circumstance which acted very prejudicially upon all the cereal crops, which were in a very backward condition. Thunderstorms occurred in this district on 4th, 5th, 13th, and 29th.

JULY.

The mean temperature was rather more than one degree above the average, and fine summer weather prevailed during the month, with the exception of a period from 13th to 18th, both inclusive. The hottest days were the 21st, 22nd, and 23rd. The rainfall was above the average, but the excess was entirely due to the very heavy rain on 13th. This was the heaviest rain which I have ever recorded in July, unaccompanied by lightning and thunder. So far as I have been able to ascertain, the largest quantity which fell in Sussex was registered at this Observatory, viz., 1·51 inches, and the amount gradually diminished both towards the east and west of it. Thus at Uck-field the amount was 1·33 inches; Forest Lodge, Maresfield, 1·37; Newick, 1·34; Haywards Heath, 1·16; Portsmouth, 1·12; Framfield, 1·20; Warbleton, 1·07. A much less quantity fell along the coast, viz., Worthing, ·68 inches; Eastbourne, ·80; Pevensey, ·89; Hastings, ·50; and Dover only ·42. The night of the 22nd was the warmest which had been experienced in Sussex since August 23rd, 1857.

AUGUST.

The mean temperature was very nearly the average, and, during the first fortnight, the weather was very fine and hot. Scarcely any rain fell till the night of the 10th. The 8th was the hottest day which has been experienced in Sussex since July, 1868. The rainfall was considerably above the average, in con-sequence of the heavy rains which fell very unfortunately during the latter part of the month, and seriously impeded the progress of corn harvest. Wind was extremely variable, and the sky was much obscured by cloud. The mean daily maximum reading of an ordinary unprotected bright black bulb solar radiation thermometer was scarcely seven degrees higher than the usual maximum in the shade. Thunderstorms occurred in this district on 19th, 24th, and 25th. The storm of the 24th was one of unusual violence. The morning had been fine, but sultry, and about 1 p.m. some very heavy masses of electric cloud appeared over the English Channel, to the S.W., which, during the afternoon, gradually approached, opposed by a brisk easterly current. It reached this Hill about 4.45, and precipitated a heavy shower. During the whole of the evening the storm was more or less violent, the lightning very vivid, and for above two hours almost incessant. Showers fell at intervals. About eleven o'clock the storm passed away to the N.E. During the height of the storm I observed some very remarkable lightning which emanated more particularly from a mass of cloud which came across the Weald, from the direction of Beachy Head, and passed to the westward of the Observatory, towards the Surrey Hills. Many flashes presented the following appearance :—

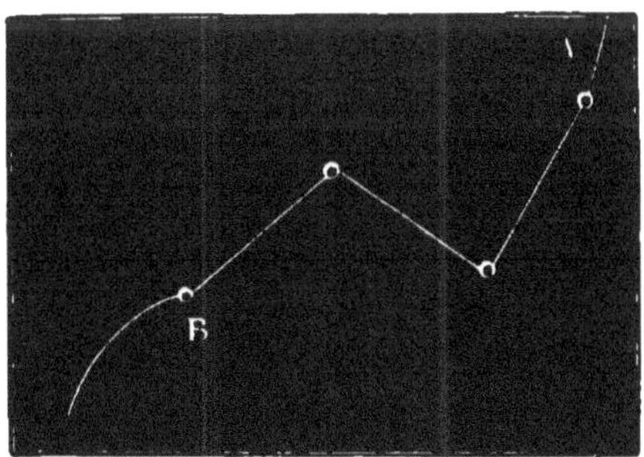

SEPTEMBER.

The mean temperature was somewhat below the average. The heavy rains which fell during the latter part of the previous month continued with but little intermission to the 15th, from which time no more rain fell to the close of the month. The last fortnight was fine, dry, and pleasant, which allowed the latter part of corn harvest and hop-picking to be completed without interruption. The equinox passed without the accustomed gales. On the 21st the wind veered to the N.E., for the first time since the beginning of June.

OCTOBER.

The mean temperature was equal to the average, and the rainfall nearly half-an-inch in excess. The finest weather occurred during the first and last week. On the 3rd the temperature was very high for the season. The wind, although variable, was chiefly from the westward. On the morning of the 8th lightning and thunder were noticed in the S.W. The 10th, 11th, and 12th were very stormy and wet. During the evening of the 17th, a number of small meteors were observed. On the 23rd and 24th distant lightning and thunder. 31st, frost.

NOVEMBER.

The mean temperature was somewhat above the average. The rainfall was considerable during the first nine days, and the amount nearly equalled the average for the entire month. From 10th to 21st the weather was particularly dry, fine, and very favourable for all agricultural operations. The wind during this period was easterly, but not cold, and evaporation from the soil was very rapid for the season of the year. The barometer fluctuated considerably, but there was no extreme reading. Vivid lightning was visible over the English Channel on the evening of the 7th and morning of 27th. Hail-showers fell on 2nd and 26th. One large meteor and many small ones were observed on the evening of 23rd.

DECEMBER.

This month was remarkably fine and dry with an unusually high reading of the barometer, particularly during the first fortnight. The mean temperature was above the average. The rainfall at Uckfield was less than an inch, or one inch and a half below the average of the last thirty years. The atmosphere, on several days, was very clear for the season of the year, more particularly on the 8th, 9th, 10th, and 28th. A brilliant meteor was visible to the eastward at 7 p.m. on 3rd. The night of the 8th was remarkably clear for astronomical observations. No rain fell till the evening of 15th. On 27th showers of hail and snow were frequent. On the 28th, during the greater part of the day, the whole of the Weald was enveloped in fog, but the Observatory, and about 100 feet of the hill below it, was entirely free. This horizontal layer of fog, with the sun shining brightly on its upper surface, presented a scene similar to that which has been obtained from a balloon after it has ascended above a large expanse of cloud. During the last week the wind at intervals blew with grew velocity, more particularly during the night of the 30th. The last day of the year was unusually mild, and warmer than many days in October and November.

1874.

JANUARY.

The mean temperature was about four degrees above the average of the last thirty years, and the highest which has occurred in January since 1866. On many days the temperature of the sun's rays more nearly resembled that of March than January. Contrary to what has been usual in many previous instances of unusual mildness at this season, the rainfall was below, instead of above, the average. The wind was, for the most part, westerly, and blew with great velocity, more particularly on the 1st and 18th. About ten a.m. of 6th two beautiful parhelia were visible; on the 7th, a prismatic solar halo. The 18th was very stormy with much rain; 28th, dense fog all day. The barometer was very high during the greater

part of the month. Although the weather was, for the mos
part, so fine, yet there was a considerable amount of moisture in
the atmosphere, as the temperature of the dew point at 9 a.m.
was less than two degrees below that of the air. In consequence of the great mildness, the following flowers were in
bloom during the greater part of the month—several kinds of
roses, African marigolds, mignonette, fuchsias, primroses,
dandelion, polyanthus, wallflower, hepatica, pyrus japonica,
vinca minor, &c. The leaves of the crocus, snowdrop, and
daffodil appeared above ground in sheltered places.

FEBRUARY.

The mean temperature of February was rather more than one
degree above the average, and the rainfall, in consequence of the
very heavy rain on the 26th, was also slightly above the average
mean of the last thirty-two years. During the first eleven days
the weather was for the most part fine and pleasant, without
any rain or snow, and with only an occasional frost at night.
From 12th to 17th was a very stormy period, with frequent
showers. During the afternoon of 25th a very cold S.E.
current of wind set in, which increased to the force of a gale
at night, and continued more or less till about 5 a.m. of 27th,
with very heavy rain during the greater part of the time. The wind
then veered to S., and some lightning and thunder were noticed
over the sea to the S.E. The most prevalent winds were those
from the westward. During the storm of 26th, the horizontal
movement of the wind amounted, at intervals, to the rate of 46
miles an hour. The various flowers which were in bloom last
month were observable also in this. Near the beginning of the
month the lark, thrush, and the blackbird were in full song.
Bees appeared during the last few days, and also a few sulphur
butterflies and small moths. The common bat came out on
several occasions after the gnats, which had rather prematurely
appeared. Abundance of toad spawn was observable during the

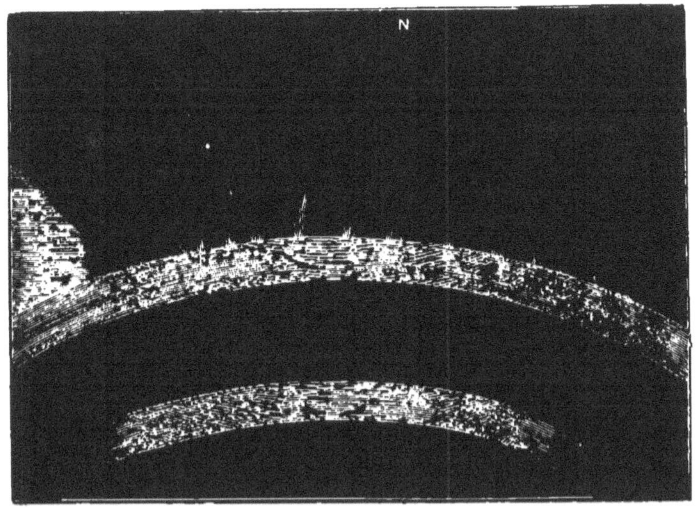

VIEW OF AURORA BOREALIS AS SEEN FROM OBSERVATORY TOWER, FEB. 4.
The Star placed among the streamers is Alpha Cygni.

last week. During the evening of the 4th, there was a grand
display of the Aurora Borealis, of which the preceding engraving
is a representation as it appeared from the Observatory tower at
intervals between 8.10 and 8.40. A second arch is very rarely
seen in the south of England. Further particulars of this
Aurora may be found in " Symons's Meteorological Magazine "
for this month.

MARCH.

The mean temperature was about two degrees above the
average, but from 9th to 12th, both inclusive, it was very low
for the season, and nearly three degrees below the freezing
point. Some snow showers fell on the 9th and 10th. On the
morning of the 11th the temperature fell to nearly fourteen
degrees of frost. The barometer continued high nearly throughout the month. The rainfall was very deficient, not amounting
to half the average. During the evening and night of the 28th
a strong S.W. gale prevailed, and the wind sometimes attained
the velocity of 45 miles per hour. The 31st was a very stormy

day, with driving rain. Westerly winds were the most frequent.

APRIL.

The mean temperature was nearly three degrees, and the rainfall half an inch above the average. Temperature generally was very equable for the season, and the month passed away without any frost. From 17th to 30th the weather was particularly fine, dry, and pleasant, several days and nights being cloudless. Winds were much distributed, but those from the westward were the most prevalent. Very stormy weather was experienced in this locality during the first four days from points between S.W. and S.E. On the 4th frequent lightning was seen, and also on 21st and 22nd. A splendid rainbow appeared on the 6th. In consequence of steady fine and warm weather during the latter part of the month, vegetation advanced very rapidly. The cuckoo and nightingale arrived during the third week, as well as some swallows, but the latter were very few in number. There were scarcely any martens.

MAY.

The mean temperature was considerably below the average—chiefly in consequence of the low temperature at night during the first three weeks. In many parts of the Weald these severe frosts seriously injured the young and tender foliage of the oak, ash, chestnut, hazel, sycamore, and even the bramble. In some gardens the potato haulm was cut down to the ground, as well as the bine of the hop plant. Had showery weather prevailed the injury would have been far greater. At Crowborough the temperature of the air was never one degree below the freezing point, but at Uckfield and Buxted five degrees of frost and upwards were registered on several mornings. This low temperature was very general over Western Europe, while in France immense damage was done by it in some of the principal vineyards. The rainfall was very deficient, and but slightly exceeded one-fourth of the average. This drought was very general throughout the county. Vivid lightning and thunder were prevalent throughout this district on the 8th and 25th. In the latter instance considerable damage was done to trees and buildings. Easterly winds were by far the most frequent.

JUNE.

The mean temperature was slightly below the average, in consequence of the great prevalence of easterly winds during the first three weeks. On the morning of the 13th there occurred in the parishes of Uckfield, Buxted, Framfield, &c., a slight frost, where some seed hay, lying abroad and just ready for the stack, was covered with hoar frost. This was a most unusual occurrence, even in parishes where late frosts are not uncommon. The rainfall was very nearly the average, and the greater part of which fell during the last week. There was electrical disturbance on the 11th and 28th.

JULY.

· This was a fine summer month, and the temperature very high during the second and third weeks, both in the shade and in the sun. The maximum temperature in the shade occurred on the 9th, but that in the sun on the 11th, when a solar radiation thermometer (in vacuo) registered 149°. The rainfall was only one-fourth the average amount. Between Uckfield and Lewes the quantity was still less, and scarcity of water for cattle became a serious inconvenience. At Uckfield rain fell on five days only, but at Crowborough on eight days, with a much larger rainfall. There was much electrical disturbance on the 9th, 11th, 23rd, and 24th. Westerly winds were the most prevalent. A fine view of the comet was obtained from the Observatory during the first fortnight.

AUGUST.

The mean temperature was below the average. With the exception of the third week the weather was cool and showery,

with much westerly wind and a high dew point. The rainfall
was about half an inch below the average, the greater part of
which fell during the first fortnight. The month was almost
entirely free from electrical disturbance, but unusually strong
winds prevailed from 9th to 15th. On the 19th large swarms
of ladybirds appeared in this district.

SEPTEMBER.

The mean temperature was two degrees above the average,
and the weather was remarkable for its great variability. The
night temperature was unusually high, more particularly during
the latter part of the month. The rainfall was somewhat
above the average, and the greater part fell during the second
and fourth weeks. Wind from due south was the most frequent, which was remarkable as being the only instance of the
equatorial current having been in excess of all others in any
month during the last thirty years and upwards. There was
much electrical disturbance on the 9th, 10th, 23rd, 27th, and
30th. Soon after 10 p.m. on the latter day a quarter of an inch
of rain fell in the course of five minutes; and after midnight
there was some vivid lightning with thunder and hail showers.
A beautiful pink Aurora was visible after midnight of the 10th,
and a bright Aurora in N.N.W. at 9 p.m. on the 16th.

OCTOBER.

The mean temperature was also above the average. There
was an entire absence of frost on the Hill, but at less elevation
severe frosts were experienced on the mornings of 5th, 6th, 23rd,
and 24th. The night temperature, however, upon the whole,
exceeded the average for the month. It was the wettest month
of the year, and therefore maintained its usual character. The
actual rainfall, too, very nearly amounted to the average of the
last thirty-two years. Southerly winds were again very frequent,
and blew with considerable velocity on the 6th and 25th. The
most severe thunderstorm of this year passed over this county

during the evening of the 15th. Between 5 and 6 p.m. a highly-charged electric mass of cloud extended across the county from south to north in a nearly straight line of forty miles, the electrical display from which for upwards of an hour was very grand. During the height of the storm the lightning was of a peculiar copper colour, but became subsequently of a beautiful violet tint. An Aurora Borealis was visible during the evenings of 7th and 13th.

NOVEMBER.

The mean temperature was somewhat above the average, as the weather was unusually warm during the first ten days. On the evening of the 10th the wind veered rather suddenly to the northward, and a slight frost occurred on the following morning. From this time to the close of the month the night temperature remained rather low for the season with an occasional slight frost. Winds were extremely variable, but the westerly were the most frequent. The rainfall was rather less than the average, and the greater part fell during the last three days. Just previously to this rainfall the atmosphere had been remarkably dry for the season, as on several mornings the temperature of the dew point was much below that of the air. During the severe gale of 28th and 29th the barometer fell to 28·684 inches at sea level. The sky was more free from cloud than is usual in this month. A slight Aurora was visible during the evenings of 9th and 13th. About 4 a.m. of the 21st I noticed the very unusual phenomenon of a **red moon-set.** The carmine colour was so bright that it attracted my notice through the window blind. The colour was formed upon the upper portions of distant fog, which was lying nearly horizontally with the setting moon. There was a slight frost, which was followed by a clear and brilliant day.

DECEMBER.

This was not only the coldest month of the year, but also the coldest December since 1844 in the south of England. The mean temperature was seven degrees below the average, and frost occurred on twenty-six nights, so that the mean night temperature was as much as five degrees below the freezing point. The fall of snow on the 16th and 17th amounted to about thirteen inches on the level, which was the deepest fall for upwards of twenty years. There had not been so much snow in *December* since the year 1836. This severe weather was very general over Western Europe. The following are all the lowest temperatures in the county of which I have received information:—Crowborough, 18°·2; Uckfield, 13°; Buxted, 12°·6; Forest Row, 9°; and Tunbridge Wells, 4°. The amount of rain and melted snow considerably exceeded the average. The barometer was low (28·663 inches) in the evening of the 11th. Some beautiful snow crystals fell on 16th and 28th. These are rarely seen except in severe weather. Lightning was visible during the evenings of 7th, 11th, and 16th. The N.W. was the most prevalent wind. The month and year ended with hard frost.

———

1875.

JANUARY.

To the severe weather of December, 1874, this month presented a striking contrast. Its mean temperature was more than five degrees above the average, and it was probably one of the warmest Januaries which have been experienced in this county during the present century. Rain fell, more or less, on twenty-one days, and the total fall was one inch above the average. The frost of the previous month gave way on the first day of the new year, when we had the finest example of a silver thaw which has been experienced in Sussex since Feb. 3, 1855. After the second morning there were only two frosts during the remainder of the month, while from the 12th to 20th, both inclusive, the night temperature exceeded the average of that for May! The prevalent winds were those between S.E. and S.W. At the end of the month crocus, snowdrop, and hepatica might be seen in bloom in sheltered situations.

FEBRUARY.

Winter returned upon us during the greater part of this month, and was more remarkable for its steady continuance than for any intense severity. The mean temperature was more than four degrees below the average, and so low a temperature had not been observed in February since 1855. Frost occurred, more or less, on twenty nights, and the lowest temperature, $20^{0}\cdot2$, was registered on the 23rd. Northerly winds were prevalent, and a high atmospheric pressure, particularly on the 5th and 15th. The rainfall was more than half an inch below the average. An Aurora Borealis was visible at 7 p.m. on the 26th.

MARCH.

The mean temperature was below the average, but the weather was for the most part seasonable and dry; the latter condition being always favourable to the grain crops. The rainfall was considerably below the average. Snow showers fell occasionally. A lunar halo was visible on the 15th.

APRIL

Was a fine month, but somewhat cold and dry, with frequent slight frosts. The wind was chiefly northerly, with a clear sky. The rainfall was considerably below the average. To the 17th vegetation generally was more backward than had been observed since the year 1837. Not a leaf was to be seen except upon the larch, honeysuckle, and bramble. A very remarkable decrease of temperature occurred on the 21st during the afternoon, and at 9 p.m. the temperature had fallen no less than 35° below the highest for the day. The highest temperature in the shade on the 21st was 74°, but on the 22nd only 41°!!

MAY.

The mean temperature was above the average; a fine spring month and entirely free from frost. The temperature of several days almost equalled that in July, and the sky very free from cloud. The rainfall was again below the average, and the wind was, for the most part, westerly. Slight thunderstorms occurred in this district, and on the 19th, in an adjoining parish, hailstones fell at noon about the size of ordinary marbles. During the evening of the 12th the cockchafer (*Melolontha vulgaris*) appeared in immense numbers.

JUNE.

The mean temperature of this month was more than a degree below the average, and the month was, for the most part, gloomy, with frequent and somewhat heavy rains, particularly in the third and fourth weeks. Slight thunderstorms were frequent in the county. The wind was chiefly westerly, and on several days moved with great velocity, particularly on 13th, 14th, and 15th.

JULY.

This month, with the exception of the last week, was gloomy, cold, and wet. The mean temperature was considerably below, and the rainfall above, the average. A large quantity of rain fell during the third week. Northerly winds and a generally overcast sky prevailed. The hay harvest was late, and very little of it was secured in good condition. Thunderstorms occurred on several days, but were of short continuance.

AUGUST.

This was the warmest and most pleasant of the summer months. Rain fell on seven days only, which, including that of the 28th, was more than an inch below the average. The wind was westerly. The barometer was high during the greater part of the month, and the variation in the readings was very trifling. Slight thunderstorms occurred at intervals.

SEPTEMBER.

During the first three weeks the weather was very fine and pleasant, but during the last nine days rain fell, more or less, on every day but one. There was frequent electrical disturbance, more particularly on the 8th, 9th, 16th, 19th, 24th, and 27th. The mean temperature was three degrees above the average, and the rainfall deficiency was one inch. The weather was stormy and unsettled on the 26th.

OCTOBER.

The mean temperature of this month was about four degrees below the average, and the rainfall considerably above the average. Some electrical disturbance was observed on the 11th, 21st, and 22nd. Both a solar and lunar halo were visible on the 13th, and a parhelion on the 21st. The wind blew very generally from the eastward, and frequently with some force, particularly on the 26th.

NOVEMBER.

This month was also rather cold and wet, the mean temperature being below, and the rainfall above, the average. It was very heavy on the 7th and 10th, causing a high flood over the low grounds in this district. On the 20th there was a great reduction of temperature, and during the last few days both frost and snow. Solar and lunar haloes were frequent.

DECEMBER.

Severe frost was prevalent during the first ten days of the month, and although the subsequent weather was much milder yet the mean for the whole month was about three degrees below the average. The rainfall was less than half the average amount. The wind was variable, but chiefly westerly. Christmas Day was remarkably fine and pleasant, and its mean temperature was $41°·6$! Heavy gales occurred on 21st and 22nd. A solar halo visible at noon on 21st.

1876.

JANUARY.

The mean temperature of January was rather more than one degree below the average. The first four days were mild and damp. During the night of the fourth a very sudden and considerable decrease of temperature occurred, from which time to the evening of the 16th was a period of continuous hard frost, with occasional snow showers. The mean temperature of each of these days was below the freezing point. On the 8th the maximum was only $23°\cdot4$! The lowest temperature for the month was recorded on the 9th, viz., $14°\cdot7$, and on grass $9°\cdot6$. From the 16th to the close of the month the temperature both day and night was about equal to the average for this season; and frost occurred on one night only. The barometer continued very high throughout the month, and on two days only was the reduced reading below thirty inches. The rainfall was considerably below the average.

FEBRUARY.

The two first days of this month were particularly fine and mild for the season; but for the 2nd, being St. Paul's day, we had to pay the penalty in the succeeding eleven days of wintry weather, thus verifying the old proverb —

> " If Candlemas Day be fair and bright,
> Winter will have another flight;
> But if Candlemas Day be clouds and rain,
> Winter is gone and will not come again."

Some beautiful snow crystals fell on the 8th. The coldest morning was the 12th, when the temperature fell to $23°\cdot6$. From the 14th to the end of the month the weather was comparatively fine and mild, with scarcely any frost. Upon the whole, the mean temperature for the entire month was about equal to the average. The rainfall was more than double the average, the chief part of which fell during the third and fourth weeks, accompanied at intervals by very stormy weather.

MARCH.

This month was cold and wet; rain fell more or less on twenty-one days, but the daily quantity was not large. Cold weather with slight falls of snow occurred during the third week. The mean temperature was below the average. A severe gale occurred on the night of the 8th, with a low reading of the barometer. On the morning of the 12th a violent gale commenced, and at intervals, during the forenoon, blew quite a hurricane. The barometer continued to fall till about 2 p.m., when it commenced to rise very rapidly. The reduced reading at 9 a.m. was 28·614 inches; but absence from the Observatory prevented my noting down the actual lowest reading, which must have been lower than the point just stated. Very stormy weather prevailed also on the 14th and 15th. The rainfall was nearly double the average.

APRIL.

This month was cold for the season, particularly during the first fortnight; and there were frequent falls of snow during the second week. The precipitation for the entire month was fully a third more than the average. On the 12th some lightning and thunder, with a shower of snowballs, about 2 p.m.; this was followed on the 13th by a violent hurricane and a heavy shower of hail and snow. The 30th was particularly cold and unseasonable, with almost continuous rain. The barometer was very low on the morning of the 19th.

MAY

Was very cold and dry during the first three weeks, with an unusual prevalence of N. and N.E. winds. The weather was more genial during the last week, which was enhanced by some refreshing showers. A solar halo visible on the 23rd. The total rainfall was not equal to half the average, and fell on seven days only.

JUNE.

Upon the whole, this was a fine summer month; nevertheless, the mean temperature was considerably below the average, as was also the rainfall. The wind proved very variable. Solar haloes visible on the 7th and 8th, and some distant lightning on the 21st.

JULY

Was a very fine, hot, and dry summer month, and the weather was most favourable for all agricultural work. The mean temperature was much above the average; but the rainfall was scarcely a fifth of the usual quantity. A sudden reduction of temperature occurred on the evening of the 17th; the maximum for the day had been 85°, but by 6 p.m. it had fallen to 58°!

AUGUST.

This was another brilliant summer month; but the actual mean temperature was not equal to that for July. The rainfall was much above the average in consequence of the heavy thunderstorm on the 19th and the stormy wet weather of the last two days. No rain fell between 4th and 17th. The air was remarkably dry on the 13th, and at 4 p.m. the temperature of the Dew Point was 31°·4 below that of the air.

SEPTEMBER

Was a wet and rather cold month, the mean temperature having been two degrees below, and the rainfall double the average. The rain was very heavy on the last day, accompanied by a cold easterly wind and a low barometer. Lightning and thunder occurred on the 6th, 7th, 16th, 18th, and 24th. On the 7th a rainbow was seen to the northward, respecting which Seneca has said—"A meridie ortus magnam vim aquarum vehit."

OCTOBER.

The mean temperature of October was about equal to the average of many years; but the rainfall was deficient, and not much more than a fourth part of the usual amount. October is the wettest month of the year in Sussex. Stormy weather prevailed on the 9th, 10th, and 11th; but from the 14th to the end of the month only one shower was recorded. Southerly winds were by far the most prevalent.

NOVEMBER.

The weather during this month was very showery, but the total quantity of rain recorded was not much above the average. The mean temperature, too, was also above the usual mean. The fluctuations of the barometer were less than usual, and the only stormy weather occurred during the last week. Westerly winds were the most prevalent. A lunar halo was visible at 9 p.m. on the 28th.

DECEMBER.

The atmospheric disturbance which prevailed over Western Europe, and the British Isles in particular, during the month of December, was of a violent and unusual character, and must have been due, in a great measure, to the contact of large masses of air of very unequal temperatures. In the south of England, southerly, and in higher latitudes, northerly and easterly, winds were very prevalent. The latter were piercingly cold, on many days, as their temperature had been much lowered by the extreme frosts which had prevailed in Norway, Lapland, and Iceland. The results of these atmospheric conditions were evinced by such violent gales of wind, excessive falls of rain, hail, snow, and inundations along this coast, as are not often experienced in the month of December. Since the commencement of my meteorological register, in the year 1842, there have been only two monthly rainfalls at Uckfield larger than that of this month, viz., Oct., 1852, and Oct., 1865. The previous heaviest rainfall for December amounted to 6·51 inches, and occurred in the year 1868. In the present instance, the amount at Uckfield was 7·95 inches, Crowborough 9·02 inches, Buxted Park 8·08 inches, Forest Lodge, Maresfield, 7·99 inches, and Tunbridge Wells 8·20 inches. The rainfall at Uckfield, of 7·95 inches, is *more than three times* the average amount for the month of December. Temperature was high for the season, and nearly four degrees above the average. Slight frosts occurred on four nights only, and to a very inconsiderable amount, as the lowest temperature in the shade was 29°·4 on the morning of the 26th. The fluctuations of the barometer were frequent and large. The lowest recorded readings (reduced) at this Observatory were 28·497 inches at 9 a.m. of the 4th, 28·667 at 1.30 p.m. of the 5th, and 28·721 at 9 p.m. of the 20th.

The following notes may, perhaps, be interesting for comparison with other localities :—1st. Stormy, with heavy rain and much lightning and thunder during the night. 2nd. Continuous light rain. 3rd. Overcast, with a violent gale and heavy rain at night. 4th. Very stormy, with frequent showers. 5th. Heavy rain during the greater part of the day. 6th. Fine, rain at night. 7th. Showery. 8th. Gloomy and colder. 9th. Fine. 10th to 12th. Overcast, with frequent rain on the latter day. 13th. Fine. 14th to 18th. Overcast, with occasional showers. 19th. Overcast day, stormy night, lightning, thunder and very heavy hail showers soon after midnight, and again at 5 a.m. on the 20th, which was followed by heavy rain till noon, which, towards evening, caused a considerable flood over the brookland between Uckfield and Lewes. 21st. Fine ; vivid lightning was observed to the eastward at 9 p.m. 22nd. Fine. 23rd. Continuous heavy rain, mingled with large flakes of snow. 24th. Dense fog. 25th. A little snow, early, then fog ; showers of rain and sleet during the evening. 26th. Slight frost, heavy rain at night. 27th. Stormy, with heavy rain. 28th. Showery. 29th. Heavy rain during the afternoon, and very stormy after 6 p.m. 30th. Rain; windy night and frequent showers. 31st. Overcast and showery, but the temperature very high for the season.

1877.

JANUARY.

The mean temperature was more than three degrees above the average, and the rainfall was the largest which I have recorded for January during the whole period of my register. The heavy rains, which were so persistent during December, continued throughout this month, so that the total for the two months amounted to no less than fifteen inches! while at Crowborough the fall for the same period was eighteen inches and a quarter! The barometer was very low during the severe storm on the 1st, but rose very rapidly during the night. Soon after midnight of the 4th a severe hailstorm passed over which aroused the whole neighbourhood. It was of short duration. During the 22 days, ending with the 10th of this month, ten inches and a half of rain had fallen. Solar haloes were seen on 23rd and 31st, and a lunar halo on 24th.

FEBRUARY

Was a mild month, with frequent rains, which, however, were not so heavy as those of the two preceding months, and the total fall was not very much above the average of forty years. The mean temperature was three degrees above the average. The weather was often stormy, more particularly on the 3rd, 12th, 20th, and 26th. The wind blew very constantly from the westward. Solar haloes occurred on the 3rd and 15th. Lunar haloes on 24th, 25th, and 28th.

MARCH.

This was a somewhat cold and showery month; the mean temperature having been one degree below, and the rainfall rather more than one inch above the average. Frost occurred more or less on fifteen nights, which gave a very decided check to the prematurely advancing foliage. The 20th was a very cold day, with drifting snow, and the highest temperature was only 35°! The wind was very fluctuating, between N. and S.W. A solar halo was seen on 23rd, and a lunar halo on 25th.

APRIL

Was also a cold month. The mean temperature was nearly three degrees below the average. The rainfall was above the average, and fell more or less on sixteen days. Thunder-storms occurred in this district on the 4th, 9th, 11th, and 22nd. In the last instance the lightning was at first of a blue and subsequently of a copper colour. A lunar halo seen on the 20th. The wind was generally from the northward. During the few warm days of the fourth week vegetation advanced rapidly.

MAY.

The weather during this month was very variable, but upon the whole it was cold, and the temperature nearly four degrees below the average. During the first week frosts of unusual severity occurred on the low grounds to the great injury of the fruit blossom and tender vegetables. Gales passed over on 17th, 27th, 28th, and 31st of greater force than usual at this season of the year. The rainfall was rather above the average; but none fell during the first nine days.

JUNE.

On the 1st we had a heavy gale, with some lightning, thunder, and hail showers. At intervals the wind was at the force of a hurricane. The 2nd was also somewhat stormy at first, but on the 3rd there was a great rise of temperature. The mean temperature was about two degrees above the average. The rainfall was less than half the usual amount, and the greater part fell during the storm of the 11th. Thunderstorms were reported on the 4th and 11th, particularly on the latter day.

JULY.

This was the coldest month of the summer, and the coldest July during the past ten years. The wind blew constantly from the westward, and the atmosphere was very calm. The rainfall was a third more than the average of many years. The largest quantity fell on the 14th. Thunder showers were prevalent in this district on the 3rd, 6th, and 7th.

AUGUST.

This was the warmest month of the summer; nevertheless, the mean temperature was below the average. The weather was very showery, particularly during the last week, and stormy on 8th, 9th, 19th, and 20th. On the 25th the rainfall amounted to nearly an inch; and the total fall for the month was nearly an inch above the average. The wind was chiefly from the southward, and the sky on several occasions very gloomy and damp. A severe thunderstorm passed to the westward on the 25th, when the lightning was very vivid. The wind was chiefly from the S.W.

SEPTEMBER.

This month was, for the most part, cold and dry, with a very great prevalence of northerly wind. The mean temperature was much below the average, as was also the rainfall. On the 2nd the atmosphere was remarkably clear, and a large number of vessels were visible in the Channel. Lightning and thunder occurred during the night. The weather was stormy on the 14th and 15th. The barometer was high, with but little fluctuation throughout the month.

OCTOBER.

This month had also a low mean temperature, but the weather was, upon the whole, very fine and dry during the first three weeks. Much rain fell during the last week, and the total fall for the month was slightly below the average of years. Very stormy weather prevailed on the 14th, 15th, 23rd, and 30th. Northerly winds were very continuous during the first nine days. The month passed away without any frost.

NOVEMBER.

This was a very mild month, and exceedingly wet. The mean temperature was two degrees above the average, and the rainfall more than double the usual quantity. It was the wettest November during the period of my register. Gales occurred on the 6th, 7th, 9th, 11th, 12th, and frequently during the last week. The barometer was very low on the 12th and 29th. The wind was for the most part southerly.

DECEMBER.

The mean temperature of this month was about equal to, and the rainfall a little below, the average. Some days were very bright and pleasant for the time of year, and the month passed away without any particular gale from any quarter. There were several frosty nights, but the cold was not severe. Westerly winds were the most prevalent. A solar halo was visible on the 28th. The last day of the month and year was very bright, with a gentle breeze from the N.W.

1878.

JANUARY.

The mean temperature of this month was rather below the average, without an instance of any severity of frost. The 26th was the coldest morning, when the recorded temperature was less than six degrees below the freezing point. The rainfall was below the average, and the greater part fell on the 27th and 28th. The wind was chiefly westerly. During the second and third weeks the weather was very fine and pleasant for the season of the year, and the barometer continued very high. The only stormy day was the 21st. As a further instance of the mildness of the season, I may mention that the following flowers were in bloom on the 11th: African marigold, polyanthus, primroses, nemophila insignis and discoidalis, yellow jasmine, &c.

FEBRUARY

Was a milder month, with a temperature slightly above the average. Although frosts were frequent at night during the first fortnight, yet they were not severe, and the greatest degree of cold was $27°·5$ on the 8th. The rainfall was slightly above the average, and the wind was very frequently southerly. The sky was much overcast throughout the month.

MARCH.

This month was cold and dry, with a high barometer. The mean temperature was nearly two degrees below the average. During the last nine days the weather was unusually cold for the end of March; frost occurred on every night, and there was a considerable fall of snow on the 28th, which, with the rainfall on the 31st, rendered the total amount for the month equal to the average.

APRIL.

In consequence of the great prevalence of easterly wind, the mean temperature of this month was more than a degree below the average. Slight frosts occurred during the first week. On the 5th there were frequent showers, with lightning and thunder. The rainfall was considerably above the average of $1·80$ inches. On the night of the 10th the rainfall was continuous, and did not cease until 3 p.m. of the 11th. A solar halo was visible on the 13th, and a lunar on the 15th. The barometer was low during the greater part of the month.

MAY.

The mean temperature was about equal to the average, and there was a great prevalence of southerly wind. The month was chiefly remarkable for the great rainfall, which was nearly double the average of forty years. The amount which fell at Crowborough largely exceeded that at Uckfield, which was, however, chiefly owing to the heavy rain which fell at the former place on 28th. The weather was very stormy for the season from 15th to 20th. On the 28th a severe thunderstorm occurred, during which a house was struck and a pony killed near the Observatory. The barometer was again rather low.

JUNE.

During this month the weather was showery, and rather cool for the season, until after the 21st, when a great increase of temperature prevailed to the end of the month, which, after the cool, wet weather of the previous month, was most acceptable to the advancing cereal crops. Several thunderstorms visited this district during this last week of hot weather, particularly on the 23rd, 26th, and 30th. The rainfall slightly exceeded the average, and fell more or less on fourteen days.

JULY.

Upon the whole this was a fine summer month, with a considerable amount of sunshine and small rainfall. The mean temperature was about equal to the average, with a very generally high temperature at night. Thunderstorms visited this district on 3rd, 8th, 21st, 22nd, and 23rd. The barometer continued high, with very little fluctuation.

AUGUST.

This was a very unfavourable time for all harvest operations in this county. The mean temperature was below the average, and there were only seven days throughout the month without more or less of rain, so that the total quantity far exceeded the average.   The barometer was very low for the time of year. This district was visited by thunderstorms on the 3rd, 6th, 16th, 24th, 29th, and 30th.   The storm on the 29th was very severe at Brighton and Eastgrinstead.   At the latter place three valuable horses were killed by lightning.

SEPTEMBER.

The first half of this month was fine and dry, but the mean temperature was rather below the average.   A thunderstorm occurred on the 8th, which, however, was more severe to the southward.   The weather was stormy on the 18th, after the heavy rain on the previous night.   The rainfall was considerably below the average, although westerly winds were the most prevalent.   The barometer was low on the 23rd and 24th. The weather was very favourable for the completion of harvest and hop-picking.

OCTOBER.

The month may be considered to have been seasonable, but stormy at intervals, more particularly on the 7th, 9th, 10th, 22nd, and 24th.   The gale during the early morning of the 22nd was very severe, but subsided at last very suddenly. Very heavy rain fell during the night of the 25th, otherwise the rainfall for the month would have been much below the average.   A slight frost occurred during the night of the 29th.   Southerly winds were by far the most frequent.

NOVEMBER.

This was a very gloomy, cold, and wet month.   The mean temperature was lower than it had been since the year 1851, although there were but few frosts at night.   The most remarkable feature was the low temperature during the day, which was doubtless owing to the great prevalence of northerly wind. The rainfall was an inch above the average.   The weather was very stormy on the 8th, 9th, and 10th.   Lightning was visible to the S.E. on the 1st and 11th.

DECEMBER

Was a very cold month throughout, with continued prevalence
of northerly wind. The mean temperature was six degrees
below the average. Frost was recorded on 24 nights, and was
very severe. On many days the temperature remained below
the freezing point, at its maximum. The rainfall was about
equal to the average, but was rather heavy during the last week.
The last day was stormy, with rain, and from 4 to 6 p.m. the
wind blew with the force of a hurricane, and increasing temperature. The total rainfall for the year was one inch and a quarter
above the average.

———

1879.

It will be apparent, from our subsequent remarks, that this
year was in some respects the most remarkable of the current
century, and its meteorological history deserves especial record.
The small amount of sunshine, the generally humid state of
atmosphere, the heavy rains in those particular months when the
reverse is so much to be desired, all tended to render this year
one of the most disastrous to the agriculturist on record. It is
probable that so unkind a year had not been experienced in
England since 1816.

Although some months of the year were extremely wet, yet
the amount of rainfall for the whole year did not very much
exceed the average of forty years, viz., by three inches only;
in the year 1852 the total amount exceeded fifty inches! but
this was, in all probability, the wettest year of this century.
I mention this fact, more particularly, on account of a prevalent
idea that the year 1879 was the wettest, as well as the most
sunless, on record.

JANUARY.

Although the concluding days of the last month and the commencement of the new year enjoyed a warmer temperature, yet

the frost returned with some severity on the 4th of this month and continued uninterruptedly to the end—the mean temperature was below the freezing point and as much as seven and a half degrees below the average of many years. It was the coldest January since 1838. The rainfall exceeded the average, but the greater part (2·05 inches) fell on the 1st and 2nd. On the 11th hard frost had prevailed throughout the day, and snow crystals had fallen occasionally. In the evening, by lamp-light, these crystals presented a very splendid aspect, every shrub appearing prismatically illuminated by them, a phenomenon which I do not recollect to have noticed before, or since. The thermometer at the time was at 20°. From the 19th to the 31st the temperature was only twice above the freezing point.

FEBRUARY.

The frost continued during the first four days, after which there was a considerable rise in temperature for more than a fortnight. The weather became colder during the last week, with some sharp frosts at night. The mean temperature was more than two degrees below the average. The rainfall was more than double the average, so that by the end of the month the soil was in a very cold and saturated condition. The 10th was a very stormy day, with heavy rain. Snow showers were frequent on 20th and 21st.

It will be seen, therefore, that the winter of 1878-9 was unusually protracted and severe. During the autumn of 1878, indications were not wanting that the ensuing winter would be, as to its general character, much colder than had been experienced for several years. Of these indications the following were more particularly observed:—(1) In Ireland, wildfowl of various kinds appeared early, and in quantities far exceeding anything of the kind either on record or in tradition. (2) On the south coast of England, some geese, wild ducks, fieldfares, and other winter birds appeared somewhat early. (3) The early disappearance of the swallow and other migratory birds. (4) The squirrel was very actively employed in collecting its winter food. (5) Wasps, although few in number during the summer, became languid, at an early period of the autumn, and sought the protection of buildings. (6) Many of the more common varieties of small birds congregated in large flocks, in the fields and hedgerows, during the month of November. (7) The fall of the leaf was later than usual, notwithstanding the early frosts. (8) The long continuance of northerly winds during November exceeded every instance of the kind on record.

The winter may be said to have commenced during the last three days of October, when the first decided decrease of temperature was recorded. On the 30th, a few flakes of snow were observed to fall, and the temperature of the air fell below the freezing point, viz., to 28°, and terrestrial radiation to 26°5.

With respect to the mean temperature of the three winter months of December, January, and February, it was 4°2 below the average of the previous thirty-six winters, and the lowest since the severe winter of 1844-45, which was considerably lower. This period of cold weather was more remarkable for its persistence than its intensity, as the temperature recorded by a thermometer, fully exposed at four feet above the soil, was never lower than 17°5.

The temperature recorded at Crowborough contrasted very favourably with that reported from places situated at a less elevation above the sea-level, and I consider it probable that the frost, on cold nights, was less intense on the heights of Crowborough (800 feet above the level of the sea) than at any other locality in Sussex. This supposition would confirm the now generally acknowledged fact that places situated on the summit of high ground, in the South of England, are less subject to extremes, whether of heat or cold, than those situated several hundred feet lower. The following Table gives the several particulars of temperature as recorded at my Observatory by two sets of instruments—one of which was fully exposed to all weathers and every kind of radiation from surrounding objects, and the other was enclosed in a structure known as Stevenson's thermometer stand. All the instruments, for comparison, were placed four feet above the level of the ground.

1878-79.	Thermometers exposed in the Open Air.				Thermometers placed in a Stevenson's Stand.			
	Dec.	Jany.	Feb.	During the Winter.	Dec.	Jany.	Feb.	During the Winter
Highest temperature	50·2	47·4	54·0	54·0	49·7	47·4	50·0	50·0
Lowest	18·5	17·5	20·0	17·5	19·3	18·8	22·2	18·8
Mean highest.........	37·6	34·7	42·7	38·3	36·0	34·2	40·6	36.9
Mean lowest	27·4	26·5	31·3	28·4	28·4	27·3	32·0	29·2
Mean	32·5	30·6	37·0	33·3	32·2	30·7	36·3	33·0
Mean daily range ...	10·2	8·2	11·4	9·9	7·6	6·9	8·6	7.7
Lowest on grass......	9·8	9·0	17·6	9·0				
Rainfall (inches) ...	2·73	3·74	4·72	11·19				

MARCH.

The mean temperature was also below the average, and had there been more sunshine the weather would have been more conformable to the spring season. Frost occurred at intervals; but from the 22nd to 27th, both inclusive, some severity was experienced with frequent snow showers. The rainfall was below the average; in fact it was the driest month since July, 1876— less than an inch having fallen. The only sunshine, of any continuance, occurred during the first few days, the remainder of the month being very gloomy and cold.

APRIL.

With respect to this month it was, if possible, more ungenial than several of its predecessors. The mean temperature was upwards of five degrees below the average, and as to the rainfall, it was nearly double the usual quantity for this month. A still larger quantity was registered at Crowborough in consequence of a heavy thunderstorm which passed over that district on the 27th. On the 12th snow fell to the depth of six and a half inches, which was a larger quantity than had fallen at any time during the past winter. Northerly winds were the most prevalent, so that, by the end of the month, vegetation generally was unusually backward.

MAY.

The mean temperature of this month did not exhibit any improvement, and the record showed a deficiency of nearly seven degrees, and also the fact that it was the coldest May on record. The temperature of the air was below the freezing point on several nights, while on fifteen nights the temperature of radiation indicated unusual severity for the time of year. Cold showers, and occasionally snow, fell very frequently, but not to any great amount until the 28th, when upwards of an inch and a half was registered.

The spring much resembled the corresponding period in 1845 and 1855, both of which had been preceded by very severe winters. In the former year the summer was, for the most part, cold and gloomy throughout, and will ever be remembered as the season during which the potato disease first appeared in this country.

Thus at the close of spring vegetation generally, and more particularly garden and cereal crops, were at least a month or six weeks later than usual, and even at that date* the foliage of the oak, ash, and poplar was not fully expanded. The fruit

* June 4th.

blossom was rendered more safe by the lateness of the season, and promised an abundant crop.

The following table gives the several particulars of the temperature and rainfall.

1879.	Thermometers exposed in the Open Air.				Thermometers placed in Stevenson's Stand.			
	March.	April.	May.	During the Spring.	March.	April.	May.	During the Spring.
Highest	65·2	64·2	73·5	73·5	62·0	56·1	66·8	66·8
Lowest	26·4	21·8	26·7	21·8	27·3	24.5	28·4	24·5
Mean highest	49·4	54·2	60·8	54·8	46·0	48·9	54·2	49·7
Mean lowest	32·8	35·2	37·5	35·1	33·8	35·9	38·8	36·1
Mean..................	41·1	44·7	49·1	44·9	39·9	42·4	46·5	42·9
Mean daily range...	16·6	19·0	23·3	19·7	12·2	13·0	15·4	13·6
Lowest on grass ...	17·8	18·5	22·4	17·8				
Rainfall	1·30	4·93	3·70	9·93				

JUNE.

The hope entertained that with the first month of summer a period of warmer temperature and more sunshine would ensue, met with a grievous disappointment. The mean temperature was about five degrees below the average, and the rainfall considerably in excess. Until the last week there were not three consecutive days without rain, while in too many parts of the country there was not even this temporary cessation. The sky was never free from cloud for a single day, and the weather, altogether, was of a most dreary character. The readings of the barometer were low for the time of year, and the wind was generally from the southward.

JULY.

During the first three weeks of this month rain fell more or less upon every day but one. It was a remarkable month even for an English summer. As the mean temperature was six degrees below the average of thirty years, we can only record that it was a dull, cold, sunless month, inducing most disastrous effects upon every kind of agricultural and garden produce. In the North of England snow actually fell both on the 4th and 8th. The rainfall was again above the average, but there was a cessation of the precipitation from the 22nd to 30th, both inclusive—an interval which had not occurred since March. At the close of the month haymaking in this district had scarcely become general. The cereal crops were in a very unpromising condition. The potato was extensively blighted everywhere, and the tubers never attained their full growth. Peas became affected with rust, and scarlet runner beans proved an entire failure.

AUGUST

Was yet another month of low, ungenial temperature and excessive rainfall, and, as regards the latter, it was by far the wettest of the three summer months. The only dry period was from the 9th to the 15th, both inclusive, but this interval was succeeded by thirteen consecutive days of heavy and almost continuous rain. Upwards of an inch and a half fell on the 19th, and exactly one inch on the 23rd at Crowborough. A less quantity fell at Uckfield. The S.W. wind was by far the most prevalent. Severe thunderstorms visited this district on the 21st, and to a less extent on the 2nd. The mean temperature did not depart so much from the average as in the two preceding months, but the rainfall exceeded it by more than two inches.

With respect to the general character of the summer I will observe that the mean temperature of June, July, and August was as much as 5° below the average temperature of our summers, and was the coldest as well as the most ungenial summer which has been experienced by the present generation. The nearest approach to it was the summer of 1860. During the ten days ending with August 28th no less a quantity than 5·43 inches of rain fell at Crowborough, and 3·65 inches at Uckfield. This immense fall of rain, in so short a space of time, produced higher floods between Uckfield and Lewes than had ever been remembered at this season of the year.

The following table will show the various conditions of temperature recorded here during the summer:—

1879.	June.	July.	August.	During the Summer.
Highest temperature in the Shade.........	68·0	77·0	75·3	77·0
Lowest..	40·4	45·0	45·0	40·4
Mean highest	61·8	63·1	65·2	63·3
Mean lowest	48·0	49·5	52·3	49·9
Mean of highest and lowest...............	54·9	56·3	58·7	56·6
Mean daily range	13·8	13·6	12·9	13·4
Mean dew point at 9 a.m.	51·3	52·6	54·9	52·9
Mean highest Solar radiation in vacuo...	78·2	78·4	80·2	78·9
Mean lowest upon the surface of grass..	44·2	46·5	50·2	46·9
Prevalent winds	S.	S.W.	S.W.	S.W.

Although the summer temperature has been cooler than in the year 1860, yet the rainfall has been less.

The following table will show the monthly fall at Uckfield, as compared with other wet summers which have occurred since the year 1842.

	RAINFALL.				WET DAYS.			
	1848.	1852.	1860.	1879.	1848.	1852.	1860.	1879.
June	3·91	7·04	4·80	3·29	18	23	18	23
July	3·01	·50	3·00	3·53	13	4	12	23
August	6·05	6·01	5·84	4·80	23	19	23	20
Total	12·97	13·55	13·64	11·62	54	46	53	66

In the year 1852, the effects of the heavy rains in June were much mitigated by the splendid weather in July. Although the actual rainfall has been less in 1879, yet the *number* of wet days *exceeds* the previous instances.

SEPTEMBER.

During the first week the weather somewhat improved. A more genial temperature obtained, and no rain fell; more than three inches, however, were registered between the 8th and 24th. Very fine weather, and almost cloudless skies, prevailed during the 25th, 26th, and 27th. The mean temperature was two degrees and a half below the average. The amount of cloud was less than in any other month of this cloudy year.

OCTOBER.

Although the temperature of this month was still below the average, yet there was a great diminution in the amount of rainfall; the month was much drier than usual; in fact, it was the only instance during the previous thirty-six years wherein the total rainfall for October had been less than one inch in depth. The really fine weather during the first fortnight was most enjoyable, but it came too late to be of any essential

service in mitigating agricultural distress. Very little frost
occurred, notwithstanding that northerly wind was so prevalent.

NOVEMBER.

This was a very cold month, and the mean temperature as
much as six degrees below the average. Northerly wind was
very continuous, with frequent hard frost, and some heavy snow,
particularly on the 20th, 21st, 25th, and 26th. The rainfall
was considerably below the average. The snow on the 21st had
the peculiar character of clinging very closely to evergreen shrubs,
whereby many branches were broken or injured. On the 26th
some snow crystals were observed, both aggregated and super-
imposed.

DECEMBER.

The last month of this remarkable year was characterised by
.severe frost, and, consequently, by a low mean temperature,
which was of the same value as in the corresponding month of
1878. On several nights the temperature fell below 20°, and
the mean was seven degrees below the average. The quantity
of rain and melted snow did not amount to half the average.
During the severe weather on the first some beautiful snow
crystals fell, but their diameter was less than usual. On the
4th a brilliant solar halo, with two parhelia, was visible soon
after noon. The hoar frost on the windows imparted a prismatic
appearance to the landscape. The frost was very severe on the
morning of the 17th. The lowest temperature at Crowborough
was 15°·4, at Uckfield 10°, and at Buxted Park 11°·5. The
barometer was very high on the 23rd.

1880.

JANUARY.

This month was very cold, but there was a considerable
amount of brilliant sunshine, and very little rain or snow. It

was the driest January since 1861. The mean temperature was several degrees below the average, but the frost was not remarkable for any intensity. The coldest morning was the 26th, when the temperature fell to 19°·6, and frost was recorded on every night but five. On the 8th a dense fog and rain prevailed throughout the day, and, as the temperature remained below the freezing point, the moisture accumulated to such an extent upon the evergreen shrubs that many branches were in danger of being broken by the mere weight of ice. The wind was chiefly from the northward. The winter was very severe on the Continent.

FEBRUARY.

The comparatively mild weather of this month was quite a relief from the severity of its predecessor. The mean temperature was two degrees above the average, and very little frost was registered. The greatest cold occurred on the morning of the 2nd, but the temperature only fell to 30°·0. The 8th was quite a mild day, and distant thunder was heard to the N.W. The weather was very stormy on the 7th, 9th, 19th, and 20th. The rainfall was more than an inch above the average. The wind was southerly.

MARCH.

This was a remarkably genial month for the season of the year, notwithstanding the great prevalence of N.E. wind ; and had it not been for the somewhat heavy rains on the 2nd and 31st it would have been one of the driest on record. Not a drop of rain fell between the 7th and 31st. A heavy gale occurred on the 2nd, and continued all day and night. Scarcely any frost was recorded. The mean amount of cloud was only 5·7. A brilliant and highly prismatic meteor was observed towards the N.W. about 8 p.m. on the 29th.

APRIL.

The weather was, as usual, extremely variable during this month. Showers were frequent during the first fortnight, but the third week was very fine and dry for the most part. During this month, also, the N.E. wind was very prevalent. In reference to shade temperature, there was no frost. The cuckoo was first heard on the 14th, and the nightingale on the 17th. The rainfall was as nearly as possible the average quantity.

MAY.

This was a remarkably dry month, during which not a quarter of an inch of rain fell at Uckfield, and the precipitation occurred on four days only. As usual in these dry seasons there was a great prevalence of N.E. wind, in consequence of which the mean temperature was somewhat below the average. The barometer was high, with but little fluctuation. No frost occurred upon the Hill, but we heard of frequent frosts upon the valley, which was very injurious to the fruit blossom. On the 20th dense haze was spread over the landscape, and thunder heard at intervals. From the 25th to the close of the month there was a considerable rise of temperature.

JUNE.

The mean temperature was below the average, and the weather generally was rather cool and unseasonable; it improved, however, during the last week. Rain fell more or less on 17 days, but the total for the month did not equal the average of forty years. Thunder was heard in this district on the 18th, 24th, and 26th.

JULY.

This month was chiefly remarkable for frequent rains, thunderstorms, and an unusual prevalence of S.W. wind. The mean temperature was below the average. Thunderstorms (but not of a violent character) occurred on the 10th, 13th, 15th, 17th, 24th, and 30th. The storm on the 15th was the most severe; a house was struck at Uckfield, and a cow at Warbleton. The rainfall was very heavy during the night of the 25th.

AUGUST.

The sky was, for the most part, much overcast, which, together with an unusual prevalence of N.E. wind, rendered this month very unfavourable for the completion of harvest. The mean temperature was about equal to the average. The highest temperature in the shade was only $76°\cdot2$ on the 10th. The rainfall slightly exceeded a third of the average quantity, which would have been still less but for the thunderstorm at Uckfield on the 25th.

SEPTEMBER.

The weather was, for the most part, fine and dry, during the first and last ten days, but some heavy rains fell between these periods. More than an inch of rain fell during the night of the 14th, and nearly one inch on the 18th, so that the total considerably exceeded the average. The wind was very equably distributed. Considerable electrical disturbance was noticed on the 6th, 13th, and 18th.

OCTOBER

Was a very cold and wet month. The mean temperature was more than four degrees below, and the rainfall nearly three inches above, the average. It was the wettest October since the year 1865. The first two days were comparatively warm, but during the night of the second there was a remarkable decrease of temperature; the difference in the minimum being 18°, as compared with the previous night. On the 9th, after several wet days, a great rainfall occurred in this county, and at Crowborough I recorded the largest daily amount during the whole period of my register which from 9 a.m. of the 8th to 9 a.m. of the 9th was $2\cdot67$ inches! Had the quantity been recorded from midnight of the 8th to midnight of the 9th it would have exceeded three inches! The amount registered at Uckfield was $1\cdot72$ inches, and at Buxted Park $1\cdot80$ inches. Soon after midnight of the 19th a heavy rain commenced, which was followed by a heavy snow till near noon of the 20th, and its average depth was eight inches. This great depth of snow was a very unusual circumstance in the month of October; in fact, there is none such on record. The foliage being still upon the oak trees, large boughs were broken off by the mere weight of snow. Another heavy rain fell on the 26th, when upwards of an inch was recorded both at Uckfield and Crowborough. The frost was not severe after the snow on the 21st; the lowest temperature was $27°\cdot6$ in the shade, and $26°\cdot6$ in the open. There was a great prevalence of N.E. wind.

NOVEMBER.

The weather at the commencement of this month was fine and bright, but the north wind was still prevalent. The mean temperature was about equal to the average. There were a few frosts at night. A considerable quantity of rain fell during the second week, and on the 16th, during a heavy gale from the S.W., the barometer fell, at sea level, to $28\cdot926$ inches at 9 a.m., and to $28\cdot807$ by 1 p.m. On the 18th there was a great decrease of temperature, followed by heavy rain and snow. At 11 p.m. the barometer had fallen to $28\cdot670$ inches. During the remainder of the month the weather was extremely variable. The rainfall was considerably above the average.

DECEMBER.

The mean temperature was above the average, and the weather generally was mild and dry to the 12th, but from that date to the close of the month there were only three days without rain; the total quantity being an inch above the average. Some slight frosts occurred during the latter part of the month. The wind was chiefly westerly. The sky was frequently densely overcast. Very little of the eclipse could be seen, the state of atmosphere being very unfavourable.

1881.

JANUARY.

This was a very wintry month; the mean temperature was about six degrees below the average, and a greater intensity of frost was recorded than for several years past. On the morning of the 22nd, the lowest temperature of the air was just 9°, or 23° of frost! while the temperature of radiation from short grass was 2°! A prominent feature of the severe frost which prevailed from the 12th to 25th, both inclusive, was the great difference between the lowest temperature of the air, at four feet from the ground, and that of terrestrial radiation, which, during these thirteen days amounted, upon the average, to 7°·5. A heavy gale and snowstorm prevailed during the night of the 17th and following day. The snow was very fine, and penetrated in a remarkable manner into the roofs of buildings and casements, which being unsuspected by many persons no precautions were taken to remove it, so that when the thaw came the ceilings of upper rooms were much injured thereby. The average depth of snow was about eight inches, but in exposed situations it had drifted to the depth of several feet. Snow crystals fell in considerable quantities on the 22nd. A prismatic solar halo was visible about 1 p.m. on the 17th. On the 31st, there was a brilliant display of the Aurora Borealis. I first noticed it at 9.45 p.m., and it continued with varying brilliancy and formation till nearly midnight.

FEBRUARY

Was a rather cold, but, upon the whole, a seasonable month; there were frequent frosts, without any great severity. The last morning was the coldest, when the temperature fell to 26°·2. The mean temperature was slightly below the average, and there was a great prevalence of northerly wind. A very heavy rain fell on the 19th: the quantity registered at Crowborough was 1·28 inches, but at Uckfield it was as much as 1·95 inches!

The total for the month was more than double the average. The barometer was low on the 10th.

MARCH.

The mean temperature was equal to the average, although, at intervals, there were some sharp frosts at night. A large quantity of rain fell during the first week, so that the total for the month exceeded the average. The weather was fine and pleasant during the third week, with a high barometer and westerly wind. Some snow showers fell on the 21st and 22nd, and the latter day was the coldest during the month; the maximum was only 42°·7.

APRIL.

The month was cold and dry, with a continuance of frosty nights and bleak N.E. wind. The mean temperature was nearly four degrees below the average, and the rainfall less than an inch: the average being 1·82 inch. A little snow fell on the 20th, and on the 26th frequent thunder showers with hail. A large solar halo was visible on the 7th, and a lunar on the 12th.

MAY.

The mean temperature was below the average. There were some slight frosts during the first night, on the grass, but the temperature of the air was not below the freezing point at any time. The chief part of the rain fell during the third week, and, upon the whole, the month was dry, with the N.E. wind very prevalent. The barometer was generally high, and the mean reading for the month was as high as 30·106 inches. On the 11th a brilliant solar halo was visible from 11 a.m. to 3 p.m. Throughout this district the appearance of the foliage of the oak before that of the ash was not only apparent, but very remarkable.

JUNE

Was a somewhat cold month, and would have been a very dry one but for the heavy rain which fell on the 5th. The mean temperature was above three degrees below the average, and the night temperature during the second week was very low for the season. On the morning of the 9th, the temperature on the grass fell just below the freezing point, but fortunately without any apparent injury to the potato haulm and other tender vegetables. The weather was more genial during the last fortnight, which very much compensated for the previous cold. Some lightning was seen during the night of 17th.

JULY

Was a fine summer month, with a high barometer, mean temperature, and small rainfall. To the 22nd, rain fell on two days only, and to a very trifling amount; the greater part fell during the last six days. On the 5th the weather was very hot, and, during the evening, frequent and vivid lightning of a bluish colour was visible to the southward. From the 6th to the 11th there was a decrease of temperature, after which warm weather returned, and continued to the end of the month. On the 15th the temperature in the sun's rays was $106°·2$, and on the 19th $101°$! The highest temperature in the shade was $91°·5$, on the 15th also. The most prevalent wind was from the S.W.

AUGUST.

This was a most unfavourable month for the harvest. The mean temperature was several degrees below the average, and from the 7th to the close of the month there were only four days without rain, which exceeded one inch in depth both on the 12th and 26th. Westerly winds were the most prevalent. On the morning of the 4th there were innumerable cobwebs both on the lawn and on shrubs. The weather was rather stormy on the 8th, 10th, 17th, and 25th.

SEPTEMBER.

A considerable amount of rain fell also in this month, and it was very heavy on the 5th and 24th. The mean temperature was below the average; nevertheless the night temperature was peculiarly high for the season. Northerly winds were frequent, with much haze on several days, particularly on the 16th. Lightning was visible on the 6th and 18th. A parhelion was visible on the 21st.

OCTOBER.

This was a cold month, with occasional frosts at night. The mean temperature was fully six degrees below the average, and there was again a great prevalence of northerly wind. The rainfall was considerably less than usual, but was heavy on the 22nd, when 1·10 inches fell at Uckfield, and as much as 1·40 inches at Crowborough. The barometer was high during the greater part of the month. Heavy gale on the 14th, but very little rain fell.

NOVEMBER

Was warmer than the previous month, and about four degrees above the average. A considerable quantity of rain fell, particularly on the 26th, viz., 1·30 inches, by which amount it exceeded the average. On the same day more than two inches (2·04) fell at Crowborough. On several days the atmosphere was saturated with moisture, and unoccupied rooms became exceedingly damp. In addition to the gale on the 16th very severe gales occurred on the 22nd, 26th, and 27th. At 2 a.m. of the latter date a terrific squall occurred, with torrents of rain and hail, which continued, with varying force, all that day and night.

DECEMBER.

The mean temperature was about equal to the average. Nevertheless there was much cold weather at intervals, with frequent, but not severe, frosts. The rainfall exceeded the average. A considerable amount of snow fell on the 9th and 10th, which attached itself in large masses to the evergreen shrubs. The weather was stormy on the 17th and 20th. On several days, both at sunrise and sunset, the brilliant tints upon the neighbouring clouds were very remarkable. From the 20th to the close of the month the atmosphere was very gloomy, but dry.

———

1882.

JANUARY.

The temperature of this month was mild, and the mean above the average. The wind was very equally distributed. The rainfall was much below the average, and the month may be considered to have been very dry, as it rained only once from the tenth to the end of the month. The heaviest rain was on the 8th, which had been preceded by a bright parhelion in the morning. The weather was so mild on the 11th that thrushes were singing. On the 12th a tortoiseshell butterfly appeared, and on the next day I noticed many primroses in bloom. The latter part of the month was dry and pleasant. The marked feature of the month was the very high readings of the barometer, of which I shall have more to say presently.

FEBRUARY.

This month was also mild, and the mean temperature nearly three degrees above the average, while the rainfall was rather less; the greater part of which fell during the last five days. The wind was for the most part southerly. The second week was particularly mild and pleasant. The barometer readings were very high to the 24th, after which the weather became stormy and wet.

At the close of this month there was a general impression that the temperature of the past winter had been many degrees above the average. It may therefore be interesting to state from the statistics of temperature, that such was not the fact. The following table will show that there were nine instances of warmer winter temperature within the last forty years. It is remarkable how soon our recollection, as regards date, of any particular weather passes away; otherwise, the majority of persons would not have forgotten the warm winters of 1868-69 and 1876-77, both of which far exceeded the past winter in warmth. It is also remarkable that of the ten instances which I quote the winter of 1881-82 was the coldest. In order to render my observations at Crowborough comparable with those previously taken at Uckfield, I have applied an approximate correction for the difference of elevation above sea-level.

Mean Temperature of the Winter Months.	
1845-46	40·7
1848-49	41·3
1851-52	40·8
1852-53	41·0
1858-59	40·8
1862-63	41·5
1865-66	41·9
1868-69	43·9
1876-77	43·4
1881-82	40·4

Mean Temperature of Each Month.	
1881. Dec...........	39·8
1882. Jan.	39·7
„ Feb...........	41·9
Mean	40·4
Mean of 28 Years ...	38·9
Difference + ...	1·5

The lowest night temperature in December was 28°·8, in January 24°·4, and in February 26°·8. After the second week in December the ground was not covered with snow during the remainder of the winter. The most remarkable features of the past winter were: (1), the unprecedentedly high atmospheric pressure; and (2), the small amount of rainfall during the *mild* winter.

With respect to the high readings of the barometer, during the third week in January, they were unquestionably the highest of which we have any satisfactory record. The following are the highest readings taken by me at 9 a.m. on each of the following days, and to which corrections have been applied for index error, capillarity, temperature to 32°, and to the level of the sea :—

1882.	Height of Barometer.
January 16......................	30·858 inches
„ 17.....................	30·943 „
„ 18................	30·967 „
„ 19.....................	30·926 „
„ 20.....................	30·763 „
„ 21.....................	30·755 „
„ 24.....................	30·723 „
„ 25.....................	30·752 „
February 20......................	30·857 „

The highest reading is reported to have occurred about 10.30 a.m. on January 18th, which I did not observe.

Since 1854 I have only recorded three instances in which the reading of the barometer at 9 a.m. exceeded 30·8 inches, viz., 1859, January 10th, 30·824 ; 1873, February 18th, 30·825; and 1879, December 23rd, 30·809. The *continuance* of high readings, irrespective of the actual maxima, was another very unusual feature, and occasioned the calm state of the atmosphere which prevailed, for the most part, during the months of January and February, contributing to the pleasure of outdoor exercise as well as to the non-interruption of agricultural labour.

With regard to the *mean* height of the barometer, during the month of January, it was exceeded so lately as in January, 1880, and nearly equalled in January, 1858. The following table, giving a list of instances since 1853 wherein the mean of any month exceeded 30·3 inches, may perhaps be interesting:—

Mean Monthly Height of Barometer at Nine a.m.	
1854. March	30·347
1857. December	30·368
1858. January	30·377
1863. February	30·347
1867. November	30·310
1873. December	30·331
1878. February	30·311
1879. December	30·342
1880. January	30·400
1881. January	30·385

If, however, we do not confine the average to the strictly calendar month, but take the mean daily readings for thirty consecutive days, viz., from January 12th to February 10th, both inclusive, the mean amounted to the extraordinary height of 30·594 inches, and from January 12th to 31st the still higher mean of 30·631 ! Again, if we taken the mean of six weeks, viz., from January 12th to February 22nd, it amounted to 30·540 ! which is greater than that of any (calendar) monthly mean on record ! !

Another point of interest is the unusual circumstance of a high barometer and small rainfall accompanying a mild winter. In the two mildest winters, viz., 1868-69 and 1876-77, the rainfall (referring to Uckfield register) was 12·04 and 17·27 inches respectively, but in that of 1881-82 only 6·83 !

As may be observed in mild winters, a great many flowers came into bloom several weeks earlier than usual. Some, such as the polyanthus, auricula, Devonshire cowslip, daisy, and heartsease, were all in bloom during the second week in January, while on February 14th I noticed the following in addition, viz.: primrose, snowdrop, crocus, wallflower, nettle, mezereon, wild strawberry, water ranunculus (var. contortus), anemone, dandelion, celandine (pilewort), ivyleaved speedwell, hazel, dog's mercury; and on 28th cuckoo flower, wood anemone, and greater stitchwort. Thrushes were in full song by January 11th, honey bee out February 12th, Toad spawn seen February 14th, when also sparrows and starlings' nests were commenced. The sulphur and cabbage butterflies appeared on 16th, and several peacocks on 20th, as well as the smaller tortoiseshell.

MARCH.

Instead of this month being unseasonably cold after the mild winter, its general character was that of continued mildness, a high mean temperature, and a small rainfall. The only heavy rain fell during the night of the 25th, and severe gale of the following morning, when from 8 to 9 a.m. it blew quite a hurricane, with drifting snow. Snow showers occurred also on the 21st and 22nd. A prismatic solar halo was visible for some time on the 20th.

As an instance of the mildness of the season I will mention that I saw a gooseberry tree in full leaf on the 13th, and on the 17th several varieties of butterflies. The wind was chiefly westerly.

APRIL.

The mean temperature was about equal to the average, while during the first half of the month the weather was fine and pleasant, notwithstanding an easterly wind. The rainfall was above the average, in consequence of the heavy rain on the 13th and showery weather during the last ten days. On the evening of the 28th I noticed some large masses of composite cloud, to

the eastward, at sunset, tinted a peculiar rose colour, indicative
of the approaching gale, which was very severe during the afternoon of the 29th. There was scarcely a trace of frost throughout the month, and vegetation advanced rapidly.

MAY.

The mean temperature was also about the average of many
years, and the month generally was warm and pleasant, with very
little rain, and the total quantity for the month was scarcely
equal to half the average. A lunar halo was visible on the 3rd,
and some electrical disturbance was noticed in this district on
the 22nd. The weather was rather stormy and wet on 25th,
after which it became finer to the end of the month.

JUNE.

It was a dripping month, and rain fell more or less on 19 days,
but we should remember that —

> " A dripping June
> Keeps all things in tune,"

and finally the total amount was not quite equal to the average.
The mean temperature was about three degrees below the
average, and upon the whole the weather was rather cold at
night. At 10 p.m. on the 1st a large lunar halo was visible,
exhibiting a mock moon with prismatic colours on the western
side—a rare phenomenon ! On the 7th a sharp hail storm,
while thunder showers were passing to the north of the Observatory. The month closed with gloomy, sultry weather, and
much haze over the landscape.

JULY.

This month was cold, gloomy, and wet. The mean temperature was upwards of three degrees below the average, while the
rainfall was more than double the usual amount, and fell more or
less on 20 days, 14 of which were consecutive. The S.W.
wind was very constant. The 5th and 6th were stormy, with

heavy rain, and just one inch was recorded for the two days. During the evenings of the 13th and 15th some very peculiar salmon-coloured clouds surrounded the sun. They had a very brilliant appearance, while some rosy tints lit up a large bank of clouds, extending horizontally to the eastward. After sunset there was a peculiar pink glow upon some clouds over the Channel.

AUGUST.

During the first fortnight the weather was very fine, dry, and pleasant, notwithstanding a considerable prevalence of northerly wind. The latter half of the month was more cool and showery, with a great prevalence of westerly wind and a low barometer. The mean temperature was nearly three degrees below, and the rainfall not equal to, the average. It was an unfavourable time for the completion of harvest and the commencement of hop-picking.

SEPTEMBER.

With exception of the 1st, 5th, and 11th, when some heavy showers fell, the weather was tolerably fine to the 18th, when some heavy rain came during the night. The mean temperature was below the average, but the rainfall was somewhat in excess. A sudden decrease of temperature occurred on the 14th, and thunderstorms were visible in the distance. On the 21st, at noon, a very low rainbow appeared in the north; its upper concavity appeared to be almost lying upon the ground. On the 28th a heavy rain fell during the night. On the 29th the air was very diaphanous, and, of course, distant objects were seen very distinctly, particularly the shipping passing along the Channel between Dungeness and New Romney.

OCTOBER.

The mean temperature of this month was about equal to the average. The chief feature was the very heavy rainfall. The record at Uckfield amounted to seven inches and three-quarters, which was the heaviest rainfall for October (1865 excepted) since the year 1852. On the 21st more than two inches fell during the 24 hours, and on the 27th more than one. At Crowborough the record was 8·30 inches. A parhelion was visible during the afternoon of the 23rd, and a bright rainbow to the eastward. A heavy gale occurred on the 24th, and about 10.15 a.m. it blew a hurricane for a few minutes. On the 26th a rainbow at noon. The last day was very fine and pleasant for the season.

On the second evening of the month there was such a very brilliant display of the Aurora Borealis as can seldom be witnessed in our latitude. The following are some details of its appearance, and that its magnitude and the area over which it was seen was very unusual is proved by the fact that it was seen, not only over the United Kingdom and Southern Europe, but also over the continent of Australia. On the evening of Oct. 2, as I was walking home, about 6h. 45m., my attention was drawn to a pink auroral glow extending from the western horizon upwards between Arcturus and Ursa Major. A somewhat interrupted auroral arch was visible from the north-eastern horizon, a little to the east of Capella, to past Arcturus on the west. At this time there was an extraordinary appearance to the south of my position. It consisted of detached patches or clouds of magnetic (phosphorescent-looking) light, nearly equidistant, and stretching across the entire sky from the S.W. horizon to a point a little north of east (probably E.N.E.). The five principal clouds were in the constellations Hercules, Aquila, Pegasus, Aries, and Taurus, but there appeared to be others stretching away upon the horizon, on either side, as far as the eye could reach. The general appearance resembled the repeated images of a chandelier in a room with opposite pier glasses. These magnetic clouds did *not* shift their position, but gradually faded away, the one nearest to my meridian disappearing first. Turning again to the northwards, there were some tall streamers extending from the N.W. horizon nearly to the zenith. At 8h. 45m. the auroral arch in N.N.W. horizon was very clearly defined. It had its greatest convexity immediately beneath Ursa Major, and extended along the horizon, as measured by a theodolite, exactly 90°. Small streamers for some time afterwards very frequently arose from the arch towards Ursa Major, and particularly in the direction of the "pointers." At 9h. 15m. brilliant streamers appeared along the entire length of the arch, and there were also some patches of auroral light here and there, which were continually shifting one after another, but always to the westward. At 9h. 17m. a cumuloid cloud passed very nearly along the line of greatest brilliancy, and presented a striking contrast, every undulation of the cloud being distinctly visible. By this time the arch had extended about 10° further to the westward. At 9h. 20m. streamers increased in brilliancy, numbers, and length, and presented a very grand and imposing scene contrasted with the dark sky. At 9h. 25m. the moon was rising, and the eastern termination of the arch had become much less bright, but the brightness increased to the westward. At 9h. 30m. the hitherto well-defined arch was very much broken up, and a few minutes afterwards there was only a diffused light to the westward. At 9h. 45m. the phenomenon had almost disappeared.

NOVEMBER.

This was another wet month, but with a mean temperature about equal to the average; nevertheless there were some rather sharp frosts during the third week, with some snow, or sleet, at intervals. The rainfall was nearly an inch above the average, and the mean reading of the barometer was low. The weather was very stormy, amounting to a gale, on the 2nd. Rain fell more or less on twenty days, and the amount which was registered from Oct. 19th to Nov. 7th, both inclusive, was 8·10 inches! Another display of the Aurora Borealis occurred on the 17th, which, so far as my own observations bear record, was not so interesting and brilliant as that of Oct. 2nd, but the red auroral hue was perhaps rather more diffused and conspicuous. On this occasion I first noticed a pink auroral tint to the westward at 5 p.m., and from almost precisely the same point as on Oct. 2. This pink tint extended very gradually to the northward. A brilliant and well-defined auroral arch was visible all the evening, but the various streamers, as seen from this Hill, were not to be compared for brilliancy, length, and numbers with those seen on Oct. 2. I believe the aurora was visible for the most part through the night; at all events, a faint arch was visible at 5 a.m. the next morning. I did not have the good fortune to see the wonderful magnetic cloud seen by Mr. J. Rand Capron and others. The night was clear and cold, with sharp hoar frost. The minimum temperature was nearly six degrees below the freezing point, the first frost we had this last autumn.

<h2 style="text-align:center">DECEMBER.</h2>

The first part of this month was cold, with sharp frosts every night during the first fortnight. Some snow fell on the 6th and 7th, and rather heavily on the latter day. The rainfall was somewhat above the average, and at Uckfield was recorded more or less on twenty-three days; the wind was very evenly distributed. The barometer fluctuated considerably, and the mean for the month, at 9 a.m., was lower than that for the previous month. Several nights were very clear, and the atmosphere in a most favourable condition for astronomical observations. The last day of the month and year was exceedingly damp, dark, and gloomy, but unusually mild for the season. Showers fell at intervals, and were more decidedly continuous after 10 p.m.

<h2 style="text-align:center">1883.</h2>

The general meteorological features of the year 1883 were not remarkable for any extreme temperature, pressure, or rainfall.

JANUARY

Was mild, with frequent fluctuations of temperature and sudden variations in the direction of the wind. Rain fell more or less on 17 days, but on no occasion was the amount large. Some snow fell on the 9th, and again on the 24th, during a gale from the S.E. A strong gale was also prevalent on 28th and 29th, which continued almost uninterruptedly on the latter day.

FEBRUARY

Was very mild also, and scarcely any frost occurred. The morning of the 17th was the coldest, but even then the lowest temperature was not more than 2° below the freezing point. A great quantity of rain fell during the first three weeks, so that the total for the month considerably exceeded the average. The wind varied very much between S.E. and W. Gales were rather frequent, especially on the 1st, 9th, 10th. The readings of the barometer were very high during the last week.

MARCH

Was the coldest month of the year, as often happens when the two or three winter months have been milder than usual. The mean temperature was nearly six degrees below the average, and therefore the coldest since March, 1865. The frost was severe during the second week, accompanied by keen northerly winds and frequent slight falls of snow. The rainfall was very much below the average. There was a great rise of temperature during the last day of the month.

APRIL.

The mean temperature was a little above the average, but the usual fluctuations peculiar to this month were not wanting. There were, however, only four frosty nights, and the greatest cold was 28·8° on the morning of the 24th. It was a remarkably dry month, and the first seventeen days passed away without a shower. A rather heavy fall of snow occurred on the 23rd, which, however, soon melted under the increasing heat of the sun's rays. This snow lay very heavily upon evergreen shrubs, some of which received injury from its weight. Northerly winds were very prevalent.

MAY.

Although there were some frosty nights during the first week, yet the mean temperature of the month was about equal to the average. After the 12th the night temperature was much warmer, and vegetation advanced very rapidly. There was, however, a frequent prevalence of northerly wind. The rainfall was rather above the average, and very heavy on the 11th during the passage of some thunder showers. During the latter part of the month there was brilliant sunshine on several days.

JUNE.

The temperature of this month was slightly above the average of the last few years, but there was very little real summer weather throughout the month. During the first fortnight there was a great prevalence of N.E. wind, and (with the exception of the rain during a thunderstorm on the 9th) an entire absence of rain. This storm was very heavy to the N.W. of this Hill, where many hop gardens and general foliage received serious damage from the fall of very large hailstones. The temperature at night was very high during the last week. The rainfall was below the average.

JULY.

This was a very dull and showery month, rain falling more or less on eighteen days; nevertheless, the total fall did not equal the average amount. The mean height of the barometer was the lowest for the year. Westerly winds were the most prevalent.

AUGUST.

This was the hottest month of the year, and the mean temperature was above the average of the other summer months.

Many days were characterized by cloudless skies and brilliant sunshine. The harvest progressed very satisfactorily. The atmospheric pressure was, upon the whole, very equable, and the mean was above the average. The first half of the month was showery, but the total rainfall was much below the average.

SEPTEMBER.

The mean temperature of this month was also somewhat above the average. There were a few fine days, but the month was, upon the whole, dull and showery. The total rainfall was considerably above the average. The wind was very changeable, but for the most part westerly. A rather severe gale occurred on the 2nd, with a considerable fall of the barometer, which was the only occasion throughout the year when the reduced reading at 9 a.m. was below 29·000 inches; viz., 28·907.

OCTOBER.

The mean temperature was about equal to, and the rainfall considerably less than, the average, although the wind was, for the most part, westerly. The month passed without any frost or any particular gale.

NOVEMBER.

The mean temperature was about equal to the average, but the rainfall was considerably in excess. The reading of the barometer was low on the 6th and 25th. On the latter occasion the weather was stormy with much lightning and thunder at midnight, accompanied by heavy rain and hail. The westerly winds were again very prevalent, but variable. Slight frosts occurred during the second week.

DECEMBER.

With the exception of some rather sharp frosts near the beginning of this month, the weather was very mild throughout, accompanied by great atmospheric pressure, particularly during the last week. A somewhat heavy snow storm occurred on the

6th, which was almost the only snow shower during the winter of 1883-4. A very dense fog prevailed both day and night during the last week, which appears to have been general over the S. and S.E. of England. The rainfall was much below the average, which is somewhat unusual when the month is characterized by mild weather.

THE PHENOMENAL SUNSETS, &c.

1883.

The beautiful phenomena which were observed during the months of November and December over the greater part of the world, in connection with sunrise and sunset, may be regarded, I think, as almost unique so far as our records extend. Readers of our various scientific periodicals must have become acquainted with several theories which have been advanced respecting their origin. The primary idea appears to have been that they were the result of the great volcanic eruption at Krakatoa, on which occasion an enormous amount of volcanic dust was forced up, retained in, and floated about, the higher strata of the atmosphere. I could never entirely accept this theory; but at the same time I do not hold the great eruption at Krakatoa unconnected with these phenomena, especially if it should be conceded that these dust particles constituted a nucleus around which frozen aqueous vapour was attached. From the vast amount of terrestrial displacement occurrent, and the equally vast amount of sea water which rushed into the chasm, an inconceivable quantity of steam, charged with the various saline ingredients of which sea water is composed, was forced up to an extraordinary height, where, on account of a low temperature, it became suddenly crystallized. These saline particles would naturally crystallize into their respective normal forms, and exhibit the various colours due to the refractive indices of their components. The colours assumed by the layers of cloud nearest the earth would doubtless originate from the refraction of those coloured ice particles situated in the upper atmosphere, which latter would of course not be visible to any one observer, unless, at his station, the emergent refracted ray reached his eye. Hence the time would be accounted for which elapsed between what would be considered an unusually fine sunset, and the after-glow.

From my exceptionally good position for observing the various phases of these very interesting phenomena, I have watched with care and attention their frequent appearance and disappearance upon the occasions of the more brilliant displays in the months of November and December.

I usually noticed that at the approach of these phenomena an extremely faint violet-tinted semi-circle or bow of 4° or 5° in diameter, appeared above and on either side of the sun; which tint would last, as a rule, not more than two or three minutes, when there was a change to a greenish hue, which continued about the same time; this was succeeded by an orange tint. Subsequently, and at an uncertain interval, the lower portion of this orange-tinted stratum assumed a red tint which was much more persistent, and finally this red stratum, together with the remaining portion of the orange, became of a very deep red, and sometimes even of a scarlet colour, producing that splendid glow along the horizon which extended many degrees both to the east and west of the point of sunset. On one occasion it extended just 90° on either side; I allude particularly to the evening of December 23rd.

The question arises why these phenomena were not *constantly* visible? I should consider that their visibility much depended upon the incident and reflected rays not being interrupted to any one observer; and as the angles between these would be very considerable, the phenomena would be seen at a very considerable height above the surface of the earth, or not at all. Extensive areas of cloud, so common during the winter season, would of course be a frequent cause of interruption. The hypothesis that the crystallization of saline particles is an important factor in the production of these phenomena is supported, I think, by the record of the displays having been at their greatest brilliancy in cold weather, as exemplified, in a remarkable manner, during the first week in December.

For several weeks past, I have frequently noticed that the upper layer of a composite cloud has been tinged of a very light salmon, or copper colour, irrespective of any particular cloud formation, and I have noticed, further, that when there has been no well defined cloud in the neighbourhood of the sun, the latter has been surrounded by a haze of aqueous vapour, of a similar tint, which has extended $3°$ or $4°$ from the limb.

1884.

JANUARY.

THE winter of 1883-84 was very mild, and its mean temperature was $2°·2$ above the average of the last eleven years. During the whole of this month frost was recorded only four times, and on one occasion only to the amount of four degrees. The readings of the barometer were much above the average, although the wind was for the most part westerly. The rainfall was above the average, and the greater part fell during the last week. On the evening of the 25th frequent lightning was visible here, and this was followed by a strong gale and heavy rain throughout the night. There was a slight sprinkling of snow on the morning of the 27th, and one degree of frost.

Referring to the subject of the phenomenal sunsets of the previous two months, I will remark that one of the grandest occurred on the evening of January 16th. On the morning of that day a dense fog rested on Crowborough Hill, but shortly before noon the fog sank somewhat, from its summit, but still enveloped the surrounding country, the Observatory alone being above it. Just upon sunset the usual violet tint became visible near the sun, and a pinkish haze above, which extended nearly to the zenith—a sure commencement of a brilliant display. Upon the horizon, and for about 3° above it, the sky soon assumed a decidedly green colour which very shortly changed to a brilliant scarlet band which extended from the S.E. to the W.N.W. points on the horizon. The whole district of the country below me was thus enveloped in fog, the upper surface of which was heaped up into irregular and undulating masses. By degrees, this surface situated to the S.W. of my position became lit up with a beautiful pink colour, by reflection from the intensely red glow upon the horizon, which being interrupted here and there by the fog undulations, these latter had the appearance of huge rocks arising from a blood-stained sea—the scene was a very remarkable one.

That the reflection was very brilliant is confirmed by the fact that on the evening in question, Capt. Wm. Noble, F.R.A.S., of Forest Lodge, Maresfield, noticed this pink tint, which, to reach him, must have penetrated the fog to the depth of 550 feet !

In conclusion I will mention that on the morning of Aug. 27th, near sunrise, I noticed a precisely similar phenomenon as regards the various tints, and their relative positions, as I did on so many mornings during the winter months, which strengthens my belief in the supposition that aqueous vapour, *under exceptional conditions*, has been concerned in the production of the late phenomena.

FEBRUARY

Was also a mild winter month. The temperature was nearly two degrees above the average. Frost was registered on five nights only, and the lowest reading was on the last morning. The rainfall was less than the average. Southerly winds were the most frequent. Very stormy weather prevailed on the eleventh, accompanied by thunder and heavy hail. About 2 p.m. on this day the darkness was very unusual for a short time. The barometric fluctuations were trifling, and the total range of its variation was less than an inch.

MARCH.

This was a very pleasant spring month, although northerly winds were somewhat prevalent. The temperature was two-and-a-half degrees above the average, and the total rainfall slightly in excess, owing to a very heavy rain during the night of the third, which amounted to nearly one inch and a quarter. Several days were almost cloudless, with a very genial warmth. On the 18th the temperature in the rays of the sun was 77°. The equinox passed without any gale. The barometer was low on the 10th and 11th, otherwise the readings varied very little throughout the month. On the 25th some sleet and hail showers fell in the neighbourhood, and a slight frost occurred at night.

APRIL.

This was a comparatively cold month, and the temperature more than a degree below the average. N.E. winds were very prevalent, and on several nights during the fourth week there were some sharp frosts; but the temperature of terrestrial radiation was not much below that of the air. The readings of the barometer were rather low, but with slight fluctuation. Rain fell more or less on fourteen days, but in small quantities, and the total for the month was half-an-inch less than the average. The drought, which continued during several subsequent months, may be said to have commenced at the close of the first week.

MAY.

This was a very fine and pleasant month, notwithstanding that the wind blew frequently from the N.E. The mean temperature was considerably above the average, and there was an entire absence of frost. The rainfall was not an eighth part of the average, although it fell more or less on seven days. None whatever fell between the 17th and the 3rd of June. The barometer continued high, but with little fluctuation after the first week. The amount of cloud was much less than the average. Some vivid lightning was visible in the S.E. during the evening of the 12th.

JUNE

Was another fine and pleasant month, although the mean temperature scarcely equalled the average of the last eleven years. The barometer continued high, with but slight fluctuation, and its entire range was less than an inch. Rain fell more or less on ten days, and in consequence of some heavy showers, during the first week, the total for the month slightly exceeded the average. The wind was again chiefly from the northward, but very slight in force. Thunder was heard on the 7th and 29th. A peculiarly dense haze prevailed on the 20th.

JULY.

This was a very fine summer month, without any excessive heat or oppressive condition of the atmosphere, either in the sun or in the shade. The mean temperature was 2° above the average. The highest temperature in the shade was 80°·2, which is relatively low for the time of year. Rain fell on 15 days, but the several amounts were trifling with the exception of that on the 24th, which was nearly half an inch. The total fall was very nearly three quarters of an inch less than the average of 42 years. Lightning was seen on the 4th and 24th, and on 25th a thunderstorm was visible to the southward. The readings of the barometer were very steady, and above their average value for the season. Winds were for the most part westerly.

AUGUST.

This was the warmest and most agreeable summer month which has been experienced in the South of England for several years. The number of almost cloudless days was very remarkable. The average amount of cloud at 9 a.m. was only 3·6

(0-10), and the mean temperature was nearly five degrees above the average of the last eleven years. The highest temperature in the shade was 88°·9 on the 11th, and in the open air 95°·2 on the 8th. Solar radiation in vacuo reached 106°·6 on the same day, while a thermometer with a black bulb contrivance rose to 148°·5. Less than half the average amount of rain fell, and very little rain (only ·13) was registered between July 28th and August 26th. The total fall for the month would have been very small but for some heavy showers which fell on the 27th. The 25th was a very remarkable day. The morning had been warm, and even sultry, and the temperature in the shade reached 78°.7. About 2 p.m. the sky became suddenly densely overcast, and at 3 p.m the darkness was so great that ordinary print could only be read close to a window. The wind was blowing strongly from the N.W. The reduction of temperature was very great : thus, at 2 p.m. on the 24th it was 87°, and at the same hour on this day only 53. The barometer at 9 a.m. fluctuated to the extent of only ·594 of an inch throughout the month. Winds were for the most part calm and very equally distributed.

It was supposed by many persons that the heat and drought of this summer had been without precedent during the last fifty years ; but I think the following extracts from my journal will show, very conclusively, that such an idea is incorrect.

I will first consider the subject of mean temperature in the shade, as follows :—

MEAN TEMPERATURE IN THE SHADE DURING THE SUMMER MONTHS.

1846	... ...	64·6
1847	... ...	63·0
1852	... ...	63·3
1857	... ...	64·6
1859	... ...	64·7
1884	... ...	62·6

During the last forty-one years there have been six other

instances wherein the summer heat has nearly equalled that of the season just terminated, viz. :—

$$
\begin{array}{lll}
1851 & \dots & \dots & 62{\cdot}3^{\circ} \\
1858 & \dots & \dots & 62{\cdot}2 \\
1866 & \dots & \dots & 62{\cdot}0 \\
1868 & \dots & \dots & 62{\cdot}0 \\
1870 & \dots & \dots & 62{\cdot}3 \\
1876 & \dots & \dots & 62{\cdot}0
\end{array}
$$

With respect to the rainfall, the following table will show that during the past forty-one years there have been four instances wherein the drought has been more severe than during the late summer :—

TOTAL RAINFALL DURING THE SUMMER MONTHS AT UCKFIELD.

$$
\begin{array}{lll}
1844 & \dots & \dots & 4{\cdot}49 \text{ inches} \\
1847 & \dots & \dots & 3{\cdot}07 \text{ ,,} \\
1870 & \dots & \dots & 4{\cdot}60 \text{ ,,} \\
1874 & \dots & \dots & 4{\cdot}65 \text{ ,,} \\
1884 & \dots & \dots & 5{\cdot}12 \text{ ,,}
\end{array}
$$

The mean summer rainfall for the above long period has been 7·07 inches; therefore the *deficiency* for 1884 has been little more than a fourth of the average (at Uckfield).

But it may be said that the rainfall was very deficient during the spring, which seriously affected the water supply for the summer months. I therefore insert the following table, which shows the amount of rainfall during the spring *and* summer months in the above-mentioned years, in all of which the amount was less than for 1884 :—

RAINFALL FROM MARCH 1ST TO AUGUST 31ST IN EACH YEAR AT UCKFIELD.

$$
\begin{array}{lll}
1844 & \dots & \dots & 7{\cdot}36 \text{ inches} \\
1847 & \dots & \dots & 6{\cdot}06 \text{ ,,} \\
1870 & \dots & \dots & 7{\cdot}69 \text{ ,,} \\
1874 & \dots & \dots & 8{\cdot}22 \text{ ,,} \\
1884 & \dots & \dots & 8{\cdot}69 \text{ ,,}
\end{array}
$$

SEPTEMBER.

This was also a warm and pleasant month. The mean temperature was between three and four degrees above the average. On several days the heat was registered 70° and upwards in the shade, and 80° and upwards in the open air. The 17th was the hottest day. The barometer continued high, with but little variation, with the exception of a depression which accompanied the heavy rain on the 3rd. The rainfall was nearly an inch above the average of many years at Uckfield, 2·75 of which fell during the first four days—a very welcome quantity after so long a drought. I believe it was the South of England only which came in for this rain, and that the drought continued in the North for some time longer. At Crowborough no less than 3·35 inches fell during the four days, 2·06 inches of which fell on the 3rd. Throughout the month the night temperature was remarkably high for the season. Barnard's comet was visible here on the evening of the 23rd.

OCTOBER.

The mean temperature of this month was very close upon the average of the last eleven years; nevertheless, many days were warm and pleasant. So late as the 16th the temperature in the shade rose to 63°, and to 77° in the sun's rays. Although the night temperature was below the average, yet there was an almost entire absence of frost. The barometer continued very high. The prevalent winds were from N.W. to N.E. The rainfall was about a quarter of the average of many years, although it fell more or less on 14 days. The 10th was the coldest day, and some slight snow showers fell between three and four o'clock in the afternoon. I saw Wolfe's comet for the first time during the eclipse of the moon on the 4th. It was not by any means a conspicuous object, even in a telescope, and was of course never visible to the naked eye.

NOVEMBER.

The mean temperature was rather more than one degree below the average, and some rather sharp frosts occurred during the fourth week, with some snow on 21st and 30th. The high readings of the barometer, which had been so conspicuous during the previous month, were higher in this. The drought, which may be said to have recurred from the second week in September, continued to the last day of this month. The total fall of rain and melted snow was two-thirds less than the average, and fell on six days only. The most prevalent winds were from N. and E. The sky was much covered by cloud. A brilliant solar halo and parhelion were observed during the morning of the 30th, which were followed by some heavy showers of snow and sleet during the evening and night.

DECEMBER.

With the last day of November the long drought, which had prevailed in England since March 10th, may be considered to have ended with the continuous rains which fell during the first three weeks of this month. In the South of England the underground springs began now to rise, and water was no longer a scarcity. The mean temperature was rather more than one degree above the average. With the exception of April, the barometer was lower than during any month of the year. The winds were for the most part westerly, and gales moderate. The rainfall was an inch and a half above the average, and fell more or less on 21 days at Uckfield. Vivid lightning was visible throughout the night of the 18th, and distant thunder was heard occasionally.

It may be gathered from the preceding tables and notes that the year 1884 has not been characterized by any period of excessive heat or extreme cold. The mean temperature has been considerably above the average, and decidedly the warmest year, in this county, since 1859, which was warmer than 1884, as were also the years 1846, 1852, and 1857. The most prominent feature of the past year has been the deficient rainfall. From information derived from various sources, I believe that an unusual drought has prevailed over the whole of the British Isles, and that it has been more severe in the North than in the South.

In my report of September 10, 1884, I gave some extracts from my Uckfield register relative to the rainfall of the past spring and summer, contrasted with other dry seasons which I have recorded therein, from which it appeared that a greater drought prevailed in the corresponding months of the years 1844, 1847, 1870, and 1874 than in 1884.

Referring to the *annual* amounts of rainfall for a long period, I find results which I have inserted in the following table, and wherein it will be shown that several drier years have been experienced in this county within our memory, thus :—

ANNUAL RAINFALL AT UCKFIELD.

1845	...	...	... 23·03 inches.
1847	...	...	... 17·58 ,,
1854	...	...	... 23·15 ,,
1858	...	...	... 19·36 ,,
1884	...	...	... 23·16 ,,

The following years were *almost* as dry as 1884, viz. :—

1844	...	...	... 23·37 inches.
1855	...	...	... 23·80 ,,
1864	...	...	... 23·48 ,,

The annual deficiency of rainfall during the above-mentioned years respectively was as follows (calculated from the average of forty-two years) :—

1844	...	...	... 6·69 inches.
1845	...	...	... 7·03 ,,
1847	...	...	... 12·48 ,,
1854	...	...	... 6·91 ,,

1855	...	...	...	6·26 inches.
1858	...	...	...	10·70 ,,
1864	...	...	...	6·58 ,,
1884	...	...	...	6·90 ,,

In the years 1847 and 1858 the drought was much more severely felt than in 1884. In the two former years the springs, wells, ponds and watercourses were dried up much earlier than in 1884. Cottagers for some months had great difficulty in obtaining the necessary supply for ordinary purposes. Farmers were put to greater inconvenience and expense, and their water-carts were constantly to be met with on the roads coming from long distances. So late even as November, in 1858, wheat sowing was suspended on account of the very hard and dry condition of the soil, while dust blew along the roads as though it were March. The above inconveniences were experienced to a certain extent only, during the past year, in this immediate locality, and chiefly in consequence of the heavy rains which fell here in September.

———

1885.

JANUARY.

This was the coldest January during the last four years, and the mean temperature was nearly three degrees below the average of the last eleven years. The sky was much covered by cloud and the easterly winds very cold. Although frost occurred on twenty-five nights, yet it was never very severe. The coldest morning was the 21st, when the temperature of the air fell to 21°, and on the grass to 16°·2, which proved to be the lowest temperature during the entire winter. Some snow fell during the third week, but a much larger quantity fell to the eastward of the Hill, and remained a long time. The total quantity of rain and snow did not amount to the average. The barometer was frequently low for the time of year, more particularly on the 11th. Distant lightning was seen at intervals during the evening of the 31st.

FEBRUARY.

This was a very mild month; the temperature higher than in any February since 1877, and nearly two-and-a-half degrees above the average of the last twelve years. The only cold weather occurred during the third week, when the temperature fell to 24° on the morning of the 21st. The readings of the barometer were low, and the month's mean was the lowest for the year, with the exception of that for October. The rainfall was nearly two inches above the average of fifteen years, at Crowborough, and nearly two-and-a-quarter inches above the average of forty-two years, at Uckfield. The wind was, for the most part, southerly, and frequently stormy, more particularly on the 2nd, 6th, 15th, and 16th. Some lightning and thunder in this district on the morning of the 2nd, during the gale. Beautifully tinted clouds were frequently observed near the western horizon after sunset on several occasions.

MARCH.

The temperature of this month was nearly one degree below the average, as well as altogether colder than the preceding month. The unusually long prevalence of north-easterly winds, which commenced on the sixth of this month, was a marked feature throughout the year. Slight frosts occurred on twenty nights, but the lowest temperature was only 26°·9 on the morning of the 10th. After the first week the barometer continued rather high for the time of year. A sudden depression occurred on the morning of the 18th, for which there was no evident reason in this immediate locality. A considerable quantity of snow fell during the night of the 21st. The amount of rain and melted snow was rather below the average, and the several showers fell on nine days only. The rainfall was heavy on the 3rd.

APRIL.

Although the mean temperature of this month was somewhat above the average of the last fifteen years, yet it was not by any means a genial spring month. The north-easterly winds were almost as prevalent as they were in March, and they were accompanied by frequent frosts at night during the first half of the month. The lowest temperature was $27°$ on the morning of the 5th, and terrestrial radiation fell to $24°·6$. The warmest period was during the third week, which was dry and pleasant. The rainfall was one inch below the average,. and, as in the preceding month, fell on nine days only. From 17th to 22nd the sky was almost cloudless during the greater part of the day. On the morning of the 20th the air was remarkably dry, the temperature of the dew point being $22°·2$ below it—viz., dry bulb $63°$, wet bulb $51°$. The amount of cloud was small, although rather more than in March. After the shower on the 28th, vegetation advanced more rapidly. Notwithstanding the prevalence of cold winds, the readings of the barometer were below the average.

MAY.

The mean temperature of this month was nearly three degrees below the average, although the north-easterly winds had given way to those from the westward. During the first three weeks the night temperature was cold and ungenial to the advancing vegetation, while occasionally a slight frost occurred. Upon the whole, the spring was a *late one*, and the daily highest temperature was scarcely equal to the average, until the last nine days. The readings of the barometer were rather low, but without much or sudden fluctuation. The rainfall was above the average, and fell more or less on seventeen days. The showers were much heavier in some parts of this district than here, with some lightning and thunder on the 22nd. On the evening of the 27th, a bright lunar halo was visible.

JUNE.

The mean temperature was more than one degree above the average of the last twelve years, nevertheless there was again an unusual prevalence of north-easterly winds during one half of the month. The readings of the barometer were very equable, but somewhat above the average height, with very little fluctuation. The long summer drought now commenced, and on many days the dryness of the air was remarkable, particularly on the 13th and 24th. The amount of rainfall was only one-third of the average of fifteen years, and fell on nine days in small amounts. Some lightning and thunder occurred on the 6th, during the night.

JULY.

This was a brilliant summer month without any extreme heat or oppressive sultriness of the atmosphere, any tendency to which was subdued by the general prevalence of north-easterly winds and frequent cloudless skies; the amount of cloud for the month having been 4·9 (0·10). On one day only did the exposed self-registering thermometer indicate a temperature of 90°, while the highest in the shade was 84°·1. The lowest temperature occurred on the morning of the 1st, 43°·2. The rainfall was even more deficient than in the preceding month, and amounted to less than a sixth of the average, so that near the close of the month vegetation had suffered considerably, while the supply of water for general purposes had become very scanty. A somewhat larger quantity fell at Uckfield than here, but even there the amount scarcely equalled one-fourth of the average of the last forty-two years. The barometer continued high throughout and remarkably steady. On four days only was the reduced reading, at 9 a.m., below thirty inches.

AUGUST.

This, the third summer month, was also remarkable for the drought which commenced and had continued, with scarcely any interruption, since the end of May. The mean temperature was nearly two degrees less than July, and, like that month, was not remarkable for intensity. Throughout the entire month the temperature in the shade exceeded 76° on two days only, while the highest registered by the exposed thermometer was 86° on the 17th. The average night temperature was not so high as usual, which was probably due to the continued prevalence of north-easterly winds. The rainfall was not a sixth of the average, but fell on eight days, on three of which the amount was only ·01 of an inch. Somewhat more fell at Uckfield in consequence of partial showers. As might be expected, the air throughout the month was very dry, and the average daily temperature of the dew point was ten degrees below it. A remarkable instance of this dryness of the air occurred about 1.30 p.m. on the 17th, when the dry bulb reading was 76° and the wet bulb 60°! The temperature of the dew point would, therefore, be 27°·4 below that of the surrounding air, in shade. The barometer remained very steady throughout the month, and its readings were somewhat above the average value.

Many years had elapsed since this county had been visited by so long and severe a drought during the summer months, while its intensity was increased by the fact that the rainfall both of 1883 and 1884 had been below the average. Notwithstanding this deficiency, the underground springs were not exhausted to such an extent as was experienced during the summer of 1884. In consequence of the paucity of wells in this district, the two public springs were scarcely able to supply all wants; nevertheless, they never absolutely failed. It is in a season like this that the value of stored rainwater is manifested, and ought to give an impulse to the consideration of this important subject.

The following Table of the amount of rainfall registered in various parts of the county will be interesting to many, whether for present information or future reference. Although Crowborough has generally the largest rainfall, yet during the late drought a less quantity has been registered here, than at any Station from which I have received a report. The comparatively large quantity which fell at Mayfield in July was owing, for the most part, to a heavy thunder shower on the 5th, which was quite local, and did not appear to extend beyond that parish and those immediately contiguous, as I was able to watch both its aggregation and dispersion. During the storm 1·34 inches of rain fell, and, if this be subtracted from the total for the month, the remainder would not equal the amount registered at the majority of the other Stations.

The summer of 1869 was very dry in the South of England and the quantity of rain which I then registered at Uckfield exceeded by 0·17 of an inch only the amount reported by Miss L. Day for the past season.

Upon the whole, the summer of 1885 may be considered to have been the driest in this county during the last fifty years.

The mean temperature of the three months was about equal to the average value. The hottest weather occurred during the fourth week in July. The warmest day was the 26th, when the temperature, about 2 p.m., was 84·1° in the shade, and 90° in the open air. As is usual in dry seasons, there was a remarkable absence of any severe thunder storms.

The Rainfall during the Late Summer, at the Following Stations in Sussex.

1885.	June.	July.	August.	Total.	Authority.
Crowborough Observatory	0·94	0·47	0·61	2·02	C. L. Prince, F.R.A.S.
Winchelsea	1·00	0·56	0·49	2·05	Miss Stileman.
Uckfield	0·82	0·67	0·68	2·17*	Miss L. Day.
Eridge Castle ...	1·18	0·05	1·06	2·29	Mr. Rust.
Lamberhurst (Scotney Castle)	1·01	0·53	0·77	2·31	E. Hussey, Esq.
Horsham	1·36	0·16	0·88	2·40	R. Sheppard, Esq.
Maresfield (Forest Lodge)	1·06	0·84	0·67	2·57	Capt. Noble, F.R.A.S.
Hastings	1·12	0·58	0·90	2·60	W. Andrews, Esq.
East Grinstead ...	0·95	0·30	1·39	2·64	W. V. K. Stenning, Esq.
Worth (Rectory) ...	1·04	0·27	1·44	2·75	The Rev. G. W. Banks.
Steyning	1·51	0·86	0·41	2·78	Colonel Ingram.
Ticehurst	1·42	0·54	0·92	2·88	Mr. J. G. Webb.
Worthing	1·41	0·77	0·74	2·92	W. J. Harris, Esq.
Brighton	1·58	0·70	0·70	2·98	Dr. Taaffe.
Warbleton (Rectory)	1·67	0·98	0·46	3·11	The Rev. G. E. Haviland.
Mayfield (Vicarage)	1·02	1·73	0·71	3·46	The Rev. H. T. M. Kirby.
Average for the County	1·17	0·61	0·79	2·57	

* The amount of summer rainfall at Uckfield upon the average of 42 years is 7·03 inches.

SEPTEMBER.

Although the mean temperature of this month was below the average, yet its general character was that of a continuance of summer, notwithstanding the frequent days of rainfall. On thirteen days the temperature of the air was upwards of seventy degrees, while the night temperature was high for the season. The only indication of frost was on the morning of the 27th. The winds were chiefly westerly, although, on several days, the wind blew steadily from the north. The long summer drought came to an end on the second day, and, with three exceptions, rain fell more or less on the fifteen succeeding days—the large amount of nearly one inch and a quarter on the 16th—and the total quantity for the month exceeded the average by one inch and a half. The barometer fluctuated to a very trifling extent, considering the number of wet days and the period of the equinox. On the second, soon after sunset, some very curious beams of a reddish colour, about $3°$ wide, ascended several degrees above the horizon near the point of sunset, while the interspaces were of a bright green colour.

OCTOBER.

This month was both cold and wet, although there was scarcely any absolute frost. The mean temperature was three degrees below, and the rainfall somewhat above the average. The sky was much overcast throughout, and the wind very equally distributed. A somewhat heavy gale occurred on the evening of the 2nd, and the weather was stormy on the 4th and 6th. A very peculiar haze was present during the afternoon of the 18th, so that at 3 p.m. the sun did not shine more brightly than the moon at full. An exceedingly dense haze was again prevalent during the afternoon of the 29th. The readings of the barometer were lower than at any other period of the year.

NOVEMBER.

The mean temperature of this month was somewhat above the average. Slight frosts occurred during the third week, otherwise the weather was, upon the whole, mild, seasonable, and dry, until the last week, when a large amount of rain fell; nevertheless, the total amount did not equal the average of the last fifteen years. The sky was much covered by cloud, and the winds were very fairly distributed, the N.E. having been the most prevalent. The month was tolerably free from any stormy weather until the last three days. A heavy gale occurred on the morning of the 28th for several hours. The mean readings of the barometer were slightly below the average.

DECEMBER.

The mean temperature was slightly above the average, and tolerably uniform throughout. The only cold weather occurred during the second week, and on the morning of the 11th the greatest cold during the year was registered, viz., $19°·5$ in the open air, and $21°·8$ in the shade. The readings of the barometer were high, and very few were below thirty inches (reduced). The winds were again very equally distributed, with an almost entire absence of stormy weather. Some snow fell on the 9th and 29th. The rainfall was two inches below the average, although it fell more or less on eleven days. Parhelia visible at 9 a.m. on 29th. The year ended with dark, gloomy weather.

INDEX.